Acclaim for the Novels of Daniel Kalla

"Kalla, an emergency-room physician, employs just enough medical realism to carry a wild tale through one cliff-hanger chapter after another."
—*Library Journal* on *Cold Plague*

"Meticulously detailed and carefully plotted."
—*Publishers Weekly* on *Cold Plague*

"Fast-paced and smartly written . . . Kalla has quickly matured into a force to be reckoned with. . . . *Blood Lies* springs several fresh surprises on the reader (including one whopping great shocker)." —*Booklist*

"A taut psychological thriller that will pull you into a world of sexual deviancy, murder, and mind games. A very good read." —Nelson DeMille, *New York Times* bestselling author, on *Rage Therapy*

"Kalla strikes again with another perfect page-turner."
—Lee Child, *New York Times* bestselling author, on *Blood Lies*

"A damn fine read." —John Lescroart, *New York Times* bestselling author, on *Blood Lies*

"Daniel Kalla expertly weaves real science and medicine into a fast-paced, nightmarish thriller—a thriller all the more frightening because it could really happen."
—Tess Gerritsen, *New York Times* bestselling author, on *Pandemic*

"An absorbing, compulsive thriller, the sort of book you could stay up too late reading."
—*The Vancouver Sun* on *Pandemic*

BY DANIEL KALLA
FROM TOM DOHERTY ASSOCIATES

Blood Lies
Cold Plague
Pandemic
Rage Therapy
Resistance

COLD
PLAGUE

Daniel Kalla

TOR®

A TOM DOHERTY ASSOCIATES BOOK
NEW YORK

This is a work of fiction. All the characters and events portrayed in this novel are either fictitious or are used fictitiously.

COLD PLAGUE

A Tor Book
Published by Tom Doherty Associates, LLC
175 Fifth Avenue
New York, NY 10010

www.tor-forge.com

Tor® is a registered trademark of Tom Doherty Associates, LLC.

ISBN-13: 978-0-7653-5793-9
ISBN-10: 0-7653-5793-3

First Edition: April 2008
First Mass Market Edition: November 2008

Printed in the United States of America

0 9 8 7 6 5 4 3 2 1

For my girls . . .
Ashley, Chelsea, and Cheryl

ACKNOWLEDGMENTS

I am so grateful for the support of my friends, colleagues, and family members who read my books from early manuscript to finished product and always provide useful feedback along with tons of encouragement. I have mentioned many of them before, but too often I've forgotten to name someone important. This time I'm going to play it safe and thank them en masse. I would have no books without them.

I do have to single out a few people for their specific contributions. Dave Allard opened my eyes to the existence of Antarctic lakes and thus inspired this novel. Dr. Marc Romney, a top-notch microbiologist, gave me a crash course in the science of prions. Nancy Stairs and Dal Schindell scoured the manuscript with keen eyes, jumping on any inconsistencies. And I am hugely indebted to the amazing Kit Schindell, a friend and freelance editor (somervillebookworks@shaw.ca), whose insights and suggestions always improve my stories.

I rely heavily on the guidance and wisdom of my agent, Henry Morrison. I would also like to acknowledge my terrific foreign rights agent, Danny Baror. And I am fortunate to have found a home in New York at Tor and Forge Books. My thanks go to Tom Doherty, Linda Quinton, Patty Garcia, Paul Stevens, and John Morrone, who give my books the chance to shine. My wonderful editor, Natalia Aponte, is the best advocate, partner, and friend an author could hope for inside the publishing world.

I would be lost without the love and inspiration of my parents, brothers, in-laws, and extended family. And, of course, my daughters, Chelsea and Ashley, and my wife, Cheryl, make life complete for me.

AUTHOR'S NOTE

The Science Behind *Cold Plague*

Imagine a lake the size of Lake Michigan buried three miles below Antarctic ice at the very coldest spot on earth! When I first heard of this natural phenomenon—the very real Lake Vostok—I knew I had to build a story around it. I decided to tie it in with a medical anomaly equally as mysterious that has long fascinated and frightened me: the prion.

Prions are infectious agents, rogue proteins that lack DNA, which defines life. But these microscopic assassins excel at destroying life. The earliest prion-related disease identified was *kuru*—a lethal brain disorder that spread among the cannibals of New Guinea through the consumption of infected human brains. In current society, Creutzfeldt-Jakob disease (CJD), though thankfully rare, is one of the most devastating disorders known. CJD kills most victims in under a year, and in that time it transforms the sufferers from healthy to demented, blind, and bed-ridden. At death, these patients' brains are so moth-eaten that pathologists use the term "spongiform" (sponge-like) to describe them. In cows, the same disease is called bovine spongiform encephalitis (BSE). But most know it by a simpler name: mad cow disease.

Lake Vostok is one of earth's largest lakes, but no one has ever seen it. Buried three miles under Antarctic ice near the South Pole, the millions-of-years-old subterranean lake might offer a prehistoric glimpse of our planet. The lake's water is kept liquefied by geothermal heat from the earth's core, and it contains enough oxygen dissolved under enormous pressure to support life on earth. Many scientists believe it houses never-before-seen life forms. For forty years—long before they knew of the lake's existence—researchers have been drilling at the Vostok site for ice core samples. In 2001, they had reached to within a hundred yards of the lake when the drilling was halted for fear that it would contaminate the pristine waters beneath. Since then, scientists have been working on a strategy for sampling the lake without contaminating it.

My story kicks off with a group of scientists successfully tapping an Antarctic lake and drawing its prehistoric water up to the earth's surface. However, they unearth a lot more than they expect!

The characters and subsequent events in this thriller are fictional, but the science behind them is firmly rooted in reality.

COLD

PLAGUE

PROLOGUE

The slivers of wind-swept ice swirled around his head, as if heralding a blizzard. But he knew it wasn't going to snow. It almost never did. Despite ice that ran miles deep below his feet, he was tramping through one of the driest spots on earth. A desert. Even in the height of the austral summer, under a sun that never set, it was usually too cold to snow. But the relentless winds kept those glimmering crystals—sundogs, as the locals called them—whipped in permanent frenzy.

And Dr. Claude Fontaine was sick of it. Sick of the endless arid expanse. Sick of the unyielding cold. Sick of the sundogs. And most of all, sick of Vishnov. But his months of toiling in this frozen hell were close to paying dividends. Despite the restricting layers of cotton, nylon, and wool, Fontaine broke into a jog as he headed for the domed structure that disrupted the monotony of ice in front of him.

The previous summer Fontaine had overseen the assembly of the insulated dome, watching the Twin Otters and LC-130 Hercules transport planes fly in the pieces. Each square-meter chunk of the three-dimensional jigsaw was clicked meticulously into place under his unrelenting scrutiny. On days when the winds kept the aerial sleds at bay, Fontaine defied the weather and stood fuming at the site. Unfinished, it always reminded him more of abandoned alien ruins than the most significant drilling spot on the planet. Somehow, his team of engineers, geologists, and technicians managed to assemble the dome before May arrived to usher in Antarctica's dark and lifeless winter. The team returned in late October. By December, they finished widening and stabilizing the old well drilled through three kilometers of solid ice. A mere two hundred meters from their target.

Today was the payoff, Fontaine reminded himself with a smile.

The ice crunched behind him, and he turned to see Georges Manet sprinting to catch up. Below the untamed locks of black hair, Manet's handsome bearded face was creased in a wild grin. His gray eyes—which, Fontaine bitterly noticed, had an almost hypnotic effect on the few women at the site—shone brighter than usual. Manet threw his arms open wide, crucifix-style. *"Claude, mon ami, un jour magnifique de changer le monde!"*

Fontaine detected a hint of mockery in his tone but chose to ignore it. He noticed that the happy-go-lucky geologist wore only a jacket and jeans. No hat, no gloves. "You know this spot once registered the coldest temperature on earth?" Fontaine said in accent-free English.

Manet waved the suggestion away. *"Seulement en hiver!"*

"Georges, it's always winter here," Fontaine snapped.

Manet laughed, verging on giddiness. "No, my friend, today is the height of summer," he said, switching to English.

Before Fontaine could answer, someone called his name from behind them. Fontaine spun to see Jerry Silver lumbering toward them from the direction of the dome.

Wound as tightly as a spring and naturally round, the American documentary producer-director was the antithesis of Manet.

"Ah, Jerry," Fontaine said, his voice now twenty degrees warmer and infused with a rich Parisian accent. "Are you prepared?"

"Yup. Three cameras," the IMAX director said. "How about you? Ready?"

"I've been ready for years, Jerry." Fontaine clapped the American on the back, his hand sinking into layers of ill-defined softness of clothing and flab. "Shall we make history?"

Without waiting for a reply, Fontaine strode briskly for the dome's arched entryway. After months spent at the site he was oblivious to the shimmering white structure that resembled a high-tech igloo dropped on the wrong pole of the planet. He pulled the key card from his neck and waved it over the sensor. A musical beep sounded and the steel door slid silently open.

Though cool enough to maintain an ice floor, the temperature warmed noticeably as soon as they stepped inside. Fontaine slipped off his gloves and hat as he surveyed the room. By his quick head count, the whole team was present. Everyone was in motion. A discordant choir of voices joined the buzz of machinery. Fontaine fed off the palpable nervous energy.

As always, his eyes were drawn to the towering platform in the room's center. Resembling a miniature oil rig, it housed the huge winch that fed a mess of cables deep into the well. Standing at the base of the platform, Pierre Anou hovered as territorially as ever. The lanky engineer, a world expert in glacial core drilling, fussed over the equipment and argued with the technicians around him.

To Fontaine's right, Akiro Tekano manned the bank of computer terminals under a massive LCD screen that hung on the wall above them. Fontaine could barely stomach Tekano, and his endless *Star Trek* references, but he wouldn't have allowed anyone else to guide his probe. In the world of robotics, Tekano was the best.

Voices trailed off and movement ground to a halt as the team members noticed Fontaine standing at the entryway. Only the steady hum of the winch filled the background, and that too stopped abruptly when Anou clicked a button in his hand. Fontaine waited until the two cameramen pointed their shoulder-mounted cameras in his direction before he offered the team his most dazzling smile. "It's been a long cold year," he said. "Time to break the ice."

The comment was met with applause and a few congratulatory hoots.

"Nothing better than a dip in the lake in summer," Manet chirped from over Fontaine's shoulder.

A scattering of laughter. Fontaine chuckled too, as he silently vowed to himself, *I am going to get rid of you, pest, at the very first opportunity.*

Fontaine headed for the bank of computers. The cameramen lowered their equipment while a blond technician with large blue eyes and a pixie-like face threaded the microphone under Fontaine's turtleneck, flushing slightly as her fingers fluttered over his chest. Fontaine returned her smile. He could still picture her lithe form arched naked above him on his cot, but he drew a blank on her name. Dismissing her from his thoughts, he turned to Jerry Silver, who paced in front of him, a jumble of nerves and excitement.

"We're going to do this from the top, right?" Silver said. "We'll cut whatever footage we don't need, but I want you to go over the details as if we've never heard—"

"Of course, Jerry." Fontaine patted his shoulder reassuringly. *You idiot!* he thought. *We've already covered this ten times.* "I will begin from the beginning, *oui?*"

Then he glanced at his robotics engineer. "Is the probe positioned?"

"Ten feet, Captain Kirk," Tekano answered in his machine-gun inflection.

Fontaine nodded. "On my cue, transfer the reformatted radar image to the big screen. Advance the probe only when I say so." He turned back to the director. "Anytime, Jerry."

Silver snapped his fingers at the cameraman and pointed to Fontaine. Both cameras focused on the Frenchman again. Fontaine stood silently, waiting. Years of lecturing at conferences and fundraisers had taught him the value of a dramatic pause.

When he finally spoke, his voice was friendly and relaxed but tinged with the promise of revelation. "Welcome to the Vishnov Research Station, only a few kilometers west of the geomagnetic South Pole." He pointed to the ground, drawing out the moment. "We are standing at an elevation of almost four thousand meters, thanks to the accumulation of millions of years of ice—ice that never melts—beneath our feet." His voice echoed slightly in the now silent dome. His pronunciation was perfect, his accent deliberately prominent—Jacques Cousteau on land. "I am standing above a massive body of water. But it was only after the invention of ground-penetrating radar that we learned of the existence of Lake Vishnov buried three kilometers below us. And what a lake she is!" He extended his palms and swept them through the air. "As big as Lake Michigan and as deep as Lake Tahoe. She is kept in a liquid state by geothermal vents at her basin that warm the water in much the same way as do volcanoes in the depths of the Pacific."

Fontaine dropped his hand to his side. "Since the Soviets opened this research station over forty years ago, scientists have drilled for ice core samples unaware that they were working above the largest geographical find of the century. By the time the lake was discovered at Vishnov, the researchers had drilled to within two hundred meters of the water. They had to stop for risk of contaminating the lake. However, we know from those samples that the ice contains oxygen dissolved under great pressure. Enough oxygen to support life."

Another pause, as Fontaine's face lit with disclosure. "And there is life in those deep core samples! Bacteria frozen in a dormant state. Microorganisms that came not from above but from the lake herself." His smile faded. "The dilemma facing scientists has always been this: How do we sample the lake without contaminating the pristine waters within? The three-kilometer-deep Russian well has been kept open with thousands of liters of Freon and other chemicals. Had we kept drilling into the lake, the toxic spill would have contaminated her water forever."

Fontaine tapped a finger above his eyebrow. "But today we have a solution." He pointed above him to nothing in the air, knowing that later, in the editing suite, Silver would add a visual for what he was about to describe. "It's called a Philberth probe. A cigar-shaped robotic drone with a heater at its tip to melt the ice and to allow it to descend by gravity. Its path freezes behind it." Fontaine pointed to the giant winch beside him. One of the cameras followed. "The probe will carry this cable into the lake." He waited two long breaths. "And for the first time in millions of years, Lake Vishnov will communicate with the surface of the earth."

"And I'll be the first person in eons to have a sip of her!" Manet cracked from across the room, breaking the solemnity of the moment.

"Merde, Georges!" Fontaine snapped.

Jerry Silver bustled over to Fontaine, waving his hands

frantically. "Don't mind him. We got exactly what we needed. You were perfect."

Fontaine mustered another smile. He looked from the cameras to the rest of the team, who stood watching him. "I think you've waited long enough. Let's sample this lake."

Heads nodded in unison. Instinctively, Silver slipped away from Fontaine's side as the cameras found him again. Fontaine nodded to Tekano. Suddenly, all the screens in the room filled with the computer-enhanced image of the probe he had described. Silvery-gray, it resembled a nose-down artillery shell buried in the whiteness of the ice. Roughly three of its lengths below the ice, the white gave way to the dark blue ultrasonographic representation of water.

Even though the image was entirely static, the prickly warmth of anticipation overcame Fontaine. He was poised on the cusp of fame. The next three meters would decide his fate.

Without looking at Tekano, he nodded a second time. On the screen, the nose of the probe started to glow faintly red. The incandescence grew steadily as its tip heated. Slowly, the shell began to nudge through the white ice. As the probe slid forward, the gentle drone of the winch broke the silence in the room.

Even Fontaine held his breath as the nose seamlessly cut through the last of the white ice and dropped into the blue water below.

"We're wet!" Tekano cried from his console.

The team broke into applause. Several members hugged. Fontaine's eyes welled up unexpectedly. He cleared the frog from his throat before staring directly into the camera that was still focused on him. "Our probe has just entered Lake Vishnov," he said in a hushed voice. "Now we will begin to withdraw samples of the water." He paused. "Let us hope they are as rich with life as we expect."

More applause.

Georges Manet hoisted his empty hand in a panto-mimed toast. "Maybe you should be careful what you wish for, Claude."

1

Philippe Manet's eyes jerked around the room. Sometimes he saw a crucifix on the wall or a pole beside his bed, and at other times there were two of them, side by side or one on top of the other. He had no idea where he was. But that was nothing new. Philippe hadn't known for weeks. He no longer recognized his mother or his sister. Sometimes he didn't even respond to his own name when the nurses spoke to him.

"The water it wills the way . . . ," Philippe began to say, but his words sputtered into a garble of nonsensical French.

He was vaguely cognizant of his own incoherence. He was also aware of the shadowy figure of a woman standing by his bed. Or was it two women?

"Georges knows, and Sylvie, too," he said to her. "The water! It wills . . ."

A smell drifted to Philippe, and he stopped trying to speak. Something pleasant, even comforting. His eyes swung back and forth over his own hand until he felt dizzy. A plume of smoke drifted above his fingers. A wisp of a memory. Then it was gone.

A soft but cold hand gripped his fingers. The woman was nearer now. There was something familiar about her, but her presence conjured a contradictory sense of vulnerability and security. She spoke to him, but somewhere between his ears and his brain the words were lost. The woman was smiling. Or was she laughing at him? Philippe could not tell.

Then he noticed the lit cigarette, or possibly two, between his trembling fingers. And that sight relaxed him as much as its welcome aroma. He wanted to bring it to his lips, but his hand wouldn't cooperate. Exhausted and nauseated from the double vision, he closed his eyes and let his head fall back on the pillow.

He began to drift off, but he was awakened by his own involuntary cough.

The odor was far more intense now. Foreign. An incomprehensible sense of danger welled inside him. His hand felt hot.

Philippe tried to focus on his fingers. The woman was nowhere to be seen—he had already forgotten her, anyway—but a flame flickered between his fingers. The pain engorged his hand. He jerked his arm away, but the searing discomfort had already spread to his back, buttocks, and thighs.

The smoke was thicker, breathing harder. Philippe gagged on the acrid smell of burning flesh, not comprehending that it was his own skin on fire. But enough of his brain function endured to experience the agony. He searched frantically for the right words. Instead of a cry for help, other words tumbled from his lips: "The water wills . . ." His cough choked off the rest of it.

He looked down and saw four legs engulfed in flames. The pain was immeasurable. With what little air he had left in his lungs, he unleashed a piercing scream.

But the roaring fire consumed his dying shriek as efficiently as it had the curtains.

2

Dr. Noah Haldane bundled his jacket tighter, fighting off the biting chill. Not only was his internal clock upended, he still hadn't adjusted to the dramatic climate change. With only a six-hour stop in Washington—to deliver his daughter, Chloe, to her mother, Anna—he had flown from the warm sunshine of Playa del Carmen in Mexico straight into a Swiss blizzard. And as he hurried along the street toward the World Health Organization's sprawling headquarters, he still couldn't figure out why he had come. Not that he didn't understand the purpose of the meeting—he knew what the WHO wanted from him—but he didn't know why he kept heeding their call.

After the ARCS virus crisis—*catastrophe might be a more apt description,* Noah thought—he had sworn to leave the WHO behind him. Though others considered his dedication to the international health agency an act of medical altruism, Noah saw nothing selfless in it. On the contrary, like an alcoholic who keeps winding up with a bottle in his hand despite well-meaning promises to himself and loved ones, Noah couldn't tear himself away from the challenge and rush he found at the front lines of infectious-disease outbreaks.

As he rounded the corner and saw the massive blue WHO flag flapping violently in the wind, Noah was filled with the contradictory mix of anticipation and dread that these urgent meetings usually brought. Approaching the main building, which always reminded him of a giant waffle standing on its side, Noah dug in his pocket for his identification.

The machine-gun-toting guards checked him through the security post out front. Inside the main foyer, he had to pass through a metal detector on his way to the elevator banks. *Welcome to the new global village,* Noah thought glumly, remembering previous visits when a simple ID badge and a nod to an unarmed guard would gain him access to any corner of the building.

The click-clack of his black oxfords against the gleaming marble floors reminded him how he missed the comfort of walking barefoot on the white sand beaches of the Mexican resort. Far more than the sand and the sun, he missed Chloe. Their vacation had given them the chance to reconnect after the upheaval in both their lives. His daughter had yet to adjust to living separate lives with each of her parents, but the trip brought her a little more of the stability she needed.

Those thoughts slipped from his mind when he turned the corner and saw Dr. Jean Nantal waiting outside his office. With bone-straight posture and silver hair, the WHO's executive director of communicable diseases was dressed as impeccably as ever in a navy suit with a tastefully understated mauve tie. Jean had occupied the director's sixth-floor office for more than twenty years, and had been with the WHO since the smallpox eradication program, but his long and distinguished face showed little evidence of his seventy years. The man was as legendary as the smallpox campaign he had spearheaded. And he was as charming as he was intelligent, which helped explain his staff's singular devotion to him.

As Noah approached Jean's open arms, he reminded himself not to be taken in by the director's infectious idealism and enthusiasm. All too often, Noah had found himself in nasty predicaments after buoyantly leaving other such meetings. Jean greeted him with a kiss to each cheek. "Noah! You look wonderful. It must be the tan."

Noah shook his head. "Jean, you make me nervous when the compliments start this soon."

"Have I become so obvious? Perhaps it is time to retire." Jean laughed cheerfully. "How is little Chloe?"

"Good. She and I just spent a fun week in Mexico together."

Jean nodded approvingly. "She's already five, isn't she?" Noah marveled at Jean's ability to recall details of his team's personal lives. "My youngest granddaughter, Antoinette, turned eleven yesterday!" He laughed again. "Perhaps it is time to retire."

"You never will."

Jean shrugged and then arched an eyebrow. "And Gwen?" he asked in a tone that suggested he was already aware of Noah's romantic troubles.

Gwen Savard, Noah's girlfriend—*ex-girlfriend*, he reminded himself—was Homeland Security's director of counterbioterrorism, or the Bug Czar, as he affectionately called her. Their paths first crossed during the ARCS crisis, when a terrorist group's attempt to spread a Spanish Flu–like virus nearly ended in a full-blown pandemic. The intensity of their hazardous high-stakes work together spilled over into their personal lives. But despite their deep connection, neither had fully rebounded from recent divorces. That emotional baggage, combined with the oppositional pull of their demanding careers, made the relationship unsustainable.

Noah suddenly had a mental image of Gwen and those

penetrating green eyes that could so easily melt his resolve. There was no denying how much he missed her.
"She's an amazing person." He cleared his throat. "But
with her work and my work . . ."

Jean closed his eyes and nodded. The career-versus-
family story must have echoed like a broken record within
the walls of the WHO building.

A voice boomed from within the office. "For the love of
all that is holy, Jean! Are you coming back in, or did you
finally stop talking about it and retire after all?"

Hearing Duncan McLeod's Scottish brogue, Noah
broke into a grin. Jean shook his head good-naturedly as
he gestured toward the door. "Best not to keep Duncan
waiting."

They stepped inside the office. Aside from the antique
oak desk and the four leather-backed chairs facing it, the
room was austerely decorated with only a few landscape-
style photographs of the African savanna and whales
breaching in the Pacific. The only photo that included
Jean was one that must have dated back at least twenty
years and showed him standing beside a robust-looking
Pope John Paul II. Noah knew that Jean could easily
have wallpapered the room with photos of himself alongside famous dignitaries, but that was not the director's
style.

Duncan McLeod sprang out of his chair to meet Noah.
With his flaming red hair and cropped beard, Duncan
looked tidier than the last time they had seen each other,
but considering his untucked shirt, coffee-stained khakis,
and lazy left eye, Noah would have been hard-pressed to
describe his wiry friend as kempt. Noah noticed that Duncan had aged in the past seven months. Or maybe he was
just tired.

"Shite, look at you, Haldane," the Scot bellowed. "Even
tanned, you still look stiffer than that two-bit actor who
played you in the TV movie."

Noah warmly shook Duncan's outstretched hand. "Nobody played me in a movie."

"Didn't you see that piece of crap movie-of-the-week?" Duncan scoffed. "Swashbuckling WHO doctor saves the world single-handedly. Can't remember what they called him, Noel Maldane or some such tripe, but he was clearly supposed to be you!" He pointed a thumb to his chest. "Meanwhile old McLeod and the rest of the grunts were written right out of history."

Noah had seen the made-for-TV movie, or at least part of it. The producers had never interviewed him, and he was so irritated by the fabrications and the liberties they had taken with the real-life events that he switched it off halfway through in disgust. "I think they meant that character to be a composite of all of us," he said.

"A composite, huh?" Duncan scoffed. "Then they should have called him Donegal McLow and given him a decent bloody accent!"

With an extended hand, Jean drew Noah's attention to the woman in the chair beside Duncan's. "Noah, allow me to introduce Elise Renard," he said. "Ms. Renard is a special envoy with the E.U.'s Agricultural Commission." Jean turned to Elise with an amused smile. "Clearly, Dr. Haldane's movie-star reputation precedes him."

Noah stepped around Duncan and offered his hand to the young woman. "It's Noah. And don't listen to Jean. He's all flattery when he wants something from us."

"Too true," Duncan said. "He called me 'invaluable' before you showed up, which can only mean he plans to toss us out of a rocket without a parachute this time!"

Elise Renard rose from her chair to meet Noah, almost reaching his six feet. Her chestnut brown hair was cut very short. Thirtyish, lean as she was tall, she had a light complexion that was scattered with freckles. With a delicate upturned nose and high cheekbones, her full lips were creased into a polite smile. Her large gray-blue eyes set off her face, but Noah sensed wariness behind those striking eyes. "It's an honor to meet you, Noah." She spoke with a light accent and her tone had a pleasing gravelly quality.

"Renard? Is that French?"

"Belgian."

"That's something, at least," Duncan grumbled. He turned to Jean, raising a stack of stapled papers from beside his chair. "No offense, but I was sick of the French even before I read this. Now—"

"On that note . . ." Jean rolled his eyes good-naturedly, showing more patience with Duncan than Noah thought he deserved. "Maybe we can turn to the issue at hand."

Noah took the seat beside Elise as Jean walked around his desk and settled into the chair behind it. He slipped on his reading glasses and then lifted the pages off the desk. "No doubt you have all read the briefing prepared on this matter, but let me give you an update. Ms. Renard—"

"Elise," she corrected.

"Mais, bien sûr," Jean said with a wave. "Elise is joining us because of the animal cases. So far, in the central region of Limousin—the heart of French cattle farming—seven cows have tested positive in the past two months for bovine spongiform encephalitis, or BSE."

"Seven mad cows?" Duncan sat up straighter. "I thought we only had four in France!"

"We only heard back from Paris this morning. The Institut Pasteur has confirmed three more positive tests."

Noah glanced at his sheet, considering the implication of the numbers. "Seven cases in two months? That's as big a cluster of BSE cases as we have seen since the nineties."

"Especially when we consider they are localized to a forty-kilometer radius surrounding Limoges, the region's capital." Jean glanced at Elise. "The E.U. is understandably concerned about this BSE emergence. It creates great uncertainty in the cattle trade industry—"

"Fucking marvelous! I'm delighted you're so concerned," Duncan turned on Elise angrily. "But where was the bloody E.U. when our cattle industry in Britain was being decimated by mad cow disease? All you did was slap an absolute moratorium on the export of British beef forever. France was the bloody worst offender of the lot in banning British beef."

Noah was about to intercede when he noticed Jean fold his hands together and lay them slowly on the desk. "Duncan, this is hardly the time or place for finger pointing," he said in a hushed voice that silenced the Scot.

Elise raised a hand. "Dr. McLeod has a point, Jean." But her expression and tone lacked contrition. "We knew far less about BSE back then. We are determined not to repeat the same errors this time. Please don't forget, Dr. McLeod, the number of cases in Limousin pales in comparison to the British epidemic of the mid-nineties."

"So far," Duncan said quietly.

Duncan's words resonated with Noah. He looked over at Elise. "Though in this case we're seeing the human equivalent, variant Creutzfeld-Jakob disease, far earlier than we did in the British epidemic."

"Exactement," Jean said solemnly. "We know of three people who have contracted vCJD in the past three months."

Noah silently digested the news of the third case that wasn't mentioned in the e-mail briefing he had received earlier. Somewhere in the recesses of his brain an alarm was quietly sounding.

"Three?" Elise frowned at Jean. "There were over a hundred human cases in Britain."

"Ah, true." Jean nodded. "But the incubation period was measured in years, decades even, not weeks."

"A rapid spread from animals to humans could spell catastrophe," Noah murmured.

Elise held up her palms, confused.

"In England, it was five or ten years after the first case of BSE before we saw the equivalent, variant Creutzfeldt-Jakob disease, in humans," Noah explained. "But in this French outbreak, it seems to have happened almost simultaneously."

She nodded. "I understand. Pardon me for appearing foolish in the presence of doctors, but can you describe the difference between CJD and *variant* CJD to me?"

Noah gave Duncan—who had remained uncharacteristically silent since his outburst—a pat on the shoulder. "Duncan's the expert on mad cows."

"It's true. Comes from years spent with the mother-in-law," Duncan said, and Noah understood that the little joke and his crooked smile were meant as a peace offering to Elise. "Creutzfeldt-Jakob has been known . . . since, well, since those two krauts, Creutzfeldt and Jakob, described it in the twenties," Duncan continued. "An exceedingly nasty disease, it mainly affects older people. Average age of onset is over sixty. Fortunately it's very rare."

"How rare?" Elise asked.

"About one in a million," Duncan said. "Though developing it is like losing the lottery. The bugger strikes hard and quickly. In under a year, it will turn a healthy person completely demented and wheelchair bound. Like full-blown Alzheimer's almost overnight. At autopsy, the poor sods' brains are so moth-eaten that the pathologists use the term 'spongiform'—Latin for spongelike—to describe them." He sighed. "But the garden variety CJD is not really considered an infectious disease."

"Unlike variant CJD," Elise said. She ran her hand through her short hair, as though she forgot there was nothing to sweep back.

"Exactly," Noah spoke up. "Variant CJD was discovered only in the mid-nineties. And though the end result is the same as for CJD—namely, death—variant CJD has quite a different course."

"Different how?" she asked.

"To begin with, the disease affects much younger people," Duncan said, slipping naturally into the tone of an enthusiastic teacher. "Average age of onset is around thirty. Also, victims show fewer signs of dementia and far more symptoms of psychiatric illness: delusion, hallucinations, and so forth. Similar to schizophrenia." He paused. "And variant CJD is invariably associated with outbreaks of mad cow disease. In fact, it occurs only in people who have eaten beef from infected cattle."

"The prion," Elise said in a near whisper.

Duncan whistled. "The little bastard is one of the great mysteries of the infectious-diseases world. Big-time evil in a wee little package. So small, it makes a virus look massive in comparison."

Noah nodded. "And the most bizarre part is that unlike other infections—bacterial, parasitical, and even viral—prions are not alive by *any* definition. They are simply rogue proteins that somehow sabotage normal functioning brain cells."

"Not alive," Jean echoed softly. "But still contagious."

Elise nodded. She glanced from Duncan to Noah, before her eyes settled on Jean. "With respect, I understand my department's worry about the outbreak in these French cattle farms, but why is the WHO so concerned about *three* cases of vCJD in France when there were over a hundred and twenty cases reported in Britain the last time?"

Jean leaned back in his chair. "Ah yes, Elise, but these French cases appeared at the same time as the cattle outbreak."

"And in the U.K.," Duncan added, "despite millions of infected cows, we only saw a hundred or so human cases. So far, in France the ratio is seven to three!"

Seven to three. Noah fought off a shudder. "We'd better find out why this cluster of vCJD has had such a short incubation period," he said. "If this prion is more contagious to humans than it was in Britain, we might be facing an infectious crisis. And not just in France."

"Or even Europe," Duncan muttered.

"How do you intend to find this out?" Elise asked.

"We'll start with the families," Noah said. "And speak to the victims themselves if they can still give us reliable information."

Jean shook his head. "None can."

"Oh?" Noah said.

"All of them are dead."

Noah went cold. The warning bells were clanging in his brain. He glanced over at Duncan, who had paled noticeably. "Shite, Jean, are you saying these people died in a matter of weeks from vCJD?" he asked.

Jean nodded.

"Are we dealing with an unknown entity here?" Duncan said, and seemed to hold his breath.

Noah was thinking along the same lines. His temples pounded as he realized that this outbreak was already behaving differently from any variant CJD previously seen. *Worse*. "What if the BSE prion has mutated and is now more aggressive and contagious than before?"

"Christ, Haldane!" Duncan stormed. "Then we haven't yet seen the tiniest tip of an extremely nasty iceberg."

"I should clarify my answer," Jean said. "Only two of the victims died directly of their disease. The third died in an accident."

"An accident?" Noah asked, taking no comfort in Jean's clarification.

Jean nodded gravely. "A fire."

3

Montmagnon, France. January 12

Pauline Lamaire stood at her kitchen countertop, eyeing the sandwich she had just constructed. She would have loved to add a slice of roast beef or, at the very least, a sliver of Brie, but her refrigerator held neither; even if it did, she wasn't about to break her self-imposed yearlong vegan diet. Not when she was starting to see sustained improvement for the first time in three years.

There wasn't much the thirty-seven-year-old had not tried. When conventional medicine failed to halt the rapid advance of her rheumatoid arthritis, Pauline turned to alternative therapies. Ignoring the advice of her doctors—in whom she had lost faith anyway—she gobbled vitamins and herbal remedies with abandon. She was willing to try almost any new treatment that she dug up in books or magazines, or through the Internet—even those she knew crossed the line into quackery. Pauline was desperate to reclaim her life. She used to run marathons, but now she had so much pain and stiffness in her knees and hips that walking a few hundred yards into town was almost impossible. She was a nationally recognized concert violinist who had not touched her instrument in more than a year.

She held up her hands and studied the knobby arthritic joints in her fingers. No question, they were less swollen and the throb had diminished. She balled her fingers and almost managed to form fists. Her heart leaped at the sight. She never would have been able to do that a month ago.

Maybe the diet is helping, she thought. However, she gave most of the credit to the new therapy she had commenced. She had been taking it for more than four months and, as promised, the results had been striking.

Did I take my morning dose? Pauline wondered. She couldn't remember. *Strange.*

Your memory would shame an elephant, her mother used to joke when she was a child. But in the past week or so she had been forgetful in uncharacteristic ways. The previous evening, she had left a tap running when she went out to the store. Earlier in the week, she had forgotten her cane at the bank. She had taken that oversight as an encouraging sign of her physical improvement, but the growing memory lapses had begun to worry her.

The smell of basil and mustard reminded Pauline how hungry she was. Shrugging off her concern, she reached for the sandwich on her plate. The edge of rye bread grazed her cheek and smeared mustard on her face. She bit through the perfectly crisp crust. As she returned the sandwich to her plate, she lost her grip. It toppled onto the floor and landed in a mess of vegetables and sauce.

"Clumsy, Pauline!" she muttered.

Both knees burned with pain as she knelt down to pick up the remains of the sandwich. Her right hand swept forward but missed the bread altogether. She tried again. This time she caught the sandwich by the crust, but no sooner had she lifted it off the ground than it tumbled from her grip.

Ignoring the spill, she leaned back against the wall and

raised her hand to her face. Trembling slightly, it felt entirely numb. She tried to form a fist again but this time the hand simply twitched, dead in response.

Sudden fear winded her. *What is happening to me?*

4

As the Airbus A321 sat on the tarmac waiting for clearance to depart, Duncan squirmed relentlessly in the seat. Beside him, Noah read the *International Herald Tribune* while trying to ignore his fidgeting friend.

"I thought the Swiss had a thing for punctuality," Duncan grumbled. And for the umpteenth time, he jerked his arm up and made a show of studying his watch. "It's been over an hour. You think the captain is waiting for France to come to us?"

Noah tapped the fogged-up window. "Not much they can do about a blizzard."

"And this comes as a surprise to them?" Duncan rolled his eyes. "I don't believe there was an ultraviolet sunscreen warning outside when they dragged me away from my beer and football match in the terminal, just to have me sit on the runway like a giant log."

Noah bit back a smile. "We both know Lufthansa has been out to get you for a while now."

Duncan sighed heavily. "I'm not terribly pleased about this."

Noah shrugged. "Would have never guessed."

"Not the bloody flight!" Duncan snapped. "The mad cow situation in France."

Despite his friend's exaggerated charade of trying to avoid every assignment the WHO sent them on, Noah knew that Duncan shared his passion for the job. However, since the meeting in Geneva, Duncan had been uncharacteristically dour. Sensing it was best to let him get it off his chest, Noah simply nodded and waited.

Duncan arched in his seat and flopped onto his side, facing away from Noah. Just as Noah began to raise his newspaper, the Scot turned back to him. "Back in the nineties, I was one of the *supposed* experts they consulted with on managing the mad cow outbreak in Britain." He paused. "They didn't listen to me then. I've got no reason to believe they will listen now."

"What did you tell them then?"

"That they were fools to think that infected cows existed only on our miserable little island. I told them to look closer at the rest of the world to see where the bugger was hiding. Their answer was to ban British beef indefinitely, and destroy a way of life for thousands of cattle farmers. It had everything to do with politics, and nothing to do with science."

Noah knew that time had proven Duncan right. Thousands of cases of BSE had been underreported or even ignored in mainland Europe before exhaustive surveillance systems were adopted. "And *'they'* are?" Noah asked.

"The new motherland." Duncan laid a hand on his chest, feigning patriotism. "The European Union."

"Aha," Noah said. Duncan's unprovoked outburst at Elise Renard, the E.U. envoy, suddenly made more sense.

"Granted, I'm not a huge fan of governments of any kind," Duncan said with a fleeting half-grin. "But the E.U.? It's not even a government. Nothing of the sort. It's no more than a huge trade monopoly with its own colorful money. I trust those bumbling E.U. bureaucrats even less than I trust the dangerous clowns who run *your* empire."

Noah ignored the anti-American dig. "And Elise Renard?" he asked.

"Works for them."

"Maybe, but Jean specifically asked us to work with her on this one."

"Jean asks a lot of us."

"Don't give me that crap." Noah's grip tightened on his armrest as his patience suddenly gave way. "He's always been there for us. And if he asks us to work with Elise and the E.U., then we work with them."

Duncan shrugged noncommittally.

Glowering, Noah grabbed for his newspaper and flapped it open noisily. He realized that part of his frustration was misdirected at Duncan. He was no happier than his colleague about having to report to a second regulatory body on their progress. And this mysterious French outbreak made him uneasy. Though the numbers of infected were still small, he sensed that the potential for something much bigger lay under the surface.

"Weeks, Haldane," Duncan said. "I don't know of a prion that manifests itself and kills its victims in a matter of weeks."

"Neither do I," Noah grunted from behind his newspaper.

"And between us, we do know a thing or two about the wee bastards."

Duncan had a point. As an infectious-disease specialist, Noah subspecialized in emerging pathogens; and Duncan was one of WHO's leading clinical microbiologists. Prion-related diseases fell within both their realms. "Let's face it, prions are the black holes of microbiology," Noah said in a more civil tone. "No one knows much about them."

"True. But with other prion diseases like scrapie in

sheep or even kuru that cannibals get from eating human brain that's been left out of the icebox too long"—Duncan joked of the brain-wasting disease New Guinea cannibals acquired from consuming infected brains—"I'm not aware of a case of spontaneous change in the disease incubation or progression. Gruesome as they are, those prions are as predictable as a clock. This thing sounds potentially explosive."

Noah's guts churned, as he tried to shrug off Duncan's ominous comment. "Microbes change all the time," he rationalized. "That's the joy of our job."

"I keep forgetting how joyful our job is." Duncan reached out and took a section of Noah's paper. "Now let me have a look at the obits. They might cheer me up."

Half an hour later, the plane finally lifted off. Noah stared out the window at the clouds enshrouding the aircraft, trying to ignore the flight's at-times-violent vibrations and unexpected drops in the turbulent air. His thoughts drifted to his family. He hadn't been able to reach his ex-wife, Anna, from his hotel room or his cell phone. He guessed she and Chloe were somewhere on the road to South Carolina, where her parents wintered.

He would have loved to have spoken with Chloe. And Anna. More than a year had passed since their separation and, though Anna had moved in with her partner, Julie, time had soothed the wounds; his sense of hurt and betrayal had ebbed until an ember of regret replaced what had once been a fire. They had grown far tighter than he ever anticipated. She told him once that their closeness was a sore point with Julie. And while Noah had grown to tolerate—even grudgingly admire—the "other woman," he took vindicatory satisfaction in knowing he was responsible for her jealousy.

Gwen had never been jealous of Noah's closeness to Anna. On the contrary, she encouraged it, reasoning that it was best for his daughter. Thinking of Gwen again, his heart sank. He was tempted to call her and run the details of the French outbreak by her. Though vCJD had little relevance for an expert on bioterrorism, Gwen had superb judgment. Once, he had gone so far as to pick up the phone and dial the first three digits of her number before hanging up, realizing it would not be fair to either of them to initiate contact.

"Finally!" Duncan shouted, waving the paper in his hands and causing the timid-looking woman across the aisle to almost leap from her seat. "It's refreshing to see a scientist more famous than you!"

Noah glanced at the paper. A half-page photo of a smiling man was inlaid with a diagram of a lake, a shot of an ice field, and an electron-microscope image of a bacterium. Noah recognized Dr. Claude Fontaine from his picture. His name and face were everywhere lately, cutting across the media spectrum from respected scientific journals to TV talk shows and even the gossip columns.

"I still don't see why they're making such a fuss over this bloke," Duncan said.

"Fontaine found organisms in a lake miles under the Antarctic ice thriving under conditions supposedly incompatible with life. Even you have to admit, that's impressive." Noah pointed at the photo of the ruggedly handsome Frenchman. "Plus he has that mug and one of those irresistible French accents. Face it. He's a media dream."

"I don't know, Haldane. You've got a cheesy smile and a ridiculous accent, too, and the press forgot you in a big hurry after the ARCS scare."

"Thank God," Noah said, and meant it. "Did you read Fontaine's article in *Nature*? Amazing how those bacteria have adapted to Lake Vishnov. Zero light, and living at the freezing point under a water pressure that would crush a tank."

Duncan shrugged. "They're not so adaptable. The little

bastards explode like dynamite when they're brought any-where near atmospheric pressure."

"Yeah," Noah agreed. "It's going to make studying them a challenge. They'll have to keep them pressurized and away from all light."

"Kind of like us." Duncan's lips cracked into a mischie-vous grin. "Under intense bloody pressure and usually completely in the dark."

At 3:05 P.M., their plane touched down bumpily on the runway of Limoges's modest airport. Noah and Duncan deplaned onto a tarmac that was even colder and windier than the streets of Geneva. They hurried inside the termi-nal, where Noah was relieved to see that no one awaited them. He preferred to avoid the (often well-intentioned) meddling from local governments and sister agencies that dogged him throughout the ARCS crisis.

In front of the airport, they grabbed the first cab they spotted. The driver's swarthy face boasted at least three days' worth of stubble, and he smelled of some kind of fried meat. Noah guessed he was Eastern European, though he had no way of knowing because the man spoke no English and barely any French. In his own basic French, Noah conveyed the address of their hotel.

In a stop-start jerky ride that would have tested the nerves of most New York cabbies, the driver wove in and out of traffic, not slowing when the highway gave way to the narrower twisting streets of the city of Limoges, built on the banks of the Vienne River. Noah fought off his growing queasiness and took in the city from the backseat of the hurtling taxi. He marveled at the medieval churches and ornate Renaissance buildings interspersed among red-roofed apartments and other more ordinary recent structures.

The driver slammed on his brakes, screeching to a stop

halfway through an intersection, barely avoiding a truck that sailed inches past the front of the car. He leaned on the tinny horn and unleashed a stream of expletives. "I was prepared to take my chances with mad cows," Duncan said, white-knuckling the door handle. "But no one mentioned the insane cabbies!"

The driver hit the accelerator as if a racing flag had dropped, and they were off again.

"You know, Richard the Lionheart was killed by a crossbow just a few miles south of here," Noah said, trying to focus on something other than his flip-flopping stomach.

Duncan pointed at the driver, who was busy working the horn. "You sure it wasn't in the back of some medieval cab that reeked of fried sausages?"

Noah chuckled. "This city has quite a history. During medieval times, it held one of the largest libraries in the known world at the Abbey of St. Martial. In the 1700s, unique clay was discovered on the riverbanks and Limoges became world famous for its porcelain. Still is today."

"Oh, Christ, Haldane." Duncan grinned. "You've been at your Frommer's tour books again, haven't you?"

Noah flashed the thumbs-up sign. When work took him to any new destination, he made a habit of reading up on the region first. Duncan teased Noah for it, but in his way, the Scotsman was eager to hear about the local color. "Limoges is the capital of Limousin, but its population is barely over a hundred thousand," Noah went on. "Apparently, Limousin has the smallest and oldest population in France's forty provinces. But the terrain is supposed to be beautiful."

"Nowadays people prefer their McDonald's and WiFi to quiet forests and babbling brooks," Duncan said wistfully.

Noah wondered if Duncan was referring to his teen-aged twin boys, but he didn't ask. His friend rarely discussed his home life, though from their few previous conversations Noah knew that the frequent travel away from home was tough on Duncan and his tight-knit family.

"On the other hand," Noah said, "this is still one of the top cattle-producing regions in France. In fact, Limousin is a popular breed the world over."

"Marvelous, Haldane. Let's just hope their trendy cows aren't responsible for the end of the world."

Before Noah could comment, the taxi skidded up to the entrance of the Grand Hotel Doré on Avenue Garibaldi. Feeling seasick as he got out, he was glad to be on stable ground despite the biting cold. He gave the pale stone exterior of the dated hotel no more than a quick glance. Providing the roofs didn't leak and the floors didn't crawl with insects, Noah didn't demand much of his lodgings. His own two-bedroom condominium just outside the Beltway in D.C. was new and bright, but since moving in more than a year before, he had not hung a single decoration on the walls, and only Chloe's room was fully furnished. Even Gwen had raised an eyebrow at the sparseness of the place.

Standing at the check-in desk, Noah consulted his watch. "If we want to catch Dr. Charron, we should get moving," he said to Duncan.

They left their bags with the teenaged bellboy and headed back out to the street. Noah was glad not to see their airport driver. Instead, a beat-up yellow Renault with taxi markings idled at the curb. They climbed in the back. Either the heater was broken or the emaciated cabbie liked the cold, because it wasn't any warmer inside, but getting out of the wind brought some relief.

After navigating the narrow downtown streets, the taxi turned onto a road that ran along the riverbank. While some of the bridges crisscrossing the river were old and pretty, Noah was underwhelmed by the Vienne itself, with its colorless black water and blandly landscaped banks. The driver turned north, away from the river, and a few blocks later, a large complex loomed around them. Duncan whistled. "Didn't expect to see *that* in a one-horse town."

Noah was equally impressed by the extent of the sprawling complex of the Centre Hospitalier Régional Universitaire, or CHRU, as the signs everywhere abbreviated the university hospital's name.

The driver dropped them off in front of the modern round entryway. In the rotunda, a heavyset receptionist directed them to the elevators down the hallway. A moment later, they walked out onto the sixth floor and passed under a sign identifying the Centre de Maladie Neuromusculaire. Noah had worked in the research world long enough to realize from the signage and the plaques alone that the CHRU had an academically important neurology department. At the end of the hallway, they reached the office of the department head, Dr. Louis Charron.

The neurologist was waiting for the WHO doctors at the door. Gaunt and with a slight stoop, Charron looked well over sixty to Noah. He had hollow cheeks and penetrating hazel eyes, and his thinning white hair complemented his long lab coat. A lit cigarette dangled from the corner of his thin lips. The sight surprised Noah, who was unaccustomed to seeing anyone smoke inside a hospital.

Charron held out a bony hand to them. "You've come from Geneva, yes?" he said in a clipped tone laced with only a trace of French accent. "I am Dr. Louis Charron. You must be Drs. Haldane and McLeod." He even pronounced Duncan's name correctly.

Noah slipped his hand into Charron's cold dry grip. "Jean Nantal told me of you," Charron said. He led them into his corner office, which had a commanding view of the Vienne as it meandered through the center of Limoges.

"So you know Jean?" Noah asked.

Charron took a long puff of his cigarette. "For years," he said in a tone that didn't clarify whether he liked the man. He walked around his desk and sank into the substantial black leather chair behind it. "Sit, please."

Noah and Duncan pulled up two chairs across from the neurologist. Charron fussed with an ashtray on the desk. "You've come about our cases."

Noah nodded. "You've had three atypical variant Creutzfeldt-Jakob patients in the past few months, right?"

"Perhaps."

Duncan rubbed a hand through his beard thoughtfully. "Jean sounded more definite."

Charron held his palms open in front of him. "No question, we've had three cases of accelerated dementia in young adults . . ."

"You're not convinced it was vCJD?" Noah asked, suddenly more on edge.

Charron took another puff and then shrugged. "If nothing else, it is a close relative."

"Did you examine the patients yourself?" Duncan asked.

"Of course," Charron snapped. "I myself made the diagnosis in the first patient. Even before I knew anything of the outbreak in the animals."

"Dr. Charron, can you give us more specifics on the victims?" Noah asked.

Charron crushed his cigarette in the ashtray, reached for the three charts stacked on his desk, and flipped open the first one. Without looking up from the chart he said, "Benoît Gagnon. Thirty-two years old. He was admitted to the psychiatric ward twelve weeks ago."

"The diagnosis?" Noah asked.

"Paranoid psychosis," Charron said. "The psychiatrists originally diagnosed him with schizophrenia. Very guarded and hostile. However, after he had a series of

seizures, they turned to me." He closed the chart. "I immediately ordered an MRI as part of the workup. The
changes in his brain's white matter were subtle, but I noticed that without question he had organic brain damage of
some kind."

Noah leaned forward in his seat. "What happened
next?"

"He died," Charron said matter-of-factly.

Duncan frowned. "From subtle white matter changes?"

"By the time of his death, there was nothing subtle
about the brain damage," Charron sighed. He reached for
the pack of smokes on the desk and tapped out another
one. "We were able to control his seizures, but in the days
that followed he deteriorated rapidly."

"From a psychiatric or neurological point of view?"
Noah asked.

"Both," Charron said, cupping his hand around the
lighter. He inhaled a long puff of smoke and then pointed
with the cigarette. "You see, he became mute. Totally.
Would not speak. Or perhaps . . . could not speak."

Noah tried to picture in his mind the young and unre-
sponsive man, but still couldn't get a feel for him. "How did
you diagnose him before you had a brain tissue sample?"

"With my forty years of clinical experience," he said
with a slight cough. "Also, I performed a spinal tap. The
fourteen-three-three protein in his spinal fluid was positive."

During the flight in, Noah had read an article on the
fourteen-three-three protein, one of the few blood tests
useful in vCJD cases. "I understand that the test is far
from foolproof," he said.

"Perhaps, but the autopsy was conclusive. His brain
showed the classic spongiform changes of vCJD."

"And the other cases?" Duncan asked, fixing his gaze
on the desk.

Charron reshuffled the charts on his desk and opened the

second one. "Giselle Tremblay from Saint Junien. Twenty-six. I wasn't involved in her care, but she was originally thought to suffer from psychosis. I suppose it was understandable. She had a history of being manic-depressive. But by the time she reached us, she was essentially catatonic. Practically no movement. She died within days. Again, the autopsy was unequivocal."

Noah's unease rose. Even beyond the aggressiveness of the disease, something in Charron's description was eating at him, but he couldn't put a finger on it. "And the third patient?" he asked.

"Ah, yes." Charron blew a ring of smoke in the air. "Philippe Manet. Thirty. A civil engineer from Lac Noir," he said without consulting the final chart on his desk. "He also presented with a psychotic episode. Threatened someone with a knife. Very paranoid. Full of conspiracy theories. This time our psychiatrists picked up on it right away."

"Picked up on what?" Duncan asked.

"The tremor in his right hand." Charron sighed. "That was the only feature that suggested it wasn't pure psychosis. They consulted me, and of course, I made the diagnosis."

"How long did he survive?"

Charron crushed another cigarette. "He was with us only two weeks before being discharged."

Noah sat up in his seat, astounded. *"Discharged?"*

"The family insisted," Charron said. "They knew he was dying. And they wanted him closer to home in Lac Noir. They found him a bed at a private hospital."

"But the lad died in a fire, right?" Duncan pointed out.

"Apparently," Charron said. "As I understand it, another patient in the hospital gave him a cigarette. Predictably, he set the whole building on fire. Two others died, too, including a staff member."

"Amazing." Noah shook his head, trying to make sense

of Philippe's bizarre death and the unsettling cluster of patients. "Earlier you referred to it as an 'accelerated dementia' and a possible relative of vCJD. You think it might be something different?" He paused. "Some new entity?"

Charron leaned back in his chair and studied the ceiling. "They died from some form of CJD-like illness. And considering the outbreak in cattle, it must be a prion-based disease. But with the English vCJD epidemic, the progression was so much slower." He drew thoughtfully on his cigarette. "Our cases behaved more like an overwhelming infection."

Noah's gut churned at the neurologist's choice of terms. "And you have no live cases?"

"Not at my hospital." Charron pointed to the window with his fresh cigarette. "God knows what is out there."

"Shite," Duncan muttered. "Would have helped to see the victims with our own eyes."

"*D'accord.* I will show you." Charron pulled open a drawer in his desk and extracted a DVD. He walked over to the TV in the corner of the room, loaded the disc into the player below it, and then returned holding a remote control in his hand.

Noah and Duncan turned their chairs to face the screen, which filled with the image of a hospital room. "This is Giselle Tremblay," Charron said.

The camera zoomed in on a woman in a yellow pajama top lying propped up in her bed, wrapped in a blanket from her chest down. With short brown hair, she had a pleasant round face and full cheeks, but the chain of drool hanging from her chin and the way her wide brown eyes deviated up and to the right dampened her otherwise attractive features.

"*Giselle?*" A soft female voice spoke from off-screen. "*Giselle? C'est Marianne. Répondez, s'il vous plaît.*"

But Giselle didn't respond. She just continued to stare up at the sky with her eyes so far back in her head it appeared she was trying to look over her shoulder without moving her head. Noah felt slightly voyeuristic watching the shell of a woman who was only days from death, but her empty doll-like presence viscerally conveyed the consequence of this brain-eating prion.

"She stayed catatonic like that for her entire stay," Charron said. "Now let me introduce Philippe Manet."

The image on the TV screen suddenly switched to an interview room. A man in jeans and a black T-shirt sat in a chair. He was young with a slim bearded face distinguished by an aquiline nose. His gray eyes darted around the room constantly. The cigarette rarely left his lips. And Noah saw that his right hand trembled on his lap.

"This was filmed on the first day of Philippe's admission," Charron said.

"Philippe, comment ça va?" asked the same female voice that had spoken to Giselle.

He shook the cigarette at the camera. *"Ça va mal!"* he spat, and then launched into rapid-fire French that Noah had trouble following.

" 'They know I'm here, you know,' " Charron translated for them in a flowing tone that was the antithesis of Manet's panicky, choppy words. " 'They will come for you just as they have come for me.' "

Noah understood the interviewer when she asked "Who are 'they'?" but Philippe's finger-waving rant was too rapid for him to follow.

" 'They are the demons who visit us,' " Charron translated. " 'They are the people who possess us. Georges knows. Sylvie does, too. The water, it worms its way into your mind. It gets into your soul. They possess me already. They will come for you!' "

The interviewer began another question, but Philippe screamed something unintelligible. He shot up out of his chair so quickly that it toppled over. Then he ran forward and out of camera range. The screen's picture seesawed from side to side as two other male voices yelled out over the commotion of a loud crash. A pair of hulking men in white hospital uniforms appeared on the screen as they wrestled Philippe back into the camera's view. One of the men righted the chair, and together they forced Philippe to sit down. Eyes wide with panic, he looked beyond the men and cried out as if speaking directly to the camera.

"'Don't you understand?'" Charron translated the words, doing no justice to Philippe's frantic tone. "'The fire. The water. They will come for you. They will come. And you will be dead, too!'"

As a medical student, Noah had seen several paranoid and delusional patients, but he never remembered a psychotic patient looking as terrified as Philippe Manet. The man's fear was so palpable it was contagious.

Charron clicked a button on the remote, and the screen changed back to the hospital room setting. Now Philippe lay in a bed similar to Giselle's and wore a similar yellow pajama top. "This is Philippe thirteen days later," Charron said nonchalantly. "The day he was sent back to Lac Noir."

"Shite," Duncan grumbled. "That's a hard thirteen days!"

Philippe's face was now gaunt to the point of skin and bones, his beard and hair wild. His hands shook uncontrollably on top of the bedcovers. His eyes gazed out at nothing, and he muttered continuously to himself in a voice that had become incomprehensibly slurred.

Noah could pick out only a few words—*l'eau* for "water" and *tête* for "head"—from the garbled speech, but he suspected that language wasn't the problem. "He's not making any sense, is he?" Noah asked.

Charron sighed. "None whatsoever. Just random words and phrases. And as you can hear, he is losing control over the ability to even form words."

"Thirteen days," Duncan repeated quietly.

Noah had a sudden mental image of hospital wards full of similarly brain-dead zombies, victims of this ultra-aggressive prion. He shook off the image and swallowed away the lump in his throat.

We can't let this thing spread.

5

Montmagnon, France. January 15

Pauline Lamaire had once prided herself on how neat and uncluttered she kept her home. Now chaos reigned. Plates, dishes, newspapers, and clothes were scattered everywhere. Her herbal remedies and other bottles were spread across the room; many toppled over with pills spilling onto the furniture and floors. The stench of spoiled milk—from a bottle left out for days—and urine—from the cat whose litter was days overdue for changing—permeated the room.

Pauline was only vaguely cognizant of the state of her house. She rarely remembered her medications, but whenever she found a bottle, she popped another dose, having no idea when was the last time she had taken one. She was, however, aware enough to know that something was desperately wrong. Her once ironclad memory grew more unreliable each day. She left notepads around the room, where she would scribble notes to herself—most of which went unread—in a script that had gone from precise and neat to barely legible.

One note beside her chair asked, WHERE IS POPO? But she had no idea what happened to her cat or even whether he was still missing. CALL DR. TANIER, another note instructed. But she didn't know his phone number and couldn't figure out where to find it. Besides, for reasons Pauline couldn't fathom, she didn't trust that Dr. Tanier or *any* medical doctor could help her.

"*You are useless, Pauline!*" a German-accented voice barked inside her head.

For days, the same voice had been nagging at her incessantly. Even in her woolly-headed state, she recognized it as belonging to her former violin teacher, Herr Strieber. The harsh Austrian had taught her from age eleven until sixteen (when Pauline had sworn to her parents that she would quit violin rather than remain his student). No matter what she did, the young Pauline could never please Herr Strieber. And she fared no better now. "*You are crippled,*" his voice spat in her head. "*And you are losing your mind. You should have listened to me. Now you are nothing. Nothing!*"

Her cat whined again, but Pauline ignored it. And again. *Or was it the doorbell?*

"*Answer it, little fool!*" Herr Strieber shrieked in her head.

She rose to her feet and staggered toward the door, feeling as if she were walking across a ship's deck in the midst of a gale. At the door, she struggled with the knob before finally pulling it open. The sunlight streamed in, temporarily blinding her.

When her eyes adjusted, she saw a woman standing on the doorstep. The attractive woman looked familiar. She was the one who brought Pauline more treatment every few weeks. Or maybe not. Everything in her head was so muddled. Still, the woman's sympathetic smile and understanding eyes eased Pauline's panic.

"You see, Pauline?" the woman said in a silky-soft voice. "I'm here now, just like I promised."

"For me?"

The woman reached out and laid a hand tenderly on Pauline's elbow. "For you."

Tears welled in Pauline's eyes. "Thank you," she sputtered.

The grip tightened around her elbow until it hurt. "I am going to take care of you now, Pauline," the woman said.

6

As he sat in the dining room of the Grand Hotel Doré and stared at the breakfast menu, Noah vacillated between the fruit-and-yogurt plate and the strawberry crêpes. Though he had been active his entire life and had never deviated more than a few pounds from his college weight, Noah had inherited his father's high cholesterol level. His doctor had been threatening him with cholesterol-lowering drugs for the past few years, but Noah had resisted, insisting he could tackle the problem with a healthy diet alone. He knew his attitude was born from foolish pride: Starting on those lifelong medications struck him as conceding his youth, something the forty-year-old hadn't been prepared to do. But recent blood tests showed he was losing the battle. Anna was right—gambling with his coronary arteries was not fair to Chloe. Silently committing to accepting the prescription, he decided to reward himself with the crêpes.

Movement caught the corner of his eye, and he looked up to see Elise Renard, dressed in a black business suit and white blouse, striding toward him. He smiled at her, but the gesture went unreciprocated.

"Morning, Elise," he said. "Did you just fly in?"

"I drove in last night," the E.U. envoy said frostily.

Noah pulled back the chair beside his. "Hungry?"

She folded her arms across her chest and made no move to sit down. "I assumed from our meeting in Geneva that we would be working together."

Noah nodded, confused by her icy deportment. "That was the general idea."

"I hear that you have already seen the neurologist who tended the victims."

"Ah." Noah suddenly understood. "I didn't realize you'd want to be present for the medical interviews. I thought you were more concerned with the livestock involvement."

"The European Union's concern lies with this entire *outbreak*," she said sharply. "If this prion affected only cows and presented no risk to humans, then my commission wouldn't need to be involved. But we are. And it is essential that I know exactly what we are facing."

"Fair enough. Sorry we started without you." He offered her a conciliatory grin and pulled back the chair beside him. "Let me give you the rundown on what Dr. Charron had to say."

She wavered a moment before she uncrossed her arms and slipped into the chair. "Thank you," she said, but the chill hadn't thawed from her tone.

Noah tried to pass her a menu, but she waved it away. "I've eaten."

He lifted his own menu. "Mind if I order?"

She shook her head, and Noah flagged down the waiter. *"Les crêpes, s'il vous plaît,"* he said, self-conscious of his pronunciation.

Elise fought back an inkling of a smile. "Spoken like a true local."

"That's nothing." Noah felt the warmth of a blush. "I speak Spanish like I was born and raised in Rio."

"But in Brazil, they speak Portuguese—" Elise stopped and grinned with understanding, but the smile didn't last. "You were saying about Dr. Charron."

"He showed us video clips of two victims. It was . . ." He struggled for the right word. "Harrowing. The man who died in the fire. Philippe Manet. We saw footage of him on his first and last day of hospitalization. On day one, he looked psychotic. Very agitated. Terrified, actually. But you could see in his eyes that he still was 'there,' you know? Thirteen days later . . . he was a muttering imbecile who couldn't move his own limbs. His body was still alive, but his brain was already dead." Shaking off the memory, he went on to recap what Charron described of the other victims and the course of their illness.

Elise toyed with a few strands of her short brown hair while she listened. After Noah finished, she asked, "Is there any evidence that the three patients knew one another?"

"No, but all three lived in Limousin."

Elise frowned. "Not that many people live in Limousin."

"I suppose. But isn't it more important to find out where they got their meat from?"

"Unless, of course, they ate it from the same table."

"Good point." Noah looked into her large eyes, sensing they were hiding more turmoil than her placid expression let on. "How are beef cattle tracked in France?"

She touched her lip with her index finger; its nail was cut short and polished a subtle pink. "Extensively."

"Can you be more specific?"

She pulled her finger from her lip. "Since 1999, all cattle breeders and farmers in E.U. nations are required to maintain complete records of where and how they procured their cows. Calves are tattooed shortly after birth so that we can easily track their origins. And every farm keeps a form of passport on each of their animals with detailed birth and travel records."

"That might be useful to us. What do you know about the seven infected cows?"

"Obviously, none were involved in human cases," she said. "They were identified before reaching the food chain. They weren't even diagnosed until *after* the first two human cases."

"Not until after," Noah echoed softly, his wariness stirring. "Unusual."

"But not unprecedented," Elise pointed out. "Considering the rapid progression we have seen, the diseased animals probably didn't show symptoms at the time they were butchered."

Noah sighed. "In other words, there must be other infected cows that will go—*or have already gone*—to the slaughterhouse."

Elise nodded. "Which is why yesterday in Paris we decided to put a moratorium on the export and sale of all French beef until we know more."

She said it matter-of-factly, but Noah realized it must have been a contentious decision. She had to be facing immense pressure from interest groups of every stripe. Admiring her poise, he reached out and touched her arm. "It was the right decision."

"Time will tell." She summoned a smile before pulling her arm away to check her watch.

"Do all French slaughterhouses routinely sample for BSE?" Noah asked.

"Legally, they have to."

"Do they keep the samples?"

"Yes." She pursed her lips and eyed him a moment, possibly even impressed. "Our labs are rechecking all samples from the past twelve months to see if we can find the source case or cases."

Noah whistled. "That's a lot of testing."

"Close to a million samples." She held up her slender hands. "What choice do we have?"

"None," he said. "Have you linked the seven involved cows to a common source?"

"Not conclusively." Elise looked over Noah's shoulder and smiled politely.

The waiter arrived and placed a plate of crêpes in front of Noah. He tried to pass a second fork to Elise, but she waved him away. "I hope you are a fast eater," she said.

His mouth watered as he eyed the flat pancakes dusted with icing sugar and garnished with strawberries. "Shouldn't be a problem. Why?"

"We have an appointment with a farmer."

By the time Noah, Elise, and Duncan—who had opted uncharacteristically to stay alone in his room for breakfast—left the hotel, the clouds had cleared and Noah saw the sun for the first time since leaving Mexico. Outside, the light was so bright he wished he'd brought his sunglasses, but the dazzling blue sky brought even colder temperatures. Bundling his jacket tighter around his neck, he headed toward Elise's car, a green BMW 330xi sedan. Noah felt as though he had stepped out into a nor'easter back home in Washington.

Elise drove east from Limoges along the narrow but scenic country roads. Though she was no match for the airport taxi driver, she drove faster and more assertively than Noah expected. He stared out the window, taking in the lush rolling countryside that was more similar to terrain he had seen in Ireland than other parts of France. They passed numerous farmhouses, all built from the same gray stone and topped with red tile roofs. After a while, the homogeneity of the architecture brought him a comfortable sense of familiarity.

Passing through the quaint village of Terrebonne, Elise slowed to point out the square across from the church. An imposing bronze statue of three soldiers towered over the town's center. "This is a well-known landmark," she said.

Noah had passed through enough French towns to know that the statue commemorated the village's young men who died on the killing fields of World War I. Duncan, who had been grimly quiet for most of the ride, pointed out the window to the plaque below the statue. "Look at all the names," he said. "Doubt there was a boy between fifteen and thirty left standing in this town at the war's end."

"Tragic," Noah agreed. "Still, if they erected a plaque listing all the victims of the Spanish Flu that followed in the wake of the war, I bet it would be even more crowded."

Elise flashed Noah a half-smile. "Of course, you have a professional bias."

"Maybe," Noah said. "But Duncan and I have seen enough to know that man-made chaos can't compete with nature's version."

"I don't buy that shite for a moment, Haldane," Duncan grunted. "There's no chaos in nature unless man is involved."

"You mean like the Spanish Flu?" Noah countered.

"Exactly!" Duncan pounded Noah's headrest from behind. "Crowded farms with nasty hygiene—humans and animals cross-contaminating each other's food and water supplies—engendered the virus. And it took the end of a world war to spread it. Don't blame nature for that."

"You have a point," Noah conceded.

Duncan sighed heavily. "Let's just hope the *current* questionable local farming practices don't cause us grief on that scale again."

Elise glanced over her shoulder at Duncan, as if she might challenge the remark, but she turned her gaze back to the road without comment and drove on.

Less than a mile past town, she turned off into the driveway of another red-roofed farmhouse that stood out from the others only because of its larger size. She stopped the car and opened her door. Climbing out of the car, Noah didn't spot anyone on the farm's grounds. He wondered if it was the subzero temperature or something else that kept everyone inside.

They hurried up the gravel pathway past the shuttered barn to the farm's front door. Elise rang the bell. Fifteen seconds passed without a response. As she reached for the buzzer again, the door opened. *"Bienvenue, mes amis,"* the man on the other side said in a slightly slurred voice. Of average height and build, he wore a tattered blue cardigan and loose sweatpants. He had thick stubble, and his thick greasy black hair was matted and looked as though it had been slept on more than once since a comb or brush had last touched it.

Elise held out her hand. *"Bonjour, Monsieur Pereau. Je m'appelle Elise Renard avec la commissione agriculture de l'E.U."* She pointed to Noah and Duncan. *"Voilà Docteurs Noah Haldane et Duncan McLeod avec—"*

The man waved his hand to interrupt. "I attended college in America—University of Wisconsin, agricultural sciences," he said in impeccable English. He turned to Noah and Duncan and bowed exaggeratedly. "I am André Pereau. It's an honor, doctors."

Breathing in the stench of stale wine, Noah shook Pereau's hand and felt the man's rough calluses slide over his palm. They followed Pereau into the common room. With the curtains drawn, the room was dark despite the sunshine. The smell of old food and cigarettes hung in the musty air. Dirty dishes cluttered the tabletop. Noah spotted at least five empty wine bottles scattered around the room.

Pereau went to the attached kitchen and flung open cabinet doors, searching from one to the next. Finally, he emerged from a lower cabinet triumphantly, bearing an unlabeled bottle of red wine in his hand. He uncorked the bottle, spilling a few drops on the kitchen floor and wiping them up with his stockinged foot. "Can I offer you a drink?" he asked.

Elise and Noah shook their heads. "Thanks, but I'm trying to cut back on my wine at breakfast time," Duncan said.

His colleagues both shot him a glance, but Pereau laughed and patted his chest. "Me? I've just started drinking at breakfast. Don't know why I ever used to wait." He waved a hand over to a particularly distressed pine kitchen table and matching chairs. "Sit, please."

Pereau carried the bottle and a glass over to the sitting area. He set the glass down on the end of the table, filled it nearly to the rim, and then plunked himself down in one worn chair. Noah and Duncan sat down on the chairs to one side of him, Elise on the other.

"They've taken them all away," he said pleasantly, sloshing his drink.

"Your cows?" Noah asked.

"I don't really care. I didn't even want to be a farmer, you know?" He grimaced. "I had little choice. The Pereaus have been farming this land for over two hundred years. I'm an only child. I was merely fulfilling my . . . destiny." He hoisted his glass and toasted the air before taking a generous swig. "Now it's done. *Fini!*"

Elise leaned forward in her seat. "Your cows were sick," she said pointedly.

"I did what I could. I fed them well. They were clean. They had a good barn. I cared for them." He looked down at the floor. "They took them all. The sheep. Even my horses. All gone."

Noah nodded sympathetically. "When did it start, M. Pereau?"

Pereau scratched roughly at his cheek. "About four weeks ago."

Noah held open his hand. "How did you know?"

"That morning I went into the barn to change the feed, and one of the cows didn't get up." Pereau stopped to drain his glass. "I thought nothing of it, until I tried to stand her up." He exhaled slowly. "She couldn't. She tried but her legs wouldn't hold her. Every time I got her up, she just kept collapsing."

"And that was the *first* indication of trouble?" Noah asked.

Pereau refilled his glass. "I suppose she had been off her feed the week before. She had not eaten well. Perhaps she was a little unsteady on her hooves. Or maybe, I'm imagining. Who knows?"

Elise tapped her lip, thoughtfully. "How old was she?"

"Eighteen months."

"When and where did you get her from?"

"End of last spring from Ferme d'Allaire." He shrugged. "A big cattle supplier near Lac Noir. All my cows come from them. Like most of the farms around here."

Elise nodded. "When did the second animal become ill?"

"Three days later, I noticed another cow staggering on her way for water." He shrugged. "Didn't matter. It was over by then, anyway."

"And the cattle feed?" Elise asked, ignoring his self-pity. "Where did that come from? Or did you make your own?"

Pereau slammed his glass down and laughed heartily. Noah and Duncan shared a confused glance. "I got it from Marceau Alimentation Animale, near Limoges." The farmer leaned closer to Elise. "And no, Mlle. Renard,

I do not supplement the food with animal by-products."

Noah suddenly understood the man's reaction. Pereau had assumed Elise was accusing him of recycling animal meat in the cattle feed, which, despite the international ban on the risky practice, some farmers still did.

Pereau lifted his glass but didn't drink from it. "I was the maker of my own undoing. I reported my case right away. I hid nothing."

"What choice did you have?" Elise pressed. "Your cows would have been discovered on testing."

"Choice?" He laughed again, spilling more wine before putting it back on the table. "I could have buried them out in the field. You would have never known. But no, I followed protocol. And now everything is gone."

Noah's throat went dry. He wondered if other farmers had already buried their infected animals. *Maybe the outbreak was far more extensive than originally thought?*

"My livestock, my livelihood, and soon the Pereau family farm," Pereau continued, brushing his hands together in the air. "All gone. *Fini.*" His voice cracked, and he reached for the glass and took another sip. "Even my wife has left."

"What happened?" Duncan spoke up.

"There was a lot of stress. Yvette was very scared of what was happening." He paused. "What might still happen."

Duncan nodded at the bottle on the table. "And the wine . . ."

"Was not helping," Pereau admitted.

"Rarely does," Duncan said kindly.

The room fell into brief silence, broken by Pereau's cracking voice. "We have been together since we were teenagers. We have been through a lot." He spoke to his glass. "Last week, I came home from the market, and she was gone."

Duncan sat up straighter. "She didn't tell you she was leaving?"

"No note. No phone call. *Rien*. Nothing." Pereau shook his head sadly. "After nineteen years, Yvette simply disappeared."

7

Normally, Detective Avril Avars would have informed the caller that someone had to be missing for at least twenty-four hours before the police would investigate. Under normal circumstances, the overworked *enquêteur* for the Gendarmerie Limoges would not have taken the call at all. However, it had come from her hometown of Montmagnon, and not only did she know the missing person in question, but the man reporting it happened to be her own doctor.

The Limoges detectives conducted major crime investigations for many of the smaller surrounding towns like Montmagnon that, while not suburbs, were near enough to logistically allow a Limoges-based investigation. Avril's colleagues grumbled endlessly about being overextended and clocking far too many kilometers on their department-issued Peugeot sedans. Even Avril, despite her workaholic tendencies, had trouble coping with the caseload.

Since her husband's death two years earlier, Avril put in a minimum of six days and sixty hours per week on the job. She knew some of her colleagues thought that, as

Limoges's only female detective and the department's sole officer of African descent, Avril felt the need to prove herself. They were wrong. The forty-six-year-old never cared much what others thought. With her only son, Frédéric, in Paris studying architecture and Antoine dead, the job helped to dampen her relentless loneliness. Mainly, though, she was slave to an obsessive work ethic inherited from her father, a carpenter, who had emigrated to France from Morocco as a teenager and tirelessly worked his way out of poverty. An unfinished job of any kind gnawed at Avril; every unsolved case weighed on her back like a stone.

Two inches shy of six feet, Avril had a full figure, but she wasn't overweight. Light brown in complexion, her face had a smattering of darker freckles that ran across her narrow nose, but her large coffee-brown eyes were her dominant feature. As the epitome of a visible minority in a near homogeneously white province, she was accustomed to the glances from strangers that became even more pronounced when she used to walk arm in arm with her lean, fair-skinned husband. Inherently strong and quietly confident, Avril was indifferent to the impact of her exotic (by Limousin standards) appearance. Few people intimidated her. But Dr. Roger Tanier was an exception.

Driving the thirty-five kilometers eastward to Montmagnon, she reflected on the unexpected phone call from the doctor. As soon as she heard his voice, her apprehension surfaced. He had never called her before, and she automatically assumed the worst—that her recent mammogram or blood test had unearthed something bad. But Tanier quickly established that he wasn't calling about her. "I'm concerned about one of my patients," he launched in, forgoing pleasantries.

"And you want my help?" Avril said, confused.

"Yes."

"How, Dr. Tanier?"

"I need you to find her."

"Find who?"

"Pauline Lamaire."

"Pauline?" Avril sat up straighter. As a teenager, she had babysat Pauline, a sweet energetic girl who never shed her perpetual smile. Avril still remembered how moved she was the first time she saw Pauline play her violin. It looked like she was holding a cello to her chin, but in Pauline's hands the instrument sang beautifully. "How do you know she is missing?" Avril asked.

"I went to make a house call this morning before clinic," he said. "She was not home."

"I see." If it were anyone else on the phone, she would have found a way to end the call right then, but Dr. Tanier had been her physician since she was a child. And she was not going to brush him off *now*. "Isn't it possible that Pauline forgot you were coming and went out to run errands instead?"

"I am not an imbecile, Avril. The woman was in no condition to have gone anywhere." He sighed. "Listen, perhaps if you come here, it will make more sense."

And so Avril dropped everything else to head back to the town where she had grown up. As she entered the outskirts of Montmagnon, childhood memories bubbled to the surface. Driving past the seventeenth-century church, she could almost hear the raised choir voices even though she had been inside only once or twice since her confirmation. She looked out the window past the town square and mentally wove her way through the lanes and shortcuts between the buildings to reach the gravel soccer pitch where she had spent so many summer hours scrimmaging with her brother, cousins, and numerous friends, including her future husband, Antoine Avars. Thirty-five years later, Antoine shattered her heart when, in a blinding storm, he crashed his helicopter into the side of a mountain.

Putting aside the usual adolescent traumas—and the

added ones that came with being one of the only dark-skinned residents of a mostly white town—Avril remembered her childhood as for the most part happy. But just as she had outgrown her favorite bicycle and her cozy bunk bed, Avril had also outgrown her hometown. Despite its proximity to Limoges, Montmagnon was now a place to return to on special occasions, like holiday visits with her father or her annual checkup with Dr. Tanier. As she pulled up to the charming little house a few kilometers past the village center, she wondered why a concert violinist like Pauline Lamaire had chosen to live in Montmagnon.

"Good day, Avril," Dr. Tanier puffed as he struggled out of his red sports car. The heavyset balding doctor, who was well into his sixties, looked ridiculous wedged inside the sporty German vehicle, but Avril, like everyone else, respected the man too much to point it out to him.

"Hello, Dr. Tanier." Avril was overcome by reflex embarrassment, because most times she saw the doctor she was on his examining table in nothing but a paper gown.

"Come," he said, striding past her on his way up the walkway to the front door.

Aware that most doors in town were left perpetually unlocked, Avril was still a little surprised when, instead of knocking, Tanier turned the door handle and stepped inside the house.

She stopped at the doorway to sniff the air. Years ago, one of her criminology professors in Paris had drilled into her the notion that competent detectives use all their senses; accordingly, Avril had come to believe in the investigative significance of odors at crime scenes. Despite the clinical scent of air freshener, she noticed something lingering beneath it—the faint stench of urine and something else that she couldn't place.

From the threshold, Avril studied the combined kitchen and living room. Several colorful oil paintings, including a series of individual fruits, lined the walls. A few photos stood on the bookshelf along with numerous musical trophies and awards. Beneath the bookshelf, a violin rested upright on a stand with the bow lying across, as if it had just been played. On the kitchen table, a cluster of magazines lay beside a vase full of tastefully arranged flowers. Spotting the ceramic water and food dishes in the room's corner, Avril realized that Pauline owned a cat. Based on the smell, she suspected its urinary indiscretion had only recently been tackled with deodorizers.

She glanced over at the white-bearded doctor. He assessed her with wrinkled brow and troubled gray eyes. "What do you think, Avril?"

"Cleaned recently. And fresh flowers. Perhaps she was expecting company?"

"At eight in the morning?" Tanier grunted, unimpressed. He pointed toward the violin. "Pauline has been nearly crippled by rheumatoid arthritis these past three years. Especially her hands. I have not seen her violin out in all that time. So why now?" He shook his head sadly. "And look!" He pointed to the sofa beside him.

Avril crossed the creaky wooden floor to get a better look. Stiffly, Tanier crouched down to his knees. Glancing at the floor, Avril spotted a single red pill lying beside one of the sofa's legs. "When I bent down to pick up this pill, I found these," he said.

Avril knelt to Tanier's level and saw several more of the same tablets scattered on the floor underneath the couch.

"Anti-inflammatory medicine that I prescribed her," he explained. "Pauline is meticulous about her medication. Especially this one. Never misses a pill. And now I find a pile of them lying loose under the furniture. . . ."

Breathing hard, Tanier rose to his feet. So did Avril. He eyed her expectantly.

She chose her words carefully. "Dr. Tanier, I agree there are unusual features here, but we don't know that

Pauline has been gone longer than this morning. In fact, we have no evidence she is missing at all."

Tanier sighed and lowered himself heavily onto the sofa. "I dropped in on Pauline three days ago," he said.

Avril waited, but when he didn't offer more, she asked, "How was she?"

He shook his head and sighed heavily. "Confused."

"In what sense, Dr. Tanier?"

"She barely recognized me. She mixed up my name on several occasions. At one point, she mistook me for her childhood music teacher." He shook his head again. "And she was acting paranoid. Suspicious of every sound around us. And this room"—he indicated it with a wave of his meaty finger—"was a mess. Food, papers, and medications everywhere. Most unlike Pauline."

Avril sat down on the couch beside him. "I see."

Tanier pointed to the coffee table, whose surface was now clear. "Her tablets were scattered all over this table. And you would not believe how many medicines she was ingesting!"

"But . . . did you not prescribe them?"

"Only a small minority." Tanier grunted. "Pauline has such terrible arthritis. She has seen so many specialists. With each one comes a new prescription. And she has turned to alternative medicines, too. She is on enough vitamins and supplements to drug a herd of elephants."

"You don't approve?" Avril asked.

He leaned forward and exhaled heavily. "Five years ago, she was a concert violinist. Now she is crippled by disease. And modern medicine has failed her. I have failed her." He cleared his throat and glanced away. "Pauline will clutch at anything, regardless of the lack of rigorous science or testing, that might offer hope. I'm worried that one of these new treatments has affected her mental state . . . Maybe she has wandered off somewhere."

Avril glanced around the room again, trying to correlate its orderly appearance with what the doctor described. "Why did Pauline ask you to come see her this week?" she asked.

Tanier hesitated. As his patient, Avril appreciated his reluctance to share confidential information. "She was having trouble with her hand," he finally said.

"The arthritis?"

"No. Something neurological. Her right arm and hand had gone numb. She was having difficulty using it."

"What did you think was wrong?"

"I did not know, but I thought it related to whatever accounted for her state of mind, her confusion and such," he said. "I wanted to send her to the hospital in Limoges for further testing, perhaps even a CAT scan, but she would not hear of it. She seemed afraid to even leave the house."

"Can you think of a medication that could explain her confusion and her arm numbness?"

Tanier shrugged. "It would be unusual, but there are such toxins. For example, lead poisoning can cause confusion and weakness of the limbs."

"I don't smell any fresh paint." Avril forced a smile.

"It was only an example," Tanier grumbled. "I have no idea what was going on with Pauline. All I know is that the woman I saw three days ago was in no condition to tidy up her house and then head out for a long morning stroll."

"I see," Avril said, still calm. "Maybe Pauline's mental state improved after you saw her. Perhaps she is in town as we speak?"

Tanier grunted his disdain for her theory. Avril shared his skepticism. Her instincts told her not only that Pauline was missing but also that she was in trouble.

8

Noah lay on the hotel bed, staring at the slivers of light that leaked through the blinds and cut zebra stripes on the ceiling. Though he had traveled the globe several times over while working for the WHO, he never adjusted to changes in time zones. Now, at 4:12 A.M., he lay wide awake and unable to decelerate his racing mind.

Noah mulled over what he knew of cases of BSE in France. Aside from its hastened course, the outbreak among humans and animals was far smaller in scale than the British epidemic in the nineties. Yet the situation gnawed at him far more than the handful of cases warranted. Another flashback of slobbering brain-dead patients from the neurologist's video clip ran through his head. *Is this really vCJD?* he wondered again. *What if it spreads faster than anything we've seen before?*

He had tried to broach the subject with Duncan earlier over dinner, but Duncan had been unusually distracted, hardly saying a word. Noah sensed something more than an unpleasant personal history with a BSE outbreak accounted for the black cloud enshrouding his friend, but given their long association, Noah knew better than to ask.

Noah glanced at the bedside phone, fighting off the impulse to call Gwen and run the situation by her. Instead, he reached for the receiver and asked the operator to connect him to a number in South Carolina. His ex-wife answered the phone on the second ring. "Noah," Anna said, her warm tone tinged with a sweet shyness that he had only noticed since their separation. "Isn't it the middle of the night for you?"

"For France maybe, but not for my internal clock," he said. "How's South Carolina?"

"Warm, thank God! Besides, it's nice to see my folks." She hesitated. "They always ask about you."

"Say hello for me." Noah had always felt close to Anna's parents. He knew that all along they had quietly pulled for Anna to reconcile with him, but they were too decent and too Calvinist to ever push their point of view upon their daughter.

"Is Chloe still up?" he asked.

"She's not supposed to be." Anna laughed. "But yeah, she's here. We can't get her out of the pool."

After a moment, he heard the clattering of the phone and then his daughter's breathless voice came on the line. "Daddy-o!"

Noah's heart leaped. "Hi, sweetie! You having fun with Granna and Gramps?"

"Daddy, I'm swimming in their pool!" Her voice surged with pride.

"No water wings?" Noah asked.

"Not even the floatie vest like Mexico!" she cried. "I can swim across on my own. Even the deep end."

"You really are my little mermaid." Proud as he was, Noah felt slightly deflated at the realization that he had missed another milestone in her life.

"I can show you at the club pool. Right, Daddy?"

"Sure, soon as we're both home," he said. "I'll race you."

"Only one arm, right?" In Mexico, they had "raced" across the pool with Chloe in her life vest and Noah swimming one-armed. "Will you be home when me and Mommy come back?"

"I hope so," Noah said, though he had the sinking feeling that his time in Europe was going to extend well beyond the seven days that Chloe and Anna were planning to spend in Hilton Head. "Are you sleeping in the pool, too?" he asked.

"No, Daddy!" she laughed. "I'd drown. I'm not a fish."

"I'm beginning to wonder," he said. "What else is happening?"

Barely pausing for breaths, she poured out the news of other exciting developments, including a detailed description of her new sundress that featured "tons of sequins," the latest fairy book series that she and her mother were reading, and the stray cat her grandparents had adopted at Chloe's urging. As infectious as his daughter's enthusiasm was, Noah hung up the phone feeling more isolated than ever.

Noah tossed and turned for another hour before he finally gave up on sleep and climbed out of bed. Just before six o'clock, he decided to take a predawn walk through the French city he had yet to explore. He slipped into his jeans and sweater and headed out.

Stepping onto the street, he was thankful for his thick gloves and lined leather jacket, though when the icy wind cut through his turtleneck he realized a scarf might have helped. Lit by the yellowish illumination from old street lamps, the sidewalk in front of the hotel was deserted. Halfway down the block, he noticed a glow waxing and waning from inside the cab of an old pickup truck—one of the more commonly seen French flatbed van-truck hybrids—parked in the shadow between lamps. As he neared the truck, its headlight flicked on and flashed him twice.

On edge, Noah stopped and pulled his gloved hands from his coat pockets. He stood still and waited, but nothing happened except the glow from inside the truck brightened and then faded. Noah inhaled a few deep chilly breaths and then ventured nearer. As he came alongside the truck, the passenger window creaked open. Cigarette smoke wafted out of the opening.

The interior lights remained off, but the sole occupant's lit cigarette and the nearest streetlight illuminated the inside enough for Noah to see the shadowy outline of the large man hunched behind the wheel. From what Noah could see when the cigarette burned brightest, the man had droopy eyes and a thick five-o'clock shadow.

The man stared at him but said nothing. Noah leaned closer so that his face was inches from the window. "Who are you?" he asked.

"Parlez-vous français?" the man said in a sandpaper voice.

"Un peu," Noah said. "Who are you?" he repeated in French.

Ignoring the question, the man said, "You are Dr. Haldane, correct?"

Noah nodded.

"I can help you," he pronounced the words slowly for Noah's benefit.

"Help me with what?"

He cleared his throat with a loud hacking sound. "I know where they come from."

"They?"

"The mad cows."

Noah leaned closer, resting his hands on the door's rusty windowsill. "Where?"

The man glanced over his shoulder before speaking in a hushed tone. "It has nothing to do with the farmers here."

A jolt shot up Noah's spine and his heart sped up. "The

mad cow problem has nothing to do with the farms in Limousin?" Noah stammered.

The man nodded impatiently.

"Then where does it come from?" Noah leaned his head inside the truck and inhaled such a mouthful of acrid smoke that he felt as if he had stolen a drag off the man's cigarette.

"Ferme d'Allaire."

Noah shook his head, confused by the language. "But you said that no farms—" He stopped, remembering Ferme d'Allaire from his earlier interview with Pereau. "The cattle supplier?" he asked in English.

"Pardonnez?" the man replied.

"The place that sells the cows," Noah sputtered in French.

"Exactly!" The cigarette bobbed up and down in his mouth. "Yes. All the bad cows come from there."

The explanation made epidemiological sense to Noah. In any outbreak, the primary goal was to track the source back to the index, or first, case that initiated the others.

"All of the cows!" the man repeated and then cleared his throat again.

"Why there?" Noah asked, almost more to himself.

He wasn't really expecting an answer, so he was surprised when the man grumbled something in French. Noah understood only snippets of the response, catching the words "feed the cows" and "illegal." He tapped the window in frustration. "Slower, please! Why did the sick cows come from Ferme d'Allaire?"

"They make bad feed," the man said, much more slowly. "They put dead cows, sheep, and pigs into the mix. It is against the law."

"But they do it anyway?"

The man nodded once.

"How do you know this?" Noah asked.

In response, the man turned the key and the engine

kicked in, churning with a loud grumble. Noah's hand vibrated on the windowsill. "Go check," the man said. "You will see for yourself."

"Are you a farmer?" Noah asked, but the man didn't respond. "Were your cows sick?"

Suddenly the truck lurched forward and Noah had to yank his hand off the door to avoid being pulled with it.

"Go check, you will see!" the man barked, and the truck rocketed off down the street, overlaying the cigarette trail with a plume of blue engine exhaust.

9

The bumpy flight on the small Twin Otter was a huge step down from the first-class comfort Claude Fontaine had grown accustomed to in the ten months since he had last seen the Antarctic. In the interim, he had been wined, dined, and feted from New York to Tokyo. But as he stood at the entryway of the "Igloo" (as the high-tech dome had been dubbed by those inside) he had the sinking sensation that he had never left this desolate unwelcoming continent.

He gave the interior a quick once-over. It was as busy as ever, though most of his original team had been replaced. Georges Manet, the wisecracking geologist, was one of the first to go. They fell like dominoes after that, including Pierre Anou, who fought back the hardest. Aside from a few technicians, only Akiro Tekano remained; even his indispensability was waning as fewer and fewer remote missions in the depths of Vishnov were contemplated for the unmanned probes.

Gone, too, were the documentary filmmakers and other media who, for a time, swarmed the site as though it were the Disneyland of the South Pole. And over an outcry that had resonated in the scientific community but fallen on deaf ears everywhere else, the academics had been purged from the site, too. The Igloo now had an industrial look and feel, which suited Fontaine. After all, the structure had transformed from a research station into a factory.

As always, Fontaine's eyes fell on the massive platform in the center of the dome. It housed the same winch and cable as before. However, the circumference of the well had been widened. A thicker, flexible plastic pipeline ran alongside the cable and through the three kilometers of ice into the lake below. The custom-engineered heated pipeline could handle a flow thirty times that of the original cable.

Fontaine turned to the tall blonde who stood beside him. Arms folded across her chest, her unreadable glacial blue eyes surveyed the site with an expression as impassive as ever. He studied her face, appreciating her striking bone structure, porcelain skin, and sensual lips. Whatever else people thought of Martine DeGroot—and Fontaine knew there was no shortage of negative opinions—no one could deny her physical beauty.

"What do you think, Martine?" he asked.

DeGroot shrugged noncommittally. "Impressive enough, I suppose," she said in the crisp Dutch accent that stirred Fontaine from the moment he first heard it. "Then again, I do not have much of a reference point to compare to."

"No need to gush, Martine," he snapped.

Bitch! he nearly added. More than DeGroot's apathetic response, Fontaine was infuriated by his own need to impress her. It had never happened before. Women had been the most dispensable commodities in his life, but now he found himself aching for validation from this beautiful and controlled biologist. Prior to meeting her, he had always been the one to turn the affection on or off like a switch. She had reversed the roles. And the more ambivalence she showed, the deeper he fell. Fontaine resented—at times hated—her for his loss of autonomy, but he was helpless to resist.

DeGroot had met Fontaine three months after he first sampled Lake Vishnov. She bedded him—Fontaine had no misconceptions about who was in control, then or now—within a day of their meeting. They had been almost inseparable since. She was at his side when he announced the discovery of the never-before-seen bacteria, *Arcobacter antarcticus,* that thrived in the sulfur-rich, freezing black waters of Lake Vishnov. DeGroot had accompanied him on the initial publicity tour after his research was published in *Nature.* The tour had evolved into a celebrity press junket with the release of Jerry Silver's IMAX documentary, which not only popularized the Vishnov discoveries but also helped launch the French scientist as a modern-day Indiana Jones. Then *The New York Times* published an editorial by a prominent astrophysicist that only added fuel to the fire. That scientist claimed that since the conditions in Lake Vishnov exactly replicated those found in the frozen oceans of two of Jupiter's moons, Europa and Ganymede, finding life in the lake as good as proved the existence of extraterrestrial life.

DeGroot's detached approach to the hype surrounding Fontaine and his discovery helped to ground him. And he appreciated that she had not only been present at the glamorous destinations and high-profile events, but had joined him now as he slipped away from the spotlight and traveled to the bottom of the earth, just as she had accompanied him to Russia to face Yulia Radvogin's wrath the previous summer.

St. Petersburg, Russia. August, four months earlier

Fontaine had visited St. Petersburg twice before, but he never found a chance to see much of the city. From what little he did take in between the airport, the hotel, and the boardroom of Radvogin Industries, he decided it might be worth exploring in the summer sunshine. However, as he sat in the ornate boardroom beside Martine and waited for Yulia Radvogin, sightseeing was the farthest thing from his mind. He had heard that Radvogin was displeased with him. And by reputation, she was not someone to cross. *Ever.* Rumor had it that despite the "narrowed coronary arteries" listed on her husband's death certificate, the former CEO, Pavel Radvogin, had in fact been poisoned for betraying his wife with one of his younger assistants. (Moscow police could never establish anything beyond the "coincidence" that Radvogin had jogged ten miles the day before his heart gave out while climbing a single flight of stairs.)

Fontaine's stomach did a rare somersault when the door flew open and Yulia Radvogin swept into the room. Tanned, with gray-blond hair and pale blue eyes, at fifty-four, the curvaceous Ukrainian woman still effortlessly exuded sensuality. And she towed her usual entourage behind her. First, the tall and skeletal chief financial officer, Ivan Milahen, loped into the room, closely followed by her perspiring and fidgety lawyer, Anatoly Beria. Both men spoke so seldom in his presence that Fontaine wondered whether they grasped much of the English spoken at the previous meetings. The same two burly interchangeable bodyguards, Myron and Viktor, brought up the rear, the outline of their shoulder holsters visible through matching suit jackets that strained to contain their muscular bulk. Though the Russian bodyguards had not both been present at recent meetings,

Fontaine tried not to read too much into this current show of force.

Nothing in Yulia Radvogin's approach suggested she was upset with Fontaine. She smiled warmly as she greeted him with open arms, grabbing him by the shoulders and kissing him on both cheeks. "How is my gorgeous scientist?" she said, pointedly ignoring Martine DeGroot. "Still the media darling, I hear."

"I'm well, Yulia." Fontaine matched her smile. "And you?"

"Trying to keep the company solvent," Radvogin said with a dismissive flutter of her hand, though Fontaine knew that her multinational corporation had announced record profits in its previous quarter.

Fontaine pointed to his companion. "Yulia, please allow me to introduce my associate, Dr. Martine DeGroot."

Radvogin's smile flickered as she turned to DeGroot with a slight nod. "Dr. DeGroot."

"Martine, please. It's an honor to meet you, Mrs. Radvogin," DeGroot said, her face lighting. "I have heard so much about you and Radvogin Industries."

"I look forward to hearing something about you, Dr. deGroot," she said, before turning back to Fontaine. "Sit, please."

Radvogin floated over to her seat at the head of the table. Her lawyer and accountant took the seats to her left. Fontaine sat in the chair to her right, and DeGroot beside him. The two bodyguards melted into the back of the room, though Fontaine felt their presence from more than just their lingering aftershave.

Radvogin reached out and laid her hand on Fontaine's sleeve. "It's been a good year for you, Claude," she said and gave his wrist a slight squeeze.

"I've had worse," Fontaine said, hoping to steer the conversation elsewhere.

"I am sure you have. Between the newspapers and the

television, I can't even keep up." She shook her head. "I understand there is talk of a Nobel Prize."

"Empty rumors, Yulia." Fontaine brushed it off with a backhanded flick. "In academics, every time a scientist makes the newspaper, there is talk of the prize."

Radvogin laughed. "Denial is the politician's confession." She pulled her hand from his sleeve. "My point is, Claude, my money and my resources in the Antarctic have brought you fame," she said, the warmth draining from her tone with each word.

Fontaine bowed his head slightly. "You know how much I appreciate your investment."

"Your appreciation is worth nothing to me." Her eyes darkened. "What is the news from the ATCP?" she snapped, referring to the Antarctic Treaty Consultative Parties, the international body that governs issues pertaining to the Antarctic.

"I met with them last week in Oslo." Fontaine took a deep breath. "As you know, based on their Environmental Protection Protocol of 1991, all oil exploration in or adjacent to the Antarctic has been banned until 2031."

Radvogin nodded impatiently. "Yes, yes."

"I told them that environmental preservation and economic development are not mutually exclusive," Fontaine said. "I argued that with the price of crude oil hitting record highs in the past twenty-four months and the global supply running low, the time was ripe for oil exploration carried out safely away from the continental shelf." He clasped his hands together. "Science and commerce, working side by side to a mutually beneficial end."

"But?"

Fontaine cleared his throat. "They didn't see it that way."

Radvogin's eyes froze over. "And *my* well?"

"I explained that Radvogin Industries would be far less

able to maintain and offer international research access to the Vishnov site without the economic incentive of oil exploration in the area."

"And?" she added in a throaty whisper.

"Yulia, they will not amend the treaty." He met her stare. "Even for you."

Milahen stopped jotting notes on his pad. Beria stopped tapping the table. A few long moments of silence passed. "Two years ago," Radvogin said as she quietly stared up at the ceiling, "you sat at this very table and promised me that if I supported your research, Radvogin Industries would be allowed access to that oil."

"I said I would do everything I could, I never promised—"

The sharp slap of Radvogin's palm against the mahogany table silenced Fontaine in midsentence. "Leave the legal technicalities to Anatoly!" she barked, thumbing at her openmouthed lawyer. "You gave me your word, Claude."

Radvogin glared at him, and Fontaine felt the eyes of her bodyguards burning into his back.

As he opened his mouth to respond, Martine DeGroot leaned forward in her chair. "Yulia," she said, surprising Fontaine by the use of her first name. "May I say something?"

"What?"

"In every setback there is opportunity," deGroot said.

Radvogin didn't reply, but her face blanched and her lip quivered with rage.

DeGroot smiled confidently. "Forget the oil, Yulia," she said as if dismissing a glass of spilled milk.

"Forget it?" Radvogin pushed herself halfway up from her seat. "You want me to forget tens of millions of dollars' worth of my own money?"

DeGroot's smile grew wider, and she nodded. Fontaine

welled with affection for the woman. Her steely poise was perfect.

"Why would I ever do that?" Radvogin hissed.

DeGroot let Radvogin's loaded question hang in the air for a few moments before answering. "Because, Yulia," she said with a laugh, "your well is sitting on something far more valuable than oil."

10

After his rendezvous with the anonymous informer in the smoke-filled pickup, Noah wandered the still-dark streets of Limoges lost in thought and oblivious to the winter chill. Near the center of the city, he stumbled across a newsstand, where he bought a copy of the *International Herald Tribune*. At the end of the block, he spotted a small bakery with a few tables inside. The smell of fresh bread and pastries drew him in. Ignoring his cholesterol level, he ordered a butter-rich croissant and an espresso and then sat down with the paper.

He had trouble concentrating on the words. Most of the articles passed through his brain like water through a sieve, but one story—concerning another leaked Al Qaeda videotape, whose spokesman promised "to rain blood and fire upon the West"—caught his attention. Since his brush with the Islamic extremist group that had propagated the ARCS virus as a weapon, he took all such threats to heart. He was certain that other terrorists must have learned from the ARCS nightmare, suspecting that for them it would serve more as an incentive than a deterrent. He thought again of Gwen Savard, who was charged with protecting her country—and, by extension, the world—from bioterrorism. More than ever, her job seemed impossible.

He looked up from the paper and noticed the gray light of early dawn seeping into the bakery. More people had emerged on the street. He glanced at his watch, which read 6:35 A.M. He left a tip on the table and left.

Heading back to the hotel, he wove his way along the city's narrow side streets, which struck him as the epitome of provincial France. He decided he would like to return one day with Chloe to explore the historically rich and diverse region. He suspected Gwen would have loved the place, too. With a sigh that froze in the air, he imagined what a romantic getaway it might have made for them had circumstances been different.

Noah stopped on rue St. Étienne to admire the striking thirteenth-century Cathedral of St. Étienne. He had read somewhere that it was the only example of Gothic architecture in Limoges. Staring at the two-hundred-foot-tall tower that loomed over him, he marveled at the ingenuity of the medieval engineers who managed to raise this massive structure at a time when the Black Death was ravaging the known world. It reminded him that scientific achievement never came easily. He tried to imagine what it must have been like for his distant predecessors, those primitive medical practitioners trying to cope with the great plague in a time of ignorance and superstition. Then as now, the unknown usually aroused the greatest fear in people, and he glumly wondered if they were now facing a new unknown in Limousin.

Walking on, he reached the historic St. Étienne Bridge that spanned the dark and silent Vienne. Though tempted to cross it, he decided he had no more time for sightseeing. Turning, he glimpsed a tall woman in black pants, nylon jacket, and hat running along the river's path toward him. He recognized her just as she called out his name.

Elise slowed to a walk and then stopped in front of him, her breath crystallizing in the air and mist steaming off her body. She hunched forward, resting her hands on her thighs as she caught her breath. Despite the sweat and lack of makeup, when she looked up and smiled, her face lit up radiantly. "I thought *I* was awake early," she said.

"I've already had a meeting."

"Oh?" Her smile dampened. "With whom?"

"I don't know."

She shed the last of her grin. "What are you talking about, Noah?"

"This morning, someone was waiting for me outside the hotel. . . ." Noah went on to summarize his conversation with the man in the truck.

Elise studied the ground in front of her. "Strange," she murmured.

"I'll say," Noah grunted. "How would he even know who I was?"

"Your face was all over the news during the time of ARCS." She gracefully swept beads of sweat off her brow with the back of her glove. "Like it or not, you are famous, Dr. Haldane."

He didn't like it at all. "Even here?"

"Of course," she said. "And this man is a farmer."

"I said he might have been. I couldn't see much of anything, except that his truck looked as though it belonged on a farm. And from what little I could make out, so might he."

"André Pereau probably spoke to his neighbors after our visit yesterday," she said. "He might have given your name to any one of them, including the man in the truck."

Noah started to walk, and Elise joined him. "Okay, let's assume he is a farmer from Terrebonne," he said. "How did he find me here in Limoges?"

She chuckled good-naturedly. "This is rural France. I

don't think it would be too hard to track down a well-known foreigner here. There are not many of you around."

Noah was unconvinced. "Why was he waiting for me outside my hotel before dawn?"

She forced a weak smile and raised her gloves helplessly. "Farmers start their day early."

"Come on, Elise."

"Obviously, he thought it was very important that you know."

"Obviously," Noah echoed, still thrown by the unusual visit. "We'd better find out if what he told me about the cattle supplier is true."

Elise kept walking without comment. Noah stopped. A few strides later, Elise stopped and faced him, her face even more flushed. "Noah . . ."

"Hold on," he said, recognizing her contrite expression. "Elise, you already knew about the sick cows from Ferme d'Allaire, didn't you?"

She looked away in embarrassment.

"Now who's withholding information?" he snapped.

"I heard only last night," she said. "I was waiting for confirmation from Brussels."

"Unbelievable." He shook his head angrily. "I'd give you my speech about how vital it is to keep each other in the loop, but I think you wrote it!"

"I'm sorry, Noah," she said quietly. "But I have superiors to answer to as well."

In a calmer voice he asked, "So all seven cases can be traced back to Ferme d'Allaire?"

She wiped her brow again. "Six."

"What about the seventh?"

"We don't know yet."

"Six of seven. That's pretty strong evidence that our index case comes from this ranch," he said. "And what about the man's claim that the feed is tainted?"

"This is the first I have heard of it."

Noah shook his head. "When are we going to see this farm?"

She pulled back the hem of her left glove and checked her watch. "In about two hours."

After eating the large croissant, Noah had little appetite left. He declined Elise's offer to join her for breakfast, opting instead for a brief nap and a long hot shower.

Pleasantly light-headed from the shower, Noah slipped into a pair of black pants and a T-shirt. He scanned the room before he spotted his gray sweater spread over the back of the chair in front of the small desk. His gaze was drawn to the mess he had made there. In addition to the original papers he had brought with him from Washington, since his arrival in Limoges a steady stream of articles and papers had accumulated by e-mail and fax via the hotel reception. He swept all the papers off the desktop and organized them in a pile beside the desk. He plugged in his laptop and logged on to the hotel's wireless server. After downloading the long list of e-mails, he glanced through them and answered only a few of the most pressing ones.

Noah closed the laptop and reached for the paper notebook lying on the desk. With each new investigation, he started a fresh journal to document his brainstorming. Having already filled several pages, he opened the notebook to the next blank page, marked by the little purple happy-face bookmark Chloe had given him as a stocking stuffer last Christmas. He began scratching notes, bullet-style, with reminders to himself and questions to follow up on, glumly realizing he had few answers for his many questions. He had covered two more pages, and could have kept going, when he glanced at his watch and realized he was already late. He marked the new page with the bookmark and shut the book.

By the time Noah reached the lobby, Elise and Duncan were waiting by the main door. As they headed out to Elise's car, Noah was relieved to see that Duncan's mood had brightened since the previous evening. "So we're off to meet the farmers who breed cattle, sheep, and Armageddon, are we?" the Scotsman remarked with a mischievous grin as he climbed into the car. "Shite! Where would this world be without French ingenuity?"

"Maybe then Scottish food would be considered a delicacy?" Noah deadpanned.

Duncan laughed uproariously and smacked Noah's headrest. "You have a point, Haldane. All things considered, we might be better off with Armageddon."

As the outskirts of Limoges gave way to the rural highway, Duncan said, "We better make short work of this visit. We're expected in Paris soon."

"Why Paris?" Noah asked.

"To see Dr. Émilie Gellier," Duncan said.

"Who?" Noah asked.

"The neuropathologist who dissected the brains of the Limousin prion victims."

"Oh." Noah nodded his approval. "That's definitely worth a visit."

"Why?" Elise asked without taking her eyes off the road.

"Pathologists are like the arson investigators who figure out from the ashes how a fire started," Noah explained. "By examining the final pathology—or tissue damage—they usually can identify the exact disease process which caused it."

"I thought we already knew what caused it," she pointed out.

Duncan leaned between the seats. "Ah, but this prion isn't playing by the rules so far."

"Exactly," Noah said. "Dr. Gellier might be able to tell us if this really is vCJD or something altogether different."

Elise's only response was a slight nod. Noah wasn't surprised. She had been subdued during the entire drive. And while he was still bothered by how she had held out on him earlier, he was warming to Elise. Beyond her addictive accent and captivating blue-gray eyes, her no-nonsense style and confident intelligence had begun to impress him. The authorities at the E.U. had chosen her carefully for this assignment.

A kilometer before Lac Noir, Elise slowed the car and then turned off on a gravel road leading to a complex of red-roofed stone buildings set back from the main road and larger than any farm they had yet seen in the region. A ceramic placard read FERME D'ALLAIRE, BIENVENUE. The car's tires crunched on the gravel driveway as they rolled to a stop in front of the large padlocked gate. A guard in military fatigues hovered nearby.

Elise rolled down her window and spoke to the guard in French before flashing her credentials. The guard leaned his head through the open window, and Noah caught a strong whiff of peppermint. The guard chomped his gum and studied Noah and Duncan for a long moment. Elise spoke up, but Noah caught only fragments of her clipped explanation.

Without a word, the guard pulled his head back from the window. He turned and unlocked the gate, allowing them to pass through. Inside, they parked in the nearly empty gravel parking lot of the complex, whose grounds were clean but somehow struck Noah as looking abandoned. The three of them walked past three identical cattle barns. The large metallic folding doors on all of them were chained shut, and Noah heard nothing from within.

Inside the main administrative building, a few clerical types milled around desks and filing cabinets, but no one spoke. A funereal pall hung over the room. Elise called out to a woman walking past them with her head almost buried in an open file. *"Pardon, madame,"* she said. *"Où est Monsieur Robichard, s'il vous plaît?"*

The woman pointed to the hallway that led off the central reception area. Noah and Duncan followed Elise down the deserted hallway. They stopped outside the second-to-last office, and Elise rapped on the door.

"Entrez!" a voice rumbled from the other side.

Elise pushed the door open. The middle-aged man with slumped shoulders, wavy black hair, and puffy eyes didn't budge from his chair behind the metallic desk. Peering over his computer screen, he stared up at them with the same indifference they had seen among the staff in the front office.

Elise identified herself and introduced Duncan and Noah. Marcel Robichard merely grunted in response. They sat down in the rickety wooden chairs across from him. As Elise described their association with the case, Robichard reached for the pack of cigarettes on his desk and lit one with a battered silver lighter that clicked loudly several times before finally flaming.

The farm's general manager exhaled a long mouthful of smoke. "I have spoken to the local authorities as well as representatives from the Ministry of Agriculture," he said in English that flowed with a surprisingly soft French accent. "Our livestock has been confiscated. Ferme d'Allaire is closed. Probably forever."

"Probably," Elise agreed. "M. Robichard, our job is to trace the source of the infected cattle. So far it leads directly back here."

Robichard stiffened in his chair and his puffy eyes narrowed. "We did nothing wrong," he growled.

"Perhaps, M. Robichard," she said frostily. "But at least six of the seven infected cattle identified were calves Ferme d'Allaire sold in the past year. That's more than just coincidence."

Robichard grunted disdainfully.

"We are going to need to see your barns, of course," she said.

Robichard shrugged. "I will have someone show you."

Elise reached into her bag and extracted a neatly printed list with numbers, dates, and other French text that Noah could not read upside down. She passed it to Robichard, who glanced at it with little interest. "Here is a list of the six infected cows that originated from this ranch along with their identifier numbers," she said. "We need the details of their genitors, siblings, and all calves born in the same season as them."

"Of course," Robichard said with a trace of cynicism. "The others have requested the same. We should have it ready by this afternoon."

Elise nodded. "We will need a list of all medications and supplements used on your herd, any organic fertilizers on site, and a log of all the animal husbandry products such as frozen semen."

"Why not?" Robichard laughed humorlessly. "Tomorrow."

Recognizing that he was wading in unfamiliar waters, Noah listened without comment. Duncan didn't say a word, either, but his amused eyes suggested he was enjoying the terse exchange.

"From where do you buy your cattle feed?" Elise asked.

"We use Marceau Alimentation Animale as our main supplier. Of course, we supplement with our own product."

"You make your own feed?" Noah piped up.

Robichard shot him a fierce look. "Most farms do," he said.

Elise tapped the desk in front of her. "I want to see where and how the feed is produced and stored. As well, we will need to seize all your existing feed."

Robichard folded his arms across his chest. "Why are you so interested in it?"

"With previous BSE outbreaks, the recycling of ruminants in the food chain has been a significant contributor to disease propagation." Elise's tone was clinical and icy.

Robichard shot up from his seat. "That practice has been banned in France for over ten years!" He shook the lit cigarette in Elise's direction. "Are you suggesting we use animal meat in our feed?"

Duncan rubbed his beard. "A wee birdie told us you're soft on that policy."

"What does that mean?" Robichard cried, waving the cigarette wildly.

"An informer came forward," Elise said.

"Who?" Robichard demanded.

"We do not know," she admitted. "But he claims you put animal meat in the feed."

"He is lying!" Robichard gripped the back of his chair as if he might hurl it. "We have not done that in ten years!"

The model of calm, Elise crossed her legs. "M. Robichard, perhaps it has happened without your knowledge," she said.

"Nothing happens here without me knowing about it," he spat. "Nothing!"

"Something *is* going on here," Elise said with an edge of her own. "All evidence indicates that this epidemic originated from your farm."

Robichard leaned over the back of his chair. "If all the cases come from here, why have we not had one sick cow on this farm?" he snorted. "Tell me, Mlle. Renard, where are all our sick cows?"

Duncan pointed out the dirty window beside the desk, through which a few yellowing fields could be seen beyond the parking lot. "Maybe they're buried out there somewhere."

Robichard's face drained of the last of its color. His eyes blackened. *"We have lost everything!"* he shouted, sweeping his hand over the three visitors. "And you come in here and accuse me of this. You have no proof. You have no right! So help me God, I will sue you."

The door opened behind them. *"Ça va, Marcel?"* a smooth female voice asked.

Noah glanced over his shoulder to see a woman of Elise's age and build standing in the doorway. With her blond hair tied in a ponytail, she wore a stylish black suit that accentuated her sculpted, Grace Kelly–like facial features.

Robichard spat out an explanation in French that Noah didn't even try to follow. The woman listened unfazed and then turned to the visitors with a polite smile. "Will you excuse us a moment?" she asked in English.

Robichard lumbered out of the room without a glance in their direction. The woman followed him and gently closed the door behind them. Noah looked from Duncan to Elise. Duncan shrugged. Elise said nothing.

They waited in silence for five minutes before the woman returned. Composed, she approached confidently. "I am Geneviève Allaire, the granddaughter of the farm's founder, Henri Allaire. I am now president. Please excuse Marcel's behavior. It is unlike him, but he has been under such enormous stress." She paused. "We all have."

"I can imagine," Noah said.

Allaire closed her eyes, showing a momentary glimpse of fatigue. Then her smile re-emerged. "So the WHO and the E.U. also believe that we are responsible for this outbreak?"

Elise shrugged unapologetically. "Mme. Allaire, are you as adamant as your general manager that it has nothing to do with Ferme d'Allaire?"

She uttered a small sigh. "By training, I am a lawyer, so I find it hard to overlook all the evidence." She held up a palm. "However, as I understand it, BSE can occur spontaneously on any farm, despite precautions."

"Certainly," Duncan said. "But not six times in a year. That takes some shoddy farming practices."

"Ah . . ." Allaire toyed with the wedding band on her left ring finger. "So naturally you've concluded that we have recycled our contaminated meat through the feed?" She said it pleasantly enough, but her eyes had gone cold.

"We did not say that," Elise said. "We are following up on information—"

"From your informant," Allaire broke in.

"Yes."

"Your *anonymous* informant."

Her skepticism was contagious enough that Noah again began to question the man's motives. Elise showed no such doubt. "What could he hope to gain by accusing you?"

Allaire shook her head. "Maybe he was an angry former employee set on revenge?"

"Does anyone come to mind?" Noah asked.

Allaire ignored the question. "Or maybe he wasn't looking to gain anything. Maybe he was trying to divert your attention *away* from something else."

Duncan glanced at Noah. Even Elise was left without a reply.

"You may have our feed, Mlle. Renard," Allaire said softly. "Why not? After all, you have taken everything else."

11

Lac Noir, France. January 17

After the altercation with Marcel Robichard at Ferme d'Allaire, his staff's attitude toward Noah and his team dipped from indifference to contempt. However, as Robichard promised, one of the farm employees reluctantly toured the visitors through the feed production plant and storage facility. The staff grew openly hostile when Elise insisted on staying in the storage room until the Ministry of Agriculture officials arrived to confiscate the feed. It was the longest three-quarters of an hour in Noah's recent memory. Even Duncan, who usually thrived on conflict, was glad to be free of the toxic atmosphere. "Much warmer out here," he muttered when they finally stepped from the heated building into the freezing wind.

They had planned to go directly to Paris to interview the neuropathologist, Dr. Gellier, but Noah suggested that since they were near Lac Noir it might be worth dropping in on the family of the prion's third known victim, Philippe Manet. The others agreed.

They parked on the shoulder of the lakeshore road in front of the Manet property. Though not exactly black, from what Noah could see of Lac Noir the narrow tree-lined lake was dark, murky, and, perhaps because of the season, foreboding. A more welcoming two-story stone house, with light gray steps and groomed lawn, stood between the lake and them. He was surprised by how far it was set back from the road on the wooded property, making the house—the last one on the road—feel secluded.

The skies were brighter now that the orange-yellow glow of the sun peeked out from behind the clouds, but the wind had not let up. Noah had forgotten his gloves at the farm, but he had no intention of going back to get them. As he walked up the long driveway, he rubbed his hands together and blew on them for warmth.

A young woman answered the door. Dressed in dark jeans and a collared shirt, she was sinewy with a flat chest and narrow hips. Her short black hair and almond brown eyes complemented her androgynous features and gave her an air of stylish sophistication.

After Elise showed her identification, the woman invited them in. She introduced herself in a fluid accent as Sylvie Manet, Philippe's older sister. She led them into a stately living room finished with decorative moldings and wainscoting and furnished with ornate classical French chairs, chaises, and cabinets.

"It's a lovely house," Elise said, glancing around.

With a modest nod, Sylvie guided them to the chairs by the fireplace. Sinking into a wingback chair, Noah appreciated the warmth of the crackling fire.

"My father was a collector," Sylvie explained. "He was obsessed with the Louis XV period. I think it is a little . . . too much for my taste."

"Your father is not alive?" Elise asked.

"He died ten years ago," Sylvie said. "This is not really Maman's taste either, but she will not change the décor out of respect for his memory. It's too bad, really. People would pay good money for much of this." She pointed to a few of the pieces.

"Is your mother home?" Elise asked.

Sylvie shook her head. "She's in the hospital. She had a heart attack last week."

"I am so sorry to hear that." Noah nodded sympathetically. "How is she doing?"

"The doctors say her heart will be okay." Her shoulders rose and fell slightly. "I am not so sure. I think it has been broken too many times now."

"Do you live here, too, Mlle. Manet?" Noah asked.

"Sylvie, please," she said. "No. I'm a biology researcher at the University of Bordeaux. I came back here to help Maman when my little brother became ill. And then when he died, and Maman had her heart problems . . ." Her words trailed off and her eyes focused on the flames.

"Sylvie, can we talk about Philippe?" Noah said gently.

"Of course," she said, still staring at the fire. "What would you like to know?"

"When did you first notice anything different about him?"

"About two months ago, Maman said Philippe had begun to act peculiarly. He started to say all kinds of strange things. He became very suspicious of everyone and everything. We were concerned he had developed a mental disorder." She looked suddenly sheepish. "I even thought he might have become mixed up with drugs."

Noah remembered Dr. Charron's video clip of Philippe wrestling with the two orderlies while screaming about fire and water. "We were told he threatened someone with a knife," he said.

"Maman," Sylvie said softly.

"He threatened his own mother?" Elise blurted, drawing a glare from Duncan.

Sylvie's eyes darted to Elise. "That was not my brother!" she said. "His brain was diseased then. Before, Philippe was so calm. Always the good boy." Eyes downcast, she smiled. "Georges and I were the wild ones."

"Georges?"

"Our older brother."

Duncan repositioned himself in his chair. "How long before the knife incident would you say that you first noticed a change in your brother?" he asked.

Sylvie considered the question. "Maman called me at work two or three days before to say Philippe was not himself." She swallowed. "I would have come right away, but I did not realize it was so serious."

Two or three days from "not himself" to knife-wielding paranoia, Noah thought. Despite the fire's warmth, he fought off the familiar chill. "Did Philippe live here, too?" he asked.

Sylvie nodded. "He was an engineer with a company in Limoges, but he did much of his work from home. You see, Philippe was born with hip problems. He had a lot of pain, much worse if he had to walk far." Her thin neck bobbed once as she swallowed. "He was supposed to have an operation in the fall."

Noah nodded. "About Philippe's diet—"

"I didn't know he was on a diet."

Noah smiled and shook his head. "No. I mean do you know if your brother ate much beef?"

Sylvie blushed slightly. "I know he liked the steaks that Maman makes. And sometimes Philippe used to have the . . ." She turned to Elise for help. *"Langue de vache marine."*

Elise's eyes widened. "Pickled cow's tongue," she translated.

Noah understood Elise's reaction. Like sweetbreads and the entrails of infected cows, the tongue typically carried the highest concentrations of prions in the case of BSE.

Duncan frowned. "Does anyone else in your family eat tongue or any organ meat?"

Sylvie waved her hands and shuddered. "I can barely eat the steak. I don't think Maman or Georges would eat the cow's tongue, either."

"Where is Georges?" Noah asked.

Sylvie rolled her eyes affectionately. "Spin a globe and choose a spot," she said.

Elise shook her head. "You don't know?"

"He e-mailed me from Canada, somewhere north of the Arctic Circle, last week," she said. "Georges is a geologist. With his research, he travels to very remote places. The North Pole, the South Pole, and everywhere in between. Sometimes we can't reach him for weeks. He did not hear about Philippe until it was too late. There was a terrible storm, and he was snowed in. He could not come home in time . . . even for Philippe's funeral."

"What kind of research?" Noah asked, curious.

"Ice."

"Ice?"

"He is a world expert on glaciers and other ice formations. He spends most of his time in the coldest places."

"I imagine they're still warmer than Limousin," Duncan cracked. "He's not been sick, has he?"

"I don't think so," she said, frowning.

"And you don't know of anyone else around here who has?" Duncan asked.

Sylvie shook her head.

"What about Benoît Gagnon or Giselle Tremblay?" Noah recited the names of the other two victims.

"Giselle Tremblay . . ." Sylvie turned back to the fire. "The name is familiar, but I am not sure why."

Noah cleared his throat. "Sylvie, they told us in Limoges that your family checked Philippe out of the hospital and brought him back to Lac Noir."

Sylvie nodded.

"Why?"

Sylvie's face shrouded with sudden anguish. "You should have seen what happened to him in two weeks, Dr. Haldane."

"We saw a few video clips of him during his hospitalization."

"So you saw what he looked like, then!" She sighed heavily and leaned back in her chair. "He was dying. Horribly. And it was hard on Maman to go back and forth to Limoges every day. She wanted him closer. She wanted him home." Her finger swept the grand living room. "Obviously, we could not care for him here. So we found a spot near us in the, um, how do you say . . . *maison de santé.*"

"Nursing home," Elise translated.

Duncan flopped forward in his chair. "Where he died in the fire?"

"It was so stupid." Sylvie glanced at the fireplace and watched the flames dance safely within the confines of the mantel. "Another patient gave my brother a cigarette." She swallowed again. "By that point, Philippe was so sick he could not even feed himself or hold a glass."

"Strange," Elise said.

"Senseless." Sylvie shook her head sternly. "The woman was demented. She was not supposed to have cigarettes, either. We'll never know how she got them. She died in the fire, too."

Noah thought again about the odd timing of the blaze, but Sylvie's intense brown eyes drew his attention. "Dr. Haldane, am I at risk for . . . you know?" she asked in a faltering voice.

He shook his head. "No family clusters of this disease have ever been reported. Even living in the same house with a victim does not put you at increased risk." He mustered a reassuring grin for her. "And since you don't seem to like cow's tongue . . ."

Her sad smile showed her relief.

They asked other questions about Philippe and his possible exposure to BSE, but his sister had little else to offer. Noah rose from his seat and the others followed. "Thank you, Sylvie, you've been very helpful," he said. "Again, I'm sorry about what your family has gone through."

Sylvie nodded gratefully. "Please let me know if I can help in any other way," she said. "I wouldn't want anyone else . . ." She didn't finish the sentence.

She led them to the front door. As they were about to file out, Sylvie said, "What happened to Philippe . . ." She looked down at her feet. "It was the worst thing I've ever seen in my life. Do you think there will be others?"

"No question," Duncan murmured.

He said it with such certainty that Noah's stomach sank.

12

More than twenty-four hours had passed without Pauline Lamaire materializing. She was now *officially* considered a missing person, but Detective Avril Avars took little solace from the change in her status. The case crept under her skin. For the first time since her husband's funeral, Avril delayed her weekly trip to Antoine's graveside to stay in Montmagnon and investigate further.

Avril and her twenty-one-year-old son, Frédéric (home from university on winter break), had gone to Montmagnon only a month earlier to visit her widowed father. Returning now brought back unwanted memories of that tense trip. Avril still felt the twinges of guilt. She and her son shared the same stubborn streak, but they had never clashed as they had during that miserable journey.

Frédéric was closer in coloring to Avril, but with his trim athletic physique and solid square face, he resembled his father so much that at times it hurt her to look at him. And like Antoine, the boy had always been mature beyond his years. From comments he made after returning home from Paris, Avril realized that Frédéric intended to propose to his high school sweetheart, Stéphane.

Avril liked the quiet doe-eyed girl, but she was convinced her son was on the verge of making a mistake. Not only did Avril think that he was far too young to marry, she could not help but see Stéphane as a provincial Catholic housewife with no goal other than to raise a large family. She envisioned so much more for her only son. The fight erupted when she told him as much.

"Maman, you make it sound as if I have to choose between Stéphane and my career," Frédéric grumbled from the driver's seat, as they drove through the outskirts of Limoges.

"Don't put words in my mouth, Freddie," she said. "Why do you need to choose at all? You're still so young."

Frédéric glanced sidelong at her. "How old were you when you married Papa?"

"Times were different," she snapped. "Besides, your father and I had a very clear vision of what we both wanted out of our lives *and* careers."

"So do Stéphane and I!"

"Really? You want to raise eight kids in a farmhouse in Saint Junien, too?"

"Eight is better than one!"

"That's not fair, Frédéric." She swallowed. "We would've loved to have had more children, but you know I—" She did not finish, but Frédéric already knew the family story of his mother's emergency hysterectomy performed to stop the life-threatening bleeding after his delivery.

Frédéric nodded grudgingly. "Sorry, Maman, you're not being fair to Stéphane. You've never given her enough credit for who she is."

"Maybe. You're doing so well at school. All your professors say so. I envisioned you making a name for yourself with a major architecture firm in Paris."

"Not drafting blueprints for new barns in Saint Junien, right?"

"Frédéric, there might be a woman out there who shares your passion for design. Someone with more . . . ambition . . . than Stéphane."

"A wife my mother can be more proud of?"

"This is not about me, Freddie!" Avril felt her cheeks grow hot with indignation. "You wanted my opinion, so I am telling you."

Stopped at a traffic light, he turned to her with eyes afire. "No. What I wanted was your unconditional support."

"You'll always have that. You know it, too." She waved her hand impatiently. "I just want you to consider what is best for *you* now."

"Not what's best for Stéphane, too?"

"No," Avril said. "At your age, what is best for you is best for her, too. If you make sacrifices for Stéphane's sake now, you may both come to regret it when it is already too late."

"Sounds like you want me to make sacrifices for your grand vision of my life," Frédéric muttered.

"You're not even trying to listen!" Avril snapped, and they fell into a cold silence that lasted for much of their stay in Montmagnon.

After weathering the visit with her father—who made matters worse by siding with Frédéric—Avril had not expected to see the town again until Easter at the earliest, but she wound up spending most of the cold January day in Montmagnon. She interviewed several of Pauline Lamaire's acquaintances, many of whom Avril knew, or at least recognized from childhood. By the time she headed back to Limoges, she took with her an appreciation of how difficult Pauline's life had become after contracting arthritis.

What Avril did *not* find in Montmagnon was any trace of Pauline's whereabouts. The search was complicated by the woman's growing isolation. By all accounts, the arthri-

tis had not only incapacitated Pauline, it also fundamen-
tally changed her. The concert violinist—once known for
her ever-present smile and carefree disposition—had become obsessed with finding a magical cure. Some of the
interviewees even guiltily admitted to, or staunchly de-
fended, their efforts to distance themselves from a woman
who grew more eccentric by the month. A few suggested
that her obsession had crossed the bounds of rationality.
One former friend, a cellist, said, "It's almost impossible
to be around her now, Detective. She lives in a world consumed by conspiracy theories, alternative medicine, and
mysticism."

Pauline's eccentricity aside, none of the interviewees
described her as confused or forgetful, though no one had
seen her as recently as Dr. Tanier had. If she was as disoriented as the doctor believed and she did wander out of
her house, then any of the lakes or woods surrounding
Montmagnon could have swallowed her without a trace.
But for Avril it always came back to the tidy state of her
house. If Pauline had simply stumbled out into the wilder-
ness, then who cleaned her house and brought in fresh-cut
flowers? Not the cleaning woman who came every second
Thursday; Avril had already checked.

Hoping to shed light on this question, Avril had asked
Pauline's closest living relative to meet her at the Gendarmerie Limoges. Pauline had no siblings, and both her
parents were long dead. Marie Lamaire was Pauline's first
cousin and, at thirty-seven, the same age. Though they
had grown up in the same town, Avril had no recollection
of the woman. And the sight of Marie standing nervously
in the foyer (wearing a black frock and her hair tied tight
in a bun that Avril would have expected to see on a woman
twice her age) did not jar any memories. However, the
detective decided that Marie, who worked at a secondhand
bookstore in Limoges, typified the provincial spinster.

She led her visitor down the colorless gray hallway and into her slightly dank office. Like the rest of the Gendarmerie building, the office was tinged with the faint smell of mold from a leak that none of the building custodians had been able to pinpoint and had long since given up trying.

Once seated, Avril explained the purpose of the interview. While the detective spoke, Marie squirmed in her chair and rarely made eye contact. "Detective Avars, I have not seen much of Pauline in the last year or two," she said.

"When was the last time?"

"About six weeks ago. I was passing by Montmagnon on my way home from Jourgnac. I had been meaning to drop off a book on Chinese herbal remedies that I had been carrying in my car, so I stopped over."

Avril reached for her pen. After being humiliated early in her career at a trial by a defense attorney, she had become a meticulous note taker. She jotted down Marie's response on the notepad in front of her. "What was the house like?"

Marie laughed anxiously. "You know Pauline, Detective. It was spotless as ever."

Avril nodded impassively, remembering Dr. Tanier's description of the mess he had found on his earlier visit. "And how did Pauline seem?" she asked.

"No different than usual." Marie uttered a quiet sigh. "Always so concerned with her arthritis." She crossed and promptly uncrossed her legs. "But she did say she was feeling a little better."

"How so?"

"She mentioned she had started on a new treatment. Pauline was always starting a new therapy of some kind. She talked about little else."

Avril noted the lack of empathy in Marie's tone. "Do you remember any details of this treatment?"

"I think she said a friend had given it to her, but I might be confusing visits."

Avril recalled Dr. Tanier's reference to new medications. "Did Pauline describe this therapy?"

"I seem to remember that it was not a pill from a pharmacy or anything like that." Marie shrugged helplessly. "If she told me more, I cannot remember."

"And the friend who gave it to her?"

Marie held up her palms again.

Suppressing an irritated sigh, Avril was about to wind up the interview when Marie spoke hesitantly. "I am not sure if it's related, but we did talk about Georges. Possibly, he suggested the treatment."

"Georges?"

"Georges Manet. Her former fiancé."

The name sounded vaguely familiar to Avril. "Is he from Montmagnon?"

Marie pursed her lips. "His family is from Lac Noir."

"You said *former* fiancé. What happened?"

"Georges is a geologist. A real globe-trotter. And very handsome, too." Her thin lips broke into a self-conscious smile as she blushed slightly. "Pauline used to travel with him on some of his trips, but after she became ill with the arthritis—"

"He broke off the engagement," Avril finished her sentence.

Marie shook her head vehemently. "No, Pauline did!"

"Oh?" Avril sat up straighter. "Why?"

"Georges is such an outdoors person." She reddened further, and Avril realized that Marie was infatuated with her cousin's ex-fiancé. "Pauline knew she would not be able to do those kinds of things with Georges anymore, that she would even hold him back. I think that is why she broke it off." She shook her head. "My cousin is nothing if not proud."

Avril jotted Georges Manet's name and underlined it

once with a sweep of ink. *Was Marie involved in her cousin's disappearance?* Avril wondered. The woman was an unlikely kidnapper. "They continued to see each other after their breakup?" Avril asked.

Marie nodded. "Georges is a wonderful man. He visits Pauline regularly. He brings her mementos from his trips. You know . . . exotic gifts." She uttered a high-pitched laugh. "Eskimo art and carvings. He even once brought her home a piece of an iceberg."

Avril frowned. "Eskimos? Icebergs?"

"Georges does his research in the far north. As I said, Pauline used to accompany him sometimes. Once, she even visited the North Pole," Marie added with awe.

Avril wondered if the woman in front of her had ever even left Limousin. "So you think Georges was the one who brought her this new treatment?"

Her narrow shoulders rose and fell quickly. "I don't recall if Pauline told me who brought it. I simply remember that we talked about . . . about Georges."

Avril rose from her chair and extended her to hand to Marie, who gripped it weakly with a wet palm. "Thank you," Avril said. "You have been most helpful."

After Marie shrank out of the office, Avril pulled out a few sheets of lined paper and began to organize her thoughts. She wrote Pauline's name in the center of the page and circled it. She drew a series of lines, like spokes, and started to connect boxes with names and notes.

"Still solving crimes with little circles and triangles?" a gruff voice grunted from the door to her office.

Avril looked up to see Detective Simon Valmont filling her doorway. Tall and overweight, Valmont had a shock of black hair. As usual, his white shirt and light blue tie bore remnants of his last meal, but at least he was cleaner shaven than the day before. An old-school detective with more than twenty years' experience and a penchant for gambling on soccer and horse races, Valmont was a chauvinist and a racist; he made little effort to hide either from the North African woman with whom he was often partnered. Despite the many reasons he gave Avril for despising him, she had a soft spot for Valmont. A widower himself, his support helped her through some of her lowest points after Antoine's fatal accident. And Valmont, who had no children of his own, was so close with Frédéric that her son referred to him as Uncle Simon.

"Want me to find you some work, Valmont?" Avril asked.

Valmont lumbered into her office. "No need. I'll find my own." He cleared his throat loudly as if trying to dislodge something that was stuck, but Avril knew it was just his vocal tic. "I hear the busboy at the café across the street hasn't been seen in half an hour. He might be at lunch, but I think I'll open a missing persons file on him just in case."

Avril fought off the smile. "You will be happy to know that Pauline Lamaire is now considered missing," she said, having already run the situation by Valmont the previous day.

"Happy? I am ecstatic."

Inspector Esmond Cabot suddenly walked into Avril's office without invitation. Short and thin, with a neatly trimmed moustache and manicured nails, Cabot was as tidy as Valmont was messy. Though he was the same age as Avril and two years less experienced, since achieving the rank of inspector that he had so coveted, Cabot protected his position like a tiger guards his kill. "Ecstatic about what, Simon?"

"That you manage to keep the most overpriced tailors in Paris in business," Valmont said, thumbing at Cabot's expensive-looking olive green suit.

The inspector ignored Valmont's gibe. Instead, he withdrew a neatly folded piece of paper from an inner pocket.

He unfolded the note meticulously. "A farmer called this afternoon to report his wife missing."

Avril frowned. "Another missing person?"

"Hang on." Valmont cleared his throat noisily again. "You still don't know that the Lamaire case is much more than a wild-goose chase."

Avril folded her arms across her chest and turned to her boss. "Who is this farmer, Esmond?"

"André Pereau. The wife is Yvette Pereau."

The names meant nothing to her. "And what makes Pereau think his wife is missing?" she asked.

Cabot ran a finger over the paper's crease as if trying to flatten out the imperfection. "She has been gone almost a week without any contact."

Avril sat up straighter. "A week? Why did he wait so long to report it?"

"Pereau originally thought his wife had left him," Cabot said emotionlessly. "Apparently, it has happened before. He admits he has a problem with the wine."

"So what's different now?" Valmont sighed.

"Allegedly, Yvette is very close to her parents," Cabot said. "She had always gone to them before. But according to his in-laws, they have not seen or heard from their daughter since she left."

"Where do the Pereaus live?" Avril asked.

"A farm just outside of Terrebonne."

Avril tensed slightly in her chair, as she realized Terrebonne was a neighboring town to Montmagnon, no more than fifteen kilometers east. *Two missing women in a region as small and remote as Limousin,* she thought. *Could there be a serial killer on the loose?*

The same growling sound came from deep within Valmont's throat again. "I bet the wife didn't want her drunk of a husband serenading her in front of Papa and Maman and the whole neighborhood, so she persuaded them to cover for her."

"Still betting, are we, Simon?" Cabot asked with a hint of accusation.

"Only on the sure things, Inspector," Valmont said defiantly.

Cabot gently fingered the edges of his moustache. "Simon is probably right," he said with patent lack of interest. "Will you have a quick look into this, Avril?"

"She already has a phantom missing persons case," Valmont said. "Only fair that I handle this one."

Avril looked from Cabot to Valmont. "I am going to be in the area on the Lamaire case anyway. I might as well look into both."

Valmont shrugged in defeat. "If you have the time to burn. . . ."

"I have nothing but time," she said with a smile, though she already had an unsettling sense that her time would not be wasted at all.

13

Paris, France. January 17

Noah, Duncan, and Elise arrived at the Gare d'Austerlitz minutes before four P.M. Stepping out of the train station into the hazy warmth of the Left Bank, Noah felt as if spring had arrived in the less than three hours since they had left Limoges. As he tucked his new gloves (which he bought at the Limoges train station to replace the pair he had left at Ferme d'Allaire) into his pocket, he even considered shedding his coat.

They began to walk the five blocks southwest of the station to the Salpêtrière Hospital, Paris's world-class neurology research center. Noah had been there once before, so when he felt his cell phone vibrate in his front pocket, he told the others: "Go ahead. I'll catch up with you."

He brought the phone to his ear. "Noah Haldane."

"Hello, Noah."

"Gwen?" Noah smiled automatically as his heart sped up. "Hi."

Elise stopped and viewed him with curiosity. Duncan gently tugged at her elbow, and she turned slowly to walk away with him. Noah moved off the sidewalk and shielded his ear from the traffic noise.

"You're in France, aren't you?" Gwen said.

"Did Jean tell you?"

"No, I just assumed when I saw the e-mail news alert this morning."

As the director of counterbioterrorism for the Department of Homeland Security, Gwen received daily, sometimes hourly, electronic alerts from the CDC and the WHO regarding infectious "hot spots" all over the planet. "They put out an alert about the mad cows, huh?" he said.

She chuckled. "Soon as I heard the WHO was involved, I knew that meant Duncan and you had to be in the thick of it."

Noah warmed at the sound of her soft laugh. "Duncan calls us 'the world's two strongest shite magnets,'" he said with a feigned Scottish brogue.

"Hey, that's not bad."

Noah didn't know if Gwen was referring to the impersonation or the comment, nor did he care. He enjoyed the affection in her tone.

"How *is* that demented redhead?" Gwen asked.

"Duncan is Duncan." He considered the remark. "Actually, he's not. Something isn't right with him."

"What's up?" she asked with concern.

"I'm not entirely sure. He's upset about this whole BSE situation. He was burned before during the British outbreak, and he thinks the E.U. is meddling again. But . . ." Noah sighed. "It's more than that. Something is going on, but he doesn't want to talk about it. And you know Duncan, he hides his emotions behind wisecracks and irreverence."

"Everything okay at home?"

"Mine or Duncan's?"

"I meant . . . um . . . Duncan's."

"He hasn't said otherwise, but then again he hasn't said much of anything."

"You're one of his best friends, Noah. He'll tell you

when he's ready. But since you brought it up, how are things at *your* home?"

"I'm a long way from home." he said ruefully. "Chloe and I did have a great trip to Mexico. Good for both of us. And Gwen, she's swimming on her own now."

She laughed softly. "I bet she's more adorable than ever."

Noah could picture Gwen's smile, green eyes aflame and lips parted widely. At forty-two, she had no children of her own. And while always respectful of boundaries, she had become fast friends with Chloe. He still felt guilty for having introduced Chloe to Gwen, only to sever the ties months later. His daughter seemed to take Gwen's absence in stride, but Noah resolved in the future to keep his dating life separate from his family, until and unless he made a permanent commitment.

"How are things with you?" he asked.

"Busy. Usual government stuff," she said, sounding evasive.

The awkwardness of their last few months together drifted back to Noah: each of them competing to out-excuse and apologize to the other for missed dates and canceled get-togethers. In the month preceding their mutually agreed hiatus, they had managed to see each other only twice—once for a hurried dinner between meetings, and once for late-night lovemaking after Noah picked her up at the airport returning from yet another overseas trip (possibly Lisbon, though he couldn't remember). They still connected emotionally and physically, but both came to realize that life as the American Bug Czar and the WHO's expert on emerging pathogens, respectively, was not compatible with building much more than a business relationship.

Gwen's tone turned professional. "Noah, how serious is this French situation?"

"It's too soon to say," he said, matching her earlier evasiveness. "The good news is that terrorists would have a tough time weaponizing mad cow disease."

"You know that wasn't my concern, Noah," she said with slight irritation.

"Yeah." Accustomed to shielding sensitive information, he wavered a moment out of habit. But he knew she would have full clearance for this information, and besides, there was no one he would rather run the situation past. Appreciating that they were speaking on a secure mobile line, he decided to fill her in. "This is different from any previous BSE outbreak." He went on to describe what they had learned in the last forty-eight hours and then added, "What happened to those people in a few short weeks . . ." He exhaled slowly. "Gwen, if this thing gets loose and erupts as quickly as it did in the first weeks, we could be talking about another global crisis."

She absorbed it all without comment. He imagined her biting her lower lip and squinting the way she always did when deep in concentration. "Well?" he asked, impatient for her impression.

"Do you think this entire outbreak traces back to that one cattle supplier?"

"It would appear so."

"Appear?"

"I don't know," Noah said, riled by the same vague unease he'd repeatedly experienced since returning to Europe. "At least six of the seven infected cows come from this farm. And it's very possible that they're recycling animal meat in the feed," he said, trying to rationalize away his doubt.

"What is it, Noah?" Gwen pushed.

Noah hesitated. "It's odd that none of their cows showed any indication of illness while still on their property."

"Maybe somebody on that farm was trying to cover it up?"

Cover-up. The term struck a chord in him. "I don't know if this has to do with Ferme d'Allaire or someplace else, but my gut tells me that we haven't seen the whole story in Limousin yet."

"Stick with it, Noah. Seems to me you have a pretty wise gut."

He laughed halfheartedly. "We'll see what shows up in that cattle feed."

She was quiet a moment. "This prion is going to keep you over there for a while, huh?"

"I think so."

"And with the ban on all French beef exports . . ."

Noah clicked his tongue. "I can already feel the frying pan heating up under me, but I've been in worse places. And frankly, beef sales are the least of my concern."

"Look, Noah, if I can do anything to help . . ."

He smiled. "Thanks. I might well take you up on that offer down the road."

"You know where to find me."

"At the very least, as soon as I get home we should go grab a coffee or a bite and catch up."

"Sure. Let's do that sometime." Her tone matched the perfunctory quality of his offer.

Suddenly self-conscious, they bade each other a hasty good-bye that was stiffer than their greeting.

Slightly melancholic, Noah slipped the phone back into his pocket and hurried down Boulevard de l'Hôpital. As he neared the sprawling Salpêtrière Hospital complex, he tried to fight back the feelings her voice had stirred. As impractical as their relationship was, he realized that he missed her more than ever.

Approaching the main entrance, he distracted himself by studying the classical seventeenth-century gray stone edifice and recalling what he had been told of its important historical significance on his last visit. Neurology was born as a specialty within the walls of this hospital.

And his own specialty of infectious diseases came into being only a few miles away in the catacombs of the Institut Pasteur.

Inside the hospital's bustling foyer, the familiar medical attire, smells, and palpable hospital hum helped to ground Noah. Weaving his way down the long hallways, he followed the signs to the neuropathology department. At the department's reception desk, he introduced himself to a young woman with blue-tinted hair and a nose ring. Unenthusiastically, she rose from her seat and led Noah to Dr. Émilie Gellier's office.

Duncan and Elise were already seated across the desk from Gellier. At the sight of Noah, the petite gray-haired woman leaped from her seat and rushed toward him. Noah doubted that she reached five feet, and her slightly stooped posture and long lab coat made her look even shorter. Though her face was etched with deep lines, her bright hazel eyes possessed a youthfulness that matched her enthusiasm. She pumped his hand. "*Bienvenue,* Dr. Haldane!" she gushed. "It's an honor to meet you."

"Likewise, Dr. Gellier."

She waved away his compliment with a tiny hand. "Come. Sit. Please join us."

"Haldane, I had no idea you caught a later train than us," Duncan groaned.

Ignoring the barb, Noah sat down beside Elise, who viewed him coolly. He sensed her reaction had nothing to do with his tardiness.

Gellier smiled warmly. "I was just telling your colleagues that I know Louis Charron from our days in training together. He is a brilliant clinician."

"If not the cheeriest," Duncan said.

"He can be quite the curmudgeon." Gellier laughed. "Do not fall for his act. Deep down he is a softie. And his wife, Clarice, is absolutely delightful. She adores him."

Elise shifted in her seat. "Dr. Gellier, can we discuss the autopsies—"

Gellier raised a hand to interrupt. "I do not perform autopsies, Mlle. Renard."

"Of course. I meant, can we discuss your findings on the patients' brains."

"We can do better than that," she said, hopping out of her seat again with surprising spryness. She hurried out through an open door that connected her office to a laboratory. After a moment of uncertainty, the others followed.

The room was a decent size but crowded with microscopes, equipment, computers, and specimens. Noah had never seen so many brains. The full length of the far side of the room was stacked with shelf upon shelf of glass jars holding brains floating in formaldehyde.

"Is Dr. Frankenstein aware that his warehouse has been relocated?" Duncan said, surveying the wall.

"It's a wonderful collection," Gellier said proudly. She waved a hand over the wall. "We have specimens over a hundred years old. Neurosyphilis, cerebral tuberculosis, even some smallpox cerebritis. There is not a neurological disorder that I know of missing from our collection."

"And the vCJD patients from Limousin?" Noah asked.

"*Ah, oui.* Come and see." Gellier turned from the wall and headed to one of the computers perched on a desk against the opposite wall. She sat down in front of a computer screen that showed a grainy black-and-white photo of a man with long sideburns and a waistcoat standing in what looked like a nineteenth-century ward. Gellier tapped the screen. "Jean-Martin Charcot," she said reverentially. "The father of modern neurology. And he worked right here on this very floor a hundred fifty years before me."

"I wonder if old Charcot freelanced for Jean Nantal, too?" Duncan said mischievously.

Giggling at the reference to the WHO director, Gellier typed in a password and the screen saver gave way to a blue backdrop covered with numerous computer icons. With a click of the mouse, the monitor filled with a schematic diagram of a large spiral molecule that Noah recognized as a protein.

"These are normal prions. Complex proteins, prominent in brain tissue." Gellier turned to Elise. "And, yes, all brains do normally contain prions. Notice the helix shape." She clicked a button and suddenly the molecule collapsed into rows of sheets. "This is a *pathological* prion. For unknown reasons, the normal alpha-helical protein is reshaped into this structure that we call beta-pleated sheets."

None of this was news to Noah, but he let Gellier explain for Elise's benefit as his eyes drifted to the specimens lining the wall. He spotted placards that read as early as 1904.

"Now, here is the amazing quality of pathological prions," Gellier went on, waving her hands excitedly. "Though not alive in any way, somehow they . . . what is the word? . . . coerce normal prions in brain cells to mimic their shape."

"You mean they turn normal prions into replicas of themselves?" Elise asked.

"Exactly!" Gellier almost hopped out of her chair. "One pathological prion converts a normal prion into its same shape. Now you have two abnormal prions that convert two normal prions into the pathological form. And so on."

Gellier clicked her mouse and a cell appeared on the screen. "This is a brain cell, a neuron," she explained. As always, it reminded Noah of a daisy with its central body and stemlike axon. "As the abnormal proteins multiply inside the neuron, they begin to crystallize out and accumulate, causing the cell to swell." Gellier tapped her mouse. On the screen, the inside of the neuron shimmered like a shaken snow globe. Then the cell grew in girth. When it reached the size of a distended balloon, it burst, showering fragments across the screen. Gellier circled the screen with a small finger. "This cell is dead. And now all these pathological proteins can go on to infect the next neuron."

"And so on," Duncan said ominously.

"Dr. Gellier, the cases in Limousin," Noah said. "Are you certain they had the same form of vCJD?"

Instead of replying, Gellier typed at her computer for a few moments. The figure on the screen split into two; each looked like the mirror image of the other. Noah recognized the two specimens as cross-sections of midbrain tissue. "I personally dissected four of the six cases of vCJD reported in France in the nineties," Gellier said without a trace of conceit. "And I examined all three cases from Limousin." She tapped at the screen. "The brain tissue on the left comes from a vCJD victim who died in Paris in 1998. And on the right, we have the brain of Giselle Tremblay from Limousin. As you can see, they are identical."

Noah looked from one to the other. The butterfly-wing-shaped midbrains were interchangeable, both of them equally chewed up with cracks, fissures, and gaping holes.

"But it's more than just the microscopic findings. The levels of fourteen-three-three protein in the brain tissues were the same between the two groups. And both tested positive for PrPres."

"I know that fourteen-three-three protein is used to screen for vCJD," Elise said. "But what is PrPres?"

"PrPres is a DNA marker for the cellular presence of the rogue BSE prions," Gellier explained. "It is like a fingerprint that they leave behind on damaged cells. It has been positive in all known cases of vCJD. And it is positive in all three of the Limousin victims."

Noah studied the screen intently. "Have you found any discrepancies between the previous vCJD cases and the ones in Limousin?"

Gellier turned from the computer to look at Noah. "One, and only one. In the tissue of the 1990s victims we saw much higher levels of phosphorylated tau protein than in the Limousin outbreak."

Noah's stomach tightened, but he said nothing.

"That's a mouthful," Duncan said. "Is it a significant difference?"

Gellier shook her head. "I think there is a very good explanation. In previous cases, the disease progressed over a period of a year to eighteen months, while in Limousin it happened over a matter of weeks. I do not think there was enough time for the phosphorylated tau protein to accumulate in the tissue like it had in earlier vCJD outbreaks."

Noah pointed to the screen. "That's the point, Dr. Gellier. What we have seen in Limousin has a completely different time course from all known prion outbreaks. Doesn't that make you think it could be a different disease?"

"I only know what I see, Dr. Haldane," she said with a smile. She hopped back to her feet, gaining little height, and hurried over to the wall of brains. She pulled one of the specimen containers down from the shelf and laid it on the counter nearby, and then scuttled back for a second brain.

The others gathered around the countertop. Gellier reached for a box of gloves, extracted a pair, and slid her small hands into them. She lifted the lids on both jars. The formaldehyde smell wafted up to Noah, and he had a queasy flashback to his first day in the dissecting lab of medical school.

Gellier plunged her left hand into a jar and pulled out the first brain. She grabbed the second brain with her right. Palms upward, she held them out to show to the others. They had the typical gray cauliflower appearance of the brain, but these particular cauliflowers looked as if they had been left out to rot. Certain areas had blackened while other sections had collapsed. Throughout, large holes penetrated the surface as if a small animal had burrowed through the tissue.

"Christ," Duncan said. "There's not much left of them, is there?"

Elise blanched slightly but her eyes never deviated from the brain. "Whose are they?" she asked.

Gellier raised her right hand. "This is a 1997 BSE victim." Then she lifted her left. "And this is Benoît Gagnon. But without the labels, I would not be able to tell one from the other."

"May I?" Noah asked, pointing to the brains.

Gellier nodded.

Noah grabbed a pair of large gloves from the far box and slipped his hands into them. Gellier carefully passed him the two brains. He could not believe how light they were in his hands. A long time had passed since he'd last held a brain, and he had forgotten that a person's nerve center—his essence—could weigh only a few pounds.

He seesawed them up and down, comparing weights. They felt the same. And when he held them up closer, so that the formaldehyde filled his nostrils, he realized that the two brains were indeed interchangeable.

Noah trusted Dr. Gellier. He knew that what she was implying—that only the same infection could produce the identical final pathology—made perfect sense.

However, for reasons he could not put into words, he found no reassurance in her clinical findings.

14

Clarice was going to be furious. Of that, Dr. Louis Charron had no doubt. The neurologist had promised his wife he would be home by eight P.M. for dinner—she was insisting on celebrating a missed anniversary—but by 10:05 P.M., Charron had yet to leave his office. Clarice would understand, though. She always did in the end. "If you want someone home for dinner every night, go find yourself a banker," he had once said with less than sentimental frankness.

"If I had only hung on to my figure after the children, I would be down at the bank right now," she had shot back.

Actually, Charron liked his wife on the fuller side. Though he wasn't foolish enough to tell her, he had thought she was too skinny when they first married. And besides, after forty-four years together, they both knew only death would separate them now.

Today's schedule had been hectic. In addition to his own unofficial investigation, Charron had to contend with hospital rounds, a full caseload in the clinic, and the monthly neuroscience faculty meeting. The entire meeting was devoted to the three cases of variant Creutzfeldt-Jakob—or, as he thought to himself, the *apparent* cases—that had made such a splash within the entire medical community of Limousin.

Charron reached again for the business card on his desk and twirled it in his hand. Indifferent to the hour, he decided to try the number once more before leaving. It rang through to a voicemail greeting. Always mistrustful of technology, Charron had no voicemail on his own line, and he had no intention now of leaving sensitive information on an answering machine. He hung up, resolving to try again in the morning.

Slipping out of his lab coat, he traded it for the suit jacket behind his door. He withdrew a package of cigarettes from the pocket, slid one out, and lit it as he headed for the staircase. Reaching the parking lot, he saw that his fourteen-year-old Jaguar was one of the few cars left in the lot. He unlocked the door and plunked down in the leather seat, enjoying the nicotine-scented smell of the car's interior as he finished his first smoke.

Charron removed and lit another cigarette before turning the ignition. As he pulled out of the lot, he again reflected on the three known prion victims. Originally, he had been proud of his diagnosis; he enjoyed reminding the younger department members that his clinical acumen was still as sharp as ever. As the novelty wore off, niggling doubt had crept into its place. Especially after he watched the third patient, Philippe Manet, wither away by the hour before his eyes. The visit from Drs. Haldane and McLeod of the WHO solidified his suspicions. Charron saw that they shared his skepticism about the disease's abnormally rapid progression. *Why else would they have come?* he wondered, resolving again to try Haldane's number in the morning.

These growing concerns, more than his official schedule, had kept him at work so late. He had stolen hours to dig deeper into the cluster of apparent vCJD cases. Forty years of experience as a neurologist told him that something was not quite right. And after visiting that farm and meeting Benoît Gagnon's partner, his suspicions had gelled. He was determined to find out what was at play in Limoges.

The xenon blue headlights in his rearview mirror drew his attention. They had grown steadily brighter since he had first noticed them a few kilometers back. Irritably, Charron crushed his second cigarette in the ashtray and glanced over his shoulder. The car was too close now. He pressed the button to roll down the window of his sedan. He stuck an arm out the gap and waved the other driver past.

"Merde! If you want to pass, then go already!" Charron yelled into the streaming wind.

But the driver did not pull out to pass. Instead, the interior of the Jaguar flooded with the blue light of the trailing car's high beams.

Charron's chest pounded with fury. He hit his horn hard, and eased his foot down on the brake so as not to be rear-ended. "What the hell are you doing, you fool?" He shook his fist out the window. *"You are driving like a maniac!* Are you trying—?"

Charron's diatribe was cut off in midsentence when he involuntarily lurched forward and his car shook from the impact against its bumper.

Anger suddenly gave way to fear. In an instant, Charron understood the car did not intend to pass.

It had come for him.

He thought of his two girls: both married and raising three of his grandchildren between them. Then his thoughts turned to Clarice. He pictured her laughing gray eyes. And he wished with his all heart that he had gone home earlier to dine with her.

15

Paris, France. January 17

With meetings in Paris planned for the morning, Noah, Duncan, and Elise opted to stay at a hotel in the historic Montparnasse district. Their dinner together was particularly subdued. Elise had been withdrawn since the interview with Dr. Gellier. And Duncan verged on mute, not even responding when Noah tried to goad him by reciting tour guide facts about Montparnasse and how it was the cultural heart of Paris in the early twentieth century.

So Noah was surprised when, upon returning to the room, he found a note under his door in Duncan's chicken-scratch: HALDANE, I'LL BE IN THE BAR. IF YOU CAN'T JOIN ME, SEND AN AMBULANCE IN TWO HOURS. MCLEOD.

Before heading down, Noah changed shirts and tried to call Chloe and Anna, but only reached Anna's father. After a pleasant but slightly forced conversation, in which Noah learned that his daughter had suffered her first bee sting, he hung up and headed to the lobby.

Stepping into the smoky and sterile lounge, Noah discovered that his friend had started without him. An empty highball glass sat on the bar in front of Duncan, and the one he was drinking from looked half full. Noah walked up to the bar beside him and slid onto the empty bar stool, but Duncan didn't acknowledge him.

"Last time I saw you drink like this was China," Noah said. "And we were facing a potential pandemic then."

"Desperate times, weren't they? But at least there are no French in China," Duncan grunted, drawing a sneer from an older man in a gray suit who sat alone halfway down the bar. "Shite, Haldane, we accomplished something over there."

"You don't think we will here?"

Duncan buried his nose in his drink. He slammed the empty glass down on the table and pointed from Noah to himself. "Three more vodka tonics!" he yelled to the bartender at the other end.

"Two more," Noah corrected. "I'll have a Fischer."

"Can't speak for you, Haldane," Duncan grunted, "but I know for sure that I won't accomplish anything here."

"Oh?"

"I'm going home," he said quietly.

"Duncan, I know this has been frustrating for you. Must feel like déjà vu, but—"

The Scot raised his hand and silenced Noah in midsentence. The bartender arrived to deposit their drinks in front of them. "It's got nothing to do with the mad cows," Duncan said, reaching for his drink.

"I don't understand."

"It's Maggie."

"Maggie? What has your wife got to do with it?"

Duncan took a long sip of his drink. "I think she might be dying," he said quietly.

Noah felt winded. *"What?"*

Duncan turned to him, his face creased in a sadness Noah had never seen from him before. His eyes misted over, but his voice held firm. "She was diagnosed with breast cancer. It was advanced when they found the lump."

Noah reached out and put a hand on Duncan's shoulder. "Oh, no. When?"

"Three months ago."

"Why didn't you tell me?"

"Shite, Haldane, I would have. I would have told anyone who'd listen to me. But Maggie—" He stopped for a long sip, almost finishing the first of his refills. "She didn't want a soul to know. She told me nothing would be worse than having to face 'all that pity.'"

Noah leaned closer, put his arm around his friend, and squeezed his shoulders. "I'm so sorry, Duncan."

"Haldane, I might be a bit drunk and maybe even a tad vulnerable." Duncan viewed him with a half-smile. "But it still doesn't mean I'm willing to sleep with the likes of you."

Smiling, Noah freed Duncan from his grip. "Why did you even come to France?" he asked.

Duncan shook his head. "Wasn't my idea." He downed the last of the glass. "Maggie thought it would be good for both of us if I got away for a while."

Noah nodded and sipped his beer with little enthusiasm.

"She had just finished the chemo and we were feeling a bit more optimistic. . . ." Duncan rubbed his beard roughly. His eyes drifted past Noah. "I got a call this afternoon from her doctor. Maggie broke her arm putting on her shirt. Turns out the cancer is all through her bones."

"Shit."

"It's 'shite,' Haldane. When are you going to learn to say the fucking word properly?" Duncan reached for his second refill.

"But she's still going to get more treatment?" Noah asked. "Chemo and radiation?"

"Of course she is," he said irritably. "And she's still full of hope. I'd never let anyone take that from her." He reached for his drink and then changed his mind. "Problem is, Haldane, I'm a doctor. I know better."

Noah could not find the right words, so he sipped his beer. They sat beside each other drinking in silence for a minute or two. "It's funny, you know," Noah finally said. "I've always liked Maggie so much better than you."

Duncan said nothing for a long moment, but then he broke into a deep laugh. "Thank you, Haldane. I needed that."

"You're leaving in the morning?" Noah asked.

Duncan nodded.

"How are the boys taking it?" Noah asked.

"They're teenage boys. Beyond the football matches and the music videos with the girls wearing only tissue paper, nothing else much matters to them." He drained the last of the other glass. "Still, it's not easy for them to see their ma go through this. She is their rock, you know?"

"Look, Duncan, if you need—"

Duncan gripped Noah's wrist briefly. "I already counted on that, Noah."

They lapsed into silence again, interrupted by the ring of Noah's cell phone. He pulled it out of his pocket and brought it to his ear. "Noah Haldane."

"Noah, it's Elise. Where are you?" she asked stiffly.

"The hotel bar."

"Oh."

Duncan glanced at Noah inquisitively. Noah shrugged and then said into the phone, "What's up, Elise?"

"The lab called me," she said. "We have the preliminary results on the cattle feed we seized from Ferme d'Allaire."

"And?"

"They've found significant traces of bovine and other ruminants' protein."

Noah felt numb at the news. "So they *were* putting animal by-products back into the feed."

"It would seem so."

"Okay. Thanks." Noah said good-bye and hung up.

Duncan stretched in his chair. "It's all beginning to fall into place, isn't it?"

Noah took another sip.

"One of their cows develops a spontaneous mutation in her prions, and presto, you've got a mad cow," Duncan said, slurring his words slightly. "They butcher that cow, run it through the grinder, toss it back into the feed stock, and voilà, a few months later you have multiple cases of a new and wonderful mad cow disease that kills everyone in a couple hours, give or take."

Noah nodded. "We have a world-class neuropathologist telling us that the victims died from garden variety vCJD, if there is such a thing. And now we have an explanation for its spread." He sighed. "It's so straightforward."

"Very."

Noah put his drink down and turned to his friend. "You really think it's that simple, Duncan?"

He shook his head. "Not for a minute."

"Me, neither."

"Might be time for me to go home, after all." Duncan uttered a heavy sigh. "My cynicism is finally rubbing off on you."

"I've learned a lot from you," Noah said. "Thanks."

Duncan shrugged in Scottish embarrassment and turned his attention back to his glass. He waved his arm in a dramatic gesture toward the bartender. "We've got a drought down this end of the bar!" he yelled.

Noah viewed his friend fondly. "Listen, Duncan, you tell Maggie she has to beat this thing, because—"

"I know, Haldane," he said with a soft laugh. "Because no one else can put up with me."

16

___

The glaring sun beat down on and reflected off the end-less sheet of ice surrounding Claude Fontaine without providing any warmth. The wind, which changed direc-tion so often that he felt encircled, penetrated his coat and chilled him to the bone. Ignoring the ice and snow swirl-ing around his head, he glanced over to Martine deGroot, who stood a few feet away, offering no more warmth than the air around her. She stared out past the horizon. Her expression tranquil, she looked as though she were at home. *And why not?* Fontaine muttered to himself. *After all, she's made of ice.*

The remoteness of the land coupled with the claustro-phobic lodgings of their aluminum hut had strained their relationship. Back in civilization, they used to have sex every day, often in public places such as theaters, rest-rooms, and parks. Martine's arousal from the risk of ex-posure bordered on fetish, but Fontaine was excited by it, too. Despite years of experience, Fontaine had never known a lover as vocal or as kinky as Martine. Nothing was taboo for her. She particularly loved to use physical restraints, to be tied with scarves or even handcuffs. But a week had passed since their last physical contact. *Why do I stay with her?* he wondered, but one glimpse of her—all white in a down coat, gloves, hat, and boots—set off the stirrings again. He wanted her as much as ever. And the helpless need disgusted him.

A choppy buzz from above pulled him out of his mood of self-recrimination. Shielding his eyes, Fontaine looked up in the sky to see a glint of silver. He was reminded of the anticipation that accompanied his frequent waits for planes carrying in the chunks of the Igloo. This time all he experienced was a mix of impatience and anxiety. He had tried to dissuade the woman, explaining that she had nothing to gain by visiting, but Yulia Radvogin did not change her mind easily, if at all. Radvogin's expectations grew with each discussion, and her threats were no longer veiled; she now made the consequences of failure deathly clear.

The whirr grew louder as the plane steadily descended. Fontaine watched the skis of the Twin Otter kiss the glass surface of the ice, hop once, and then skid only slightly as it roared nearer. The Otter came to a stop thirty feet away.

Fontaine hustled toward it. He reached the plane just as the door popped up and three steps flipped down. In a puffy coat that made him look comically oversized, one of Radvogin's brawny bodyguards—Viktor, Fontaine guessed—pounded down the steps. The colossus locked his impassive brown eyes on Fontaine. Then he held De-Groot's gaze for a moment, before his eyes did a quick scan of the barren surroundings. Assured there were no imminent threats, he stood to the side and turned back to face the plane.

Wearing a long sable coat and hat, Yulia Radvogin glided down the steps and onto the ice. The pilot and the other bodyguard, his arms laden with luggage, followed after. Radvogin greeted Fontaine and DeGroot with kisses to each of their cheeks. Stepping back from her, Fontaine noticed something different about the woman. Awe danced in her pale eyes. "Now I have been everywhere," she said.

"Welcome, Yulia." Fontaine pointed in the direction of the settlement that housed all Vishnov's inhabitants. The "village" of matching white aluminum huts that resembled a high-end trailer park was a vast upgrade from the hodgepodge of decrepit relics from the Soviet era that used to occupy the site. "As I warned you, this is not exactly the Four Seasons, but may I show you to your lodgings?"

Radvogin's familiar authoritative expression replaced the look of wonderment. "I did not travel this far for shopping and a manicure," she snapped. "Show me to the Igloo."

"It's quite something, Yulia," DeGroot said, showing an enthusiasm for it that she had never shared with Fontaine.

"Lead the way, darling." Walking past Fontaine, Radvogin locked arms with DeGroot as they headed east toward the domed structure.

Fontaine followed a few steps behind the women, humiliated at his lesser place in the pack. Despite their first awkward meeting in St. Petersburg, Yulia had taken a shine to Martine, and it seemed that she could do no wrong. Fontaine bore the brunt of the woman's impatience and frustration, while most of the credit for the venture fell to DeGroot. He forced the bitter thoughts from his mind. *Think of the money,* he reminded himself.

With the two women chatting like old friends, they crossed the equivalent of two football fields to the dome. Built several hundred meters from the rest of the settlement, the dome was once the only sight that broke the landscape of ice looking eastward from the runway. However, with each week, more vehicles—from snowmobiles and Caterpillar loaders to huge pickups and ultramodern snow trucks—surrounded the Igloo. The area outside the dome now looked like a snow-covered shopping mall parking lot, except all the parked vehicles possessed tracks in place of wheels.

Radvogin stopped a few feet before the Igloo's entry, and the others came to a halt beside her. Despite the cold, she slowly surveyed the scene, first studying the trucks parked around it and then focusing on the structure. She stepped closer to the rounded wall and ran her glove over its smooth surface, as if checking for cracks or flaws. Finally, she backtracked a few steps and nodded once with satisfaction. Without a word, she turned and headed for the entry.

Fontaine pulled his key card from under his jacket and waved it over the sensor. The white steel doors parted. They walked inside the research-station-cum-factory, where they were greeted by the hum of activity. Fontaine offered up his most charming smile. "Yulia, welcome to Radvogin Industries' southernmost plant."

Radvogin didn't reply. Her eyes scoured the room, skipping from the banks of computers to the people, circling and finally resting on the oil-rig-like platform in the center of the well that drew eyes like metal to a magnet.

Fontaine pointed to the platform. "And that is *your* well."

She flashed him an indecipherable look. "The most expensive well ever built."

"The most lucrative, too," DeGroot pointed out.

"Let us hope so, Martine," Radvogin said with slight menace. She turned to Fontaine. "Walk me through the production process again."

"Please." Fontaine pointed ahead. Radvogin strode across the ice floor toward the platform, and the others followed. Since the original scientists and engineers had all been cleared from the site, Fontaine had not even bothered to learn the names of the technicians who replaced them. In their matching blue uniforms, the men around the platform looked interchangeable to him. And he preferred it that way. Fontaine didn't need another group of prima donnas threatening his prosperity.

He walked up the six steps leading to the winch and waited for Radvogin and DeGroot to join him on the platform. He ran a hand over the smooth cylinder that was wound with black cable as wide as an air duct, giving it the appearance of a giant spool.

"This is the original cabling we used to tap Lake Vishnov. It's still functional," he said with a hint of pride. He turned to the even thicker gray plastic pipe that emerged from the landing and ran down the other side of the platform and along the ice to a tank against the far wall that was the size of a mobile home. Beside the tank, the wall was lined with shiny metallic barrels that resembled futuristic oil drums. He ran his boot across the top of the pipe. "We had this low-temperature flexible piping especially designed for our purposes." He pointed to the tank. "With a water pressure of five hundred psi, we can refill our main tank in half an hour."

Radvogin stared at the piping by her feet, unimpressed. "I remember signing the check," she said. "I understand how a well works. What is not so obvious to me is how we get the water off this continent."

Remember the money! Fontaine mustered another smile. "Let me show you." He crossed the platform and took the far set of steps down to the ice floor. He followed the gray piping to the tank. The others joined him in front of it. He knocked on the side of the tank and it echoed slightly in response. Then he moved to the containers lined up beside it. He lifted one off the ground with one hand. "These drums weigh nothing empty, but when full they hold two hundred liters." He dropped it to the ground with a light thud. "Our LC-130 Hercules transport planes can fly sixty of these barrels at a time to the coast."

"Twelve thousand liters," Radvogin calculated aloud.

DeGroot nodded. "With a fleet of four planes, we can load a cargo ship in three days of sorties."

"But not year round, Martine," Radvogin said.

"That is true," Fontaine said. "For decent weather and safe shipping, our window of opportunity is from mid-November to mid-March."

Radvogin squinted hard at him. "So the window is rapidly closing this year."

"We still have two months," Fontaine said. "The transports will begin in two days, and we will dispatch our first ship by the end of the week."

The muscles around Radvogin's eyes relaxed. "But the transport costs alone—"

Fontaine dismissed the concern with a wave of his palm. "Are well factored into the price of a bottle of the Lake."

"*Providing* people are willing to pay more for the Lake than they would for a bottle of Châteauneuf du Pape," Radvogin challenged.

"They will! More and more restaurants are selling designer-label waters as if they were varieties of fine wine." DeGroot's glacial eyes lit with excitement. "Yulia, this is the purest drinking water any person has ever sampled. Millions of years old, it has been completely spared from all of man's pollution. That is not true of another drop of water on the planet."

Radvogin turned to her. "And you're convinced people will pay so much for the privilege of drinking it?"

DeGroot laughed. "Yulia, from San Francisco to Tokyo, and every city in between, they will be climbing over each other to get bottles of this."

Fontaine's bitterness toward DeGroot dissipated. He remembered again why she made such a useful partner. "Martine is right," he said. "And imagine the hysteria when word gets out about the restorative powers of the water."

Radvogin ran her fingers across her cheek. "You honestly believe those stories?"

"Believe it?" Fontaine held up his arms. "I've seen it myself. People with chronic pain that didn't respond to any medication are suddenly pain-free after drinking water from Vishnov."

"How do you, as a scientist, possibly explain water with healing powers?" Radvogin demanded.

Fontaine shrugged. "I've reviewed the chemical analyses. Vishnov is hypermineralized with a unique cocktail of sulfur, chloride, carbonates, calcium, iron, magnesium, and various organic acids."

DeGroot put a hand on Radvogin's shoulder. "It works, Yulia."

Radvogin smiled at the other woman. "So you two have found the fountain of youth at the South Pole?" Her eyes hinted at mockery. "The only fountain *I* trust in is the one at my plastic surgeon's clinic."

"Not necessarily the fountain of youth." DeGroot removed her hand from the other woman's shoulder. "More like the pot of gold at the end of the rainbow."

"Let's hope you're right," Radvogin said. "And you're certain the water is safe?"

Fontaine nodded. "We have tested the water exhaustively. From chemical content to acidity, the water is pristine."

"What about those organisms you found in the lake?" Radvogin asked.

"*Arcobacter antarcticus?*" Fontaine blew out his cheeks. "They are utterly harmless, but even if they weren't it would not matter."

"Oh?" said Radvogin.

"They can survive only under enormous water pressure. Those cells explode long before they reach anywhere close to atmospheric pressure."

"Still, we are taking no chances," DeGroot added. "We

will treat the water with heat and ultraviolet sterilization prior to bottling."

"Good," Radvogin grunted. "Believe me, you don't want a lawsuit on *my* hands."

Fontaine glanced at DeGroot with his first genuine smile of the day. "I am a little thirsty now." He reached behind one of the drums and pulled out a small clear plastic drinking bottle that had no label. He offered the bottle to Radvogin, but she shook her head. He held it out to DeGroot, brushing it up against her chin.

She pulled her head away and brought her hand up to his. She gave the back of his hand a fleeting squeeze, sending a shock wave of arousal through him, and then gently pushed his hand and the bottle away. "I can't afford the sticker price." She smiled.

Fontaine shrugged and then toasted each of them with the bottle. "Your health," he said. He brought the bottle slowly to his lips and took a long sip. After weeks of drinking Vishnov's water, its crisp, subtly metallic flavor— different from any water he'd ever tasted—was growing on him.

17

Paris, France. January 18

Noah woke to hammering in his forehead and queasiness in his stomach. A bitter acidic taste filled his mouth. Only fleeting images from the previous evening spent with Duncan drifted back to him. Reminiscences of Maggie had kept them planted in the bar, and soon Noah's empty beer bottles gave way to full glasses of single malt scotch. He had no recollection of how or when he stumbled back to his room. He could not imagine what shape Duncan, who must have outdrunk him two to one, must have been in.

Noah had met Maggie only a handful of times, but he had felt connected to her from their first encounter over lunch at Jean Nantal's home. Quieter and more diplomatic than her husband, Maggie was still as perceptive, strong-willed, and funny. She was the epitome of robust with a pleasant round face and kind hazel eyes. Noah could not imagine her riddled with cancer. His heart went out to Maggie and Duncan. He wondered how his friend would cope if his wife died. Their bond was unbreakable. Of course, Noah had once thought the same of his marriage, too, but even before Julie arrived to complicate their situation, he recognized that he and Anna were on shaky ground.

With his easygoing charm, blue eyes, and quick smile, Noah had attracted women effortlessly, but before Anna, all his girlfriends were his age and shared his interests. In college he dated women in his undergrad sciences program, and from med school on he dated fellow doctors in training. Then, in the senior year of his infectious-diseases residency, he met Anna at a party. She shattered the mold. Six years younger than he, she was an artistic, free-spirited master's student in English literature. Their relationship was more volatile and sexually charged than any he had known previously. Only after Chloe was born did they settle into a more predictable routine. Noah was the one who pulled away first, toppling into a dark funk that even he didn't understand. Anna had fought to keep him close, but his remoteness and frequent travel had worn her down. Eventually, his wife—who had never hidden her self-described sexual confusion—fell for their neighbor Julie, whom Noah still suspected of actively pursuing Anna during their marital crisis.

Looking back, the evolution of their relationship from lovers and spouses to co-parents and friends now seemed natural to him. He had the urge to call Anna and share Duncan's heart-wrenching news, but glancing at the bed-side alarm clock, which read 7:04 A.M., he realized it was still the middle of the night in South Carolina.

He sat up on the side of the bed, and the pressure on top of his head increased. Swallowing back bile, he rose to his feet and headed for the shower. By the time he stepped out of the bathroom, the message indicator light on his phone was flashing. He pressed the button to retrieve messages and soon heard Elise's soft accent on the line: "Noah, I'm going downstairs now for breakfast. Duncan and you are welcome to join me if you would like to." He detected a hint of shyness to the request.

Noah dialed Duncan's room, but there was no answer. He called the front desk and was told that Dr. McLeod had checked out an hour earlier. He wondered if his friend had caught a wink of sleep between the bar and his departure.

Elise was studying the menu when Noah reached her table in the corner of the dining room. Her short hair was clipped to the side, and Noah noticed that her eye shadow and lipstick were more generously applied than he had previously seen. While it gave her face a more sophisticated and sexy touch, Noah preferred what he had seen before: the scattering of freckles on top of her milk-and-honey complexion. He wondered if the added makeup was attributable to their impending meeting with her boss.

They exchanged polite but subdued greetings. As he slipped into the chair beside hers, she asked, "Will Duncan be joining us?"

Noah shook his head. "He had to go home urgently."

She tilted her head. "Is everything all right?"

He hesitated, remembering what Duncan had told him of his wife's desire for privacy. Realizing it wouldn't matter what he told Elise, he chose to respect Maggie's wishes anyway. "A family issue. He's gone home to sort it out."

Clearly dissatisfied with his explanation, Elise turned back to the menu. "You like crêpes, don't you?" she asked.

"Normally." Regardless of his cholesterol issues, with hangover in full flight, he wasn't tempted. "Not this morning."

She lowered the menu to chest height. A smile cracked her lips. "You look a little bit . . . worse for the wear . . . , is that the expression?"

"Yes, and I do." Noah smiled. "Duncan and I got into a heavy conversation at the bar. Not the smartest place to start one of those."

Elise put her menu down. "Were you discussing this BSE outbreak?"

Noah shook his head. "Family."

Her smile brightened again. "Ah, yes, family. Those conversations often lead to drink, *oui*?"

"*Oui*," Noah sighed. "Speaking of which, I don't know anything about your family."

"There is little to tell," she said matter-of-factly. "I grew up in Brussels. My mother and father both work for the Bank of Belgium. A very boring middle-class upbringing."

"Any brothers or sisters?"

"A sister, two years younger than me." She sighed. "Hélène is the smart one. She married a very rich man. But I win, too. She has given me two adorable nephews."

"You're not married, are you?"

She shook her head and her cheeks flushed slightly. "I have . . ." Her words trailed away and her eyes fell to the table.

Noah moved to safer ground. "And why the E.U.?"

"Excuse me?"

"Why did you choose to work for the European Union?"

"Ah." The embarrassment left her features. "I studied biology and animal sciences at university. I was even considering a faculty position, when a friend told me about a job opportunity with the E.U. in the Agricultural Commission. I was attracted to the mix of science and politics."

"An explosive mix," Noah said. "Do you enjoy it?"

She licked her lips, considering the question. "You mean now or before this BSE crisis?"

"Either."

"Yes," she said. "This is a stressful time, but it is also the biggest challenge of my career."

"The most trying assignments in my job have usually turned out to be the most rewarding."

She smiled and showed him another glimpse of shyness. "Noah, would you mind if I asked a question about your life?"

"No time, sorry." Noah winked as the waitress arrived at their table.

Elise ordered a vegetarian omelet, while Noah opted for only a cup of coffee. After the waitress left, Elise leaned forward in her seat. "Do you have a photograph of Chloe?"

Noah was happy to dig one out of his wallet. In the two hours he had spent in his condo between Mexico and Europe, while scrambling to pack and answer a slew of e-mails, he had printed a wallet-sized shot of Chloe from their trip together.

Elise took the snapshot from his hand. She nodded approvingly as she glanced from the photo to Noah. "I see the resemblance . . . except the hair."

Noah laughed. "On our flight down, all Chloe talked about was getting her hair done in cornrows. We had barely touched down, and she found a woman at the hotel to braid it. Far as I know, she's still wearing them."

"She is lovely," Elise said, passing the photo back to Noah.

"She looks a lot like her mom," he said.

Elise tilted her head again, and Noah read the unspoken question in her eyes. "We split up last year," he said.

Elise nodded. Again, her eyes searched his for more details but she didn't ask. "The travel away from your daughter must be difficult."

"Nature of the beast, I'm afraid." Noah shrugged, feigning acceptance. "I have yet to see a new infectious threat break out in the Washington area. Thank God."

Having opened up more to each other than in any previous conversation, they fell into a brief clumsy silence before they turned to more familiar territory. "What will happen to the Allaire farm?" Noah asked.

"It will be closed, of course," she said. "We will gather the evidence and soil samples we require. And then the buildings will be demolished."

Despite their dubious farming practices, Noah felt a pang of sympathy for the distraught manager and the stoic president, Geneviève Allaire. Their situation reminded him of André Pereau, and how this prion shattered his life.

The waitress placed Elise's omelet in front of her. Elise attacked the plate, while Noah sipped his coffee and watched her eat. "Did you miss dinner last night . . . and lunch . . . and breakfast?" he teased.

She dabbed at the corner of her lip with a napkin. "I get hungry when I am nervous."

"About meeting your boss?"

Without answering, Elise checked her watch. "The traffic might be bad. We should go."

She signed the bill to the room and they headed outside to find a taxi. Under crystal blue skies dotted with benign white clouds, Paris was at her travel-guide best. Noah noticed that the temperature had cooled, though it was still balmy compared to Limoges. The bellman hailed a cab. The old cabbie greeted them with a hacking cough as they climbed in the back. He grunted unhappily when Elise gave him their destination, and then he jerked the car out onto the road. The traffic was lighter than Elise had predicted and the sulking cabbie drove them from Montparnasse to the Ministry of Agriculture building on rue de Varenne in less than ten minutes.

They arrived early for the meeting. Noah stood across the street and admired the ornate engraving and detail of the Ministry of Agriculture building's classical design. "You do that often," Elise remarked.

"Do what?"

"Stare at buildings."

"Your buildings in Europe have so much more history than ours."

"Too much." She smiled. "When I go to America, I appreciate how well-heated your buildings are and how many electrical outlets they have. Here, I am always looking for places to plug in my laptop."

Noah smiled. "We always appreciate other people's backyards more."

They crossed the street and walked up the stone steps to the main entrance, where the armed guard recognized Elise with a nod and asked only for Noah's identification. After clearing security, Elise led Noah down the hall to an ornate staircase. They climbed three flights of stairs and then passed through double doors into a large office. She stopped to greet a plump older woman at the desk without introducing Noah.

Elise pointed down the corridor. "This is the French agriculture minister's office, but he is away today. We're meeting in the conference room with Javier."

"Javier?"

"Javier Montalva, the minister of agriculture for the E.U.," she said, looking away. "My boss."

They walked down a corridor to another set of double doors. Inside the conference room, the warm light flooded in from the wall of windows looking out on the main boulevard. A long mahogany conference table filled the length of the room. Noah estimated that there were at least thirty leather rolling chairs encircling it, but all were empty. The room smelled of coffee and pastries. Noah saw neither, but his interest in them reminded him that his stomach had settled and his hangover abated.

Elise pointed to two chairs near the end of the table, and they sat down beside each other facing the windows. At the sound of voices, they turned to see one door swing open. A man in an olive suit and black patterned tie swept into the room. Behind him, to Noah's surprise, strode Jean Nantal. "Jean?" Noah said, rising to his feet.

"Ah, Noah." Jean flashed his paternal smile. "I am almost

as surprised as you are. I happened to be in Paris visiting my daughter and her family when Javier called. No more than an hour ago."

Javier Montalva y Casas approached Noah with his hand outstretched. With a flawless smile, gelled wavy black hair, and sculpted cheeks, the man moved with the confidence of someone unaccustomed to hearing the word "no." The scent of his cologne reached Noah before his hand did. "Ah, Dr. Haldane, what an honor it is to finally meet you!"

"Thank you, Sr. Montalva."

Montalva, who Noah guessed to be in his late forties, clasped the back of Noah's hand with his left and squeezed it between both palms. "Please, call me Javier," he said with a Spanish lilt.

"And I'm Noah."

"Your reputation truly precedes you, Noah. Your work on the ARCS virus was nothing short of heroic." Montalva released his grip and turned to Elise. "Elise." He took her by both shoulders and kissed on her either cheek. *"Bienvenue à Paris aussi."*

"Javier," Elise said and reddened slightly.

Noah and Elise sat back down in their seats and the two other men sat across from them. Montalva smiled at Noah again. "I understand your participation in Limousin has been invaluable."

Noah gave Montalva a doubtful look. "I don't know that I've been much help."

"Not so." Montalva's hand swept through the air. "I understand you led the investigation back to Paris, where the victims' autopsies proved that this outbreak is, indeed, vCJD and not an unknown prion."

"That was Dr. McLeod's lead. Besides, nothing is proven yet." Noah understood that Elise had to update her superior at regular intervals, but he was still annoyed that she had briefed Montalva on their discussion with Gellier prior to this meeting.

Montalva waved away Noah's doubts. He turned to his subordinate. "Elise, wonderful work with Ferme d'Allaire. Further testing has confirmed that their cattle feed was loaded with bovine protein." He shook his head gravely. "That farm was a ticking bomb."

"Thank you," Elise murmured with a coyness Noah had not heard before.

Montalva interlocked his hands. "As we now have identified the cause and the source of both the bovine and human cases in this outbreak, we can move toward eradicating it."

"It's a little premature to say we have identified the source," Noah pointed out.

"Oh?" Montalva's eyes narrowed slightly. "Why is that, Noah?"

"We have yet to establish any connection between the three known human cases and Ferme d'Allaire."

"Except that they all lived within thirty kilometers of the farm," Elise said.

"And would have presumably eaten beef products originally from there," Montalva said. "After all, they are the largest cattle supplier in the province."

Noah shook his head. "But we have no reason to believe the cows were sick while still on Ferme d'Allaire."

"Ah, but who knows what else they were hiding in addition to illegal feeding practices?" Montalva said knowingly. "Besides, the infected cows were sold as calves. Is it not true that vCJD can take years to show up?"

Jean spoke up. "In the past, yes." He rested a hand on Montalva's sleeve. "But in this case, Javier, we are seeing both a shortened incubation period and an accelerated course of illness."

"And what about the seventh infected cow?" Noah asked. "We still don't know where it acquired its infection."

Montalva's very white smile resurfaced. "Actually, Noah, as of this morning we do."

"Where?"

"There was some confusion at the farm where the cow died," Montalva explained. "The record keeping was not . . . how should I say . . . ideal. Several of the cattle's 'passports' were confused. However, we have sorted the records out. The involved animal did indeed come from Ferme d'Allaire."

"Good." Jean nodded. "All seven cows. That certainly helps us pinpoint the source."

"I couldn't agree more, Jean," Montalva said.

Despite the minister's friendliness, his politicianlike manner grated on Noah. He glanced over to Elise. Something had changed in the envoy. Even her body language, which had always been as direct as her speech, had become more submissive in the presence of her superior. She sat lower in her chair, fidgeted with her nails, and for the most part avoided eye contact.

Montalva looked from Jean to Noah. "Obviously, I have neither the authority nor the expertise to tell you how to conduct your investigation." He turned to Elise, his aqua-gray eyes smoldering with purpose. "However, from the E.U.'s point of view, we need to focus on continuing to trace and render *all* cattle without exception that came from Ferme d'Allaire in the past three years."

"I agree," Noah said grudgingly.

"And once we are satisfied we have found those animals, then we can look at lifting the ban on French beef."

"Hold on!" Noah sat bolt upright in his chair. "It's too early to consider lifting the ban. We don't know nearly enough about this outbreak."

Montalva held a hand out toward Noah as if offering him an escape from quicksand. "Noah, there have been no new human cases reported in almost a month . . ."

"A month?" Noah held up his palms. "You just said BSE is a disease measured in years."

Montalva smiled patiently. "And Jean just said that this outbreak is accelerated. Yes?"

"Make up your mind, Minister!" Noah snapped. "On Ferme d'Allaire, you say the disease has a long incubation period. But at the butcher shop, it's gone in a month. Which is it?"

There were no pearly teeth now. When Montalva spoke, his lips were tight and his voice low. "Do you have any idea what percentage of the E.U.'s budget is allotted to my department?"

Catching a warning glance from Jean, Noah bit his tongue and shook his head.

"Forty-five percent." Noah said nothing, and Montalva continued: "Agriculture . . . farming . . . is still at the heart of the European economy. Not only have we paralyzed the French cattle-farming industry, we have sent shock waves through all of Europe and beyond. The continent's entire infrastructure could be seriously impacted."

Noah inhaled deeply and then said, "And what impact would it have on the continent if cases of brain-eating disease began to spread outside of Limousin?"

"That is why you are here." Montalva smiled again, though his eyes were cooler than ever. "We will not lift any bans until it is safe to do so."

Noah merely shrugged.

The conversation drifted to the logistics of tracking all the cows that originated from Ferme d'Allaire. Montalva explained that while the E.U. would continue to oversee the testing, the French Ministry of Agriculture would do the groundwork. When Montalva finished, Jean addressed the issue of the human cases. "Noah, Elise, we hope you will continue your investigation in Limousin to see what else you can learn from the families of the victims and the medical staff who cared for them."

Elise nodded at the table, while Noah said, "We will also need to follow up with veterinarians who examined the diseased cows."

Montalva frowned. "Why is that?"

"In any outbreak involving animal vectors—or carriers—we always consult the involved zoologists."

"I see." Montalva glanced at his watch. "I think we have covered the essentials this morning. Perhaps we should plan to meet again in three or four days to review the situation?"

As they were leaving, Jean grabbed Noah's arm and led him down the hallway. When they were out of earshot of the others, he said, "You must understand, Javier and the others at the E.U. are under enormous political pressure."

Noah shook his head. "It's always the same, Jean. You know that. They're always so concerned that we will threaten their economy with our quarantines and restrictions."

"They never realize how much worse the alternative is, do they?" Jean smiled. "But as we bumbling bureaucrats go, Javier is one of the smarter ones. He won't do anything rash out of political interest."

"I hope you're right."

Jean reached out and laid a hand on Noah's shoulder. "Duncan told me about Maggie," he said with deep sadness. "It does not sound hopeful."

Noah swallowed. "It isn't."

"Duncan is a survivor. He will find the strength to carry on." Jean shook his head. "This has not been a good week. You of course have heard about Louis Charron?"

"The neurologist?"

"Yes. I was a few years ahead of him in medical school. A first-class neurologist. And underneath his bark, he was a good man, too."

"Was?"

"You haven't heard?" Jean said. "He was rushing home

from the hospital last night when he lost control of his car. He died instantly."

"My God, how awful," Noah said. "I had planned to see him again when we got back to Limousin. He was the only doctor who had examined all of the human cases."

"Maybe one of his colleagues or residents had as well?"

"Maybe," Noah muttered, but his thoughts were focused on all the accidents and death associated with the outbreak. Everyone touched by this prion seemed to face nothing but misery.

His stomach knotted again, but this time the hangover wasn't to blame.

18

Avril Avars leaned back in her chair and silently assessed André Pereau. Clean-shaven, but wearing an old cardigan and reeking of wine, he sat across from her with his hands folded on his lap and trembling slightly. Avril assumed Pereau had driven himself to her office. Had she not requested his presence, she might have taken the man downstairs for a Breathalyzer exam. She was frustrated by the indifferent attitude toward drinking and driving that was so prevalent in the region; she had attended far too many crash sites and seen too many bodies in the morgue because of the cavalier mix. Earlier that very day, she had heard of another victim, a prominent neurologist, who had fortunately killed only himself when he was so intoxicated that he veered off a straight road and directly into a tree.

Pereau looked around the room, sniffing. "Do you have a mold problem in your office, Detective?"

The question snapped Avril from her thoughts. "I am surprised you can smell it," she said, unable to hide her disdain. "All I smell is stale wine."

Pereau squinted at her. "I have not had a drink since last night." He raised his shaky hands above the level of her desk. "These are steady as glass when I *have* been drinking."

"Hmmm," Avril said noncommittally. She reached for the wallet-sized photograph on the desk in front of her and studied it again. With fair skin, sculpted cheeks, and wide eyes, Yvette Pereau's ethereal attractiveness was evident. And yet, from the ten-year-old photo alone, Avril inferred a fragile quality in Yvette, who stared at her like a startled kitten.

She lowered the photo to the desk. "M. Pereau, please tell me about the last time you saw your wife."

"It was the Monday before last."

She picked up the pen that lay on top of her notepad. "What time?"

"Around ten o'clock. We had eaten breakfast together. Afterwards, I went into town to run errands."

She jotted down the date and time. "What sort of errands?"

"To pick up some supplies."

"For the farm?"

"No point." He shook his head. "By then, my farm was closed. Finished."

"Because of the mad cow disease?" Avril asked. She was still digesting the news she had heard about the Pereau farm being a possible source of the mysterious illness. Though she was uncertain of its relevance to Pauline Lamaire's disappearance, instinct told her that it probably played some role in Yvette Pereau's sudden departure.

"Exactly," he said. "The farm has been condemned by the Ministry of Agriculture. All my animals removed and destroyed."

"So what supplies were you going to pick up in town?" she asked.

Pereau shrugged. "Food, household items, that sort of thing."

"Wine?" Avril offered.

He nodded slightly. "Yes. That, too."

"My colleagues suggested that your wine intake had something to do with Yvette's departure."

"Undoubtedly." Pereau clasped his hands together. He looked up at Avril, his sad eyes not the least defensive. "I thought the same, too. At first."

Avril deliberately ignored the opening, wanting to review the events chronologically. "How was that last breakfast together?"

He forced a laugh. "The eggs were on the runny side."

"M. Pereau . . ."

"It was tense, Detective." He sighed heavily. "All our meals after the first cow became sick were like that. We were facing ruin. Yvette was very scared." He looked away. "So was I."

Avril could easily picture the woman from the photo being terrified. "In retrospect, you didn't notice anything different about her that morning?"

He shook his head.

"And when you came home from town?"

"She was gone."

"She didn't leave you any kind of note?"

"No."

"Has she been in contact since?"

"Not a word."

Avril tapped her pen on the half-empty page. "You knew right away that she had left. How?"

"Most of her clothes were missing. And she took both of our big suitcases." He paused. "She was in a rush, too."

"How do you know?"

His hands trembled more. "She left a few things behind. Some of her makeup and her hair dryer." He glanced down at his shaking hands. "I don't know why she would have left her boots."

"Her boots?"

"Yes, she usually wore them whenever the snow threatened." Pereau looked up at her. "And as you know, these days that is a constant threat."

"Was the house locked when you came home?"

"We never lock our house."

No surprise, Avril thought. She tried another approach. "Did you find anything else out of place?"

"What do you mean, out of place?"

"Anything moved or broken?"

"Broken?" He frowned. "No, nothing. Only the luggage was gone."

Avril nodded. "And did she take a car?"

He shook his head. "Someone must have driven her."

"Or she hired a car." Avril knew there were a few people in the area who ran under-the-table taxi services, primarily during what little tourist season they had in the summertime. It would be easy enough to check. She jotted a note to herself to do so. "Earlier, you said that you thought your drinking was the reason she left you. But not now?"

"No."

"Why?"

"Her parents." Pereau held open his hands. "I assumed all along that she would have gone home to her parents in Saint Martin Terressus. That's where she always went."

Avril understood. "Yvette had left you before?"

Pereau closed his eyes and nodded. "But she always came back." Avril said nothing and he continued. "Usually within three or four days. This time, I waited over a week before I called them. They had not seen her, either. Not even a phone call."

Avril had to agree the act seemed out of character for a woman who had fled to her parents' house after all previous fights with her husband. "You've checked with other friends?"

"We live outside a small town, Detective," he explained,

unaware that Avril had grown up in a neighboring town of similar size. "Yvette does not have many friends, but those who will take my calls"—he looked at his hands again—"say they have not heard from her, either."

"I will need their names," Avril said.

"Of course."

She wrote the list as he dictated the names to her.

"M. Pereau, I have to ask," Avril said unapologetically. "You don't know of any men with whom your wife was friendly?"

Pereau chuckled softy, as if responding to a private joke, but his expression was devoid of indignation. "Not lately."

"When, then?"

"Seven or eight years ago." He shook his head and sighed. "Yvette is a lovely woman. And we've been together almost twenty years. . . ."

"Who was he?"

"Nobody. A summer student who was helping on the farm. A mere tryst." He waved it away with his shaky hand. "It's long forgotten."

Clearly it wasn't. Despite his casual response, Avril could see in the farmer's eyes that the wound was still fresh. "Do you know his name?" she asked.

"Pascal . . ." He looked up at the ceiling as if struggling to produce the name that was probably etched in his brain. "Etellier. Pascal Etellier."

"Do you know where M. Etellier lives now?"

Pereau rolled his eyes and grunted in contempt. "Somewhere miserable, I hope."

Avril decided to take one final stab with Pereau. "Do you know Pauline Lamaire?" she asked.

"The violinist from Montmagnon?"

Avril held her breath. "That's her."

"Only by reputation. I've never met her, but I understand she hasn't been well lately. I hear she no longer plays the violin."

"No, she doesn't," Avril said, burying her disappointment. She put down her pen and rose from her seat, preparing to end the interview. As she walked around the desk, Pereau remained in his seat, staring at the floor. "What is it, M. Pereau?"

He didn't make eye contact. "I don't know if it is even worth mentioning."

"It always is," she said, standing over him.

"Yvette became so fearful after, you know, the people from the ministry came," he said. "I think the whole trauma made her a little paranoid."

Silent and still, Avril waited for more.

"Yvette grew more and more suspicious that someone was deliberately doing this to us. Trying to ruin our farm. Ruin us."

"Why would someone want to ruin you?"

"That was my question, too, but she could never answer." He exhaled, and Avril resisted the urge to recoil from the pungent smell of stale alcohol. "She remembered seeing a person leaving our barn a few weeks before the first cow fell sick."

Avril leaned back against her desk. "And Yvette thought it was related?"

"Not at the time, no. She wasn't even concerned. We have people coming and going, dropping off supplies and so forth, all the time." He shook his head. "But Yvette didn't recognize the woman. And the more suspicious she became, the deeper her belief grew that the visitor was somehow related to the illness."

"Did she tell you anything about the woman?"

"Only that she was an attractive young woman in jeans," he said. "I assumed she was a courier for one of our suppliers, but Yvette thought she was too elegant."

Avril nodded. "Your wife thought that this anonymous woman had somehow infected the cows?"

"It's ridiculous, I know. Yvette wanted to go to the

police." Pereau uttered a self-conscious laugh. "I convinced her it was madness." He looked away and added, as if speaking to himself, "You couldn't infect cattle with mad cow disease, even if you wanted to."

Avril stared at the farmer, wondering what to make of the revelation when a loud knock at the door drew her attention. "Excuse me, M. Pereau," she said, as she hurried to the door.

Detective Simon Valmont stood waiting for her in the colorless hallway, soup stains on his jacket and a broad smile on his face. "Sorry to interrupt," he said without sounding apologetic. "It looks as though you and the farmer are having a good heart-to-heart in there."

"Wonderful," she snapped. "All we need are candles and mood music."

"Don't pounce too fast, Avril." Simon laughed. "He might not be single yet."

"Oh?"

Valmont dug in his pocket and produced a folded and slightly crumpled piece of paper, passing it to Avril. She unfolded it. Though the language was foreign, possibly German, she recognized the hotel receipt. "What is this?"

"Elemental police work," he said in a tone of feigned modesty. "I had to miss a couple of horse races, but I tracked down Yvette Pereau for you by her passport."

Avril shook her head in surprise. "Where did you find her?"

"She flew last week from Limoges to Amsterdam, through Paris. Paid cash for the ticket. And then she stayed five days in the Hotel Zanbergen."

"Was she alone?"

His smile widened. "Not according to the people in the rooms below and beside her."

19

Chapelat, France. January 18

Noah and Elise hardly exchanged a word during the smooth train ride from Paris back to Limoges. He stared out at the dark French countryside, his mind skipping from one unsettling subject to another. He thought of Duncan and Maggie and imagined how difficult his friend's homecoming must have been. Noah was reminded how much he missed his own family. Especially Chloe. It seemed as though years, not days, had passed since they built sand castles, played in the pool, and rolled messy fajitas together. Though he desperately wanted to see his daughter again, Noah sensed that, contrary to Minister Montalva's reassurances, his work was nowhere near finished in Limousin.

Eventually, the gliding motion of the train overcame his racing thoughts, and he was lulled into sleep. He awoke to find Elise staring at him with a slight grin fixed on her full lips.

Noah rubbed his eyes. "When does this plane touch down?" he said.

Her smile grew. "I wish I could sleep like that."

"Was I snoring?" he asked sheepishly.

"Not at all," she said. "A whistle blew a little while ago. And at one point the brakes screeched. You did not budge. Me?" She touched her chest lightly. "I am a very light sleeper."

Noah grinned. "Anna used to say that she could detonate dynamite on her side of the bed without waking me. My daughter, Chloe, sleeps like that, too."

"I wake up every time someone rolls over beside me in bed," she said, without a trace of embarrassment.

"Elise, you were—I don't know—quieter at our meeting with Javier than I expected."

"Was I?" She tapped her lip with her index finger.

"I've come to expect more assertiveness from you."

She stopped tapping and frowned, but playfully. "You consider me pushy?"

"No, but you usually stand your ground."

"And I did not in Paris?"

"Not like other times."

She considered the comment. "Javier is not always the easiest man to please."

Ignoring the possible double entendre, Noah said, "He seemed very pleased with your work so far."

"You only saw his public face."

Noah remembered the Spaniard's unyielding smile and realized, as he had suspected at the time, that Montalva would be less restrained behind closed doors. "So he's not satisfied with our investigation?"

"I did not mean that," she said. "His expectations are always high. He would like us to wrap this up as quickly as possible."

"And with as little fallout as possible for him and his commission," he added.

"Yes, that, too."

"How long have you known him?" Noah asked.

"We've worked in the same department for over five years, but I've only worked directly under . . . with . . .

Javier for the past fourteen months." She studied her polished fingernails, rubbing her thumbs over the tips of the other fingers. "Javier cares deeply about his job and the people he serves."

What color is his toothbrush, Elise? Noah wondered without voicing it. He leaned nearer to her. "Are you as convinced as your boss that what we found at Ferme d'Allaire completely explains this outbreak?"

She touched her lip again, considering the question. "Not entirely convinced, but I am more willing to consider the possibility than you seem to be."

For a moment, he wondered if she was right—maybe stubbornness was fueling his skepticism—but he shook off the doubt as quickly as it came. "I've been doing this for a while, Elise. Sometimes, even when the evidence is not there—or in this case, *is* there—you still have to trust your gut when something doesn't seem kosher."

She tilted her head from side to side. "At what point do you accept the evidence?"

"When I am convinced." He leaned back in his seat. "Besides, we're a long way from completing our investigation. We still have to speak to the families of the other two known victims, Benoît Gagnon and Giselle Tremblay."

"I agree."

"And I want to speak to the veterinary pathologist who examined the infected cows."

"You said that in Paris." Her expression hardened. "You've seen the postmortem reports. They were conclusive."

"I don't care," Noah said. "I want to hear directly from the doctor involved. And I need to know what other tests were run on the animals' blood and spinal fluid."

Elise opened her mouth but closed it without comment, just as an automated voice announced that the train was approaching Limoges. When the train rumbled to a stop in the station, they grabbed their bags and headed outside.

There were no cabs waiting out front, and the air had not warmed one degree since they had left. Noah put his knapsack down on a wooden bench against the wall, opened the zipper, and searched through it until he found his new gloves at the bottom. He had just slipped the second one on when he noticed a man in a black suit stepping out of the station's entry.

Tall and heavy with a stooped posture, the man looked to be in his mid-fifties. From twenty feet away, they made brief eye contact, and then the man turned and headed in the opposite direction. Noah watched him go. Just before rounding the street corner, the man slowed a moment to bring a cigarette to his mouth. As he hunched over to light it, Noah had a sudden sense of déjà vu. His heart leaped into his throat. He had seen that same profile in silhouette, stooped behind the wheel of the French-style pickup truck parked outside his hotel.

Noah dropped his half-zipped bag on the bench. "Hey, you!" he called out and raced for the corner where the man had just turned. He rounded it in time to see the man loping across the street. "Hey, hold on!" Noah shouted. *"Attendez!"*

But the man did not wait. He reached the old pickup truck on the other side and flung open the driver's door. With surprising agility, he hopped into the driver's seat and slammed the door shut. The truck's lights flicked on and its engine uttered a rattling roar.

Noah ran onto the road and straight for the vehicle. When he was ten feet away, the tires screeched and it lurched out of the parking spot.

Noah stood in the middle of the road, blocking the truck's path and waving frantically for the driver to stop. But the truck wobbled as it veered to the left and then shot across the median into the oncoming traffic lane to weave around Noah. He spun to watch it pass. It backfired once with a loud crack and then left a plume of blue smoke in its wake as it bounced back onto the right side of the median.

Elise caught up with Noah in the middle of the street. "Was it the man from outside the hotel?" she asked breathlessly. "The farmer?"

His heart still thudding in his ears and nostrils filled with exhaust smoke, Noah simply nodded.

20

*

*W*ellness. Nikolas Cupierdo sometimes still winced inwardly on hearing the name of his own spa. *If my buddies in South Philly could see me now . . .*, he had thought more than once. Still, Cupierdo was a born salesman. He had made it to Rodeo Drive, riding a health-and-fitness wave that he was oblivious to before arriving in L.A. With a combination of street smarts and an almost prophetic ability to predict the next fad—and helped by the unfounded rumors that he had trained Demi Moore and Bruce Willis in the nineties—Cupierdo had reached the top of the wellness industry. He now counted some of Southern California's richest and most famous among his faithful clientele.

As Cupierdo surveyed his large but cramped storeroom—filled with boxes of vitamin supplements, herbal remedies, and high-end exercise accessories—he realized with deep satisfaction that he needed to find more space in a neighborhood that carried one of the most prestigious zip codes in the country.

"There's no room to breathe in here," Michael Jefferson

grunted, pulling Cupierdo out of his thoughts. The astute young African-American who had become Cupierdo's most trusted employee threw his hands up in the air. "Nick, where the hell are we going to put ten thousand bottles of water?"

Cupierdo flicked a finger at the existing stock. "Time to get rid of this stuff."

"You smoking something you're not sharing?" Jefferson chuckled. "This is our bread and butter, dude. What else can you mark up three hundred percent and still sell out of?"

"The Lake!"

"Great, more water." Jefferson scoffed. "What flavors does this crap come in?"

"Natural. No flavors. And it's not just any water, Mikey." Cupierdo smiled. "We're talking about a purity no one has ever before seen or tasted." His eyes lit up, and he slipped into salesman mode. "Picture this, Michael. Antarctic water protected by miles of ice for millions of years. Water that has never been in contact with human pollution. Not so much as a single molecule of smog!" He held up a single finger. "Not only that, this water contains a unique concentration of minerals and organic acids. It's as natural a health product as you will ever *unearth*." He stressed the last word for effect.

"Yeah, yeah," Jefferson said, unimpressed. "You really believe that shit?"

The excitement drained from Cupierdo's face and his hands dropped to his side. "To be honest, I don't care if the bottles are filled from a rusty tap in Cleveland." He thumbed at the door leading out to the lobby. "Point is, *they* will believe it. And they'll beat down our door for a sip of this stuff."

"At a hundred bucks a bottle?"

"One fifty," Cupierdo corrected. "And that's just the

introductory price. I've already got commitments for most of the stock before it's even arrived. I might have under-priced it." He laughed. "Trust me, Mikey, we're going to have a hell of a time keeping up with the demand."

21

As soon as they reached the Grand Hotel Doré, Noah said a quick good night to Elise and headed straight up to the same room he had stayed in before leaving for Paris. At the small desk in the corner, he sat nursing a Coke from the minibar and trying to figure out what the pickup driver was doing at the train station. *Was it just a coincidence?* he wondered. If not, then how did the man know where to find them? And most disturbing, *why did he run?*

Realizing he could not answer any of the questions, Noah decided to update his own notes and tackle a few nagging concerns. He rose from the chair and walked to the corner of the room where his notebook lay under the stack of articles, faxes, and printed e-mails, too bulky to carry to Paris for a one-day trip. He'd left the papers and notebook in the room, taking only his lightweight laptop computer with him.

Noah picked up the stack and carried it back to the desk. He dug through the files, looking for the article he had read on biochemical markers of vCJD. He found the paper and scanned through it until he spotted the section concerning phosphorylated tau protein. The article confirmed that all previous cases of vCJD had shown pronounced elevation of the protein in the sufferers' brain tissue. He considered Dr. Gellier's explanation that the Limousin victims had died so quickly that there had not been time to accumulate the chemical, but he still wasn't satisfied.

Noah moved the other papers out of the way and freed his notebook from the pile. He flipped it open and leafed through the pages, looking for a fresh sheet. It took him a moment to realize that Chloe's happy-face clip-on bookmark was missing.

He dropped out of his chair and onto his knees. Scanning under the desk, he spotted the purple bookmark where it had fallen behind the far leg of the desk. He patted the carpet until his fingers grasped it. As he brought the clip to eye level, he remembered marking his page right before racing off to meet Duncan and Elise. The bookmark could not have fallen out on its own.

Someone had gone through his notes.

Noah examined every page of his notebook and each loose paper but noticed nothing else missing or displaced. He got up and combed the room, looking under the bed and scouring the drawers and closet, uncertain what he was looking for and doubtful he would recognize it if he saw it, but still compelled to look.

Once he finished his search, he walked empty-handed back to the desk and reached for the phone. He began to dial Elise's room number, but stopped before punching in the last digit and placed the receiver gently back into the cradle.

How did the truck driver know where to find me? he thought again. *And how would anyone have known I would be in Paris for a day?* The only people who came to mind were Jean Nantal, Elise Renard, and Minister Javier Montalva y Casas. And Jean was beyond suspicion.

Noah glanced at his watch and calculated the time zones. Distrusting the room's phone, he reached for his cell. As he was about to dial, he saw the MISSED CALL text message on the screen, though the voicemail indicator light was not on. He pressed the LIST button and scrolled through the numbers. The last two calls both came the previous evening from the same phone number, between 9:15 and 10:15 P.M., when he must have been in the bar with Duncan. Though he didn't recognize the number, he realized that the area code was local. *Who in Limoges would call twice but leave no message?* He tried the number, but the line rang repeatedly without answer. Finally, he hung up.

Studying his phone's screen, he chose the fourth number down on the speed-dial list. The line rang five times before Noah heard Gwen's familiar voicemail greeting. He almost hung up, but after a moment's pause, he said, "Gwen, hi. It's Noah. I just . . . um . . . wanted to run something by you. Nothing urgent. Call me back when, or if, you have a chance." He clicked the END button and tossed the cell phone onto the bed in disgust. "Smooth, Haldane!" he groaned.

Feeling confined in the small hotel room, he paced the floor. He considered going for a walk, but he did not want to chance another rendezvous in the dead of night with the truck driver or anyone else, so he fought off his claustrophobia and stayed put. It occurred to him that help might not come soon, if at all. Duncan was gone. And he no longer fully trusted Elise. There was no one left to turn to.

Determined to find more answers in his stack of papers, Noah hurried back to the desk. He laid the papers out in sequence and picked up the first article. He reread every word on the subject of BSE and vCJD as he scribbled through several more pages in his notebook. Finished, he carried the book over to his bed. As he lay in bed reviewing his own chicken-scratch, he could not escape the prickly sense of violation, knowing that someone else had read the thoughts and ideas intended only for himself.

Eventually fatigue overcame him, and he drifted off with the notebook on his chest.

He awoke before dawn, still dressed, though the book had fallen to the floor beside him. After his shower, he changed into a sweater and khakis and went downstairs to the dining room.

Relieved not to have run into Elise in the restaurant, Noah sat alone at a table and read the *International Herald Tribune* while waiting for his breakfast. On page two, a detailed article updated the Limousin outbreak under a headline that dubbed it: THE VIENNE UNKNOWN. Noah snorted when he read that "unnamed sources" within the E.U. claimed that the investigators had located "with confidence" the source of the prion. He could imagine the insincere smile and Spanish lilt behind that anonymous tip.

The waitress deposited a bowl of steaming oatmeal in front of him. Noah downed another coffee and picked at the food for a while before he pushed it aside and picked up the second newspaper, *Limousin Matin,* Limoges's local daily. Scanning the pages for any more information on the situation, he stumbled across an article on Dr. Louis Charron on page six. But he struggled to translate the French. As best he could tell, the article lauded the man's academic accomplishments and read more like an obituary than a report of a car accident. Near the end, Noah made out a brief mention that both alcohol and high speed were involved in the single-car collision that killed Charron.

"Tu lis en français aussi, maintenant?" a familiar voice interrupted his thoughts.

Noah lowered the paper to see Elise standing over him in a black blouse and gray slacks. Her smile was radiant.

He was filled with a conflicting mix of wariness and familiarity. "Hello, Elise," he said coolly.

Without invitation, she slid into the seat across from him. "May I?" she said, taking the newspaper from his hand.

He pointed to the article on Charron. "I was trying to read this."

She began to read and translate aloud on the fly. " 'At 11:30 P.M., Dr. Louis Charron—the head of neurology for CHRU in Limoges—lost control of his Jaguar, drove off an embankment, and slammed into a tree. The sixty-seven-year-old physician died instantly. . . .' "

Noah listened in silence. Though her translation was far more fluid than his, he learned nothing new. Finished, she put down the paper. "Sad, isn't it?" she said.

"Hmmm," Noah agreed. He consulted his watch. "What time is Benoît Gagnon's partner expecting us?"

"Ten o'clock."

Noah rose from the table. "I'm going for a quick walk. How about I meet you in the lobby at a quarter to?"

"All right." Elise squinted, seemingly taken aback by his abrupt mood.

Noah left without another word to her. As he wandered through downtown Limoges, he reflected on the science of prions. The more he had read about the rogue proteins, the more contradictory their nature seemed. Not alive by any scientific criteria, these proteins mimicked the fundamental mechanism of life—self-replication—solely to accomplish one purpose: the destruction of life. They were nature's perfect Trojan horses.

Despite Dr. Gellier's assertions, Noah was more convinced than ever the prion that killed Philippe Manet, Benoît Gagnon, and Giselle Tremblay was not one the world was familiar with. *Yet.* And from the tampering in his hotel room and his run-in with the skittish truck driver, Noah strongly suspected that people outside his own team had taken a deep and troubling interest in this prion, too.

Walking without a specific direction, Noah found himself standing at the foot of the St. Étienne Cathedral. No longer did he view the church's looming tower as an architectural marvel. Now it struck him as foreboding and somehow symbolic of the many mysteries and unanswered questions that this city and its surrounding province concealed.

Chilled and uneasy, he turned and headed back for the hotel.

He reached the entrance at 9:40 A.M. Elise was already waiting outside. She hailed a taxi, and they drove wordlessly through the downtown area. The taxi slowed on a cobbled street that boasted a row of distinguished heritage buildings. The driver let them off in front of the corner building, and they walked up to the entryway's decorative glass door. Elise pressed the intercom button that read DIEPPE ET GAGNON.

Inside, the smell of fresh flowers and potpourri in the lobby followed them up the grand staircase to the second-floor apartment. Michel Dieppe was leaning against the doorjamb of his apartment. Lean with short hair, Dieppe had a goatee and faint acne scars. He wore a bright checkered pullover with black pants, but despite his colorful outfit, Noah noticed profound sadness in the man's blue eyes.

"You must be Mlle. Renard and Dr. Haldane," Dieppe said in flawless English. He led his guests into the stylish apartment, decorated with warm furnishings and colorful oil paintings—an eclectic mix of landscape, Postimpressionist, and abstract art.

After they were seated on the leather divans in the living room, Dieppe leaned back against a pillow and rested a hand behind his neck. "You want to know more about Benoît?"

Noah nodded. "I understand you and Benoît Gagnon were partners?"

"He was my husband, Dr. Haldane," Dieppe said with a glimmer of defensiveness. "We were together for over eight years. That is a long time in our community."

"In anybody's community," Noah said, making Dieppe laugh softly. "Michel, were you with Benoît when he first showed signs of sickness?"

Dieppe bit down on his lip and looked away. He didn't answer for a few moments. "You must understand, it came out of nowhere." He sighed. "One day, I will never forget it. A Sunday morning." His hand plucked at the threads on the pillow beside him. "Benoît had slept in. I was making breakfast when he marched into the kitchen and accused me of spying on him for the police. I thought he was joking. I laughed. And he . . ." He touched his cheek. "Benoît hit me in the face. And then again. He just attacked me . . . punching, kicking, spitting . . ." He shook his head and his gaze fell to his lap. "He was normally so gentle. This was nothing like him."

"Of course." Elise reached out as if to touch him, but her hand stopped short of his, and she withdrew it. "What happened after?"

Dieppe cleared his throat. "My neighbors heard the screams—mine and his—and phoned the police. It took three officers just to contain him. They wanted to take him to jail, but I convinced them that this was not Benoît, so they took him to the hospital."

"And then, Michel?" Elise asked gently.

"The doctors thought that Benoît was crazy. Schizophrenia, they told me. And I believed them, too. He really was acting insane." He shook his head again. "Nothing like my Benoît."

"But then he had a seizure?" Noah prodded, remembering Dr. Charron's description.

"Not just one, Dr. Haldane!" Dieppe sat up straighter.

"It was two days later. Benoît was in the psychiatric ward. I was sitting with him in his room, reading to him. He was much calmer by then. Even making sense. Much more like the old Benoît. Then suddenly, he collapsed in his bed and his arms and legs began to jerk and shake. His face turned dark blue. Spit and blood flew from his mouth. . . . It was so awful. He had convulsion after convulsion." Dieppe reached into his pocket, pulled out a handkerchief, and dabbed at his eyes before continuing. "It took hours, but finally the doctors managed to stop his seizures." He closed his eyes and shook his head. "It was too late, then."

"Why too late?" Noah asked.

"By that point, Benoît was already damaged." He touched the side of his own temple. "He was confused. He didn't recognize friends . . . his own family."

"And you?" Elise asked.

"He seemed to recognize me almost to the end." Dieppe shrugged. "It was hard to tell because soon after the seizures, he stopped talking. The doctor called it, how do you say, cata—"

"Catatonia," Noah offered.

"Yes. They said he could no longer speak, but I don't think that was it."

Noah leaned closer to Dieppe. "What do you think, Michel?"

His lips cracked into a smile and his eyes welled up. "I think he was so afraid of the nonsense that came out of his mouth every time he tried to speak that he just stopped talking altogether. I think it was less painful for him."

Noah nodded sympathetically.

"It was such a terribly cruel way to go, for both of us," Dieppe said wistfully. "It was like watching him dissolve, piece by piece. Sometimes, I would go for a coffee—or even a smoke—and when I came back there was less of Benoît than before I left. It happened that quickly."

They lapsed into a few moments of silence, broken by Elise. "Michel, did Benoît eat much red meat?" she asked.

"Not in the hospital. He would have choked."

"No, before he became ill."

Dieppe chewed his lip, thinking. "Not too much. We both liked a steak now and then, but we ate far more seafood and vegetable dishes than red meat."

"How about beef delicacies like calves' liver, sweetbreads, or cow's tongue?"

Dieppe scrunched his face in disgust. "Definitely not! Neither of us would touch those."

"Okay, in the months before Benoît became ill, which butcher did you use for your meats?"

"I'm very particular about my meat," Dieppe said. "I only buy from Boucherie Lebeau."

"In Limoges?" Elise asked.

"Of course." He waved at the window. "Right down the street."

"And you and Benoît ate most of your meals together?"

"Most, yes. Except, of course . . ." Dieppe looked out the window without finishing.

Elise raised an eyebrow. "*Except,* Michel?"

"Eight years we were together," Dieppe said. "Right out of university. It was bound to happen to one of us—maybe even both of us—at some point."

"What was?" Noah asked.

Elise nodded, her face lit with understanding. "Benoît had an affair," she said.

"It was just a . . . what is the English term . . . ?"

"A fling?" Noah suggested.

"Exactly!" Dieppe nodded vehemently. "Benoît told me later it was nothing. Just sex." He sighed. "I found the e-mails on his computer." He rolled his eyes. "The silly fool had told me his password. I don't know why he did not expect me to look. Or perhaps maybe he wanted me to catch him. I wonder sometimes."

Noah nodded. "So you broke up?"

"Only a few weeks, really. Then he came home, as I always knew he would." He nodded to himself. "Benoît soon found out how difficult Philippe was to be with."

Noah straightened at the mention of the name.

"Philippe?" Elise asked. "Do you mean Philippe Manet?"

"All I know is that his e-mail address is Philippe_M99." Dieppe paused. "Funny, that old doctor asked me the same question."

Noah tasted acid in his mouth. "Which doctor?" Noah snapped. "Not Dr. Charron?"

"Exactly. He came to see me."

"When?" Noah demanded.

Dieppe thought about it. "Three days ago. Anyway, I told him I didn't know what the thief's last name was. God knows what I would do if I ever ran into him."

"Do you know anything else about this Philippe M?" Noah asked.

"I know he lives in the town of Lac Noir. There can't be many Philippe M's in a town of that size."

Noah looked past Dieppe and out the window at the foreboding gray skies. "No. There can't be."

22

———

Avril Avars was lost. Though she spoke fluent English and scraps of Arabic from her Moroccan heritage, she did not understand a word of Dutch. And as the sheets of rain pelted the streets, she had trouble finding any locals willing to stop long enough to offer directions to the Hotel Zanbergen. The soggy map in her hand offered nothing but confusion. So Avril wandered the narrow sidewalks, crossing bridge after bridge over the many canals, while trying to make sense of the few addresses she could spot on streets that had remarkably similar polysyllabic names that all ended in *gracht*.

Avril knew she had overstepped her authority by leaving Limousin. Detective Valmont had vociferously tried to talk her out of the trip. Twenty-four hours earlier, he had sat in her office with his feet on her desk. "Avril, I don't object to the odd trip to Saint Junien or Felletin, but isn't Amsterdam a bit beyond our jurisdiction?"

"Possibly, but who else is going to check?"

"I do not want to jump to conclusions, but I would imagine that the Dutch have some kind of organized police system," he deadpanned.

"Simon, you don't even believe Yvette Pereau is actually missing," she said with a sigh. "Imagine what our colleagues in Amsterdam would think if I tried to explain this to them."

"Exactly what I think," he grumbled. "There is no evidence of a crime here."

She sighed. "That is why I have to go."

Valmont jerked his feet off the desk and sat up straighter in his seat. The flippancy gone from his face, he studied her with unusual intensity. "I know you hate loose ends," he said. "But listen to me for a change, Avril. We found the woman. She went off on a little sex romp. She was bored and lonely and had a drunk for a husband. It's no crime. Why not let this one sit for a while, yes?"

Avril did not argue further with Valmont. She had tried to follow his advice, spending her day searching for some trace of Pauline Lamaire or confirmation that Yvette Pereau had simply gone off with her lover. But she found neither. She even tracked down Yvette's former lover, Pascal Etellier, who had not seen her in years. With an attitude that verged on scorn, Etellier said that Yvette was so racked by remorse after their brief affair that he could not imagine her doing it again. Avril also spoke to Yvette's mother; she confirmed everything the husband had said. Unlike André—who, crushed as he was by the Dutch hotel receipt, at least accepted that his wife might have run off with another man—her mother was adamant Yvette would not have behaved so impetuously. The woman's tangible worry fueled Avril's determination. She caught the first flight out earlier this morning and, four hours later, now found herself lost, drenched, and hungry in a Dutch downpour.

Stepping off a bridge onto a busy corner that she had already passed at least once, she spotted the small sign for the Hotel Zanbergen hanging from an old brick building squeezed in between two others.

Inside the lobby, wallpapered in burgundy and warmed by an open fireplace, Avril asked to speak to the manager. Five minutes later, she stood at the registration desk interviewing Maarten Van Doorn. Middle-aged and cadaverous, Van Doorn wore a dark suit and had a thick thatch of greasy blond hair and heavy-framed glasses. To Avril, he looked better suited for undertaking than hotel management. However, from his eager-to-please and efficient manner, Avril soon recognized the qualities that must have made him an excellent manager.

They commiserated on their respective cities' abhorrent recent weather, and then Avril established the purpose of her visit. She passed Van Doorn the out-of-date snapshot of Yvette Pereau that the husband had lent her. The manager studied the photo for a few seconds. "This is the woman," he finally said in his impeccable French.

"You're sure?"

Van Doorn nodded.

"But you see so many guests . . ."

"Of course, Detective Avars. At the Zanbergen we pride ourselves on the personal service we offer. I try to greet every new guest myself, when possible." His business smile faded. "But with Mme. Pereau, it was something more."

"What was that, Mr. Van Doorn?"

"She seemed . . ." He frowned. "Exceedingly tense to me."

Which might fit with someone about to embark on an affair, Avril thought, slightly deflated. "And she was alone when she checked in?"

"Yes."

"I was led to believe she was with a man," Avril said. "A man who was not her husband."

"Ah, yes. There were one or two noise complaints in the early morning hours from neighboring rooms," he said diplomatically. "To be honest, that . . . ah . . . revelation came as a surprise to me, considering how anxious Mme. Pereau was when she checked in."

"Really?" Avril said. "In my experience, adulterers are often nervous in public places. I would imagine especially so in hotel lobbies."

He chuckled knowingly. "Detective Avars, I've worked in the hotel business my whole life. To a certain extent, affairs drive our industry here in Amsterdam. I try not to judge, but I think now I can spot a tryst from across the lobby. Usually, only one person checks in. And while it is true he or she might be nervous, it is somehow different. There is guilt, to be sure—often they avoid eye contact, not wanting to be recognized—however, there is excitement and anticipation, too. Mme. Pereau acted nothing like that."

"You think she was afraid?"

"Exactly so! Almost as if . . ." He stopped and frowned again. "As if she needed help. I asked her as much, but she insisted she was fine."

"Did you see Mme. Pereau after check-in?"

"Not that I remember, no. Though I wasn't here the morning she checked out."

Van Doorn turned to the plump plain-faced blonde beside him whose name tag pinned to her red blazer read KALIE. She had been typing at a computer since Avril arrived, oblivious to—and possibly not understanding—the French conversation beside her. Van Doorn showed Kalie the photo of Yvette and addressed her in Dutch. She studied the photo and then viewed the manager warily. They launched into an unexpectedly long discussion. By the end of it, the clerk's voice had dropped to a near whisper and her face had flushed slightly.

The manager turned back to Avril. "Kalie was here that morning, but Mme. Pereau did not check out herself. Apparently, a gentleman paid in cash for the room and charges."

"Oh?" Avril glanced over to Kalie, whose cheeks were still colored. "But there is more?"

"Yes." Van Doorn cleared his throat. "The rest is almost . . . gossip. I am not sure how reliable it would be."

Avril grinned. "I will put a star beside it in my report."

Van Doorn nodded, appeased. "One of our chambermaids—who is not working today—told Kalie that she inadvertently walked in on . . . something . . . in the room."

"Walked in on what, M. Van Doorn?"

"Apparently, there was no do-not-disturb sign on the door. And the maid was in the middle of her late-morning cleaning in that section. It was perfectly understandable that she should enter."

"Of course, she was only doing her job," Avril said, trying to cloak her impatience. "I understand. What did she see?"

"There was a woman. Naked." He cleared his throat. "And she was handcuffed to the bed."

Avril gripped the edge of the desk. "Handcuffed?"

"That is right. And there was a very large man standing over her."

Her stomach knotted. "And the maid didn't report this to anyone?" she said.

"Oh, no, no, no!" The manager waved his hand and smiled apologetically. "You misunderstand, Detective Avars. It was clearly a . . . consensual act. A sexual game of some sort."

"I see." Though her mental image of Yvette Pereau did not jibe with the concept of someone who dabbled in bondage, in her professional experience Avril had learned never to jump to conclusions about people's sexual practices. Again, she felt a slight letdown that this lead was not panning out better.

Kalie said something to Van Doorn in Dutch and

pointed at the photograph. He nodded and turned back to Avril. "It is interesting, though."

"What is?"

"The maid had seen Mme. Pereau on the day she checked in. She told Kalie that woman in the handcuffs was definitely not her."

Not Yvette! Avril thought as her grip tightened on the desk. "Where was Mme. Pereau?"

Van Doorn turned and asked Kalie. The young clerk merely shrugged in response.

Avril pointed to the photo. "Has Kalie seen Mme. Pereau since?"

The manager asked in Dutch, and the clerk shook her head blankly.

"M. Van Doorn, would you please phone the maid for me and see if I could arrange a time to speak to her myself?" Avril asked.

"Of course," Van Doorn said in his accommodating tone. "Excuse me a moment, while I find her number."

He disappeared into a back office. Avril waited, bubbling with the excitement of a fresh lead, though concerned for its implications. Questions swirled in her head. Who was the woman having sex in Pereau's room, and where was Yvette? Were the disappearances of Yvette Pereau and Pauline Lamaire related? *Could it be some kind of serial sex crime?*

Her thoughts were interrupted by the familiar tinny Chopin melody ringtone of her cell phone. She stepped away from the desk and dug the phone out of her purse. The call display read PARIS but did not provide a specific number.

"Bonjour," she answered.

"Maman?"

"Frédéric!" Avril said, warmed by the sound of her son's voice. They had not spoken as often as she would

have liked since their pre-Christmas clash in Montmagnon. "How is school, my love?"

"Not good, Maman."

Something in his tone immediately launched her anxiety. "What is it?"

"Maman, they say that you have to stop what you are
doing!" he said in a ragged voice that was nothing like his
usual flowing delivery.

Her heart leaped into her throat. "*Doing*, Frédéric? I
don't understand."

"Your investigation, Maman," he labored to say. "About
those missing women. They told me to tell you to stop
looking for them."

Avril fought off the tears and clutched the phone tighter
against her head, desperate to keep her son on the line.
"Frédéric, who is *they*?"

"They say they will not harm me if you cooperate," he
said as if reading from a script.

A clamp squeezed around her heart. The anguish was
excruciatingly reminiscent of the moment she received
the call about Antoine's crash.

*Frédéric, my baby! Oh please, please, God, anything
but this!*

Somehow she managed to maintain a calm tone. "Everything will be okay, Frédéric. Are you all right?"

"I have to go now."

"Frédéric, let me speak to them!"

"Maman, it's the only way. Stop your investigation.
Please!"

"*Anything!* Just let me speak to—" Before she could get
out another word, the line went dead.

23

Limoges, France. January 19

For twenty minutes after leaving Michel Dieppe's home, Elise and Noah did not exchange a word. The cloud cover was thick and the natural light was gray as dusk, but despite the snow flurries and the menacing wind gusting around them, they reached a silent understanding that they would walk back to their hotel.

Halfway down the rue de Consulat, Elise stopped on the sidewalk outside one of the grand buildings lining the street. Noah walked a few steps farther before slowly turning to face her. He waited for her to speak.

"Noah, just because Benoît Gagnon and Philippe Manet happened to know each other, does that really change anything?"

Anger pushed away Noah's disquiet. He avoided eye contact with Elise and stared instead at the snowflakes accumulating on the sidewalk. "Sounds to me like they more than just *knew* each other," he said.

"No question."

"Variant Creutzfeldt-Jakob disease—any prion disease, for that matter—is not sexually transmitted."

"I am aware of that," she said coolly, standing her

ground. "But the two victims might have shared the same food, *non?*"

"Doesn't fit," Noah said, measuring his words. "In almost two hundred previous human cases, there have never been any reported clusters or associations between the family and friends of victims. So why here—when we've only identified three victims—are two of them intimately linked?"

She held open a palm. "Obviously this throws another . . . what is the expression? . . . wrench into the situation."

"I could open up a hardware store with all the wrenches I've collected since I came here," he said, but there was no levity in his tone.

"We discussed this before. Limousin has a small population. At some point, we were bound to discover associations between the people involved."

Noah locked eyes with her. "What is it with you, Elise?" he asked quietly.

She shook her head. "Me?"

"Why are you so desperate to write everything off as coincidence?"

Elise folded her arms across her chest. "What makes you say that?"

"Right from day one, you and everyone at the E.U. have wanted this to be just another outbreak of BSE with a few human victims as collateral damage."

"Why would we want that, Noah?" she said frostily. "As you have seen, this is a disaster for the European agricultural community."

"Maybe the alternative is even worse."

"What *alternative?*"

Noah wasn't sure how to put his darkest thoughts into words, so he simply shook his head and said, "I don't know."

Elise raised an eyebrow. "Is it not possible that after your experience with the ARCS virus and those terrorists . . ."

"Yes?"

She uncrossed her arms. "That perhaps you are more . . . suspicious now?"

"You mean paranoid?"

"I mean what I said."

"Maybe I was naïve before my experience with ARCS. Maybe I am jaded now. Who knows?" He narrowed his gaze. "What I do know is that my experience tells me all is not what it appears here. It's like this whole time we've been trying to wedge together a jigsaw puzzle with the wrong pieces."

Elise clasped her hands in front of her. "You say that, and yet we have heard that the recent victims looked exactly like previous vCJD sufferers on autopsy. And we've found a central cattle supplier—proven to produce dangerous and illegal feeds—as the source for all known infected cows."

Noah leaned closer to her. "Yes. But we also have a disease that spreads with the speed of a common cold, and kills as fast as any virus. Nothing like a prion."

"I thought that microorganisms constantly mutate."

"Mutate, of course. Subtle changes that occur over time. They don't become new diseases overnight!" He numbered the points with his gloved fingers. "Now we have victims who are sexually involved. There are supposedly infected cows coming from a farm that has never been known to have a symptomatic case. People touched by the investigation into this prion have been dying in fires and car accidents. *And* we have an informant who tracks me to my hotel in the middle of the night, and then spies on me at a train station."

"You don't know that he was there to spy on you."

"Just another coincidence, right?" Noah snapped. "Like the fact that someone searched my room in Limoges as soon as we left for Paris."

Elise's mouth fell open. "What are you talking about?"

"Somebody broke into my hotel room and combed through my notes and research papers."

She closed her mouth, but her eyes were still wide with surprise. "How do you know? Is anything missing?"

"No, but I had a marker in my notebook. It was moved."

"Could that not have been an accident? Maybe when the hotel maid was cleaning—"

"No!" Noah was so frustrated by her reflex rationalization that he didn't bother explaining how secure the clip was. He fought off a scowl and calmed his voice. "It is strange, though."

Elise pursed her lips and viewed him warily. "What is?"

He stared at her for a long moment. "That someone seems to know where I am at all times."

Her eyes darkened. "Are you implying that *I* might have told someone?"

"What I am saying is that very few people know my schedule in France."

Their breath crystallized between them for several seconds. "Except me?" she whispered hoarsely.

"And Javier," Noah said. "He seems very well apprised of what we are up to."

"He is my boss!"

"Is that all he is?"

Elise glared at him, fire in her eyes. "You have no right," she said between gritted teeth. Tears suddenly welled up and spilled down her cheeks. She spun away from him and stormed off.

Noah watched her stride away. His anger suddenly dissolved, replaced by guilt. With shoes sliding on the slick sidewalk, he broke into a jog after her. He reached her at the street corner, where she stood waiting for a break in the traffic. He laid a hand on her shoulder, but she shook it away without turning. "Leave me alone, Noah," she said softly.

His hand fell off her shoulder. "I am sorry, Elise. I was out of line."

The traffic cleared momentarily, and Elise hurried across the street without acknowledging the apology.

Noah watched her go. He stood, immobilized, in the same spot as the pedestrian light cycled through two more color changes. Feeling his phone vibrate in his pocket, he dug it out and brought it to his ear. "Noah Haldane," he barked.

"Catch you at a bad time?" the familiar voice said.

"Gwen?" he said. "What's going on?"

"I don't know," she said, amused. "You called me, remember?"

"I did, didn't I?" he said, pleased to hear her voice.

"You said you wanted to run something by me." Her tone grew more serious. "What's going on over there, Noah?"

"I'm not sure." He moved away from two other pedestrians waiting for the light and stood off the edge of the sidewalk. "I think the situation is more involved than it first appeared." He gave her a quick update of the recent events, including the break-in.

"Shouldn't you go to the police?" Gwen asked.

"With what? A farmer who ran from me, and a bookmark that was moved in my hotel room?"

"C'mon, Noah," she said. "You are obviously being shadowed."

Shadowed. He bristled at the word. "If I am, then it's probably the E.U. or the French government keeping tabs on me."

"Why bother if you're already with one of their envoys?"

"Maybe they don't trust Elise?" But he did not believe his own explanation.

"Hmmm. And would a government send a grizzled farmer to tip you off about the cattle supplier, and then have him wait for you outside a train station?"

"No." With wind biting at his neck, he turned up the collar of his jacket.

"Other factors are at play here," she said. "Noah, you need to be careful, you understand?"

"We're talking about me, Gwen." He summoned a chuckle. "Remember? I'm the one who runs out of collapsing buildings ahead of the women and children."

"The way I remember it, you saved me from that building."

"Yeah, but you were hit on the head. I could have told you anything afterwards."

"True," she said with a light laugh. "Maybe chivalry is dead, after all."

"Long dead," Noah said. "Enough about me and France. What's new with you?"

"Usual sky-is-falling kind of stuff that fuels this town." She told him of the latest bioterrorism threats worrying the authorities in Washington.

As Noah listened to Gwen's matter-of-fact description of recent threats—anthrax, smallpox, Ebola, and botulism being just a few—he was reminded again of the momentous responsibility that she shouldered with such poise. "I guess a few mad cows and an angry farmer don't seem so bad compared to your load," he said.

"Noah, there are people here who can cover for me for a couple of days. Why don't I come over there and see if I can lend a hand?"

Feeling as isolated as he ever had, Noah longed to have her by his side. He pictured her thoughtful eyes and captivating smile. He had a flashback of Gwen walking naked in that effortlessly sexy way toward him where he lay in the bed. But he forced himself to shake off the mental image. "Gwen, France is outside of the Bug Czar's jurisdiction. Your crown wouldn't shine as brightly here."

"Crown?" she scoffed. "I don't even get a decent dental plan with this job."

Noah laughed, hiding his disappointment that she didn't put up more of a fight.

"You keep me in the loop, Noah Haldane."

"Dead center, I promise."

"And Noah . . ." Her voice dropped. "Be careful, all right?"

As he hung up, he glanced at the call display that showed Gwen's cell number. The sight reminded him of the two missed calls from the same local phone number two evenings earlier. He tried the number again, but the line rang unanswered, just as before. As he was hanging up, an idea hit him.

He hurried across the ____ and continued toward the hotel. Three block___ __ ___ he walked past the cybercafé he had spotted befo.__ He ordered an espresso and sat down at an empty terminal. Struggling with his French spelling, he had a few missteps before he found his way to the website that provided reverse-phone-number searches. He typed in the number from his cell's display of missed calls. The system paused as the hourglass icon hovered on the screen, and then it coughed up a name: Dr. Louis Charron.

The implication hit him like a punch.

Noah studied his cell phone screen again. Charron called for the second and last time at 10:07 P.M. He thought back to the French newspaper article about Charron's car accident. He remembered it said that Charron died before midnight, which meant that little more than an hour after trying *twice* to contact Noah, the neurologist had been so drunk behind the wheel that he veered off a straight road and slammed into a tree.

Noah's veins filled with ice.

What the hell is going on here?

24

Yvette Pereau was dead. So was Pauline Lamaire. Detective Avril Avars was sure now. She did not know why, nor did she care any longer. Only finding Frédéric mattered.

On autopilot, Avril had left the Hotel Zanbergen and headed directly to the Amsterdam airport. During the choppy flight to Paris, she repeated her Our Fathers and Hail Marys and every other prayer that she could dredge up from childhood memory.

She kept repeating those prayers up until the moment Frédéric's roommate let her into their small Left Bank apartment. When she stepped inside her son's empty bedroom, the impact of his abduction dug into her like a knife to the belly.

As she sat on Frédéric's unmade bed, she was aware of the faint scent of his deodorant. She remembered her son as if watching random clips from the video footage her husband had faithfully shot: those tottering first steps, his adorable four-year-old Christmas suit and bowtie, lying in bed with the six-year-old Frédéric as his measles-induced fever blazed, watching Antoine and a teenaged Frédéric battle it out on the soccer pitch, and helping her son stuff all his bags in his beat-up old Citro'n before he headed off to university. Aside from the physical resemblance, he had so much of Antoine's character in him: the same quiet strength and generous nature.

She rocked back and forth on the bed. *Will I ever see him again?* Even in the depths of her mourning for her husband, she had never known such fear or helplessness. *Please, God, don't let them hurt my son!* she thought for the thousandth time.

"Mme. Avars?" The voice jerked her from her misery. "Are you all right?"

Avril gave her eyes a furtive wipe, as if rubbing sleep from them, and then looked up to see Frédéric's roommate, Jacques Beauchamps, studying her from the doorway. The boy—a brilliant mathematician according to Frédéric—had spiky blue hair and a small boltlike stud through one nostril and another through his lip. Though she did not know Beauchamps well, Avril thought of him as a nice kid and a good friend to her son.

She cleared her throat and forced a smile. "I'm so tired from my flight that I'm thinking of having a nap in Frédéric's bed."

"Wouldn't do that," Beauchamps said, stepping into the room. "These mattresses are made of rocks. Your back will never be right again." He winked at her. "Plus, I don't think he washes his sheets enough."

"Thanks for the warning." Avril rose to her feet. "Listen, Jacques, I wish I had told Frédéric I was coming. I am in Paris only for the afternoon. Are you certain you don't know where he is?"

"Had dinner with him early last night. Then he took off. Haven't seen him since." He grinned and bit down on the stud in his lip. "Told me not to wait up."

"Why?" Avril shot, and then forced her voice calmer. "Was he meeting someone?"

Beauchamps glanced around the room conspiratorially. "Mme. Avars, you know Freddie and Stéphane broke up soon after he got back from the Christmas break?"

"No, I didn't," Avril said, rocked by another wave of guilt for meddling in her son's love life.

Beauchamps winked again. "You can't blame Freddie for catching up on lost time."

"I understand, Jacques." Avril swallowed back her bile. "So he had a big date last night?"

"Must have been." He smiled. "Freddie didn't come back this morning."

"Did he tell you anything about the girl?"

"No 'girl' about it." Beauchamps chuckled. "This was an *older* woman."

"How old?"

"I didn't see her, but Freddie made it sound like she was a lot older. Maybe thirty or something, you know?"

"Anything else?"

Beauchamps shrugged. "He said she was really hot."

"Where did he meet her?"

"In the library. Can you believe that?" Beauchamps laughed. "If I knew you could meet babes by going to the library, maybe I would start studying."

Avril's heart beat even faster. "She was a student?"

"Freddie made it sound like she was a grad student, or maybe a prof." Beauchamps held up his palms indifferently, as if the details beyond her age and looks were insignificant. "She just marched right up to him, told him she thought he was cute, and asked him to have a drink."

Avril snapped her fingers, her chest hammering. "Where, Jacques?"

Beauchamps looked taken aback by her sudden ferocity. "Didn't say." Suddenly, the boy's face clouded over with suspicion. "What's the big deal, Mme. Avars?"

She conjured a smile. "Just an overprotective mother not

willing to let go of her boy yet." She pulled a small notepad and pen out of her jacket. She jotted her cell number down on a blank page, tore it off, and handed it to Beauchamps. "Listen, Jacques, I will be in the city all day. I was really hoping to see Frédéric. I have something important to tell him. So if you see him—or if you hear *anything* about his whereabouts—you call. *Promise?*"

Beauchamps bit the stud in his lip and nodded.

Avril hurried out to the hallway and down the narrow staircase. Tears streamed down her cheeks before she even reached the street.

How am I going to keep it together? she wondered as she rushed along the wet sidewalk, weaving through the foot traffic. But she already knew. *For Freddie.*

Two blocks closer to the train station, she barely heard the Chopin melody over the street noise. Frantically, she dug in her pocket and grabbed for her phone.

"Maman?"

"Baby!" Her knees almost buckled as she ducked into the relative privacy of the alcove of the nearest building and cupped the phone tightly against her ear.

"Maman, they have further instructions for you." His voice was even weaker than the last time, and each hesitant word ripped at her heart.

"Frédéric, are you all right?"

"Yes," he said, but his tone was unconvincing. "Maman, you have to do as they say."

"Baby, let me speak to them."

"They won't talk to you."

"Frédéric, I *have to* speak to them."

"No, Maman."

Her throat filled and she couldn't keep the sob from her voice. "Frédéric, I love you so much, but I have to hang up now."

"Maman!"

Avril clicked the END button on her phone. She leaned

back against the wall, feeling as though the building had just collapsed on top of her.

It was the worst gamble of her life, but now Avril could do nothing but wait. Each silent second that passed was more painful than the last. She stood absolutely still, wondering every moment if she had just killed her son.

After ten agonizing minutes, she heard the soft Chopin melody. Her hand shook wildly as it shot for the phone. "Yes?"

"Detective Avars?" the metallic voice said.

Avril immediately recognized the use of an electronic voice changer. The sound was too distorted for her to tell if the caller was male or female. She willed her slamming heart to slow. "Yes."

"I am with Frédéric now."

"What do you want from us?" Avril growled.

"We want to send Frédéric home to you. We do. But we need your help."

"I'm listening."

"We need you to close your investigation on the two missing women."

"Consider it closed," Avril said. "I will write an official report and send it anywhere you want. It will be done. Then you will send him home, right?"

"All in good time." The tinny words were as emotionless as the sentiment behind them. "We need that report, but we will require a little more assistance from you than simply that."

"What kind of assistance?"

"We are not sure."

The rage surged through Avril, and she fought the urge to smash her phone against the wall. "What does that mean?" she growled.

"It means you have to be patient," the voice said. "I know that is difficult, but we think people will come to see you."

"Which people?"

"Investigators. Maybe doctors or even E.U. officials interested in the Limousin situation."

Of course, the mad cow disease outbreak! Avril remembered Yvette Pereau's husband's description of how his wife had become suspicious that someone had tampered with the farm. It had to be a cover-up. Her mind racing as fast as her heart, Avril asked, "And what do I tell them?"

"Nothing," the artificial voice said. "You have not come across anything out of the ordinary. And if the outside investigators have, then you must convince them that it *is* ordinary."

"And if they don't come at all?"

"Then we will send Frédéric back to you."

"Let me speak to him again."

"In good time, Detective."

"Now!"

There was a long pause, but Avril was crestfallen when the tinny voice spoke again. "We have your son. You do not. We do not want to hurt Frédéric, but we will if you force us. To ensure his safe return, you have to go back to Limoges and behave as though nothing is different. Tell absolutely no one. When the outside investigators arrive, convince them there is nothing to find in your sleepy province. And as soon as they leave, Frédéric will come home."

"I will do everything you say." Avril took a long slow breath. "I am an excellent detective. If Frédéric is harmed in any way, I will find you. I assure you. And I will—"

The line clicked, and she heard a beep. Her caller had already hung up.

25

We are late" were the only words Elise uttered when Noah met her in the hotel lobby. With one look, she made it poisonously clear that she was not interested in further discussion. For the thirty-kilometer trip west from Limoges to Saint Junien, only the radio's soft instrumental music masked the tense silence between them. Behind the wheel, Elise's eyes were locked on the road ahead, never once glancing in Noah's direction. He stared out the passenger window, barely conscious of the lush countryside. He still reeled from the news that Dr. Charron was trying to reach him within hours of the neurologist's fatal car crash.

As they neared the turnoff for Saint Junien, Noah spotted in the side mirror the same black Mercedes hanging a few hundred meters behind them as he had seen ten kilometers earlier. *Are we being followed in broad daylight?* Noah watched it intently, but when Elise turned off for the town, the Mercedes cruised past without following. His vigilance subsided slightly.

Through the passenger window, Noah noticed that Saint Junien was the prettiest town he had seen yet in

Limousin. Set among the pastoral rolling hills, the town's Romanesque buildings and historic houses looked as if they had sprung from the pages of a brochure or coffee table book.

Elise parked on the street in front of a row of stone houses with ivy snaking up the side. Silently, they climbed out of the car and walked the short gravel pathway to the door of the house. A willowy woman dressed completely in black greeted them at the door. She had wild gray hair and paint-spattered fingers. Noah wondered if she was an artist.

Elise made introductions, but Annette Tremblay did not shake hands with either visitor. Instead, she turned and led them into a living room that was crammed with sculptures, ceramics, and oil paintings, confirming Noah's first impression. She cleared two canvases off the chairs, creating enough space for the three of them to sit down.

Noah studied one of the landscape paintings that stood propped against the fireplace. Though depicting a sunny meadow, the splash of colors gave the painting a visceral wildness. "Did you paint this?" Noah asked.

"Hmmm," Tremblay grunted.

"Evocative," Noah said. "It reminds me of van Gogh."

"Dr. Haldane, if I want to talk art, I can do so with the paying American tourists at my gallery," Tremblay said in heavily accented English. "You came here to speak about my daughter."

Elise nodded somberly. "We're sorry for your loss, Mme. Tremblay."

Tremblay rolled her eyes but said nothing.

"Did Giselle live with you?" Noah asked.

"At times," Tremblay said.

"Was she living with you when she first showed symptoms?"

Slow to answer, Tremblay rubbed her face. "Yes."

"Can you tell us what it was like?" Elise asked.

Tremblay grimaced. "Picture hell, Mlle. Renard. That was what it was like."

Elise held out her palms. "Please . . ."

"Giselle went mad." Her eyes darted to Noah. "Just like your friend van Gogh."

"It would help us if you could be more specific," Elise said a little more firmly.

"Not sleeping. Not eating. Coming and going at all hours. And the paranoia! Giselle was convinced everyone was trying to poison her."

"Poison her?" Noah said.

"Yes," Tremblay snapped. "She thought her ex-boyfriend had poisoned her water, and we were all trying to kill her with it. She stopped drinking anything. I thought she might die of thirst. That was why I took her to hospital."

"Not because of her erratic behavior?" Elise asked.

Tremblay shook her head. "Giselle was manic-depressive. I had seen her act strangely before. All the doctors ever did was increase her lithium. I would have done the same, but I could not make her swallow the capsules."

Noah nodded. "And once she was hospitalized?"

"Of course, you must already know." Tremblay sighed. "Giselle grew worse and worse. Within a few weeks, she could not walk or even talk. She was just a . . . vegetable." She swallowed. "If I was braver, I would have taken a gun. It would have been less cruel."

"It must have been so very difficult for you." Elise reached out to touch Tremblay, but the woman recoiled from her hand.

"For me?" Tremblay squinted at Elise in outraged disbelief. "I went through nothing compared to what my daughter endured. *Nothing.*"

"Of course." Elise's hand fell to her lap.

Moments passed. "It was cruel irony, that this should happen to Giselle," Tremblay finally said.

"How so?" Elise asked.

"Giselle did not eat beef," she murmured.

Noah sat up straighter. "Was she a vegetarian?"

"Not entirely, but she did not like meat. She ate steak perhaps once a year. And that one time was enough for her to get sick. . . ."

Noah suspected that something with less infinitesimally small odds had to be at play. He leaned forward in his chair. "Did Giselle know either Philippe Manet or Benoît Gagnon?"

Tremblay shrugged. "My daughter was a pretty girl. And she *knew* many men, you understand. Especially when she was manic. What does it matter now?"

Noah fought back his urgent impatience. "I don't think that Giselle would have dated either man, but both are from the region," he said. "Do you recognize the names?"

Tremblay shook her head.

Noah stood to his feet. "Okay, well, thank you for your time, Mme. Tremblay."

Elise rose, too, but Tremblay leaned back in her seat, indifferent to her guests' impending departure. "The months before she became sick, Giselle was doing better. Almost a year had passed without an *episode*. She had a good job at the restaurant." She glanced at Noah with unconcealed hostility. "And then she fell in love with a man and everything went to hell."

"The boyfriend?" Elise asked. "The one she thought was trying to poison her?"

"The bastard went off on some scientific research trip and never came back. Giselle was heartbroken."

"Research?" Elise asked. "What did he do?"

Tremblay frowned. "I think he is a geologist or some such nonsense. I know that he really did bring her water from somewhere. Told her it was special. That it would help with her mental illness." She fired Noah another angry glance. "The way he treated her in the end . . . it was no wonder she thought the water was poisoned."

But Noah was oblivious to her resentment. His heart was pounding in his throat. "A geologist? *Was his name Georges Manet?*"

26

Though it was nearly midnight, Yulia Radvogin and Martine DeGroot walked away from the settlement in the brightness of early twilight. Time of day meant almost nothing at the height of the austral summer; it would not get any darker in the Antarctic for weeks to come.

Their boots crunched through the rare fresh dusting of snow onto ice that ran four kilometers thick and was built up from an accumulation of millions of years' worth of compressed snowfalls. Below the ice floor, Lake Vishnov gently swayed with an almost imperceptible tide that, like the planet's oceans, was dictated by the movement of the moon. And somewhere in the lake, a pipeline ran down from the Igloo, like a straw dipping into the world's largest Slurpee.

After a hundred or so meters, DeGroot turned to Radvogin. "You wanted to discuss something, Yulia?"

"Claude is not well?" Radvogin countered, ignoring DeGroot's question without slowing her pace.

"Something he ate, I'm sure," DeGroot said. "He'll be fine."

"No doubt. I've been here less than two days, and I'm

desperate for some fresh fruit and vegetables," Radvogin said with a sigh. "All this dried and canned food cannot be healthy. And it reminds me too much of my childhood in Kiev, living under the boots of those hopeless communists." She snorted in disgust. "Fresh produce did not exist for my family. It was saved for the commissars and the other *loyal* party members. The scum."

DeGroot chuckled. "Fresh produce and corrupt communists, is that what you wanted to discuss?"

Radvogin shot DeGroot a look that wiped the smile off the younger woman's face, though when she spoke, her voice was pleasant and conversational. "You remember when we first met in St. Petersburg?" Radvogin asked.

"Of course," DeGroot said. "I was awed by your natural authority."

Radvogin was indifferent to the compliment. "That day, you and Claude first presented your scheme for saving my investment here in the Antarctic. . . ." Her words drifted and her gaze fell on the horizon of ice.

DeGroot waited in silence.

"Claude is a competent enough scientist, I suppose," Radvogin continued. "Ah, but once he had that first taste of fame, he began to imagine himself as something more. Some kind of tycoon, I think. But he is not and never will be much of a businessman. I would have buried his Antarctic lab—and him, too—last summer."

"But you didn't."

Radvogin stopped and turned to DeGroot. "Because of you, Martine."

"Me?"

"From that very first meeting, I recognized something in you."

"A little of yourself, maybe?"

Radvogin laughed. "See, I wasn't mistaken! You remind me so much of myself from when I was . . . how old are you?"

"Thirty-two."

"Twenty years ago." Radvogin exhaled a puff of mist like it was cigarette smoke. "I had not even met Pavel yet, but I was already blinded with ambition. Exactly as you are." She turned to DeGroot, her pale eyes afire. "I didn't need Pavel to reach the level I have. Just as you don't need Claude."

DeGroot considered the comment. "Probably not, but they do make themselves useful from time to time."

Radvogin shook her head. "Only for a while. Trust me. And then you find a way to get rid of them." Her voice dripped with implication.

DeGroot nodded.

"Listen carefully, Martine." Radvogin's eyes locked on DeGroot like a missile engaging its target. "Perhaps because you remind me of myself, I do not trust you at all."

DeGroot shrugged, as if to say that wasn't her problem.

Radvogin swept her gloved hand back in the direction of the settlement and the Igloo. "I am committed now. You understand? It's not just the hundreds of millions that I have poured into the development of the infrastructure here in the Antarctic."

"No?"

"I have committed to advertising, shipping, bottling, distribution, and on and on. None of it can be undone. And the costs of this venture make oil exploration look cheap in comparison. I may be the CEO and majority shareholder of Radvogin Industries, but I still have to answer to the board. And the board is worried."

DeGroot tapped the back of one glove against the palm of the other. "The board has seen only the costs and none of the results yet. I have seen the product, Yulia. It is spectacular! In a few weeks, the Lake will reach the shelves of the best stores around the world. Can you imagine how quickly demand will grow for such pure water that possesses built-in healing properties?"

"I am banking on it."

"And so you should," DeGroot cried. "You've seen the results. They are phenomenal."

"I have seen nothing," Radvogin grunted. "I have only heard these stories from Claude and you."

"You don't believe us?"

"Belief is one thing, trust another." The older woman's eyes constricted. "For example, maybe you can explain what happened to the money."

"What money?"

"I've had Ivan Petrovich review the books for me," she said, using the traditional Russian name of her senior financial advisor. "According to him, there are millions of unaccounted dollars lost on this project."

DeGroot squared her shoulders to the woman. "What are you suggesting, Yulia?"

Radvogin leaned closer. She exhaled heavily enough to share the faint smell of pickled herring on her breath. "I am suggesting"—she emphasized each syllable—"that someone is fucking around with *my* money. And believe me, Martine, that is a deadly undertaking."

DeGroot didn't back off an inch. "We haven't embezzled from you, Yulia."

"Then where did my money go?"

"Research. Testing." DeGroot paused a moment and stared deep into Radvogin's eyes. "And *persuasion*. The kind of things you probably wouldn't want to see on your books."

"Things that come without receipts?"

DeGroot nodded.

"I will let it go." Radvogin pulled her face back from DeGroot's. "For now."

"Thank you, Yulia."

Radvogin turned and strode in the direction of the Igloo. DeGroot waited a moment, and then hurried to catch up with her. Without looking over to her, Radvogin said,

"Martine, even at thirty-two, if I were in your shoes I would recognize one thing about this whole venture."

"Which is?"

Radvogin's head swiveled and her eyes bored into De-Groot. "That I would not survive failure."

27

Saint Junien, France. January 19

As they pulled away from Annette Tremblay's home, Noah was gripped by a sense of time bleeding away, especially now that they had unearthed a connection between the known victims. With all the unexplained occurrences, Noah realized Gwen was right: He had to go to the police. And he planned to, though he had yet to decide whether to let Elise in on his intent.

Elise broke the chilled silence. "It's surprising, *non*?"

Noah turned slowly to look at her. "What's that?"

"That the Manet family is somehow the link to all three victims."

"We have to find Georges Manet. Urgently."

She nodded without looking at him. "And we need to visit the sister again."

"Yes." He studied her profile with her lightly freckled skin and perfectly upturned nose. Even when she was brooding her attractiveness still shone through. "I don't think Giselle Tremblay could have beaten the odds that badly."

"It would appear not."

"I *mean*," Noah stressed, "for her to acquire vCJD from

eating steak—and muscle is by far the lowest-risk tissue for prions—once a year . . . the odds are too small to imagine. Same for Benoît Gagnon."

Elise didn't try to argue. "You think she was poisoned by Georges Manet?" she asked, her tone unreadable.

Noah shrugged. "I would like to know more about that water he gave her, though. In the videotape I saw at the hospital, Georges's brother Philippe talked about water, too."

Elise glanced at him. "But he was . . . psychotic, no?"

"So I supposed," he conceded. "Psychotic patients often share remarkably similar paranoid delusions— transmitters in their dental fillings, the Devil stalking them, loved ones trying to poison them, and so on. But this is yet another huge coincidence."

Elise showed a hint of a smile. "Another wrench, too. You think there is any room left in your hardware store?"

Noah showed her a slight smile. "The shelves are pretty full."

Elise's cell phone rang, and she pulled one hand off the wheel and dug it out of her coat pocket. "*Allo?*" She paused a moment. "*Ah, Maurice. Ça va?*"

Noah listened, trying to translate Elise's side of the conversation. They exchanged a few more pleasantries. Then Elise mentioned Noah's name and asked Maurice whether he would mind if she put him on speakerphone. After a moment, Elise hit a button on her cell phone and the speaker hummed with low static. "Professor Maurice Hébert with the Institut National de la Recherche Agronomique, allow me to introduce Dr. Noah Haldane with the World Health Organization," she said and then glanced at Noah. "Maurice performed the autopsies on many of the involved animals."

"It is a pleasure, Dr. Haldane," Hébert gushed. "I am a true admirer of yours."

"You might be the only one in France," Noah said.

"Nonsense, my friend! You must have been under enormous pressure with the ARCS virus. I thought you handled it beautifully." Hébert's smooth French accent reminded Noah of Jean Nantal, and he warmed to the veterinarian immediately.

"Thank you."

"Elise tells me you are interested in the cows with bovine spongiform encephalitis, yes?"

"That's right." Noah measured his words. "We are seeing some inconsistencies in the human vCJD cases in Limousin."

"I understand that people are dying very rapidly of their disease," Hébert said. "Much quicker than anything seen before."

"Exactly," Noah said. "Have you seen the same in the cows?"

"Of course, my friend, it is a little different with animals. We destroy them at the first sign of illness." Hébert chuckled. "You probably cannot get away with that in people."

"Probably not," Noah said. "Still, what is your impression of the brains you have seen so far?"

"My impression is that, without question, all the cases have been classic for BSE."

"Nothing out of the ordinary?" Noah asked.

"Absolutely nothing." Hébert paused. "Except possibly that compared to other cases I have dissected, the brains I have seen so far are in relatively early stages of the disease."

"Early?" Noah's stomach knotted. "That is the opposite of the human cases."

"Ah, but it is apples and oranges, my friend," Hébert said. "In the region, everyone is on the lookout for new bovine cases. As a result, we are more likely to catch the infected cows earlier. And, of course, the cows responsible for the human cases were butchered and went to market. We will never know what their brains would have looked like under a microscope."

"Good point," Noah said, but his gut didn't settle. "What do you make of the relatively few cases—seven so far—diagnosed among the region's cattle?"

"That is unusual," Hébert admitted. "As you know, in the other outbreaks with human cross-infectivity we saw significantly higher rates of infection among the livestock."

"They are still early in the testing in Paris." Elise spoke up. "It is possible they will find many more cases among the destroyed cows that we were not aware of."

"Vraiment, Elise," Hébert agreed. "And we cannot forget the possibility that some farms might not have been so forthcoming."

"You mean, they might have hidden other infected cows?" Noah said.

Hébert's heavy breath whistled through the speaker. "People do stupid and reckless things when they are afraid."

"Very true," Noah said, thinking of more than just desperate farmers. "Maurice, I assume you measured the standard chemical levels."

"Of course," he said. "The fourteen-three-three protein and PrPres markers were both positive, as expected, in the bovine spinal fluid."

"And what about the levels of phosphorylated tau protein?" Noah asked.

Hébert's breath caught noisily in surprise. "We don't normally test for that in animals."

"But you can?" Noah asked.

"Of course," Hébert said. "Though, I do not see the point. It is always elevated in BSE."

"I know." Noah thought of how the molecule was *not*

elevated in Limousin's human cases. "But do you mind confirming that for me?"

"For you, my friend?" He laughed again. "There is no test I would not run. Give me twenty-four hours. I will have your answer."

28

Seoul, South Korea. January 19

Han Soo Kim closed the shutters across her shop's windows. Her husband, a businessman who had inherited his fortune, had leased the prime space for the boutique health store on Fashion Street in the ultrachic Cheongdam district. Kim knew that her husband viewed the venture as nothing more than a pricey distraction for her—his third, and much younger, wife. She was determined to show him otherwise. Kim desperately wanted to be free of the disdainful glances from the other wives in their social circle. She was not merely a trophy and she intended to prove it, pouring her heart and soul into her store.

Kim turned from the window and hurried back to her laptop computer, her chest swelling with anticipation. For the first time, she had let herself dream about branching out with several more shops across Seoul and throughout the peninsula.

She studied the online order form that filled the screen. Unlike Kim, most of her patrons had never known anything but prosperity. They would not blink at the one-hundred-thousand-won price tag she planned to charge per bottle of the Lake.

Pure Antarctic water enriched with natural minerals was exactly the kind of product that would cause a stir among Kim's clientele. And she knew that these women were nothing if not competitive. When one or two of them bought a few bottles, the rush would be unstoppable.

Then no other wife would be able to accuse Kim of surviving on her youthful good looks alone.

Her fingers trembled with excitement as she tapped on the keyboard, changing her order from one thousand to two thousand bottles.

29

By the time Noah and Elise reached the hotel, the sun had begun to set. When the slow elevator finally opened on the fifth floor, Noah nodded his good-bye to Elise and left without another word.

Inside his room, he had a quick glance around but saw nothing out of place. The reassurance was hollow, though. He knew that his "shadow" would be unlikely to leave another calling card. The thought even occurred to him that the displaced bookmark might not have been an oversight. *Did someone leave it for me as a warning?* he wondered grimly.

Exhausted from the emotional roller coaster of the day, he longed to climb under the covers, but he could not shake the sense of time sifting away. He reached into his jacket and extracted the notebook that he now carried with him everywhere. He scribbled pages of notes from the interview with Benoît Gagnon's lover and Giselle Tremblay's mother, including a description of Giselle's and Philippe's similar obsession with water.

Satisfied, he closed the notebook and stuffed it back into his jacket. He glanced at his watch and calculated that it would be one o'clock in the afternoon in South Carolina. He picked up the phone and dialed Anna's parents' number from memory.

"Hi," the little voice chirped.

"Chloe!"

"Daddy-o!" she shrieked.

Noah was flooded with affection. "Chlo, how's my girl? I heard a bee stung you. You okay?"

"A hornet, Daddy, and it was no biggie," she said with a worldliness she must have absorbed from one of her favorite preteen, or tweenie, shows that she watched religiously. "The hornets won't get me again, because I can swim underwater now."

"Cool."

"Mommy says we have to go home in two days, but I want to stay here."

"Don't you miss home?"

She hesitated. "Will you be home, Daddy?"

The innocent words tore at his heart. "Not for a little while longer."

"Then I want to stay here. It's too cold in Washington. Why does anyone live there?"

"Good question." Noah laughed.

They discussed school and friends, and for fifteen minutes the vCJD crisis slipped out of mind and Noah relived the carefree happiness of their Mexican vacation. Then he asked, "Hon, can I speak to your mom now?"

"Her and Julie went shopping with Granna. Gramps is here. Want to talk to him?"

"That's okay, Chlo," Noah said, brought down to the earth by the reminder that Julie had fully replaced him on this family vacation. "I love you. Can't wait to see you again."

"Right back atcha, Daddy-o!" she said, stealing another line from one of her shows.

Noah ordered a light dinner from room service. He

decided that the WHO could splurge on a nice bottle of wine and chose a pinot noir from the Alsace region. While waiting for dinner, he opened his laptop and read his e-mail. He was pleased to see a brief message from Gwen sent from her BlackBerry that read: GOOD TO TALK TO YOU TODAY. MY OFFER STILL STANDS. REGARDLESS, COME HOME SAFE SOON. GWEN.

He thought for a moment and then began his reply. RIGHT BACK ATCHA, he typed, recycling Chloe's phrase. APPRECI-ATE THE OFFER, BUT IT'S NOT NECESSARY. FAR RATHER SEE YOU AT HOME. I MIGHT EVEN SPRING FOR DINNER.

Then he composed a brief e-mail for Jean, which read: JEAN, WE NEED TO DISCUSS DEVELOPMENTS IN PERSON. HERE OR THERE?

He exited his e-mail and launched the Internet browser. He searched for the Limoges police department and found an address and phone number for Gendarmerie Limoges. He decided there was no point in calling them until morning when he was more likely to reach a detective.

Dinner arrived and Noah picked at it with little appe-tite. He had just filled his second glass of wine when the bedside phone rang. He reached for it. "Noah Haldane," he said.

"It has been a long day," Elise said without a word of greeting. "I deserve a glass of wine. I think you do, too."

"I'm holding mine already."

"Wine is better shared," she said. "Will you join me at the bar?"

"As you said, it's been a long one. I'm beat," he said, thinking it might be best not to see Elise until he had spo-ken to the police.

"Of course." She cleared her throat. "I will see you in the morning, then."

The trace of vulnerability in her voice was enough to break his resolve. "You know what? How could another glass of wine hurt?"

"I will save a table."

Noah finished his second glass of wine and then headed for the door. With his hand on the handle, he had a sudden twinge of suspicion and went back to grab his jacket and the notebook tucked inside.

By the time Noah reached the bar, Elise had already claimed the corner table. A bottle of red stood on the tabletop and an empty glass awaited him on the other side. Wearing jeans and a black blouse, she sat holding a wineglass that was down to its last drops. He noticed her flushed cheeks and the uncharacteristic carefree sparkle in her eyes. He assumed she was beyond her first glass.

She raised the glass to him. "Welcome."

He smiled as he dropped onto the stool across from her. A waiter arrived and refilled Elise's glass and, with a nod from Noah, filled his, too. They toasted silently. Noah had a sip of the subtly dry wine. Elise cleared her throat. "I am sorry, Noah."

He shook his head. "I was the one who overstepped my bounds."

"And I was the one who overreacted." She smiled disarmingly. "You just . . . touched a nerve. . . . Is that the right expression?"

Noah nodded.

She looked away. "Javier and I do have a history," she said quietly.

"Elise, you don't have to—"

"It is so common, it is almost expected for people of his standing," she continued as if Noah had never spoken. "Affairs here are more . . . accepted . . . than in America. But I never saw myself as being someone's mistress! Javier and I worked so many long hours together. I wish I could blame him for what happened. The truth is that it was as much my fault. I broke my own rules." She smiled down at the table. "I know that he is a politician inside and out, but he is also a charming, caring man. And we fell in love." Her smile faded and her voice dropped. "Or, at least, *I* fell in love."

Noah fingered the stem of his glass. "Is it over now?" he asked gently.

Elise shrugged. "I thought so. He has a young family. We both knew it was for the best that we stop. And for months we did, but then that night in Paris, before our meeting, he came to my room to talk. . . ." She shook her head. "It should never have happened."

Noah finished the last of his glass. "It's never easy, is it?"

Elise looked up at him, her eyes slightly reddened but still burning. "You wanted to know why I was not 'more assertive' at our meeting. I think it was maybe because I was confused, distracted . . . and a little embarassed." She drained her glass again and placed it gently on the table. "I hope that doesn't make you uncomfortable, but I felt I needed to tell you. I want you to be able to trust me again."

Noah met her stare. "And I want to trust you."

"You do not, though," she said with matter-of-fact frankness.

"I think there's a leak on our side."

She viewed him impassively. "And I am it?"

"Not necessarily. But somewhere in the chain of command in the E.U., I believe, sensitive information is getting out to the wrong people."

The waiter came by and refilled both of their glasses. After he left, Elise leaned forward in her chair and spoke in a quieter tone. "I agree, Noah, that is one possible explanation."

"One?"

"Has it occurred to you that the leak might be on *your* side?" she asked.

Noah straightened, taken aback. "At the WHO?"

"Why not?" she said. "You have been keeping Jean abreast of our investigation, have you not?"

"Jean?" Noah laughed at the thought. "I would trust my life in his hands. In fact, I have."

"And you are probably right to do so," she said. "Surely, Jean reports to others in the WHO. Your information would be shared, *non?*"

"Jean does not have to report to anyone at the WHO. And he's extremely discreet," Noah said with an edge, but even as he spoke the words he realized she had a point. He could not disregard the possibility that the leak could have happened through the director's office. Troubled, he drained the rest of the glass.

She studied him. Her smile was as warm as any he had seen from her. "Noah, I am not the enemy," she said.

He sighed. "There is so much left unexplained here in Limousin."

"We are making progress, *non?*"

The waiter arrived again and poured the last of the bottle into her glass. Wordlessly, Elise nodded for a new bottle, and the server picked up the empty one and headed off to replace it. Already buzzed from the wine, and longing for someone to vent to, Noah said, "Dr. Charron was trying to reach me."

She tilted her head. "When?"

"The night he died. Within an hour and a half of his death."

Her forehead creased into a deep frown. "Wasn't he drunk when he died?"

"Exactly."

"Did he leave a message?"

Noah shook his head.

She put down the glass and touched the tabletop gingerly as if it might be too hot. "Then how do you know he called you?"

Noah told her about the missed calls on his cell phone. And then he said, "You never met him, Elise, but believe me: He was not the kind of guy to call unless he had something important to share."

She nodded. "Maybe he wanted to tell you about his conversation with Michel Dieppe, and how he discovered the relationship between the two male victims?"

"Maybe," he said gravely. "Or maybe he had uncovered something else."

Her mouth parted in surprise. "Dr. Charron's accident? You don't think that someone might have . . ."

"I don't know."

Her hand trembled slightly as she brought the glass to her mouth.

"Elise, I am going to the police with what I know." He realized it might have sounded as though he defied her to stop him, but he did not qualify the remark.

"I think we have to."

Her unexpected agreement relaxed him. "Maybe we are on the same side, after all." He laughed.

Her frown gave way to another grin. "I have been trying to tell you that."

She raised her glass, and they clinked rims. "To new beginnings," she said.

"Salut," he replied.

Elise's cheeks burned redder. "You mentioned that you and your wife separated last year. I know it is none of my business, but I was wondering—"

"Another woman," Noah said.

"Oh," Elise said with surprise. "And have you and this woman—"

"I wasn't the one who left for the other woman."

Elise squinted in confusion. Then her eyes lit with understanding and she fought back a laugh. "I—I am sorry," she stammered. "I don't mean to make light of it. I just did not expect that."

"You didn't expect it? How do you think I felt?" Noah

said, and after a pause, they exploded in uproarious laughter.

As they finished the second bottle of wine, their conversation drifted toward more drunken confidences. They exchanged horror stories of previous romances gone awry. And Elise's Belgian accent grew more pronounced as she began to slur her words slightly. "You know that evening when Javier came to my room in Paris?" she said with a conspiratorial tone. "I phoned him."

"Oh?" Noah lowered his glass.

"I had seen Duncan and you in the bar earlier." She looked down. "You had not invited me. And I was feeling a little left out."

Noah reached across and patted the back of her hand. "We were discussing heavy family issues. I don't think you would have wanted to join us."

She grabbed his hand and gave it a squeeze.

Noah squeezed back before releasing the grip and pulling his hand back. "Listen, Elise. It's late. And we're drunk."

She nodded. "And tomorrow is a big, big day. *C'est ça?*"

"*Oui.*" Noah looked up and pantomimed signing to the waiter, who hurried over with the already printed bill. With a drunken squiggle, Noah left a generous tip.

On the way to the elevator, Elise swayed slightly on her feet. A couple of times, she leaned into Noah before she regained her footing. The elevator was empty when they stepped inside, but Elise stood very close. Noah pressed the buttons for the fifth and sixth floors. The doors closed. As the elevator jerked into motion, she stumbled forward and caught herself bumping against him. But rather than step back, she leaned even closer. Her wine-scented breath tickled his cheek. And when her eyes found his, they were inviting. She parted her lips a fraction and then pressed them against his.

Noah returned the kiss, enjoying the warm wetness and the sweet taste of her lips. Her tentative pressure gave way to a deeper kiss, and her arms wrapped around his back.

The implication of their contact hit Noah with a start, as sudden sobriety descended on him. He pulled his face away from hers and gently wriggled free of her embrace. Holding her arm in his hands, he said, "Elise, this is not . . ." But he ran out of words.

She backtracked two steps and stared at the floor. "Of course," she said softly. "It would be inappropriate."

The pleasant taste of her breath still lingered on his lips, but in his mind, Noah pictured Gwen's alluring smile, eyes brimming with desire and her upper teeth gently biting down on her lower lip. Confused, he mumbled, "I think it might look different for both of us in the morning."

She viewed him almost wistfully. "Lately, I have come to dread the mornings."

30

The sky couldn't decide between snow and rain, so instead flip-flopped between both. The wet flurries clung to Avril's coat and soaked through to her skin. Oblivious to the cold, she stood at her husband's grave and stared at the white lilies that lay by his headstone. Antoine had never had much interest in flowers, but the lilies were her favorite; she brought them with her every visit, regardless of the season.

Avril was grateful for the miserable weather. It kept everyone else away from the sprawling cemetery, located on the western outskirts of the city. For the first time since Frédéric's abduction, she felt safe to speak her fears aloud.

"This is my fault, Antoine. If I hadn't interfered in his life, Frédéric would have not broken up with Stéphane. Then that awful woman wouldn't have been able to lure him away like she did." The detective in her realized that the kidnappers would have probably found other means to get at her son, but the insight didn't diminish her crushing guilt. Avril glanced over to the empty plot beside her husband's grave. "I would crawl in there right now beside

you, Antoine, if I knew they would only let him go, but—"
The words caught in her throat, and a tear joined the icy
streaks coursing down her cheeks. "Once I do everything
they need of me, they will kill our boy and then they will
come for me." She swallowed. "And if I don't do as they
ask . . ." She could not even finish the sentence.

Avril wiped the wetness from her cheeks. "I will find
him, Antoine, but I need time. It's the only way. I have to
stall. If I can somehow keep those E.U. investigators
around here, then maybe . . ." Kneeling lower, she touched
the lilies' already soggy petals and let her fingers brush
over the muddy grass of the grave. "Someone told them I
was investigating those missing women. Perhaps it was
one of the people I interviewed in Montmagnon about
Pauline? Perhaps even Yvette Pereau's husband or her former lover?" She shook her head so hard that drops of
precipitation sprayed from her hair. "No. It must have
come from somewhere within the Gendarmerie. Only another policeman could have known what I was up to.
What threat I might pose." She recalled André Pereau's
description of his wife's concerns. "Yvette Pereau wanted
to go to the police, Antoine," she whispered. *"Perhaps
she did!* Maybe that was why she 'disappeared.'"

Avril touched the grass over his grave again. "Our
boy . . ." She looked up to the heavens, but she was done
praying. She straightened up and wiped the dirt from her
fingers. "I don't know whom to trust. I will have to do this
alone."

She blew the headstone a kiss and then turned away.
She hurried across the grass to the parking lot, her boots
noisily sinking in the sleet and mud with each step. Her
foot had barely touched pavement when she heard the
Chopin melody from her pocket.

"Maman."

Her pulse shot up. "Frédéric, are you all right?"

"I am okay." His voice was calmer than before. "The

phone booth at the corner of the rue Jean Jaurès and rue du Temple, Maman."

"What about it?"

For a fleeting elated moment, she thought Frédéric might be waiting there, but the hope was dashed as quickly as it rose. "Be there in five minutes, Maman." His tone verged on detached, and Avril feared that he was in a state of shock.

"Listen to me, Frédéric," she said. "Everything will be okay. Just do as they say, and you will be home soon."

"Five minutes," he repeated emotionlessly, and then the line clicked.

Sliding on the sleek pavement, Avril sprinted for her car. At the door, she fumbled with the keys before dropping into the driver's seat. She started the engine and hit the accelerator. The tires skidded a moment before the car lurched out of its parking spot.

As she wove and dodged through the mercifully light traffic, Avril understood why the kidnappers had sent her on this wild ride. She had intended to trace her own cell phone to pinpoint the source of the calls, but they must have thought of that. By giving her an impossibly tight time frame, she had no time to organize a trace on the pay phone, either.

She checked her watch. Six minutes. *Merde!*

She took the corner hard onto rue du Temple. Her car slid, bounced off the curb, and almost slammed into the lamppost beside it. As soon as the wheels straightened, Avril punched the accelerator and the car fishtailed down the street. She swerved up to the designated intersection and hopped out of her car, leaving the key in the ignition.

The phone was already ringing when her hand gripped the receiver. "Yes?" she spat.

"Detective Avars?" It was the same electronic voice as the previous call, but Avril had no way of knowing whether the person behind the voice changer was the same.

"Yes," Avril puffed.

"Have you told anyone else about our *situation*?"

"No."

"You are a smart woman, Detective Avars."

You will learn just how smart, Avril thought. "Frédéric did not sound right when I spoke to him just now."

"He is fine."

"He better be."

"Detective, you are in no position to threaten."

"Think of it as a promise," Avril said through clenched teeth.

"No need," the tinny voice soothed. "Frédéric will be home soon."

"When?"

"Within a day or two." The caller paused. "Unless, of course, you try to find him. In which case, he won't come home at all."

Avril swallowed away the sudden lump in her throat. *Be calm,* she told herself. *Think.*

"Have you completed your investigation into the missing women?" the voice asked.

"I have."

"And?"

"There is no evidence of foul play in Pauline Lamaire's disappearance," Avril said. "Perhaps she got lost on a walk and fell into one of the rivers, lakes, or gullies near her home. Perhaps she has traveled off somewhere in search of a miracle cure for her arthritis. Regardless, it is no longer a police matter."

"And Yvette Pereau?"

"Is not missing at all. She merely ran away from her husband to meet a lover in Amsterdam. She told me as much when I interviewed her yesterday."

"Will your colleagues now consider the matter closed?"

"They already do."

"Good," the caller said. "Now we need you to stay close to the Gendarmerie."

"Why?"

"We believe your visitors will arrive soon."

"Who?"

"An American doctor, Noah Haldane, and a Belgian woman, Elise Renard," the caller said. "When they come, you are to ensure they end up in your office."

"And how do I do that?"

"Be resourceful, Detective. Think how it will expedite Frédéric's release."

Avril exhaled slowly, considering her next move.

"Remember, Detective, you are to convince the visitors that there is nothing out of the ordinary in Limoges."

"What if they have evidence to the contrary?"

"They will not. At most, they will offer you a few coincidences."

Avril's thoughts raced. "If I dismiss them too easily, that might make them suspicious, true? I will at least need to appear to follow up on their information."

There was a pause. "If it is necessary, but you will do it quickly and convincingly."

"Of course." It was the opening she sought. "Meantime, I need guarantees."

"Guarantees?" the voice rattled.

"Frédéric is to call me twice a day, at eight A.M. and eight P.M.," she said. "If I do not hear from Frédéric at those times, I will assume . . ." She swallowed again. "The worst. And I will take all that I know to anyone who will listen, including the visitors."

"Listen, Detective, you are toying with your son's future—"

"I will speak to you at eight o'clock," she cut the caller off in midthreat. With a trembling hand, she deposited the receiver back into the cradle.

"It's the only way, my love," she whispered.

31

Limoges, France. January 20

The doors to the elevator opened, and Noah spotted Elise, legs crossed and reclining on a couch while reading a magazine. His head throbbed and he still could taste the wine in the back of his throat. The memory of their sensuous kiss also reminded him of how abruptly their night had ended, and the self-consciousness he felt grew with each step nearer.

Elise lowered her magazine and rose to greet him. There were slight bags under her eyes, but her cheeks held a healthy flush and she looked otherwise as fresh as her citrus fragrance smelled. Her polite smile didn't hint at any of the discomfort that Noah was experiencing. "Did you sleep all right?" she asked pleasantly.

"I'm not sure if 'sleep' is the right word for it, but I was out for a good while." He broke off the eye contact. "And you?"

She shrugged. "I usually sleep well after wine."

"Then you must have been in a coma last night."

Her eyes widened in momentary amusement. Despite his embarrassment, Noah was struck again by her natural beauty. He cleared his throat. "Listen, Elise, I wanted to, um, clarify about last night. I hope you understand—"

"We were drunk, Noah. It happens." Her offhand dismissal of their encounter bruised his ego, but Noah was relieved to hear that the evening would not spill over into their professional relationship. "Sylvie Manet is expecting us." She turned and headed for the door.

Noah followed. "You spoke to Sylvie already?"

"This morning. She sounded eager to see us again."

"Why eager?"

"She wanted to discuss her brother."

"Philippe?"

Elise shook her head. "Georges. Sylvie is worried about him."

Noah's back tightened. "About what?"

"She said she would explain in person."

Stepping out of the hotel, Noah was hit by a gust of moist wind. Though the air temperature had warmed considerably, the dampness brought a different kind of chill. They hurried halfway up the street where Elise's BMW was parked. Together, they swept the wet snow off the windshield and climbed inside. As Elise pulled out of the parking spot, Noah checked over his shoulder, searching for a black Mercedes, but he saw only two or three cars and a couple of vans.

Two blocks later, they turned onto a busier street, and in the side mirror Noah spotted a silver Audi sedan that made the same turn ten seconds behind them. The sight of the car cemented his resolve. "After we see Sylvie, we're going to the police," he said.

Elise glanced sidelong at him. "As I said last night, I agree that it is time we do."

Noah had not intended it as a challenge, but rather than explain he held up a hand in apology. "Glad we agree."

Sylvie Manet met them at the door to her Lac Noir family home and led them into the ornate living room, explaining that her mother was still in the hospital. Following Sylvie's example, Noah and Elise sat down in the wingback Louis XV chairs in front of the fireplace, which sparked and crackled even louder than on their previous visit, but Noah was glad for the warmth. Like Elise, he declined Sylvie's offer of tea.

Sylvie wore a gray sweatshirt and jeans. With her short black hair gelled back against her head, she looked scrubbed and free of makeup. Her slender hands cupped a mug of tea close to her flat chest. As she listened to Noah and Elise describe how her family linked all three of the vCJD victims, her brow furrowed and her intense almond eyes burned with concern.

"I have never heard of Benoît Gagnon," Sylvie said. "No surprise, though. Philippe never discussed his love life. Georges and I knew for ages that our brother was gay, but he insisted on hiding it from Maman." She sounded disappointed. Studying her androgynous physique and style, Noah wondered if Sylvie might share her brother's sexual orientation. "Philippe never brought any of his boyfriends home."

Elise nodded.

"And the water?" Noah asked.

Sylvie sipped her tea slowly. "During Philippe's illness he used to go on and on about water and fire, but it never made much sense. I thought he was . . ."

"Delusional?" Elise offered.

"Something like that," Sylvie muttered.

"What about Giselle Tremblay?" Noah asked.

"I knew her name sounded familiar before." She nodded to herself. "Georges mentioned her once or twice. A local girl, I believe."

"From Saint Junien," Elise said.

"That's right. When he came back to town last summer, he began dating her. I don't think it was too serious, though."

"Why do you say that?" Elise asked.

"Georges was heading back to the Arctic to spend the fall and winter there on a new research project." Sylvie sighed. "My older brother is a charmer, but with his research and travel, he never settles down. He has not had a serious girlfriend in years. Philippe and I used to tease him that ice is far more precious to him than people."

"Do you know anything about the water that Giselle's mother claims Georges gave her?" Noah asked.

"This is the first I have heard of it. Though, most of last summer when Georges was home in Lac Noir, I was working in the lab in Bordeaux. I hardly saw him." Sylvie frowned. "You don't think it's related to her illness, do you? It was only water, Dr. Haldane."

"We are simply being thorough," Elise said.

But Noah knew there was more to it than just thoroughness. "Where was Georges before the summer?" he asked.

Sylvie squinted in concentration. "I get confused. Was he in the Arctic last spring? I am not entirely sure. And in the winter he might have been in Antarctica. He often does research there during our winter, their summer."

"Does he routinely bring back samples from his expeditions?" Noah asked.

"I am afraid my brother is a real collector." Sylvie offered the kind of embarrassed smile reserved for discussing a close relative's eccentricity. "Not only research samples, either. He also brings back Eskimo art and all sorts of things he stumbles across on his trip. Since I am a biologist, he often brings me home samples of the arctic flora." She turned her palms up. "Even though it's of no real use to me."

"Sylvie, we need to speak to Georges," Noah said urgently.

Sylvie put her mug down on the table in front of her. The worry creased her face deeper than before. "Ever since your last visit, I have been trying to reach him. He hasn't replied to any of my e-mails."

"When did he last write?"

"Two weeks ago."

"Where was he?" Noah asked.

"He has been stuck for months at an observatory north of the Arctic Circle. A place called Axel Heiberg Island." She sighed. "It is dark twenty-four hours a day there now. The storms have been particularly bad this winter. The icebreakers have not been able to get through. I am worried about him, Dr. Haldane."

"Is he with others?" Elise asked.

"I don't know," Sylvie admitted. "He mentioned earlier that he was traveling with a graduate student. But Georges often does his research alone. I am afraid he is somewhat of a . . ."

"Lone wolf?" Noah offered.

Sylvie grimaced. "Pardon me?"

"It means someone who likes to work alone," Noah explained.

"D'accord." Sylvie nodded. "He is very experienced in living in extreme climates. This is not the first time he has been snowed in. And he always carries enough food and supplies to last a winter."

Noah eyed her steadily. "But?"

Instead of answering, Sylvie rose from her chair and hurried toward the staircase at the far end of the room. Noah and Elise watched her go and then turned to one another with the same bewildered expression. They heard the patter of rapid footsteps on the floor above them, and a few moments later Sylvie came rushing back into the room, clutching a piece of paper.

She handed it to Noah. It was a printout of an e-mail, though the text was in French. Elise leaned over and gently pulled the page from his hand. "From your brother?" she asked.

"Yes," Sylvie said.

Elise studied the page. "From twelve days ago." Then she began translating for Noah. " 'Dear Sylvie. Conditions are no better. The storm shows no sign of letting up. I don't know when I will be able to get out. And the ships cannot reach me for weeks, maybe months.' " Elise paused. " 'I never minded the constant darkness before. I used to sleep so well, but I am hardly sleeping now. I keep thinking of Philippe. He was dying so horribly, and his big brother was not there for him. Not even at his funeral. I feel awful about that. And now Maman is in hospital, and I cannot see her. If anything happens to her . . . Syl, I am embarrassed to tell you, but I cry all the time now. I am not getting any research done. Maybe it's because I don't sleep but my thinking is not clear. And I am having trouble remembering things.' "

Elise glanced up from the page and briefly locked eyes with Noah. He knew Elise was wondering, as he was, if Georges might already be infected with the prion.

Elise returned her attention to the page and resumed her translation. " 'All I want is to come home to be with you and Maman. I don't know how much longer I can wait this out.' " She cleared her throat and then continued. " 'Ah, listen to me complain. I sound like an old woman, don't I? I am going to stop feeling sorry for myself now and try to get back to work. In the meantime, cheer me up, Syl, and tell me what is new and exciting in your life. Send my love to Maman. Love, Georges.' " She lowered the page.

Noah turned to Sylvie. "You haven't heard from Georges since?"

Sylvie shook her head. "His messages have sounded like that for a while. I thought he was depressed because of Philippe, Maman, and the storms. Then you came to see me with all this talk of the prion." She stared at him, her eyes searching his for reassurance. "You don't think that what he said about his memory troubles . . ."

Noah measured his words. "I don't know, Sylvie, but we have to find him soon."

"I even tried to raise him on his satellite phone, but I could not get through." Sylvie folded her thin arms across her chest and seemed to sink into her chair.

Noah mustered a smile. "We'll find him. Meanwhile, we need to know more about that water he brought home last summer. Do you have any idea where Georges kept his research samples?"

Again, without replying or even looking at Noah, she rose from her chair. This time there was no urgency in her step as she trudged toward the kitchen. Noah and Elise followed. Sylvie stopped in front of the refrigerator and opened the freezer door. She rummaged through the crowded contents. When she pulled her hand out, she held a labeled freezer bag.

Noah took the small bag from her hand, surprised by the weight of it. He read the words on the label aloud: *"Arctic, échantillon 0411B2307."*

"Échantillon means sample," Elise translated for him.

He raised it up to eye level and studied the translucent hunk of ice with its bluish hue. Staring at it, he wondered if the source of the death and suffering in Limousin might somehow be suspended among its glacial crystals.

Sylvie found a small cooler in the cupboard and they packed the little bag in ice. Silently, she walked her visitors to the door. They offered her a few hollow reassurances about her brother. With a promise to contact them as soon as she heard from him, Sylvie shut the door behind them.

The cooler carefully stored in the backseat of her car, Elise drove them away from Lac Noir. Once on the highway, Noah checked over either shoulder but did not spot any silver or black sedans in the vicinity. Elise looked at him out of the corner of her eye. "Do you think that piece of glacier holds the answer to this outbreak?"

"No idea." Noah turned to her. "But we'd better get that ice off to the Institut Pasteur for urgent analysis."

She nodded almost imperceptibly.

"Elise, let's assume there are people deliberately meddling with this investigation."

"All right."

"Why?"

"I can think of one possibility," she said. "After all, the cattle trade is a major industry in France. In all of Europe."

"I realize." Noah's eyes were drawn to the mirror, as he again searched for a tail. "The French cattle trade is already in disarray. The ban aside, the public is spooked. Beef sales always plummet after an outbreak of BSE." He turned back to Elise. "So how does derailing our investigation help the industry?"

"You heard Javier. Now that we've pinpointed the source to Ferme d'Allaire, the E.U. is considering lifting its ban."

Noah nodded. "I see. If other farms have been hiding their sick cows, and they can make Ferme d'Allaire the sole scapegoat . . ."

Elise tapped the steering wheel. "Then maybe they can minimize the financial damage."

"And maximize the human risk," Noah said, almost wishing it were so simple. "It still doesn't explain what happened to Louis Charron."

"We don't know that anything more than alcohol and poor judgment were involved in the accident."

Noah grunted. "You think Charron was calling me because he didn't want to drink alone?"

"He wouldn't be the only one to make that mistake," Elise said, flushing slightly and focusing her eyes back on the road.

He shook his head. "Charron had something important to tell me. I am certain of it."

"Maybe he came to the same conclusion we did," she said. "Maybe he found something that pointed toward a cover-up of the extent of this outbreak."

Cover-up. The word resonated deep within Noah. "Wait a minute, Elise. What if . . ."

"What, Noah?"

He hesitated to put his thoughts into words. "What if the mad cow disease is a red herring?"

"A red herring?" She squinted. "I do not understand."

"I mean, what if the illness among the cattle was used to mislead us?" Noah nodded to himself. "Don't forget, the bovine cases came after the human case. And you heard what your friend Maurice said. The affected cows have not shown nearly as advanced a stage of the disease."

Elise viewed him silently.

"All the human victims are now connected," Noah went on. "Then there is the issue of the water that seemed to affect Philippe Manet and Giselle Tremblay. And, just maybe, Georges Manet, too."

Elise's head snapped toward Noah. Her eyes darkened. "Are you suggesting that the human victims did not get their illness from the infected animals?"

Noah nodded. "We have to at least consider it."

"Then where did the infected cattle come from?"

"What if *that* is the cover-up?" Noah dropped his voice lower. "What if someone staged the outbreak in cattle?"

Her jaw dropped fleetingly and her eyes went wider. "You honestly think someone would . . . *fake* . . . a mad cow disease outbreak?"

"How else would you conceal a cluster of human prion victims?"

Elise's features smoothed as she turned back to the road, her eyes focusing on the hill that her car was now climbing. "Your theory creates more questions than it answers. How do you go about staging a BSE outbreak? And why would anyone want or need to cover up a human out-break?"

Noah shook his head miserably. "I don't know."

He turned back to the side mirror. At first, he saw nothing. But then, almost fifteen seconds after their car had plateaued, he saw the silver glint of an Audi sedan crest the same hill.

32

———

Claude Fontaine's fingers fumbled with the zipper of his small suitcase. The tips felt numb, as if frozen, but Fontaine had not left the warmth of his insulated aluminum hut. He studied his hands. They trembled slightly. Anxiety bubbled in his gut. *I need to get off this godforsaken continent!* he thought. He reached for the zipper again and managed to catch hold of the metal fastener.

Dressed from head to toe in a snug black ski suit, Martine DeGroot closed the final snap on her own small case and deposited it on the floor. She folded her arms across her shapely chest and regarded Fontaine. "Do you need help?" she asked.

"I can close a fucking suitcase!" he snapped.

She flashed him a nasty smile. "Oh, you are most welcome, darling."

He stopped wrestling with his suitcase and looked down at his trembling fingers. *Are you and that other bitch somehow responsible?* he wondered. *I know you're working together. You're going to squeeze me out of Vishnov. That is the plan, isn't it?*

"What is wrong, Claude?"

He glanced around the room, unable to shake the conviction that someone was eavesdropping on them. "Where is Yulia? Is she coming with us?"

DeGroot squinted at him.

"What is it?" he demanded.

"Yulia left yesterday," she said slowly. "We saw her plane off, remember?"

But he didn't remember. "Of course," he mumbled, determined not to show weakness in front of DeGroot.

"Claude, your color is not good," she said matter-of-factly.

"I feel fine," he said, conscious of DeGroot's skeptical gaze. "I just need to get the hell out of Antarctica." He reached for his suitcase and almost missed the handle, but his numb fingers managed to wrap around it. "When does our plane leave?"

"Five minutes sooner than the last time you asked."

Fontaine shrugged, but the cramping in his stomach intensified and he fought off a cold sweat. He had no recollection of asking. *What the hell is happening to me?* "Martine, is everything on schedule for the shipment of the Lake?" he asked, desperate to ground his muddled thoughts.

"Stop worrying, Claude. The first shipment will leave next week on time."

"And Manet?"

DeGroot nodded.

"We have not heard in weeks," Fontaine said, though his memory was so clouded he had a moment of doubt.

"There is nothing to hear," DeGroot soothed. "Everything is on schedule." Her sudden smile filled with invitation as she took a step closer to him.

Fontaine stared into the glacial blue pools of DeGroot's eyes. He recognized the spark of her arousal, and he felt suddenly turned on. Images of her handcuffed to the bed while wearing nothing but her snow boots danced in his brain. But he wasn't sure if they were from memory or fantasy. "We still have half an hour." She reached for the zipper and slowly slid the fastener down her chest, revealing the perfect alabaster skin beneath. As the zipper lowered inch by inch, she closed the gap between them. "Why don't you use some of your anger constructively?" she asked throatily.

The front of her jacket fell open. She leaned against him, pressing her firm breasts into his chest and licking his upper lip with a sweep of her tongue.

Fontaine grabbed her shoulders, but the numbness was so intense that he could barely feel the contact. Panic ripped through him and doused his arousal. He shoved her away with both hands.

DeGroot stumbled back a step before catching her balance. Her eyes shot up and locked onto his. Her lips parted a fraction, her breathing heavier. Her smile widened, and she ran her fingers over one of her nipples. "Oh, I see. You want it a little rougher. Do we have time for that?"

Fontaine stepped back and glanced from side to side, feeling suddenly caged in the aluminum hut. "Get away from me, Martine," he whispered.

DeGroot's grin assumed a vicious quality, but she held her ground. "Hard to get, huh?" She blew into his face. "That is so unlike you, Claude."

Sweat broke out on his forehead, and Fontaine backpedaled until he bumped against the wall. With his frozen hand, he tried to steady himself against the narrow bookcase, but he knocked it over. "Get the fuck away, Martine!" he shouted.

The lust drained from her face. Dropping her hands to her side, she stood with the jacket hanging loosely off her shoulders. "Claude, what the hell is wrong with you?" she demanded.

"You!" Fontaine said, trembling now. "You and that other bitch. You've done this to me, haven't you?"

"Done *what*?" DeGroot asked impassively.

"This." He raised his shaky numb arm and pointed it at DeGroot. "You are poisoning me, aren't you? You want all the money for yourself. And . . . and . . ." He scoured his brain for the name but drew a sudden blank. "And that woman. I will be dead before the ships even leave here."

A scowl darted across DeGroot's lips, but then her expression softened. "Claude, you are hyperventilating. Slow down your breathing."

Fontaine tried to wipe his soaked brow, but his wooden hand knocked clumsily against his cheek before it found his forehead.

DeGroot zipped her jacket closed and then broke into a loving smile. "No one is poisoning you, Claude. I am your partner—in business and in life. You remember?"

Fontaine managed to slow his breathing and steady his balance. "All those things that Ukrainian woman said." He was unclear of the exact threats, but he knew they were menacing. "She was going to kill me if we screwed up. And that day when you went onto the ice with her . . ." Fontaine's voice trailed off, unsure whether the memory was real or imagined.

"I told you, Claude," DeGroot said. "Yulia was worried about our expenses. We cleared it all up. You have nothing to fear from her."

"And . . . and what about these?" Claude said, staring at his trembling hands.

DeGroot came nearer, though there was nothing seductive in her approach. "You said it yourself. You need to get out of here. Everything will be better when we get back to Paris."

He wiped his brow again. His breathing slowed as he felt the anxiety seep away.

DeGroot pressed against him again, but this time she wrapped her arms around him and hugged him maternally.

"Everything will be okay, Claude," she cooed. "I will take care of you now."

Fontaine wanted to cry with relief. He sank his fingers into the fabric of her jacket, but he might as well have pressed them against the ice outside. They were dead now.

33

Oblivious to the musty smell and the frequent clicks and bangs of the radiator on the far side of the room, Avril sat at her desk and distractedly scanned her backlog of e-mails. The memory of that last phone call with her son's abductors occupied her thoughts. She wondered if she had jeopardized his life even further by placing demands on them. *What choice did I have?* she wanted to scream.

She forced herself to think like a detective, not a mother. *How did they know I could reach that phone booth within five minutes?* Limoges is a relatively small city, but not every two points are within five minutes of each other. *Either they already knew where I was or they are watching me,* she decided, and the hair on the back of her neck stood.

As she reached the page that showed the most recent e-mails, the subject line of one from near the top of the list caught her attention: FAMILY. She did not recognize the sender—Paris_Parent66. Overcome by fresh unease, she double-clicked the mouse and the screen filled with a photograph of Frédéric.

Avril's stomach plummeted. Ice flooded her veins and nausea overwhelmed her. *My boy!*

In the photo, the barrel of a gun was nuzzled against Frédéric's temple. In front of his chest, he held up a sign printed in red marker in his own handwriting that read DO NOT SCREW WITH US, AVRIL. More than anything else, his expression haunted her. His lips were set firm and his eyes stared directly into the camera. She did not recognize fear or even anger on her son's face, only resignation. She reached out and touched his face on the screen.

"Hey, you're looking kind of white for a black woman," a voice grumbled.

Avril snapped back in her seat. She fumbled with the mouse to close the e-mail and then looked up to see Simon Valmont standing at her doorway. "Oh, Simon, hello."

He nodded to her. The lined skin around his eyes creased deeper. "I hear you closed those two missing-woman cases."

Though the computer screen now displayed only the Gendarmerie's screen saver, the image of her son with a gun at his head burned in her mind. She willed herself to focus. "I found Yvette Pereau in Amsterdam," she said.

He hacked one of his habitual throat clearings. "Yet another bored housewife who found true love, huh?" Valmont rolled his eyes. "And what about the other one?"

"Pauline Lamaire? She was very confused from her medications. I think she wandered off, maybe into a gulley or the forest. Some hiker will probably stumble across her remains one day." She sighed. "Regardless, it's a matter for Search and Rescue, not the police."

Valmont trudged the few steps to the chair across from her desk and plunked down noisily. "Still, Avril, knowing you, I imagined we would have to pry the files from your cold dead hands before you would ever give up on either of them."

She conjured a smile. "I'm learning."

"Are you?" He toyed with the end of his dirty tie and then looked up accusingly at her. "What is going on, Avril?"

Her toes tightened below her desk. "Nothing."

"Is that so?" Valmont let go of his tie and it fell crooked over his paunch. "Ever since you returned from Amsterdam, you are different. I have never seen you so distracted."

She wanted desperately to share the news about Frédéric, but she had already risked too much by antagonizing her son's abductors. She did not know who was watching her or from where. She still suspected the original leak came from within the Gendarmerie itself. And she decided the walls were too thin to risk telling her friend.

"I suppose I am a little sad the way things turned out," Avril said as nonchalantly as her voice would allow. "With Pauline possibly dead, and Yvette having run off on her poor husband—"

"That's better than dead, is it not?"

"On balance, I suppose." She feigned a laugh. "I am just a hopeless romantic."

Valmont viewed her for several long seconds. "You are not a particularly good liar, Avril."

"It's Frédéric," she said in a whisper.

"Frédéric! What about him?"

She hesitated. "He is having trouble at school. I am not sure he is going to survive the term."

"Ah, he's a smart boy." Valmont waved her worry away with a big palm. "He probably needs to get out in the world for a bit. He has always been too serious for his age. Trust me, this may well turn out to be the best thing to happen to him."

If only, she thought miserably.

Another figure appeared at her door, but unlike Valmont,

Inspector Esmond Cabot came nowhere near to filling the space. Dressed impeccably in another one of his tailored navy suits with expensive-looking black brogues, Cabot stepped into the room. "I need one of you for a case," he said by way of greeting. "It's a politically sensitive one."

Valmont looked over his shoulder at his boss. "Politics? Isn't that your specialty?"

Cabot ignored the barb. "I have an American from the WHO and an E.U. official down in my office."

A cold rush swept through Avril. "Regarding what?" she asked.

"They're concerned people are meddling with their investigation into this mad cow crisis. Frankly, I doubt there is much to the complaint, but I'll need one of you to check it out."

Valmont uttered a noise that sounded like an engine trying to catch. "Aside from placing a couple of bets on football matches, all I have in my calendar this afternoon is an appointment to rough up a drug dealer. This sounds more interesting."

"No," Avril snapped, and then immediately shrugged it off, trying to mask her eagerness. "I just closed my last case."

"Don't worry, Avril." Valmont laughed deeply. "I have a whole stack of new ones I can share. You could even beat up my drug dealer. It would be good exercise."

Cabot tapped his fingers together, wavering. "Simon did ask first . . ."

Her mind raced. "Does the American speak French?"

"Not much, as best I can tell," Cabot said.

She turned to Valmont. "Have you learned English in the last week?"

"Yeah, that and Portuguese and Vietnamese," he grumbled. "It's been a slow week."

"Esmond, I spent a year in London," she said.

Cabot looked from Valmont to Avril. "She has a point.

Besides, Simon, I cannot afford an international incident on my desk. Avril might be a better fit."

"It's decided, then." Avril rose from her seat and walked past the two men. Valmont flashed her a glance but said nothing.

Almost light-headed with anxiety, Avril followed Cabot into his spacious corner office, which did not smell of the same mold problem that plagued the rest of the building. The large windows had a street view with a glimpse of the cathedral in the background, and the walls were plastered with photos of Cabot posing obsequiously with numerous dignitaries.

Avril walked around the desk, and the man and woman both rose to meet her. The woman was tall and strikingly pretty with voluptuous lips and a model's cheekbones, but Avril sensed a withdrawn quality to her. The man was more welcoming. With tousled brown hair, warm gray-blue eyes, and a slightly crooked smile, he was handsome without effort.

Cabot beamed his public smile. "Detective Avril Avars, allow me to introduce Dr. Noah Haldane with the World Health Organization, and Ms. Elise Renard with the European Union," he said in English. He moved his hand from Avril's direction to the other two. "Detective Avars is one of our best detectives."

Avril smiled politely. "A pleasure to meet you." She shook both their hands.

Cabot made a show of checking his watch. "Ms. Renard, Dr. Haldane, if I had known you were coming I would have cleared the afternoon, but unfortunately I have a meeting already scheduled."

Despite the inspector's apologetic tone, Avril suspected his meeting was invented, and he was already distancing himself from any potential fallout related to the international visitors. After he hurried from the room, she sat down behind his desk. She reached for the notepad and pen sitting on the neat desktop and then looked up at the others. "Do you mind if I take notes?"

Noah shook his head, and Elise said, "Please."

"Can we start from the beginning?" She held up her pen.

"Detective Avars, I work for the Agricultural Commission of the European Union," Elise said. "Dr. Haldane is a world authority on infectious diseases."

"Of course, Dr. Haldane," Avril said deferentially. "The ARCS virus."

Elise nodded impatiently. "We were sent here to investigate the regional outbreak of bovine spongiform encephalitis, or BSE."

"Mad cow disease?" Avril asked, tensing at the words. *What does this have to do with my son?*

Elise nodded. She recapped the local situation, and explained how their trail had led them back to Ferme d'Allaire as the likely source of the infected animals and tainted beef.

Noah tapped his chest. "My role is to establish how BSE is related to the human cases that were thought to be a form of variant Creutzfeldt-Jakob disease, or vCJD."

Avril flexed her toes tightly. " 'Thought to be'?" she said.

"I am not convinced that the human victims fit the criteria for vCJD." Noah went on to offer her a brief summary in lay terms of prion diseases and to explain how the Limousin cases deviated from other vCJD sufferers.

As Noah spoke, Avril slipped fully into detective mode. She was beginning to recognize a connection between the illness and the women's abductions, but she kept her suspicion from her face and tone. "The science is fascinating, and to be honest, beyond me." Her lips formed a sympathetic smile born from years of deflecting trivial, irrelevant, and sometimes unhinged complaints. "But, with respect, I still do not see the role for a police investigation."

Noah glanced at Elise, who nodded her encouragement. "There have been several unusual coincidences and events relating to our investigation," he said. "Too many."

Avril frowned. "Coincidences?"

"For starters, it appears the victims are all linked through one family."

"A family here in Limoges?" Avril asked.

Noah shook his head. "From Lac Noir. The Manet family."

Avril's gaze dropped to the notepad in front of her to hide her surprise. "M-A-N-E-T?" she asked, buying time. Overcome by déjà vu, she remembered jotting the same name when Marie Lamaire mentioned the ex-fiancé of her cousin Pauline.

"Yes," Noah said. "Philippe Manet—one of the victims—had an affair with another victim, Benoît Gagnon. And the third victim, Giselle Tremblay, was the former girlfriend of Philippe's older brother, Georges. A geologist who researches polar ice."

"Giselle's mother says that Georges Manet provided her a sample of water from one of his research trips," Elise said. "He told her it had therapeutic properties."

Avril buried her head in her notes while her heart thudded in her ears. She recalled Marie's description of the mysterious new therapy for arthritis that someone, likely Georges, had given Pauline shortly before the woman became confused. Was this water the same 'therapy'? she wondered.

"The issue of water comes up over and over again," Noah said.

Avril cleared her throat, still not daring to look up from the page. "And have you interviewed Georges Manet?" she asked.

"Only his sister, Sylvie," Noah said. "Apparently

Georges is snowbound above the Arctic Circle on a research project. But Sylvie gave us an ice sample that he brought home last summer. We're having it analyzed now."

Blank-faced, Avril looked back up at the others. "Can you not reach Georges by radio or e-mail?"

"We are trying to track his whereabouts from his satellite phone signal. In the meantime, he has not replied to his sister's e-mails in almost two weeks."

Avril wondered if Georges Manet had suffered the same fate as Pauline Lamaire and Yvette Pereau. "You mentioned other coincidences?" she said.

"Someone broke into my room at the Grand Hotel Doré."

"A theft?"

Noah shook his head. He dug in his pocket, pulled out his notebook, and showed Avril the happy-face bookmark clipped inside, explaining how he found it dislodged upon returning from Paris. "Whoever broke in must have been looking for my notes."

Avril tilted her head from side to side. "Certainly, it is one explanation."

Noah eyed her with a trace of impatience. "You can think of others?"

"A clumsy or perhaps curious maid? But it is worth looking into." She wrote a note on the pad. "What else?"

"We think we are being followed," Elise said.

"Oh?" The words jabbed at Avril's heart, reminding her of her own desperate situation.

Noah described the tall stooped man in the pickup truck who waited for him outside the hotel and then later ran from the train station. He added a description of the black Mercedes and silver Audi he had spotted over the past days.

Avril realized that none of these sightings were coincidental. From her anonymous caller, she knew someone had to be keeping a close tab on the investigators. She made a mental note to check for a black or silver car on her own tail. If she could corner the driver of one of them, maybe he could lead her back to Frédéric. Meanwhile, she needed time and that meant stringing along the two investigators. She looked from Elise to Noah and said, "German sedans are very popular in this region. If you had a license plate for them or that truck . . ."

Noah exhaled heavily. "I think they're smarter than that."

Avril put down her pen. "From what I understand from the newspapers, it seems to me the financial stakes in this mad cow situation are great. True?"

"Very," Elise said.

"So I could see why people in the industry might be taking an active—possibly even illegal—interest in your investigation," Avril said. "It could explain much of what you have described."

Noah folded his arms across his chest, clearly dissatisfied. "The Ferme d'Allaire findings have been way too convenient," he said.

"How so, Dr. Haldane?"

"Maybe the human victims have nothing to do with the cows." Noah said. "What if there is a conspiracy to cover up an outbreak of a new disease among humans?"

Avril nodded patiently, as if soothing a frustrated child, but her ears burned and her chest thudded. "A new disease spread by water?" she said, making her tone as skeptical as possible.

Noah nodded vehemently.

"And how would you go about infecting the cows?" Avril asked.

"I don't know," Noah admitted. "Deliberately feed them tainted food? Or maybe just inject it into them. It would be faster."

Avril thought of the anonymous woman whom Yvette

Pereau spotted leaving their barn. She wondered if the woman had come to inject Pereaus' animals. "It is quite a theory, but do you have any evidence?"

Noah didn't reply, but Elise said, "Only what we have described so far."

"Hmmm, I see," Avril said. "And the motive?"

"We don't have one," Elise said.

Avril pushed her notepad away from her. "Still, these are very serious accusations, and of course, I will make them my priority to investigate—"

"Louis Charron," Noah snapped.

"Excuse me?"

"Dr. Louis Charron," he said. "He shared our suspicion that the human cases might not be vCJD. And he was trying to phone me the night he died—an hour before he drove his car into a tree. Does that make any sense to you, Detective?"

"Ah, Dr. Charron." Avril remembered the report of the neurologist who was so drunk he drove off a straight highway. Instinctively, she recognized his death was tied in, but her thoughts raced to come up with a cover story. "A tragic case. He was an important physician in Limoges." She sighed again. "But, of course—"

"Of course, what?" Elise said.

"Wine and Dr. Charron." Avril shook her head. "Actually, I think brandy was his Achilles' heel. He should not have been driving at all after all the previous charges."

"Charges?" Elise said.

"I believe it's called 'DUI' in America?" Avril said. "Dr. Charron had been caught on at least four previous occasions drunk behind the wheel. If not for his reputation, and of course his lawyer, he would never have kept his license." She sighed again for effect. "In the end, I do not believe we did him any favors."

Elise looked over to Noah. He did not comment, but from the way his head hung slightly, Avril knew that she had succeeded in breaking some of his conviction.

Feeling every inch the fraud, she reached for her note-pad again. "Thank you both so much for bringing this to our attention. It will, of course, be my priority now. I will see if I can find anyone matching the description of your truck driver." She paused to pretend to read her own notes. "I will speak to Sylvie Manet and see if I can reach Georges Manet myself. And I will certainly follow up at the hotel on the break-in."

"Thank you," Elise said.

Avril rose from her seat. "I consider this matter very serious, but you will need to give me some time to follow up on all these many leads. Perhaps we can discuss this again in a few days?"

Noah stood up and met her handshake. He stared her in the eye. "We have some follow-up of our own to pursue."

"Of course. Let us make sure we keep each other apprised." But what Avril wanted to say was: *Don't get yourself killed, Doctor.*

34

Limoges, France. January 20

The cloud cover had thickened while Noah and Elise were inside the Gendarmerie. They walked back out into an ominous flat gray light that made it seem as if dusk had decided to descend a few hours early. With his hands tucked in his pockets and his eyes fixed on the slushy sidewalk, Noah trudged away from the Gendarmerie confused, disappointed, and even more on edge than before the meeting. Despite her benign smile and intelligent eyes, Detective Avars had worn her skepticism like blush. Her doubt was contagious. Now Noah wondered how much his own imagination factored into his theories.

When they reached the car, Elise spoke up. "Noah, she took our concerns seriously. I am certain she will investigate."

"Let's hope," he muttered. "In the meantime, I don't think we can just stop and wait to see what she uncovers."

"I agree. But do you not think we should stick to our areas of expertise, and let Detective Avars handle the police work?"

Elise walked over to the driver's side while Noah reached

for the door handle on the passenger's side. He paused to look across the hood at her. "Tell me, Elise, where does our investigation end and the police work begin?"

"Well . . . the victims' families and that ice sample . . ." Her words petered out.

"It's not so cut and dried, is it?"

Elise climbed into the car without comment. Noah got in, too. As they pulled out of the parking spot, he said, "It could take days for the lab in Paris to run tests on that hunk of ice that Sylvie Manet gave us," he said.

"What do you see as our next step?" she asked tersely.

"Georges Manet."

"And until we reach him?"

"*If* we reach him," he said. "You saw his last e-mail to his sister. We don't know what condition he is in." He looked out the window. "We need to find out more about where he was and what he was working on."

"Where do we begin?" Elise said distantly.

"Speak to his colleagues." Noah stared out at the city's streets, which had become depressingly familiar to him. "He is a researcher. He must be affiliated with a university."

Her shoulders rose and fell. "Maybe."

He turned and viewed her classic profile, catching another whiff of her citrus perfume. An image of their passionate kiss with the promise of more floated to mind, but he shook it off. "We also need to speak to someone close to Dr. Charron. Somebody who knows what he was looking into before he died."

She frowned. "Surely that falls into Detective Avars's area of expertise?"

"His car accident, maybe. Regardless of how he died, he was trying to reach me shortly before his crash. I want to know why."

Elise opened her mouth as if to speak, but closed it without remarking.

They drove the rest of the way to the hotel in silence. As they passed through the lobby, someone called out: "Elise! Noah! *Bonjour.*"

Noah recognized Jean Nantal's voice before he turned to see his mentor approaching from across the room. At his side, Javier Montalva y Casas strode with the confidence of a man who considered himself the most important person in the vicinity. They all shook hands, but Noah did not return either man's smile, annoyed at Montalva's unannounced presence.

"Is it too early for a drink?" Montalva asked with a wink, squeezing every drop of Mediterranean charm out of the gesture.

"I think I might stick with water today," Elise said with a half-smile to Noah.

They headed to the hotel bar and claimed the same corner table where Elise and Noah had shared moments of drunken intimacy the evening before. Jean and Montalva ordered red wines, Noah a Fischer, and Elise a bottle of sparkling water.

They exchanged small talk—carried mainly by Montalva and without any contribution from Noah—while waiting for their drinks. After they arrived, the minister said, "I understand the two of you continue to make brilliant progress in your investigation."

Elise seesawed her head from side to side. "With progress come complications."

Montalva toasted them with his glass. "Still, establishing that the three victims knew one another was very impressive detective work."

Noah had a sip of his beer. The lager tasted cool on his lips, but his stomach responded with queasiness, an aftershock of his recent hangover.

With a paternal smile, Jean looked from Elise to Noah. "Perhaps we could ask you to bring us up to date?"

Elise glanced at Noah, who nodded his approval. She efficiently recapped their findings of the past three days, including the recurring issue of the water, their visit to the Gendarmerie Limoges, and Noah's hypothesis that the human cases were not directly related to the bovine outbreak.

Montalva's reaction was unexpectedly subdued, and Noah was filled with the dark suspicion that Elise had already privately briefed her boss on all of it. "So am I correct in assuming that the detective was not swayed by your conspiracy theory?" Montalva asked.

Ignoring the minister, Noah turned to Jean. "Did you know that Louis Charron had a habit of drinking and driving?" he asked.

Jean's face creased with surprise. "Louis? *Mais non!* Are you certain?"

"The police are," Noah said. "And right before he got blind drunk and drove off a highway, he called me."

Montalva leaned in closer.

The skin tightened further around Jean's eyes. "What was he calling you about?" he asked.

"I don't know," Noah said. "I never received the call, and he didn't leave a message. But don't you think that's a big coincidence?"

Montalva relaxed in his seat. "Noah, you seem unwilling to accept that coincidences do happen."

Noah put his beer down on the coaster and turned the bottle slowly until the label faced him. "Minister, I am just not willing to assume that *every* unexplained loose end is merely coincidence."

"Well said." Montalva nodded, unfazed. He reached for his wineglass. "Let me see if I understand your issues here. You have a wandering bookmark, a skittish farmer, two German sedans, the connection to the Manet family, and a hunk of Arctic ice?"

Noah bit back a sneer and reached for his beer. He could not deny, though, that despite the man's condescension, Montalva had summarized the bulk of the evidence.

"No one would be happier than me if you were right." Montalva held out his free hand to Noah. "I am responsible for the well-being of the European agricultural community, and this crisis has decimated our sector." He moved his hand to his chest. "If this outbreak has nothing to do with livestock or farming, my commission would benefit more than anyone."

Noah stared at the man, searching for a hole in his logic. "You don't believe that it is possible the human outbreak is not related to the bovine cases?" Noah asked.

"I would have." Montalva studied his glass. "Except for the nine calves."

Noah slammed the bottle back on the table. "What calves?"

Montalva offered an almost apologetic smile. "We only heard back from the Institut Pasteur this morning. Nine more calves that were rendered from Ferme d'Allaire have tested positive for the prion."

Noah's gaze darted over to Jean.

The Frenchman nodded. "It is true. None of them showed symptoms, Noah, but they were all incubating the prion in their nervous tissue."

"This was one of your primary concerns, Noah. That the Allaire farm never had a case of its own. Now they do." Montalva nodded sympathetically. "I would very much love for you to be right, but, my friend . . ." He reached out to him again. "If this disease is related to polar ice or water, how would so many cattle be infected on Ferme d'Allaire?"

"It would have to involve a large-scale cover-up," Noah said.

"Ah, a cover-up," Montalva echoed, raising his eyebrow slightly.

"Yes," Noah murmured. "One that reached very high up."

"Very high, indeed," Montalva said with a hint of amusement.

Jean glanced at the Spaniard with slight annoyance. "I think it is premature to rule out any explanation at this point," he said. "Perhaps we should discuss our next steps."

Noah said nothing more as the others discussed the ongoing logistics of the investigation. Montalva concluded the discussions with more platitudes and a promise to reconnect soon. On their way out of the bar, Jean reached for Noah's elbow and gently tugged him aside at the bottom of the steps. When Elise and Montalva were out of earshot, Jean said, "Noah, I owe you an apology." He bowed his head slightly. "I had no right to bring Javier to our meeting without telling you beforehand."

"No doubt the minister insisted," Noah said.

Jean waved the excuse away. "That is irrelevant. Please accept my apology."

"Accepted." Noah showed his mentor a fleeting smile. He lowered his voice. "Jean, what do you make of all of this?"

Jean smoothed back his silver hair, considering the question. "It troubles me. On the one hand, there are too many anomalies compared to any other prion outbreak," he said thoughtfully. "On the other, the explanations are almost too readily available." He met Noah's gaze and offered a reassuring smile. "But more important, I trust your judgment, Noah. If you have such deep concerns, then I know there is legitimacy to them."

Noah was filled with a revived sense of purpose. "Despite the findings at Ferme d'Allaire, every ounce of my experience and intuition tells me that something else is going on here in Limousin."

"Including a cover-up?"

Noah nodded and then glanced over his shoulder to ensure that they were still alone. "Jean, I'm not certain whom I can trust any more."

"You mean Javier?" Jean asked calmly.

"Him . . . the locals . . . even Elise." Noah sighed. "To be honest, I'm not even sure information hasn't been leaking out through our channels."

Jean's shoulders drooped a fraction. "Within the WHO?" he said.

Noah nodded.

Jean was quiet for a few moments. "If that is how you feel," he said slowly, "then perhaps we should discuss these matters only face to face, without leaving any electronic or paper records for the time being."

Noah reached over and laid a hand on his mentor's sagging shoulder. "Now I owe you an apology."

Jean smiled and straightened to his usual bone-straight posture. "Nonsense. I have always tried to instill the importance of security and discretion in my staff. Until we know there is no leak on our side, then it is a sensible precaution."

Noah pulled his hand away from Jean's shoulder just as Elise came hurrying back toward them, holding her cell phone out to Noah. "It's Maurice," she said.

He brought the phone to his ear. "Hello?"

"Noah, *bonjour*!" Professor Maurice Hébert gushed. "Am I catching you at a difficult moment?"

"No," Noah said, too impatient for pleasantries. "Do you have the results?"

"Of course," Hébert said. "In all the bovine brains from Limousin infected with BSE, the levels of phosphorylated tau protein are markedly elevated. It is just as we expected."

Not "we"! Noah's temples thudded and his left hand formed a fist. "Maurice, the phosphorylated tau protein levels weren't elevated in the brains of the human victims supposedly infected by the same prion."

"Is that so?" Hébert said, his tone suddenly concerned. "How do you explain the discrepancy?"

"I can't. Listen, Maurice, say that I wanted to inoculate an animal with the BSE prion."

"Why would you want to do so?" Hébert said in a hoarse voice.

Noah ignored the question. "Hypothetically, could it be done?"

"More than hypothetically. I have done it myself in the laboratory."

Noah's fist tightened. "How would I go about doing it?"

"How quickly would you want to see symptoms in the animal?"

"As soon as possible," Noah said. "In weeks or less, if possible."

"Then you would have to take the highest concentration of prion—ideally from the brain tissue of a fresh BSE victim—and inject it directly into the cerebral system of a subject."

"So I would have to inject the prion through the cow's skull?"

"No, no, no. You could inject it into the thecal sac at the base of the cow's neck that communicates directly with the brain. It is easy. The animals do not even require sedation."

Noah felt the acid creep up the back of his throat as he envisioned the procedure. "So all it would take is a sample of BSE and a quick stab with a long needle?" he said, almost to himself.

"Exactly so," Hébert said. "Though surely, you would need a good reason to do it."

"I can think of one, Maurice," Noah said in just above a whisper.

35

Driving erratically, Avril accelerated on the open stretches of highway and then abruptly slowed, sometimes screeching her brakes after each bend or turn, hoping to unmask her tail. With her thoughts racing as fast as her car, at one point she glimpsed a black sedan, possibly a Mercedes, in her side mirror. But the car turned off long before Lac Noir.

The highway grew deserted, and Avril's thoughts drifted back to her last interview. The tall woman from the E.U. appeared to accept Avril's deflections and denials, but Dr. Haldane was a different matter. She might have shaken his certainty, but she had not weakened his resolve. She recognized the glint of determination in his eyes; it was a feeling she knew well from personal experience.

Avril was aware that discouraging this doctor would take time. She prayed that Frédéric's abductors would also see that. If so, Haldane's tenacity might help save Frédéric's life. As soon as the investigators departed Limousin, satisfied with the manufactured explanation for the outbreak, Avril suspected that her son would be killed.

And so would she. She needed to ground Haldane and Renard in the province and keep them invested long enough for her to find Frédéric.

"Don't screw with us." Those words were as clear in her brain as the sky above. She had deleted the e-mail from her hard drive, but she could not shake the mental image of her son holding up the sign, a gun to his head. And his expression still sent shivers up her spine. She had seen the same look on the faces of suspects before they tried to flee or go for their guns. It was the look of someone with nothing to lose. "Please, Frédéric, do not try anything rash," she murmured. "Let me sort this out."

She turned off the highway onto the road leading into Lac Noir. Steering through the town, she checked the address written on her notepad. She found the street and spotted the location, though the house was concealed by trees on the sprawling property.

She hesitated before climbing out of the car. *I am only doing what they asked of me,* she reassured herself. She remembered her own words to Frédéric's abductors: "I need at least to appear to follow up on their information." Of course, if by going through the motions she managed to unravel the conspiracy, then she would possess the ultimate bargaining chip for her son's life.

Sylvie Manet met her at the door to the house. Avril had never before seen the lean woman with the captivating brown eyes and androgynous features; she would have remembered that striking face. For her part, Sylvie Manet did not appear surprised in the least by Avril's unannounced visit or, like many others meeting the detective for the first time, the color of her skin.

Sylvie led Avril into the ornate living room and over to the antique chairs beside the large fireplace. Though it did not appeal to Avril's taste, the furniture and decorations gave the room a somber authority. And the warmth of the fire and the lingering pine scent from the logs by the mantel helped to relax her slightly. Avril sat in one of the wingback chairs. "I am sorry for your loss, Mlle. Manet," she began.

Sylvie nodded her appreciation. "It has not been the best year for my family."

Mine, either. "I met earlier with Dr. Haldane and Ms. Renard. I understand they have come to see you."

"Twice." Sylvie broke into a sad smile. "They wanted a piece of my brother's glacier."

"So they told me."

Sylvie glanced from side to side as if someone might listen in on what she was about to disclose. "They seem to think that some kind of exotic water or ice might factor into the goings-on here in Limousin."

"What do you think?"

"I always assumed that Philippe acquired his illness from the tainted beef. But I have to admit that it is strange how often water, ice, and my older brother come up in the context of the victims of this illness."

"They tell me that you still have not reached Georges."

Sylvie's eyes darkened with worry. "I've sent several e-mails, but they've gone unanswered for almost two weeks. And I cannot reach him on his satellite phone."

"Surely his phone or other equipment has a GPS locating chip in it?"

A helpless frown creased Sylvie's features. "Maybe, but even if they could locate him, I am not sure anyone could reach him in the Arctic storms."

"Winter in the Arctic, that must be something." Avril nodded grimly. "Georges is a scientific researcher, isn't he?"

Sylvie forced a lighthearted chuckle. "What other kind of research is there, Detective?"

"Of course," Avril said. "I mean, his research is academic in nature. He doesn't work for the government or industry?"

"Ah, no!" Sylvie broke into a smile. "Georges is a bit of a socialist. He would never work for the private sector. And he trusts governments even less! He is an associate professor with the Institut de Physique du Globe de Paris."

Avril nodded. "And Philippe?" she asked.

"Was a civil engineer in Limoges."

"Did he have any kind of physical disability or ailments?"

Sylvie stiffened in her seat momentarily. "Why do you ask?"

I am clutching for anything that may lead to my son's kidnappers! Avril thought. She shook her head, as if it were all idle speculation. "I hear that Georges gave the water to Giselle Tremblay with the promise that it possessed some kind of curative property for her psychiatric . . . instability. I wondered if maybe he was using the water as a kind of naturopathic remedy?"

Sylvie looked down at her interlocking hands. "That doesn't sound like Georges. He is very rigorous about his science."

"And Philippe?" Avril prodded.

"Philippe was born with a congenital hip problem. It gave him quite a lot of pain. In fact, he was due for surgery next autumn."

"I see." Avril showed little reaction, though she realized it was far too much of a coincidence that Georges gave the water to three people—Pauline, Giselle, and Philippe—all of whom had chronic illnesses of some kind. "Do you know Pauline Lamaire?"

"Georges's former fiancée?"

"Yes."

"Of course." Sylvie looked up at her with even more concern. "What does Pauline have to do with any of this?"

"I just closed a missing persons case on her. Coincidentally, Georges's name came up during the course of that investigation."

"Oh?" Sylvie said softly. "In what respect?"

Avril considered her words. "It was probably nothing, but Pauline's cousin told me that Georges used to bring her back mementos from his research trips."

"Not only Pauline," Sylvie pointed out. "He brought them home for Maman, Philippe, me, and other people."

"I realize that," Avril said, "but Pauline has quite advanced arthritis. I wonder if he might have given her some of the same water he gave Giselle."

Sylvie was quiet for a moment. "Wait a minute," Sylvie said. "Is Pauline . . . sick?"

"We don't know. She's still missing. There was no evidence of foul play, so it's no longer a police matter."

Sylvie looked at Avril with a knowing nod. "You think Georges might have given all these people what he thought was therapeutic water, when actually it was tainted with this horrible prion. Right?"

"It's only one theory," Avril said, though her suspicions ran far deeper than the tone of her voice let on. Even if it were true, she knew it did not explain why people were being abducted and murdered across Limousin. There had to be more. Still, she did not want to tip her hand to anyone, even Sylvie. "Figuring out what is or isn't in that water is not my responsibility. My job is to follow up on Dr. Haldane's allegation that someone is meddling with *his* investigation."

Sylvie ran a hand through her short hair. "Is that true? Is someone interfering?"

Avril shook her head. "I am really not sure. Like me, Dr. Haldane might be letting his imagination get the best of him." She raised her shoulders and held up her palms as if to say that her heart wasn't in this, but she was obligated to see it through. "Do you happen to know a middle-aged man—a big man, stooped in posture—and a smoker—who drives an old gray truck? He might be a farmer?"

"A middle-aged farmer?" Sylvie laughed. "That is practically the only demographic left in this province."

Avril forced a smile. "But no one specific comes to mind?"

Sylvie thought a moment. "I'm sorry, no."

"And can you think of anyone around here who drives a gray Audi or black Mercedes sedan?"

"I know a professor at the university who has a silver Mercedes convertible." She sighed. "He is about seventy and arrogant as can be. I would be surprised if he even knows where Lac Noir is, or Limoges, for that matter."

Avril rose from her seat. After bidding Sylvie good-bye at the door, she stepped out into the biting wind, her mind racing as fast as the air whipping around her. She had no doubt that Georges was handing out contaminated water. *Why is he or anyone else so desperate to conceal his tracks?* she wondered.

She got into her car and pulled away from the Manet home, following the same route back to the highway along the quiet streets of the town as she had taken before. *Think motive!* She focused on her criminology fundamentals: Why do people commit murder? Money, sex, drugs, jealousy, fear of exposure, or any combination of the above led to the vast majority of violent crimes. No such motives jumped out in this case. Someone had gone to extreme measures—abducting people and engineering a mad cow outbreak—to hide the truth about the water. And yet, there was nothing criminal about handing out untested, unproven "therapeutic" water; at most, it was ill-advised experimentation.

Experimentation! The word stuck in her brain. What if Georges or others were testing the water because they intended to gain from it somehow? Maybe they planned to publish the finding as some kind of new natural cure that he had uncovered in the polar ice? Or, possibly, he or someone else planned to sell it as such? Mad cow disease would definitely not be an acceptable side effect for a commercial product.

Could that really be it? Avril thought with a quick glance in her rearview mirror. At that moment, she spotted a black Mercedes sedan rounding the corner behind her.

36

⌒

As they headed northwest along the Avenue Saint Surin, Noah again checked his side mirror. Nothing. He looked over to Elise, who had hardly said a word since leaving the hotel. Eyes fixed on the road, she was lost deep in her own thoughts.

Noah thought back to the scene in the hotel lobby. After he had ended the telephone conversation with Maurice Hébert, the others—even Javier Montalva—waited wide-eyed, impatient for the news. Noah explained that the brains of the BSE-infected cows had accumulated a fingerprint-like protein not seen in the human victims. "This essentially proves we're dealing with two separate infections in the humans and the animals," he concluded. Montalva responded with predictable skepticism and doubt, but Noah couldn't help but take some satisfaction from the wounded pride in the minister's eyes. Jean Nantal had been far more accepting of the significance, vowing to expedite the analysis of Georges Manet's ice sample.

The silence inside the car finally got the better of Noah. "Elise, why so quiet?"

Staring at the road ahead, she said, "It is all so complicated."

"The prion illness?"

"All of it."

He wondered if the proximity of Montalva, her intermittent lover, had provoked Elise's moody introspection, but her clenched jaw and straight-ahead stare discouraged him from broaching the subject. Instead, he said, "You know what I don't understand?"

She glanced at him. "What is that?"

"If it turns out that the human victims didn't get sick from eating beef, wouldn't that be the best possible outcome for your Agricultural Commission? Your boss said so himself."

She nodded.

"So why wasn't the minister happier to hear it?"

"Maybe it is. . . ." She sighed. "I don't think Javier is overly fond of you."

Noah grunted a laugh. "You don't say?"

"He is a proud man," Elise said, rising to his defense. "Perhaps you don't intend to, Noah, but I think in his eyes you undermine his authority."

"Maybe there's a little intent on my part," he admitted.

"A case of one too many alpha males?" she said with a touch of levity that didn't last. "Though Javier is far too competent to let his feelings affect his judgment."

"Then what?"

She took a hand off the wheel and touched her lip. "By nature, he is very cautious in accepting statistics or studies of any kind."

"You mean he doesn't believe Maurice's results?"

"More likely, he doesn't yet trust *your* interpretation of them."

Noah viewed her for a long moment. "Do you?"

She turned to him with utter impassiveness. "You are a brilliant man, Noah."

"But?"

"At times, I think you let emotions affect your professional opinions, too."

He resisted the urge to argue. "You don't believe that we're dealing with two separate disease processes in the animals and humans?"

"Of course, it's possible," she conceded. "But the idea that someone at Ferme d'Allaire stuck needles loaded with prions directly into cows' brains seems—"

"Far-fetched?"

"Dramatic."

"Fair enough," he said. "I wish I could think of a less dramatic explanation. Can you?"

"We need to know more."

Elise turned onto the Avenue Albert Thomas. Noah stared out his window at the collection of modern orange-roofed brick buildings that made up the science and technology campus of Limoges University. The tidy group of matching structures reminded him of a small Ivy League school. And the association brought a wave of homesickness, not only for his own academic and clinical work, but even more so for Chloe. Gwen, too. With his desire re-awakened in the elevator the night before, Noah longed to see her again. Confusion reigned in him. Though still unsure how far he could trust Elise, he found her more attractive than ever. He even questioned how much her relationship with Montalva factored into his own dislike of the man.

Noah pushed the thoughts from his mind as Elise pulled into the parking lot on the far side of the campus. Following a map that she extracted from her jacket pocket, she led them to a smaller building with a sign above the entrance that read GÉOLOGIE.

They walked through the front door into the lobby. The faint smells of science—solvents and other chemicals ubiquitous in labs—drifted to Noah's nose. Elise stopped

a passing female student laden with a bulky backpack
and asked directions. The girl pointed toward the staircase and rapidly mumbled something that Noah had trouble understanding.

Downstairs, they followed the corridor to a steel door
near the end. Elise rang the bell beside the door. A man in
jeans, turtleneck, and Harry Potter–style wire-rimmed
glasses answered. Medium height and narrow-chested, he
had a small paunch. Long brown hair flowed past the
smooth whiskerless skin on his friendly face. He stepped
aside to welcome them into his lab. "Ah, you must be the
bigwigs from Geneva and Brussels," he said in the flat accent of Northern England.

"Professor Milton?" Elise asked.

"Assistant professor. No tenure," Milton said. "Please call
me Jeremy. It's less painful that way."

Elise introduced them. Noah was surprised by the
chilliness of Milton's damp, bony grip. "Sorry, I was mess-
ing about in the freezer," the geologist said, as if reading
Noah's thoughts.

Noah looked over and saw that beyond the desks, computers, and other gadgetry he didn't recognize, the far
wall of the room was hidden behind a bank of silver refrigerators and freezers.

"I'm doing a study on glacier firn—immature polar
ice—kind of a hybrid between snow and ice. Anyway, it
takes up a lot of freezer space."

"You don't sound local, Jeremy," Noah said.

"Depends on whether you consider Leeds local." Milton nodded to Elise with an impish grin and a wink. "Just
ask Ms. Renard here. We're all one close-knit family in
Europe."

Elise returned his smile. "Like any healthy family, we
have our differences."

"Especially mine. I married a girl from Limoges. And
I've never looked back. 'Course, she won't allow me to

look back. I'm barely allowed to look sideways." He laughed again as he blew on his hands to warm them. "But you've come about old Georges, haven't you?"

"Yes," Elise said. "Is he a colleague?"

"Georges? I'm not in his league—he's world-class—but I've known him since our postdoctoral days. Crazy as he is, he's a mate. And we both dabble in paleoclimatological research."

"Excuse me—" Elise started.

"The study of climate changes," Milton explained. "In our case, through glacial ice records."

"Is Georges based out of Limoges, too?" Noah asked.

"No." Milton waved his hand away. "He uses our little provincial university—specifically my lab—for storage. He's on faculty at Institut de Physique du Globe de Paris. With tenure, mind you. La-de-da!" He laughed. "He's hardly there, either. Most of the time, he's in the field."

Milton walked them over to counter space at the back of his lab. He offered them stools, but both refused. "Do you know where Georges is now?" Elise asked.

"Last I heard, he was still in the Arctic on Axel Heiberg Island."

Noah nodded. "His sister has had trouble contacting him. When was the last time you heard from him?"

"Good question." Milton's neck tensed with a grimace. "Been at least a month or two." His upper body relaxed. "I've hardly noticed, though. His e-mails have grown so tedious."

"What do you mean?" Elise asked.

"For a Frenchman, Georges has quite a sense of humor. Very irreverent, too. I used to look forward to his e-mails, but lately they are all business. No fun at all."

"Business?" Noah asked, his interest piqued. "About his research?"

Milton shrugged. "Mainly he wants to ensure that his precious samples are okay."

Noah looked over to Elise and caught her eye fleetingly. "Water samples?"

"Not unless the backup generator has gone out in the last hour!" Milton laughed. "His *ice* samples."

Noah nodded, a little deflated. "Did he store any water in your lab?"

"Water in a freezer?" Milton glanced at Noah as though he were simple. "No. Only ice."

"Jeremy, can we see his samples?" Elise asked.

Milton shrugged and turned for the wall. He walked over to the scratched and dented freezer, twice the size of most American refrigerators, in the far corner of the room. He dug in a pocket, pulled out a crowded key ring, and flipped through various keys until he chose one. He slid the key into the lock and opened it with a light click. Then he pulled open the door. Inside, the four levels of shelves were stuffed with clear bags holding blocks of ice of various sizes, shapes, and colors. A light mist of frozen vapor wafted out the open door. "Georges would fill all my freezers if I let him."

"Why doesn't he keep the samples at his lab in Paris?" Noah asked.

"When he stays with his family in Lac Noir, this is a more convenient satellite research lab." Milton's narrow shoulders shook with laughter. "More convenient for him, not me!"

"May I?" Noah pointed to the samples.

Milton nodded, and Noah reached inside the freezer and pulled out one of the bags. It was labeled with the same blue ink as the one Sylvie Manet had given them and read: ARCTIC, ÉCHANTILLON 0314G3117. No heavier than the ice from Sylvie's freezer, its weight was still sobering in Noah's hand. *What kind of microscopic monster is hiding in these crystals?*

Elise pointed at the label. "What does the number refer to?"

"George had his own referencing scheme for his samples. He tried to explain it to me once, but I almost nodded off. The first four digits refer to the month and date. The lettering has to do with years. Beyond that?" Milton shook his head and chuckled. "He told me it was the only way he could remember where the ice came from, but I think he was afraid someone was going to steal his precious glacier."

Noah put the sample back and pulled out another larger one with a similar alphanumeric tag. He studied the large blue chunk. "That must be a deep core sample," Milton said. "At least a hundred meters, probably five hundred."

"How can you tell?" Elise asked.

"The blue hue," Milton said, slipping into a professorial tone. "Glaciers are made of layers of ice sheets laid down over tens of thousands of years. The deeper the ice, the older it is and the more pressure it has on it. The air bubbles are progressively squeezed tighter and the molecules are more and more compressed, making it less translucent. Thus the darker color."

Noah put the sample back on the shelf and reached for another. He read the label, but put it back when he saw that the alphanumeric characters were nearly identical to the previous ones. He randomly picked through several more samples until he reached for one from the bottom shelf. It had the same whitish-blue appearance of the others, but it was labeled ANTARCTIC, ÉCHANTILLON 1122H2147.

"Antarctic?" Elise asked, reading the label in Noah's hand.

Milton took the sample from Noah. "Georges spent last winter near the South Pole. He came home with all kinds of exotic core samples from glaciers there."

"Exotic?" Noah said. "It looks just like the others."

Milton waved the bag in front of Noah and Elise. "Night and day," he said. "For us geologists, that's like saying that polar bears and penguins are indistinguishable."

"You can tell the ice apart with your naked eye?" Noah asked.

"Most of the time, yes," Milton said. "But with simple equipment like mass spectrometers or gas chromatography we can easily determine the gas content of the ice. The relative content of carbon dioxide, formaldehyde, nitrous oxide, helium, and chlorocarbons, among others, would tell me in minutes whether a sample was Arctic or Antarctic ice."

"So by looking at a piece of a glacier, you can tell me where it comes from?" Noah asked, intrigued.

"Up to a point. I could easily tell if it came from an ice cap in, say, Greenland versus Alaska. And by looking at the relative isotope of hydrogen and carbon, I could date the sample to within a few years of when it was laid. However, I couldn't pinpoint the precise sampling site, if that's what you mean." Milton sighed. "It's not a treasure map."

Noah thought about the labels. "So Georges was in the Antarctic last winter, the Arctic last spring, and here for the summer."

"Yes, but don't forget our winter is their summer in the Antarctic." Milton's brow creased. "Take it from me, Noah, you do not want to spend winter in the Antarctic."

Noah returned the sample to the freezer. He shut the door, ensuring the latch was secured. "Georges probably wouldn't appreciate it if we melted his ice samples," he said half jokingly.

Milton clicked the padlock into place. "I don't know," he said. "Georges melts the ice all the time. The git likes to drink unprocessed glacier water."

"Why?"

"He's obsessed with the idea of water purity," Milton said. "Remember that below about thirty or forty meters, most glaciers will consist of snow from a time before the industrial revolution."

Noah nodded. "Before air pollution."

"That's the general idea," Milton said. "I'm not convinced it makes any difference, but Georges sure is."

"You last saw him this past summer?" Elise asked.

"Only a few times. I spent most of the summer in Greenland at a coring site. When I came back in late August, we went for a pint shortly before he left for the Arctic. He was utterly scatterbrained, even for Georges, but very excited. Told me it was all very hush-hush. He promised to fill me in later, but he never did."

"Are there any other colleagues who might be in contact with Georges?" Elise asked.

Milton clicked his tongue, considering the question. "There's a bloke he has done a lot of deep core sampling with. I've met him once. Adaire . . . Allen . . . Anou." He snapped his fingers. "Pierre Anou. An engineer. Tall bugger. From around here somewhere, too, I think."

Noah nodded. "You haven't seen Georges since you had that drink together?"

"Didn't even hear from him again until I e-mailed to let him know he had forgotten to arrange transport for some of his larger ice samples. By then, he was in the Arctic. He wrote back with arrangements for transporting them to Paris. As I said, he has been all business ever since."

Noah glanced back to the freezer in the corner. What kind of business?

37

Sitting in his twelfth-story corner office, Trevor Ayling stared at the menus until his eyes hurt, realizing again how deeply he regretted hiring the temperamental Italian executive chef for the cruise line. Originally, Ayling viewed it as a coup to have stolen Luca Rossi from one of Rome's highest-profile restaurants, but the fiery Tuscan's demands and pigheadedness grew by the day. They had hit a stalemate. And only four days before the *Buckingham*'s maiden transatlantic voyage. Much as Ayling would have liked to sack the chef, he knew it was impossible. The ship had been completed six months behind schedule and hundreds of millions over budget. The last thing the *Buckingham* needed was a crisis in her kitchen.

"Trev, do you have a moment?" a voice asked.

Ayling looked up to see Martin Downs, the prematurely gray-haired CFO, standing in his doorway. In his trademark blue suit and striped tie, the lanky accountant's narrow shoulders sagged lower than usual. Ayling immediately knew Downs had another budgetary concern. The man was an insufferable micromanager. Stifling a sigh, Ayling put the menus down. "Of course, Marty. What can I do for you?"

Downs cleared his throat. "It has come to my attention that you've placed a rather . . . er . . . expensive order for water."

Ayling nodded. "The Lake."

"I see, yes," Downs said stiffly. "But surely the other brand waters—Evian and what have you—would be far cheaper."

"Marty, this isn't some precious bottled French water. We're talking about the Lake here," Ayling said. "Haven't you seen the adverts?"

Downs shook his head as his shoulders slumped further.

Ayling mustered his patience. "This water has been drawn up from miles under Antarctic ice. No man has ever tasted it until now. It's all the rage among the spa and health store set."

"I see, Trev." Downs cleared his throat again. "That's all well and good, but we're talking over half a million pounds for water . . . albeit exotic water."

Ayling rose slowly to his feet. "At one hundred sixty thousand tons and over twelve hundred feet, the *Buckingham* is the largest cruise ship ever built."

"I am quite aware of that."

"Marty, more than four thousand people, from royalty to movie stars—not to mention an entire classroom of handicapped children, as part of that Children's Dreams foundation—will be aboard. The media is watching this one very closely. This is the biggest liner launch since—"

"The *Titanic*?" Downs said with a rare trace of irony.

"The *Queen Mary II*," Ayling corrected. "Listen, Marty, if we serve them three-hundred-pound-a-bottle champagne no one will even notice! But imagine the PR windfall when word gets out that we lavished our guests—from rock stars to poor handicapped kids—with the most virgin water on the planet?"

Downs hesitated, digesting the argument.

"Pure Antarctic water." Ayling touched his fingertips together. "Imagine the splash *that* will make with the press on board!"

Downs shook his head. "From below the Antarctic ice, is it?" His lips broke into a humorless smile. "Wasn't it ice that caused the *Titanic* a spot of trouble?"

38

Limoges, France. January 20

Geneviève Allaire had asked to meet at a small café in the city center, suggesting that it might be less "disruptive" for her family than if the investigators were to interview her at her home. Remembering the way she toyed with her wedding band, Noah wondered if Allaire had young children or, possibly, marital troubles, but she had not elaborated and he had not asked.

Elise had darted expertly across town from the university to the chosen café, but they still arrived fifteen minutes late. Inside, the place was three-quarters empty. Geneviève Allaire sat alone at a table by the window wearing a long black down coat, despite the café's warmth, and sipping from an espresso cup. As they reached her table, Allaire rose to shake hands. Nothing in her polite greeting indicated any remnant of the tension with which their previous meeting had ended.

Noah and Elise sat down on either side of her at the round table. Neither ordered coffee. With her blue eyes and delicate facial features, Allaire was as pretty as Noah remembered, but she looked somehow different. Her blond hair was not pinned back and now fell loosely past her shoulders, but her cheekbones looked even more prominent and her face more drawn.

"Thank you for seeing us on short notice," Elise said.

"My pleasure." Allaire showed a trace of a rueful smile. "I am not so terribly busy with my work anymore."

Elise nodded. "Yes, of course—"

"The farm is closed. It is to be demolished," Allaire went on as if describing an old car that she had to junk. "I am not worried about my family. We will get some kind of settlement from the government. Besides, my husband owns a law firm in Limoges. It's our employees that concern me." She shook her head. "Some of them have been with the farm since my grandfather ran it. I am not sure how they will cope."

Noah shifted in his seat, disconcerted by her graciousness in light of the questions he was about to ask. "Mme. Allaire, we wanted to discuss the . . . um . . . contamination of your farm."

Allaire sipped her espresso. "I have no idea how that prion spread through my farm," she said matter-of-factly. "Or how animal by-products ended up in our cattle feed."

Elise leaned forward in her chair. "There is only one way for it to happen."

Immune to the implicit accusation, Allaire shrugged. "Mlle. Renard, Ferme d'Allaire recorded over two million euros in profit last year alone," she said. "Do you really think we would risk all that to save a few euros by recycling sick cows into our cattle feed?"

Elise was unswayed. "You are the president of a large company," she said. "I imagine you were not involved in the daily processing of your cattle feed. Is it not possible that some overzealous employee decided to save the farm some money?"

Allaire shook her head. "I do not—did not—oversee

those details, but our manager, Marcel Robichard, did. He would never allow that to happen."

Elise leaned back. "Then how do you explain what our lab found in your feed?"

"That is your issue, not mine," Allaire said, showing the first hint of an edge. "I have my own ideas, though."

Noah held out a palm. "Such as?"

Allaire's unfocused gaze drifted past Noah. "I cannot imagine a more effective way to get rid of our farm."

"You mean industrial sabotage?" Elise frowned at the other woman. "Are you suggesting one of your competitors might have set this up?"

Allaire's shoulders rose and fell again.

"Why orchestrate an epidemic?" Noah asked. "Kind of self-destructive for any of your rivals, isn't it? Wouldn't it be easier to just burn down your farm?"

"Depends on *who* the competition is." Allaire's blue eyes lit with intensity. "Cattle farming is a global industry. What if some person or group wanted to paralyze the Limousin trade? Or, perhaps, the entire French or even E.U. cattle industry?"

Good point, Noah thought. As a motive, international industrial sabotage made sense, but only if the human cases traced back to the cows, which Noah knew that recent evidence argued against. "Mme. Allaire, we think someone went to great lengths to set up your farm."

"Great lengths," Allaire echoed. "I agree."

"Last time we met, you hypothesized that someone might be using the BSE cases on your farm to divert our attention from something else."

"Yes, but from what?" Allaire asked.

"What if the entire cattle outbreak was orchestrated to explain away the human cases?" Noah suggested.

"Explain away. . . ." Allaire's mouth hung open a fraction. "You mean the human cases came *first?*"

Noah glanced at Elise, who stared back poker-faced. "We think so," he said to Allaire.

"And someone made our beef cattle appear responsible?" she said, awestruck. "By contaminating the feed to make them sick?"

Noah shook his head. "That would take far too long."

"So how were our animals infected?"

"By injecting BSE directly into their nervous system."

"That's ridiculous!" Allaire said, snapping out of her astonishment. "How could anyone inject so many of our animals without our knowledge?"

"That's a good question," Noah said.

Allaire went very still. "Are you accusing us . . . me . . . Dr. Haldane?" she asked in a hushed tone.

"We are trying to make sense of this mess." He met her angry stare, refusing to back down. "And we have to look at every possibility."

Her expression softened. "It could not happen like that," she said. "Not right under our noses. Too many people would have to be involved."

They fell into an abrupt silence, broken by Elise. "Mme. Allaire, do you know Georges Manet?"

Allaire looked over to Elise slowly. "The geologist?" she asked warily. "I haven't seen him in years."

Elise glanced at Noah, her wide eyes betraying her surprise.

"How did you know him?" Noah demanded.

"We met in Limoges, maybe ten years ago." Allaire spun her wedding band with her thumb. "We dated for a while. We were very young. It would not have lasted. I had no interest in settling down with a researcher who spends most of his time at the most inhospitable points on the planet." She stared down at her ring. "Besides, Georges met someone else."

"Oh?" Elise's shoulders straightened. "Who?"

"I don't remember her name," she said with a tinge of

spite. "I heard she is a concert violinist who lives—or at least used to live—in one of the surrounding towns. Last I heard, they were engaged."

"And you have not seen him since?" Noah asked.

She stopped toying with her ring. "I have run into him a few times in the city."

Noah's temples drummed. "Did he ever give you any samples of water or ice?" he asked.

"Water? Ice?" Her frown dampened Noah's exhilaration. "No. We barely spoke, Dr. Haldane."

On the ride back to the hotel, Noah silently grappled with all the information they had uncovered in the past hours. He struggled to package it into one plausible explanation, but it wouldn't fit.

As soon as they arrived, Noah went straight to his room, anxious to call home. Opening the door, he headed for the phone. He dialed Anna's parents in Hilton Head, but heard only their static-filled answering machine message. "Hi, it's Noah. Hope the sun is out and the hornets gone," he said, trying to sound upbeat. "Anna, please try me on my cell."

Noah put the receiver in the cradle. It had barely stilled when he grabbed for it again and dialed Gwen's cell number. After five rings, he heard her familiar voicemail message. Frustrated, he hung up without leaving a message.

He took off his jacket, hung it on the back of the chair, and then dug his notebook out of his pocket. As he glimpsed the happy-face clip-on bookmark, he was reminded how someone had broken into this same room, trying to decipher what he knew. Suspicions washed over him again. He wondered if the same person or people were involved in Dr. Charron's accident, or related to Georges Manet's mysterious ice and water. Why had anyone gone to such measures? *What did they hope to gain?*

The question gnawed at him like a sliver trapped under his nail.

Suddenly dog-tired, Noah grabbed the pen from the desk and opened a new page in his book. He wanted to summarize what he had learned in the past few hours before sleep threatened to smudge the mental record. After filling in two pages, he was on the verge of nodding off when he heard shuffling outside his room. Suddenly alert, he gently laid his pen down and turned to the door.

Three loud bangs on the door hurled him out of his seat.

39

Lac Noir, France. January 20

Avril's breath came in short staccato bursts. Her suddenly moist hands stuck to the steering wheel. Glancing in the rearview mirror, she could still see the black Mercedes behind her, but it had fallen farther back now. Right where she wanted it.

The wind and icy rain had given way to a heavy wet snow that had begun to accumulate on the highway, making it slick and unpredictable.

Avril's hands tightened on the wheel as she gently depressed the accelerator. The speedometer's needle increased from ninety to one hundred ten kilometers per hour. She eased her foot back. A bead of sweat ran by her eye as she visualized the road ahead. In her mind's eye, she could see the short wooden bridge over the river followed by the slow gentle curve to the left. After a climb up a long tree-lined hill, the road would level and turn harder to the right. Then, a few hundred meters after the turn, she would reach the farm on the right side of the road. The row of pines on the roadside might be enough to conceal her car.

Only if I give myself a good enough head start, she thought.

She pressed her foot harder on the gas pedal. Her Peugeot 406 police sedan picked up speed, but it rattled and the tires skidded when it hit the always-icy bridge. Avril gripped the wheel harder, and held her breath. Another furtive check in the mirror confirmed that the Mercedes was well back now. Veering into the gentler curve, she lost sight of her tail altogether.

She floored the accelerator, and the back tires fishtailed slightly. Hitting the hill, the front tires grabbed a bite of the snowy road. The car jolted forward and gained speed as it shot up the hill.

She flew over the crest at the top of the hill, almost airborne. She relaxed her foot off the gas pedal but resisted the urge to brake before the sudden bank right. As she leaned into the steep curve, the tires slid out and she dug her fingers into the steering wheel so hard that they pulsated. Turning into the skid, she managed to straighten her car just as she spotted the dirt road entrance to the farm.

She pumped her brakes and made a quick check over her shoulder. No sign of the Mercedes. To her relief, she saw multiple tire tracks along the farm's driveway, meaning hers would mix in with others. She turned into the driveway. As soon as she cleared the gate, she spun the car left and drove parallel to the highway along the strip of parking spaces partially hidden by a row of snow-dusted pines. She slowed to a halt behind the thickest cluster of trees.

Staring through the cracks between the pines, she did not have to wait long before she glimpsed the black car zipping past. She jerked the gearshift into reverse and backed up toward the entry. At the driveway, she reversed toward the house until the nose of her Peugeot had straightened out and faced the highway. She shifted gears back to drive and eased out, stopping at the edge of the road. She peered to her right, but there was no sign of the Mercedes before the next bend, so she pulled out onto the road. Running her forearm across her damp brow, she realized she was now facing the trickiest part of the maneuver—reversing roles, tailing her tail. She hoped to follow the black car all the way back to Frédéric.

As Avril drove along the highway, each second that passed without sight of the Mercedes heightened her dread, but she never let her car exceed one hundred kilometers an hour despite the welling panic. She drove almost two kilometers before she rounded a corner and, on the open road in front of her, spotted the Mercedes about half a kilometer ahead.

Avril saw that the Mercedes was moving at a crawl and realized that the driver must have been searching for her. But it was too late. The car's brake lights suddenly dimmed and the back wheels skidded into action.

He is going to run!

Her breath caught in her throat. She felt paralyzed by indecision. If the Mercedes escaped, she might never find another lead back to Frédéric. *But if I am caught following the car* . . . It was too awful to consider.

Not even aware that she had decided, she stabbed the accelerator with her foot. With a groan, the car lurched forward and the snow tires bit the road.

Avril lost sight of the Mercedes down another dip in the highway, but she knew there was nowhere to turn off for the next five kilometers. Gripping the wheel as tightly as if she were hanging off the railing of a high bridge, she kept the gas pedal floored. As her car slid around another curve, the road straightened and she spotted the black car in front of her. Her heart lifted in her chest. Her chance to catch him was coming; the highway was about to snake again heading into the approaching hills. *I can do this,* she resolved.

As she reached the winding section of the highway, Avril had to back off the accelerator. Even so, her performance

vehicle slid in and out of the curves, brushing precariously close to the side of the hill on one side and the lip of
the road on the other. Despite her aggressiveness, she did
not gain an inch on the Mercedes, whose driver weaved
through the turns with obvious skill.

Her hopes fading, she entered the last series of curves
with the realization that the black car was most likely going to outrun her. She did not even see it clip the edge of
the road. By the time the nose of her Peugeot straightened
around the corner, the Mercedes was fishtailing wildly a
few hundred meters in front of her. Then it slid into a full
spin, making two complete revolutions on the snowy highway before it smashed into the guardrail and its back tires
dropped off the side of the road. It slipped backward,
coming to rest on the embankment. Pointing back at Avril,
the car was tilted precariously to its side, as if it might flip
at any moment.

Avril pumped her brakes as she neared the derailed
vehicle. Through the waning light she saw the silhouette
of a large man in the driver's seat. She could not make out
his face, but his hand was clutching the left side of his
head as if it were bleeding.

She stopped thirty feet from the black car. Mouth dry
and heart rate sprinting, she reached her hand into the
purse beside her and pulled out her handgun.

Now or never, she thought, her fingers tightening around
the gun's handle. Just as she reached for the door handle,
the Chopin ringtone suddenly sounded from her cell
phone. Hand trembling, she ignored the first three rings
but could not hold out through a fourth. Still gripping the
gun in her right hand, she picked up the phone with her
left and clicked the answer button with her thumb.
"Yes?"

"Maman . . . they are going to . . . kill me," her son said
haltingly.

"Baby! No!" Avril froze.

There was a slight clatter and then the electronically altered voice spoke into the receiver. "Detective, would you like to hear your son die?" the person asked in a chillingly level tone.

"God, no!" Avril spat. "Please. Tell me what to do."

"Same phone booth as last time. Ten minutes. You don't answer the phone, Frédéric dies." *Click.*

Numb, Avril glanced at the clock. Ten minutes to get to the other side of Limoges in these road conditions would require driving even more recklessly than she had the past ten minutes. Avril gunned the engine and roared past the upended car without another glance at it.

Twelve minutes later, she skidded into the curb by the phone. Jumping from her car with lights on and driver's door wide open, she slid and skated on the pavement as she raced toward the ringing pay phone. Avril grabbed for the receiver. "I'm here," she said breathlessly.

She heard only slow breathing on the other end for a long while. "How many fingers and toes do we need to send before you understand how serious we are?"

"I understand," Avril said. "I swear I do."

"I am not fully convinced," the voice said and then went silent.

Avril heard a heart-piercing cry, followed by her son's muffled choking voice. "You won't get away with this," Frédéric sputtered. Then another series of agonizing screams and more words that were now unintelligible.

Avril's hand shook wildly on the phone. *"No. No. No . . . ,"* she pleaded.

"Do you understand, Detective?"

"I do!" she cried. "I swear."

"Don't you ever try to approach one of our cars again."

"I won't," she said hoarsely, tears starting to flow.

"The doctor and the woman came to see you today," the caller said in a tone that abruptly turned conversational. "What did they want to know?"

Avril did not hesitate. "They know this is about more than simply a livestock-related infection." Tears running down her cheeks and what felt like an anvil strapped to her heart, she went on to describe what Haldane and Renard had told her of the mysterious illness and their suspicions of a cover-up in the region. "Dr. Haldane thinks the infection is related to glacial ice samples that Georges Manet brought back with him."

The caller did not comment.

"I have told you everything," Avril said. "Let me speak to Frédéric. Please."

"He is sleeping now." A soft metallic chuckle. "Why did you go to see Sylvie Manet?"

"Because I had to," Avril spat, before willing herself calmer. "I did everything I could to discourage Haldane and Renard, but they are persistent." She swallowed. "Especially Haldane. I warned you that I would have to respond to their complaints."

"Then *appear* to respond, but don't try to solve anything. It will only hurt Frédéric more."

Avril wiped the tears from her cheeks. "To be convincing, I have to provide answers they will believe."

"You are a smart woman. Come up with answers, Detective." The voice said. "But leave it at that if you want your son to live."

"Listen to me," Avril said through gritted teeth. "I am all that is keeping those investigators in check."

"Do you think so?"

"They are important people with international reputations," Avril continued, her ire overcoming her caution. "If they do not believe or trust me, they can easily go over my head. Or maybe they will sound the alarm to the Police Nationale or Interpol or someone else that you won't be able to control no matter who you abduct or kill!"

"Don't be too sure, Detective."

"We are talking about high-ranking officials with the

WHO and the E.U.," Avril snapped. "I will keep them in the dark. I promise you. But the only way I can stall them is by continuing my investigation." She took a deep breath. "But if you lay one more hand on my son . . ."

"What will happen, Detective?"

"I will go to the Police Nationale myself."

"Frédéric will die before you get through their door."

Avril did not push further. She had made her point. "Understand this. You cannot make these people simply disappear without a trace like you did Pauline Lamaire and Yvette Pereau."

"You might be surprised, Detective."

40

Noah gripped the cool metal of the door handle. Hesitating, he scanned the room for anything that could pass for a weapon. His eyes focused on the iron that lay on the top shelf in the open closet. The door shook with three more heavy knocks. Noah took a long silent step toward the closet.

"For Christ's sake, Haldane, I'd have an easier time rousing my dead grandmother!" the voice boomed. "Open the bloody door."

"Duncan!" Noah turned back to the door and yanked it open.

In a jacket and jeans, his red hair damp from snow and hanging messily over his forehead, McLeod stared back at Noah with a wisp of a smile. Noah flung his arms around the Scotsman.

"Enough already." Duncan wriggled free of the embrace. "What are you, Italian? Can't you take no for an answer?"

"Woe is me." Noah stepped aside to let Duncan enter. "What's the news with Maggie?"

"They had already put a pin in her shoulder by the time

I got home." Duncan headed straight for the minibar beside the desk. "She's out of the hospital now." He leaned over and foraged through the minibar, pulling out a pair of two-ounce scotch bottles and jiggling them between his fingers like they were bells.

Noah waved off the offer. Duncan poured himself a scotch in a tumbler from the top of the bar, leaving the other bottle unopened beside the clean glasses.

"Duncan, the situation sounded . . . very dire when you left."

"It still is, Haldane." He cleared his throat. "Shite, it's a fucking disaster. But Maggie's spirit is strong and she's a fighter."

"I never doubted that, but what are you doing back here so soon?"

"I was driving Maggie bonkers at home. Apparently, I don't make much of a nurse."

"Hard to imagine," Noah said.

"No doubt you're bloody Florence Nightingale incarnate," he grumbled, as he downed his glass in one long gulp. "Besides, Maggie and the boys have gone off to stay with her mother on Black Isle for a few days. I would have gone, too, but I didn't think it would be fair to leave Maggie widowed *and* orphaned by the end of our stay at *that* woman's house!"

Noah laughed. "You think it's safer here?"

Duncan left the empty tumbler on top of the minibar and trod over to the chair by the desk. He sat down and hung his head. "I'd never have left her, Haldane, but Maggie insisted. And once her mind is set . . ."

With Duncan's flippancy gone, the gravity of Maggie's condition again sank in for Noah. "The change might be good for you, too."

Duncan ran a hand through his sopping hair. "Listen, Noah, if anything happens at home and I need to go in a hurry—"

"Of course." Noah nodded. "Still, it's good to have you back on the job." He raised a smile. "Though I already miss the quiet."

"Tough shite," Duncan muttered. "Truth is, Haldane, without me your life is boring and forgettable."

Noah shook his head. "You have no idea how much I wish that were true right now."

Duncan's shoulders straightened. "I've heard snippets from Jean, but I need the whole story. What the hell is going on in this province that time forgot?"

Noah sat down on the bed across from Duncan. "Our instincts were right," he said. "This is anything *but* a BSE outbreak. In fact, I think the cows are an afterthought."

Duncan rubbed his beard fiercely, but said nothing as Noah went on to give him a thorough recap of the happenings in the days since the microbiologist had left France.

When Noah finished, Duncan pointed to the nightstand by the bed. "Pass me the Bible, will you?"

"The Bible?" Noah frowned. "Have you found religion?"

"No, but I want to double-check something." He sighed. "I don't remember seeing your name in there before, but Armageddon sure as hell doesn't seem to want to happen without you along for the ride."

Noah laughed. A weight lifted from his shoulders as his sense of isolation lessened. He had not realized just how much he missed working with his friend.

"What's the latest with our Belgian envoy?" Duncan asked.

"I'm not sure. I think Elise is under even more pressure than we are."

Duncan raised an eyebrow. "The two of you didn't economize on hotel rooms in my absence, did you?"

"No," Noah murmured, remembering their brief elevator exchange. "Her boss, Minister Javier Montalva, has been an impediment at every turn so far."

"Those fucking E.U. politicians! Always on the lookout for the nearest sandpile to stick their heads in." The creases around his eyes deepened and his expression darkened. "By the sounds of it, there have to be other people involved in this grand whitewash. Locals. At the very least, some of them must know a hell of lot more than what they're letting on."

Noah glanced at the notebook on the desk and thought of the displaced bookmark. "No question," he said.

"Doesn't sound like anyone is too interested in what's lurking under the rocks around here."

"Not even Detective Avars. She struck me as a sharp investigator, but I suppose no one likes to dig up skeletons in their own backyard."

"Far better to just fill the yard with fresh bones! Haldane, do you trust Ms. Renard?"

Noah paused. "I think so."

Duncan snapped his fingers. "Don't give me that. You're not the 'think so' type."

"Elise has toed the E.U. line all along. I think she's been instructed to. And maybe that's all there is to it."

"But . . ." Duncan rolled his finger in a get-on-with-it gesture.

"She has been slow to accept any of this as out of the ordinary." Noah absentmindedly smoothed the bedsheets beside him. "And the whole time we've been investigating, it has felt like someone is always one step ahead of us."

"You wonder if maybe she is feeding someone information?"

Noah shrugged. "Don't know, but I wouldn't be surprised if the leak came from somewhere within Elise's department."

"Fucking European Union! Has to be the all-time stupidest marriage of convenience."

"Elise suggested that the leak could be coming from within the WHO," Noah said.

"Really?" Duncan looked down at his hands, considering the possibility. A small grin broke across his lips. "I don't buy it. You and I both know that our creaking bureaucracy takes six months and a thousand e-mails to plan a bloody Christmas party. Could you imagine those idiots trying to subvert an international investigation?"

"My point is: We just don't know who is involved," Noah said. "And until we do, we shouldn't trust anyone."

Duncan's gaze was now unfocused. "I hardly ever do," he said distantly.

Noah rose to his feet. "You must be hungry."

Duncan shook his head. "Appetite isn't a big problem for me these days."

Noah pointed at the minibar. "Another drink?"

Duncan stood up from the chair, sweeping the drops of melted snow from his forehead. "Shite, even liquor isn't the panacea it once was." He summoned a grin. "I'm in grave danger of becoming the world's first failed alcoholic."

Noah opened his mouth to respond but the ring of his cell phone interrupted him. Duncan picked up the phone and passed it to Noah. "Noah Haldane," he said as he brought it to his ear.

"*Allo*, Noah," Jean Nantal said with less than his usual warmth.

"Jean?" Noah said. "Are you still in Limoges?"

"No. I'm in Paris."

"More meetings?"

"Noah, I am calling from the Institut Pasteur."

"At this hour?" Then it suddenly hit Noah. *The ice sample!* He squeezed the receiver tighter. His heart thudded in his ears.

Duncan grimaced. "What is it?" he demanded.

Noah stared at Duncan but spoke into the phone. "Jean . . . you're calling about Georges Manet's glacier sample, aren't you?"

"It's all very preliminary—"

"You found the prion in that ice, didn't you?"

41

Meribel, France. January 16

When he came to, Claude Fontaine had no idea where he was. His mouth felt full of sand and his head throbbed as if rousing from a staggering hangover, but, strangely, his mind was clearer than it had been in days. The room came into focus. Lying on the sofa, he surveyed his surroundings. The peaked ceiling above him sloped dramatically down to the low walls on either side of the room. Beside him, the open fireplace roared with a load of wood. The blast of warmth washed over him. Despite his headache, disorientation, and a vague sense of peril, he found the heat from the flames comforting.

Must be a ski chalet, Fontaine thought. He loved to ski. He had spent many winter nights in various chalets in the Alps, though he had no idea if this place had been one of them. He was flooded with nostalgia, though there were no specific memories attached to the feeling.

Fontaine struggled to sit upright. Several glasses and two empty wine bottles were scattered on the coffee table in front of him. Then he saw the white powder dusting the tabletop. A line of the powder seemed to point right at him. *Cocaine.* He had a vague recollection of trying the drug before, but it held no temptation for him now. The sight only fueled his disquiet.

He stared at the full wineglass nearest him. Concentrating hard, he reached for it, knocking the glass with a shaky hand. It wobbled and listed before he managed to grip it between both his palms. He saw that his hands held the glass, but he could barely feel the contact. He brought it to his lips, but he spilled almost as much as he managed to swallow.

The sound of voices from the attached room drew his attention. He immediately recognized the clipped feminine tone, but it took a moment to remember her name: *Martine*. The other voice, deep and spoken with a heavy Russian accent, was also vaguely familiar. They spoke English. Despite being bilingual, Fontaine had trouble following the conversation.

"It's almost two o'clock," Martine deGroot said. "He might wake at any time, Viktor."

"So?" the Russian said.

"*So,* I would like to have this done before then," deGroot snapped.

"He is not going anywhere. What does it matter if he sleeps or not?"

"It matters to me," deGroot said. "I do not particularly want to do this at all, let alone with him conscious."

Though he was unable to follow the meaning of the conversation, a sense of ominous threat flooded Fontaine. He took another slurp of his wine, bobbling the glass.

"She wants it done," Viktor said. "So we do it."

"But he does not have to be awake. Is that so hard to understand?"

"Not so hard," Viktor replied with a touch of petulance.

"Let's not fight, Viktor," deGroot said, her tone suddenly contrite. "Is the car packed?"

"Yes."

"I will be waiting for you there," she said with a touch of invitation, before her tone hardened. "Remember, Viktor. Everything must burn."

"It will."

"There cannot be anything left. You understand?"

"It will burn."

What must burn? Fontaine wondered. The glass dropped out of his hand, bounced off his leg, and thudded against the coffee table without breaking. His thigh felt wet and he looked down to see the dark stain on his jeans.

When he looked up, DeGroot stood across the room from him, dressed completely in black. "Claude, you're awake," she said pleasantly.

"Where am I, Martine?" he asked in French.

She walked closer. "Meribel."

"Meribel . . . ," he repeated, bewildered. Then he remembered. "The mountain."

"That's right," DeGroot said. "You wanted to ski again."

Fontaine took her word for it. "I love the snow here. It's beautiful. So soft. Nothing like that ice of the Antarctic. So hard. So endless."

DeGroot smiled, but the gesture only heightened Fontaine's unease. "I have to go now, Claude," she said.

"Not yet," he said, aware of a sudden sense of finality. "The water . . ."

"It's all taken care of, Claude," she reassured him.

"The Lake, Martine." Without understanding why or how, he knew that everything happening to him was connected to Vishnov. "Tell me about the Lake."

"The first cargo ship has already sailed from port. Tomorrow, it will reach Argentina, where the water will be treated and bottled." Her eyes lit. "In a few days, the Lake will be in stores—"

Fontaine waved a hand wildly to interrupt. "No! Tell me about the water. It's in the water, isn't it?"

DeGroot folded her arms and studied him silently.

As if a fog lifted inside his skull, Fontaine suddenly had a clearer understanding of his predicament. Without recalling the specifics, he remembered that he had lost trust in DeGroot. She was the one who pushed him into the idea of bottling the Lake, promising unimaginable wealth and fame. She had struck the deal with Manet, and insisted on being the sole liaison. And she had won the support of Yulia Radvogin, forcing a deeper wedge between Claude and the CEO.

Eyes cold, DeGroot stared at Fontaine without responding.

"What's in the water?" he begged. "Please tell me."

"I told you not to drink it. I told you to wait until it was sterilized."

Sweat broke out on his brow. "Why did I need to wait? What is in the water?"

DeGroot looked over her shoulder. "How much longer?" she asked in English.

"Five, maybe ten minutes," Viktor called back.

DeGroot turned back to Fontaine. "Some of the people Georges gave the water to in France became sick," she said.

"Sick? What do you mean 'sick'?"

"They call it Creutzfeldt-Jakob disease," she said with a slight shrug.

The name rattled inside his brain for a few moments until it stuck. As porous as his memory was, he recalled the monstrous affliction with a shudder. The microbiology department where he earned his PhD was one of the leading research centers for CJD. "The prion disease?" he whispered.

"Yes."

"From the water?"

"It would appear so," DeGroot said indifferently. "Technically, I believe the prions are carried inside the *Arcobacter antarcticus* bacteria that you discovered."

It took Fontaine a moment to make the association. "But the Lake—"

"Will be perfectly safe." She backhanded his concern away. "We are pretreating the water with heat, light, and chemical sterilization."

Fontaine felt no better for the explanation. Something was wrong in her logic, but he could not put his finger on it.

Sweat poured off him. He looked at his numb hands. The realization hit him with the impact of a gunshot. "I have it, don't I?" he croaked. *"I have the prion!"*

DeGroot pursed her lips and nodded.

"Oh, God . . ." He rocked in his seat clumsily.

DeGroot checked her watch again. She moved nearer but stopped at the coffee table. She grabbed an empty glass and filled it from the open bottle. She knelt near him. He smelled her fruity cologne and recoiled in his seat. She pushed the wineglass closer to his lips. "Listen to me, Claude," she said sternly. "There is medicine in this wine. It will help you relax."

"Relax?" he asked, panicky. "Why do I need to relax?"

"It will make things easier for you."

Fontaine was too distressed to fight her. He put his lips around the rim and slurped at the wine as she tilted the glass for him. He gulped at the glass, spilling some and choking on the last mouthful.

"What is going to burn, Martine?" he asked when the rim left his lips.

She put down the glass and shook her head slowly. "Nothing." She straightened to her full height and looked down at him. "I have to go now, Claude." She turned and headed out of the room. "Good-bye," she called over her shoulder.

Fontaine's eyes were feeling very heavy. His mouth felt frozen, as if he had been to the dentist. The room began to spin. As his eyes drifted shut, it suddenly hit him. "Heat and light won't help," he slurred. "Prions aren't alive."

The room went dark. "I don't speak French," Viktor said in his heavily accented English.

"*You can't kill prions . . . ,*" Fontaine said, and then everything went black.

42

Avril woke at 5:05 in the morning, surprised to discover she had slept for almost three hours.

Frédéric!

She sprang out of bed, determined not to waste a moment of the day. She threw on a housecoat and slippers and headed for her kitchen. Though she had not eaten more than a couple of pieces of bread and a slice of Camembert in the past two days, she was not hungry. However, she needed a café au lait to ward off a caffeine-withdrawal headache. She filled a small saucepan with milk and put it and the kettle on the flame. While waiting for the milk to heat, she switched on the laptop computer that she kept stationed on the kitchen counter.

Avril rarely used her computer at home, preferring to use the broadband Internet access at her office instead of the sluggish dial-up connection. This morning the wait seemed interminable as her laptop buzzed and beeped before the three long bells finally announced that the modem had logged on. Nerves raw, she watched the new messages accumulate at a snail's pace, certain that another e-mail from her son's captors was about to surface. Her breath caught in her throat when she spotted the message from Paris_Parent66 on the list. Finger trembling, she clicked the mouse on the subject line.

The tears started before the photo finished downloading.

Dazed, Frédéric stared back at the camera through only his left eye. His right eye was dark purple and swollen shut. Crusted blood caked over both nostrils. His entire upper lip was so swollen that it looked as though it were attached to his nose. His T-shirt was covered in blood.

Monsters! I will kill you. I will make you pay! Avril sobbed, clutching her head in her hands. *Oh, Freddie . . .*

Avril stared at the photo for almost a minute before she noticed the message typed below it. She scrolled down and read the text.

> THE NEXT PICTURE WE SEND OF FRÉDÉRIC, HE WILL BE DEAD. STOP TRYING TO FIND US.
>
> WHEN THE INVESTIGATORS RETURN TO TALK TO YOU AGAIN, YOU WILL ACCEPT WHAT THEY TELL YOU ABOUT THE GLACIER. YOU WILL ENSURE THE DISCUSSION IN-CLUDES ONLY THE ICE. YOU WILL KEEP THEM AWAY FROM ANYTHING ELSE TO DO WITH LIMOUSIN. YOU WILL DO THIS, OR YOUR SON WILL MOST CERTAINLY DIE.
>
> ACKNOWLEDGE THAT YOU UNDERSTAND THIS E-MAIL.

Her hand still shaking, Avril overshot the REPLY icon twice before clicking it. Fighting the urge to unleash a tor-rent of rage and threats, she typed the word "understood" and then hit the ENTER key before she could add any more.

Avril closed the e-mail program and shut the lid of her laptop, unwilling even to face its blank screen. She stared at her cell phone on the counter, immobilized by sudden indecision. She knew that his captors would never volun-tarily release Frédéric, but she could not bear the thought of being responsible for any more of his suffering.

You are a detective, think like one! she reminded herself. "What would I do if this were someone else's son?" she said aloud, trying to distance herself from her whirlpool of emotion.

Avril could think of only one answer. She scanned the kitchen with a quick check over her shoulder, ensuring the blinds were shut, and then reached for her address book. She found the number, picked up the phone, and was about to dial when she slammed it back on the cradle. *What if they've bugged my landline?* She glanced at her cell phone lying on the counter but decided that, with cell phone scanners readily available, even that was too risky. Instead, she jotted the phone number down on a piece of paper and tucked it into her purse.

She downed two cups of coffee before the shaking finally stilled. She showered, changed, and hurried out to her car. Another few inches of snow had accumulated overnight. Lost in her thoughts, she barely noticed the deep freeze as she scraped the snow off the windows.

The local gas station was still closed when Avril arrived. Confirming with a quick scan that she was alone, she rushed to the phone booth outside. She dialed the operator, who connected her to the number in Paris.

"Hello?" a voice said groggily after the fourth ring.

"Étienne, it's Avril," she blurted.

"Avril?" murmured Inspector Étienne Breton of the Police Nationale. "It's not even six o'clock."

"I am so sorry to wake you, but I need an urgent favor."

"Must be, huh?" His tone sounded concerned. "What is it, Avril?"

She fought to contain the urgency in her voice. "I need you to trace a series of cell phone calls for me."

"Hmmm," Breton said. "Do you mean calls that originated from a particular cell phone?"

"No," Avril said softly. "I have the cell phone and the

number. I want you to trace the source and location of the calls *to* that particular number."

"That's a bit of a sticky area without a magistrate's order." He sighed. "What is the number?"

Avril recited her own cell number. "There should be no legal worries," she added.

"Why is that?"

"Because it's my mobile phone."

There was a pause. "Avril, what the hell is going on?"

Her mind raced to come up with an excuse. "Étienne, I am being threatened."

"Threatened?" Breton echoed. "And you don't know who is behind these threats?"

"No."

"Come on, Avril," he said. "I need more. Are you in real trouble here?"

"I wish I could tell you more, but I cannot. Not now." She cleared her throat. "Étienne, please trust me on this."

"How long have I known you, Avril?"

"Twenty years, at least." She summoned a laugh. "We were only children when we met."

"Not children, but not yet middle-aged, either. I used to tease Antoine back then that one day I would steal you away from him. I was only half joking." He went quiet for a few moments. "Give me a few hours. I will see what I can come up with."

She swallowed. "Thank you, Étienne."

Avril hung up and rushed back to her car, confirming with another glance that no one was around to watch her.

During the drive into work, other cars joined hers on the snowy roads, but she avoided checking for familiar vehicles in her rearview mirror. She assumed she would still be followed, but undoubtedly whoever was tailing her would be more careful. Besides, even if a black Mercedes or silver Audi stopped right in front of her, she would not approach it. She could not allow Frédéric to endure any more torture because of her. Instead, Avril focused on the e-mailed instructions. *How could a piece of glacier incite such illness and death?* she wondered. However, she kept coming back to the same question: *What is it that they want me to keep Haldane and Renard away from?*

Aside from Pauline Lamaire and Yvette Pereau—whose disappearances she had already put to rest—the only answer that came to mind was Ferme d'Allaire. She remembered reading an article on how officials from the Ministry of Agriculture were combing every inch of the farm for clues about the source of the possible mad cow outbreak. *What could anyone at the farm possibly hide from those investigators?*

She slapped the steering wheel in sudden realization. *Not what, who! Who are they trying to hide?* If Haldane was right about the cover-up, then someone inside the farm had to be involved. Someone who could lead Avril to Frédéric's kidnappers.

Avril arrived at the Gendarmerie Limoges at least an hour before the day staff. She headed toward her office in the dim light leaking through the small translucent windows of the otherwise dark hallway. As she passed Valmont's office, she noticed light from within. She ducked her head through his door. Her hulking colleague sat stooped over his desk and stared at his computer screen with a pen clamped between his teeth like one of his unfiltered cigarettes. When he noticed Avril at his door, surprise creased Valmont's features, but his expression relaxed and he soon broke into a sarcastic grin. "You still look whiter than I remember," he said, pulling the pen from his teeth. "How are things with Frédéric?"

Avril felt flooded with brief confusion before she remembered the invented story of her son's school problems. "Oh, it is day-to-day."

"A break from school might be the best thing for him

in the long run," Valmont grunted and then cleared his throat with one of his vocal tics.

Avril glanced around her to ensure that they were indeed alone.

Valmont frowned. "Come on, woman, out with it," he said.

Avril bit her tongue. Desperate to tell Simon, she still believed that Frédéric's abductors had somehow infiltrated the Gendarmerie. She did not feel safe raising the matter inside these walls. She shook her head. "It's the anniversary of Antoine's . . . accident," she said, even though it was still three days away. "I was hoping you might join me after work at the cemetery to mark the occasion."

Valmont cocked his head in surprise and reddened slightly. His eyes fell to the keyboard in front of him. "Certainly, Avril, I would be . . . er . . . honored to."

Avril tracked down the names of Ferme d'Allaire's directors through the company's website and she managed to find addresses for most of the people listed.

Frantic not to antagonize Frédéric's abductors, she prayed that if they learned about her inquiries into the farm—which was inevitable if they had someone on the inside—she could argue it was part of her effort to dissuade Haldane and Renard from nosing around themselves.

As she hoped to use surprise to her advantage, she decided to drop in on the directors unannounced. Her first stop was at Geneviève Allaire's imposing mansion on the northwest outskirts of Limoges. At the gilded wooden doors, she rang the doorbell three times, but no one answered.

She drove directly from the Allaire home to that of the farm's general manager, Marcel Robichard. For the second time in two days, she found herself cruising along the streets of Lac Noir, though Robichard's old stone house was on the opposite side of town from the Manet family's.

At the door, she heard faint TV noises from inside, but she had to pound on it before Marcel Robichard answered. He was dressed in a bathrobe and reeking of cigarette smoke, his uncombed shock of black hair puffed up more on the right side of his head than the left. "What do you want?" he snapped.

"M. Robichard?"

His eyes narrowed. "Who are you?"

"I am Detective Avril Avars. I need to ask you some questions relating to Ferme d'Allaire."

Robichard stood his ground. "I have been over this a hundred times," he whined.

"Then it will be easy for you," Avril said. "Listen, M. Robichard, I am obliged to follow up on issues raised by the investigators with the E.U. and the WHO."

"What *issues*?" he asked.

Avril shrugged as if the whole investigation were a big nuisance to her, too. "They allege that someone is tampering with their investigation." She sighed and rolled her eyes. "I promise I will not take much of your time."

Robichard turned and walked back into the house. Without a spoken invitation, Avril followed him down the narrow hallway. As she approached the living room, the smell of smoke grew stronger and she recognized the sounds—cheering and commentary—of a televised soccer game. She stepped into the cold austere living room, just as Robichard flicked off the sleek flat-screen TV mounted above the mantel. "I tape the matches and watch them in the morning," he explained as he put the remote control down on the arm of the well-worn chair facing the screen.

He settled into the same chair and reached for the pack of cigarettes resting on the other arm. Avril sat down on the weathered sofa beside him. "Nine more calves, I hear," Robichard said without looking at her.

"Excuse me?" Avril said.

He reached for the lighter and clicked it five or six times before the flame finally emerged. He lit the cigarette between his lips and inhaled a long drag before speaking. "I was told that nine more calves on the farm tested positive for mad cow."

"You don't seem surprised."

He coughed. "Nothing surprises me anymore."

"Can you explain it?" she asked.

"Explain it? I never even saw it." Robichard snorted. "All those supposed cases of mad cow disease and not one actually sick cow on our farm. How do *you* explain that?"

Avril searched his eyes for a hint of evasion, but she saw none. "I don't understand your industry enough to even begin to try," she said. "What about the contamination found in the cattle feed?"

"We did not supplement our feed with animal products. I have no idea how it showed up." He paused for another drag of his smoke. "Or even if it showed up."

"*If?*"

"All these positive tests and yet not one sick animal," he said. "How do you know someone in the lab or at the E.U. is not falsifying results to make our animals look responsible?"

"I do not," she said, realizing that his hypothesis might have weight. "Besides, it is beyond my jurisdiction. I am simply following up on the allegation that someone is interfering with the scientific investigators."

"They have no right to complain," Robichard grumbled in disgust. "Look what their interference did to our farm."

Avril nodded empathetically. "Dr. Haldane has raised the possibility that the human cases are not at all related to the outbreak in the cows."

Robichard's frown deepened but he said nothing.

"He even speculates that the cows might have been infected to cover up the real source of the human cases."

Robichard crushed the butt in the clay ashtray beside the pack of cigarettes but still did not comment.

"Dr. Haldane suggests that these conspirators might have even injected the animals directly with the mad cow disease."

"*Injected* them?" Robichard fumbled with the pack, almost knocking it on the floor. He managed to steady it and extract a new cigarette. "That is craziness," he muttered as he grasped for his lighter.

Avril's toes tensed inside her boots. To avoid eye contact, she glanced at the mantel and again noticed the large TV mounted above. It looked new and expensive, so out of place relative to the rest of the sober furnishings.

Robichard stopped clicking his lighter and eyed her guardedly. "What is it, Detective?"

Her heart pounded in her chest, but she feigned weariness by rubbing her eyes and exhaling heavily. "M. Robichard, I have a very full agenda. Real criminals—murderers, thieves, and rapists—to catch. Frankly, I do not have the time or energy to follow up on the wild ideas of some foreign doctor, but my boss is being pressured by his boss and so on. You understand?"

Robichard appeared to relax slightly in his chair. He clicked the lighter a few more times until it finally produced a flame. "I know the feeling," he said as he lit the cigarette.

"Just so that I can reassure the others, you are saying it is not possible that someone injected the cows at Ferme d'Allaire?"

He sucked aggressively at his cigarette. "I've never heard of such a thing."

"All right, but supposing someone managed to sneak onto the premises—"

"I used to practically live on that farm." Robichard gestured with his cigarette, indicating the sparsely furnished living room. "Believe me, Detective, no one could sneak onto the farm without me hearing about it."

"I understand."

"And no one injected my animals. It's all nonsense."

"Of course, but I had to ask." She dismissed the idea with a toss of her wrist, but her chest thudded and her blood chilled remembering his flustered initial response. She had been a detective too long to overlook that moment of exposure.

43

⌒

Noah woke to the shrill ring of the room's phone. As he reached for the receiver, he glanced at the bedside alarm: 7:10 A.M. "Hello," he croaked.

"Morning, Noah," Gwen Savard said pleasantly. "Hope I didn't wake you."

He smiled to himself. "Matter of fact, you did, but thanks. I didn't set my alarm. Normally, I don't need to over here."

"Sounds like you've adjusted to the French time zone."

"Let's not get carried away, Gwen." He yawned. "Hey, must be late in Washington."

"You know me, I'm a night owl."

"An early bird, too." He remembered those times waking up in Gwen's bed to find that she had already left for a meeting or a predawn workout.

"What can I say? My job leaves more than a little to be desired." She laughed. "Were you trying to reach me yesterday?"

He realized she would have seen his number on her call display even though he had not left a message. It reminded him of Charron's fateful calls.

"You still there, Noah?"

"Just groggy," he said. "It was nothing urgent, Gwen."

"Oh, all right." There was a note of strain in her voice, and Noah felt the distance widening between them again. "I just wanted to make sure you didn't need any help from me and that you were, you know, okay."

Determined not to let the conversation lapse into another series of awkward platitudes between former lovers, he said, "Listen, Gwen, this might not be the time or place . . . but I wanted to tell you that I really miss you."

"Oh, that's . . . um . . ." Her voice faltered. "Very sweet of you to say."

Embarrassed, he cleared his throat. "I was hoping it might mean a little more than that."

"Of course it does, Noah," she said, her words more assured. "It's just unexpected."

Noah realized that she might be dating someone else. "Look, it's not a big deal." He forced a laugh. "I think I've probably been reminiscing over too much French wine. Please don't—"

"Noah, I think about you all the time. I miss you, too." She sighed. "But don't you remember how much our jobs kept getting in our way?"

"Sure, I remember. I just don't care. I'm tired of my job, Gwen. And I'm sick of how often it keeps me away from the people who matter most."

She was quiet for a moment. When she spoke again, her tone was soft and uncharacteristically vulnerable. "Are you saying you want to give this—us—another try?"

"I think I am," he said, surprising himself. "Not like the last time, though. I don't want to put our relationship a distant second to our careers."

She paused a moment. "My life has been on the back burner for so long that I was beginning to think it had just evaporated. I'm ready for a change, too."

He warmed at the thought of reconciliation. "And not to

break my word eight seconds into this offer . . ." He chuckled. "But I won't be able to come home to Washington for another few days at least."

"Ah, and here I was hoping you'd be under my window with a guitar tonight."

"Why? Do you like the sound of cats fighting?"

"Okay, no guitar." She laughed. "But it would be nice to be in the same time zone."

"Soon, Gwen."

"Good." Her tone turned professional. "Now tell me what's the latest in France."

"Gwen, we've traced the human cases back to a geologist and his glacier," Noah said somberly.

"A glacier?" Gwen's voice cracked with surprise. "That's what this is all about?"

"We don't know yet." Noah told her about the traces of the prion found in Georges Manet's ice sample and his connection to all the known victims. "There are still so many unanswered questions."

"Like how did BSE break out simultaneously in cattle?"

"Among others, yes."

"Noah, I'm thinking that as the Bug Czar maybe I actually have a professional reason to join you over there."

"As tempting as the idea is, no, you don't," he said, almost regretting the words as they left his lips. "Let me finish up as fast as I can here. Then I'll come home and we can start over."

Gwen wasn't swayed. "Someone has gone to a lot of trouble to create a smoke screen in that province. When they find out that you're beginning to see through it . . ."

His guts tightened as he digested her warning. "It's not only me, Gwen. The WHO and the E.U. are also involved. There's protection in numbers."

"Yes, but you told me that you don't know how much you can trust the people on 'your' side."

"I trust Jean. And Duncan."

"Is Duncan back there with you?"

"Yes. Speaking of whom, I have to meet him downstairs." He thought of Maggie's illness. "Listen, Gwen, I am going to get Duncan to give you a call. There's something you should hear from him."

"Is he all right?" she asked, concerned.

"Be best if you heard it from him."

"Hmmm." Her dissatisfaction with his answer was obvious, but she didn't press the point.

"I better get moving."

"Go. But take care of yourself, Noah Haldane!" Shyness crept back into her tone. "I've got no else around here to sweep me off my feet."

He pictured her animated green eyes and lip-biting smile. Without a second thought, he blurted, "I love you, Gwen," as he hung up.

Noah felt a slight glow as he bounded out of bed and headed for the shower. He had no regrets about the conversation. He longed to be with Gwen again. His only concern was his daughter. Chloe loved Gwen, but she had only just adjusted to her absence. He would have to find a gentle way to reintroduce Gwen into her life.

For the first time in days, he headed to the lobby more preoccupied with personal than prion-related issues. When Noah entered the same restaurant that had provided most of his sustenance for the past week, he saw Elise and Duncan already seated in the corner table with coffee cups in their hands. For once, they appeared to be chatting amiably. She looked as lovely as ever in her black suit and white blouse, but after his conversation with Gwen, Elise's looks were academic to him now, as if he were noticing a pretty woman on a passing bus.

Duncan wore a casual jacket and his hair was combed, but the layers of darkness under his eyes made him look more sleep-deprived than ever. Those eyes lit mischievously as Noah reached the table. "Ah, Haldane, I hope we're not cutting too much into your vacation by getting you up at this ungodly hour. Were you planning on a porcelain factory tour after a wee lie-in and a buffet brunch?"

Noah smiled. "No, I thought today would be a pool day."

"Wouldn't be the least surprised." Duncan laughed. "Shite, Haldane, expect a call from Satan any time now. That deal you signed with him must be coming due."

Unamused, Elise glanced impatiently from Duncan to Noah. "I think we need to focus on the recent developments."

"Agreed." Duncan slurped his coffee. "Let's talk killer glaciers."

"One that could be almost anywhere in the Arctic," Noah said.

Duncan nodded. "Yup, that's the bugger."

"So either we find Georges Manet or we decipher his referencing system," Elise said flatly.

"Why not?" Duncan grunted. "And once we've done both, we'll build a perpetual motion machine and find the lost continent of Atlantis in time for lunch."

Before Elise could respond, Noah said, "We need to rush the analysis on the samples Georges stored in Jeremy Milton's lab. That might help."

"In fact, I spoke to Dr. Milton right before I came down here," Elise said.

"Oh?" Noah frowned. "About?"

"Pauline Lamaire."

"Who the hell is she?" Duncan asked.

"Georges Manet's former fiancée," Elise said. "I couldn't reach Sylvie, so I tried Dr. Milton. He gave me Pauline's name. She still lives in Montmagnon." She frowned. "Or she did, until a week or so ago."

"What does that mean?" Noah asked.

"I tried to phone her, but her line has been redirected to the Gendarmerie Limoges. Apparently she has been missing since last week."

"Missing?!" Duncan slammed his cup on the table. "She's probably with Georges."

The knots tightened in Noah's neck. "Why would Georges be with his *ex*-fiancée now? He was seeing Giselle Tremblay last summer. And his sister told us he hasn't had a serious relationship in years."

"So what's your grand theory?" Duncan demanded.

"I don't have one," Noah said miserably. "But it's another unexplained happening in this sleepy province that has already chewed through several lifetimes' worth of coincidences."

Duncan blew out his lips. "Another missing woman, too. Like that poor sod of a farmer whose wife disappeared on him."

The comment tweaked Noah's memory. Without a word, he dug in his pocket and pulled out his notebook. He flipped through the pages until he found the entry he was searching for.

"What is it, Noah?" Elise asked.

"The timing is all wrong. . . ."

"How so?" Elise demanded.

"That farm!" Noah pointed to his own notes. "André Pereau told us that he bought the affected calves from Ferme d'Allaire in the 'late spring,' at least six months before they showed symptoms."

"Shite, that's right!" Duncan nodded. "If his cows were injected at the Allaire farm, they would have become sick much earlier."

"Exactly," Noah said. "Long before any people had shown symptoms from Georges's water."

Elise's brow crinkled in bewilderment. "So the animals were never injected?"

Duncan broke into a small grin. "*Or* Pereau's cows were injected somewhere other than the Allaire farm."

Parked outside the rundown stone farmhouse in Terrebonne, Noah reached to open the car door, but Elise's voice stopped him. "Shouldn't we call Detective Avars before going any further?"

"Did you happen to notice the shape the fellow was in last time we were here?" Duncan said. "Standing upright was a challenge for him. I don't think he poses a huge threat to us."

Noah nodded. "We can't waste any more time, Elise."

Prickling with anticipation, Noah climbed out of the car and scanned the grounds, but they were as deserted as on their last visit. At the entry, Elise rapped on the old wooden door. After a few moments, the door opened. André Pereau looked thinner but, dressed in jeans and a turtleneck, he was clean-shaven with combed hair. Noah smelled only aftershave, no wine. "Ah, welcome back, *mes amis*," Pereau said pleasantly.

He led them into the common room, which, unlike on their previous visit, was clean and without an empty bottle in sight. Duncan surveyed the room and nodded his approval. "How long have you been dry?" he asked.

Pereau shrugged. "Four days."

"A long four days, I'm sure." Duncan smiled. "Has your wife come home?"

"Not yet."

Duncan nodded kindly. "Have you found her, then?"

"In Amsterdam."

"Why would she go to Holland in January?" Duncan asked. "Why would anyone?"

"She went with another man," Pereau said.

"Oh." Duncan nodded sympathetically.

"I can't blame her," Pereau continued without a trace of

anger or embarrassment. "It was a stressful time for her here. Those last months I spent more time with the bottle than with Yvette."

Noah noticed the slight tremor in Pereau's hands and recognized the signs of alcohol withdrawal. He wondered if Pereau's sudden sobriety was spurred by the hope of winning his wife back. Duncan reached out and patted Pereau on the shoulder. "Sometimes, even humans make better company than the bottle."

Pereau grinned sadly. "I miss her."

Elise spoke up. "M. Pereau, we need to ask a few more questions about your cattle."

The farmer led them back to the worn chairs they had sat in before. His face clouded with an expression of utter defeat. "I have nothing left to tell you."

"There are some inconsistencies in the timing of this outbreak," Elise said.

Pereau shrugged.

"When exactly did you take possession of those cows from Ferme d'Allaire?" she asked.

"Same as every year." Pereau sighed. "The first week of June."

"And the first sign of illness in the animals?" Noah asked.

"Not until the middle of December."

"Six months." Noah shook his head. "That's way too long."

Pereau frowned. "Too long for what? I do not understand."

"We don't think tainted cattle feed made your animals sick," Noah said.

Pereau held out his palms. "So what did?"

"We suspect somebody might have deliberately injected the animals to infect them," Noah said. "And if so, illness would occur within weeks, not six months later."

Pereau's face blanched and his jaw fell open. The tremor

in his hands became a shake. "*Mon Dieu,* Yvette was right!"

"About what, M. Pereau?" Elise demanded.

"The woman at our farm," he said in a hoarse voice. "It must have been her!"

"*Woman?*" Duncan snapped. "What bloody woman?"

"Yvette didn't even tell me until after the cows became sick," he said, his voice shaky. "She had seen a woman coming out of our barns two or three weeks earlier. Yvette grew convinced that this woman was involved with the illness in some way. Of course, I thought it was absurd. People were always coming and going." His voice cracked. "I even wondered if my wife was losing her mind under the stress."

Elise stiffened in her seat. "Did Mme. Pereau recognize the woman?" she asked quietly.

Pereau's gaze dropped to his lap. "No."

Noah shuffled in his seat. "Did she describe her at all?"

Pereau shook his head slightly. "Only to say that she was young. And attractive."

"What about her hair?" Noah pressed. "Or her coloring? Was she tall? Thin? Anything distinctive?"

Pereau held up his tremulous palms. "All I remember Yvette saying was that even though the woman wore jeans and an old shirt, she looked out of place in the barn."

Duncan grimaced. "What does that mean?"

"That she was too elegant to be working on a farm or as a courier."

Noah thought back to some of the attractive women he had encountered during the investigation. A stranger might have described any one of them as "elegant."

"Why didn't you or your wife tell someone about this woman?" Elise demanded.

"But we did!" Pereau said defensively. "Or at least, I did."

"Who?" Noah asked.

"The detective who investigated Yvette's disappearance," Pereau cried. "The one who found her in Amsterdam."

Noah's throat went dry. He didn't need to ask which detective. He already knew.

44

The road conditions deteriorated steadily during Avril's drive from Lac Noir back to her office. The highway had not been cleared and the snow fell so heavily that her visibility was very limited. Despite the all-wheel drive and snow tires, her car skidded in places on the deserted road.

Avril was barely conscious of the treacherous highway. In her mind, she carefully reviewed the interview with Marcel Robichard. She had had to muster every iota of restraint to leave without challenging him. She was certain the man was involved in whatever happened at Ferme d'Allaire—and by extension, her son's kidnapping—but she had nothing even close to proof. Even if Robichard was involved, she knew that he wasn't the mastermind. He might not even know where Frédéric was held. Or he might not talk. Regardless, confronting Robichard could lead to Frédéric's immediate death. A gamble she wasn't willing to chance.

Avril decided that the best strategy was to connect Robichard to those responsible, either by following him physically to them or through his electronic trail of phone records or financial statements. However, gathering data on Robichard without drawing the attention of someone inside the police department would be another challenge. And she wondered if her patience would hold. *Just twenty-four hours,* she vowed to herself. *And if Robichard does not lead me to Freddie by tomorrow, I will stick a gun between his eyes to make him tell me.*

Avril parked in the Gendarmerie's near-empty parking lot and hurried up to her office. She sat down at her computer and logged on with trepidation, but her pulse slowed after she confirmed that no new e-mails had come from Frédéric's abductors. She opened the Web browser and searched for electronics stores in the Limoges area. She had seen the Sony label on Robichard's flat-screen TV, but she had no idea of the model number or the size of the screen. If she could figure out when and how Robichard purchased the TV, it would solidify her suspicions and provide potential ammunition for a confrontation.

A rap at the door interrupted her research. "Come in," she called out as she closed the search window on her computer.

The door opened and Inspector Esmond Cabot, his hair immaculately coiffed and his blue suit perfectly pressed, stood at the doorway. "Avril, I was wondering if you have finished dealing with our international visitors?"

Avril shook her head. "I am still working on it."

"We are getting a little behind in the rest of our case-load."

Avril stared at her superior with unconcealed annoyance. "You will be the first to know when I am finished, Esmond."

Cabot nodded, but he hesitated at the door. "Have you found anything yet?"

Avril shook her head.

"Do you need any help?" Cabot asked.

Avril hesitated. She had no intention of involving

Cabot, but she could not remember him ever offering to help before. "Thank you, but no, Esmond. I have it under control."

Cabot nodded and left.

As Avril watched him go, her thoughts churned with renewed suspicions. *Is Esmond the mole within our department?* Cabot fit her imagined profile. He knew about the missing women in Limousin. And Yvette Pereau could have approached him with her concerns about tampering on her farm. Or one of the junior officers might have apprised him of Yvette's complaint.

Avril tasted acid in her throat. *Did someone make Esmond an offer he couldn't refuse?*

She was mulling the idea over when Simon Valmont trooped in through her open door. "What did Esmond want?"

"To know if I had finished with the mad cow disease investigators," she said. "He even offered to help with the investigation."

"Help?" Valmont chuckled. "We *are* talking about Inspector Cabot, correct?"

"Not like him, is it?"

"People change, you know?" Valmont snorted. "Magic spells and brain transplants, those kinds of things." The levity left his eyes. "Avril, when will you be finished with all this nonsense?"

"Soon, I hope," she said softly. "Why?"

"I am drowning under the backlog without you." His heavy exhalation turned into one of his throat-hacking tics. "And now I have to traipse out to bloody Lac Noir."

Avril sat up straighter. "What's going on there?"

"Sounds like a suicide."

Skin afire with pins and needles, Avril forced her voice to cooperate. "Do you know anything about the victim?"

Valmont shrugged disinterestedly. "I've got the name

in my office. The neighbor apparently heard a gunshot and called it in. The constable tells me that the victim was the manager for that cattle supplier the E.U. closed down. Sounds very open-and-shut. The fellow loses his lifelong job and then puts a bullet in his brain. Not such a bad way to go, all things considered."

Avril's mouth was too dry to speak. She had only left Robichard's house ninety minutes before. *How did they get to him so quickly?*

"I have to head out in this blizzard to confirm that the death was a suicide," Valmont grunted. "You want to come along to keep me entertained in case radio reception is poor?"

Avril shook her head. "I can't. The investigators from the E.U. are coming to see me."

Valmont shrugged again and headed for the door.

"Simon," Avril called after him. "Will you still be able to join me at the cemetery later today?"

He nodded with his back to her and disappeared out the door.

The Chopin ringtone of her cell phone drew her attention. She glanced down and saw that the caller display read PARIS, FRANCE. Her heart leaped into her throat. She grabbed her purse and jacket, expecting to be sent racing across town to one of many phone booths. "Yes?" she answered anxiously.

"Avril, it's Étienne," said Inspector Breton of the Police Nationale.

She relaxed her grip on the phone. "Étienne, what did you find out?" she asked, too impatient to worry about cell phone scanners.

"I wish I could be of more help," Breton sighed.

Avril swallowed. "You couldn't trace the calls?"

"Of course we could."

"Then what?"

"The calls originated from multiple cell phones—or maybe it was the same phone with the GSM card switched. It's impossible to know."

"Étienne, please . . ." Avril said anxiously.

"Many types of mobile phones carry their activation on interchangeable GSM chips," Breton explained. "Those chips are the phones' 'identity.'"

"Replace the chip, and the phone has a brand-new identity, I understand," Avril said, aware of the technology but frustrated by the news. "But surely you can trace where the calls originated and who registered the GSM chips in the first place?"

"I wish it were that easy, Avril," Breton said. "Unfortunately, it's still legal in numerous E.U. countries to sell anonymous GSM chips for cash. You can even buy them over the Internet."

Crestfallen, Avril said nothing. As an investigator, she should have foreseen that the people holding Frédéric would be too sophisticated to allow themselves to be traced. Still, she had staked her slim hopes on their having made a mistake. With Robichard's death, she had nothing else left.

"Avril?" Breton said.

"Yes?" she breathed.

"There is something more to this, isn't there?"

She didn't reply.

"Tell me."

"Étienne, you can't help." Her voice cracked and she felt the tears welling. "I am not sure anyone can."

"But if you're in danger . . ."

Snap out of it! She fought off the tears. "Étienne, thanks for your concern, but I think I have might have overreacted. I will be fine."

"Overreacted? Someone is phoning you from all over Limoges to threaten you on different GSM cards and you—"

"What did you say?" she cut him off urgently. *"Limoges?"*

"Of course. I tracked the cell tower that relayed the phone calls. All those calls have come from within your vicinity."

Oh my God, Frédéric is somewhere here!

45

Terrebonne, France. January 21

Focused on his swirling thoughts, Noah lost his footing in the snow that had accumulated on the pathway while they had been inside the farmhouse. He righted himself just as Duncan reached a hand out to him. "Haldane, you been drinking Pereau's castoffs?" Duncan quipped.

Noah ignored the remark. "His wife saw her."

Duncan nodded. "We better find the wife. Even if it means going to bloody Amsterdam."

"If she's there," Noah said.

"What are you suggesting, Noah?" Elise asked.

Noah thumbed back to the house. "You heard André. Detective Avars is the only person who has spoken to his wife recently."

Elise spun to face him. "Do you think the detective lied about that?"

"I'm not sure." Noah studied Elise. In her stylish red leather coat and matching beret, she was undeniably elegant. The suspicion bubbled in his gut again. He glanced away. "This thing reaches far and wide," he muttered.

They loaded into the car, and Elise pulled out onto the slippery road. Noah stared out the window, but the snow fell so heavily that he could barely make out the farms and fields that bordered the highway. Though it was only midday, the light was as dim as twilight. And Noah felt chilled despite the heat blasting from the car's vents. He kept his eyes glued to the side mirror.

A few minutes after leaving Terrebonne, Noah spotted another car in the mirror. With the vehicle holding steady a few hundred feet behind them, he could not distinguish its make or color. All he could see was the xenon headlights. Noah's grip tightened on the armrest. From those headlights alone, he knew it had to be a late-model luxury sedan, possibly an Audi or Mercedes. He glanced over his shoulder at Duncan with concern.

"What is it, Haldane?" Duncan asked. "Did it suddenly occur to you that I'm two years overdue for my turn to sit in the front?"

Noah pointed out the back window. Duncan looked over his shoulder. "Is that one of the cars you've seen before?" he asked.

"Maybe." Noah turned to Elise. "Slow down."

She glanced at him. "What if it is them?" she asked urgently.

"If it's *them,* then they're trying to tail us, not catch us."

"How do you know?" she asked.

"They would have caught us by now if they'd wanted to," Noah said. "Let's see what happens if we slow down."

Duncan leaned between the seats. "Do it, Elise."

Elise eased her foot off the gas. Noah craned his neck to stare out the back window. As their car lost speed, the one behind them matched the deceleration. Both vehicles crawled along the highway for another quarter of a kilometer. At the first turnoff they passed—a small road that was largely hidden behind the precipitation—the trailing car veered off and disappeared into the blowing wind and snow.

Duncan broke the tense silence in the car. "Haldane, I think someone means business."

But who? Noah wondered as he stared at Elise out of the corner of his eye. Her face was set in an impassive stare, but he noticed that her hands trembled slightly on the steering wheel.

His phone vibrated in his pocket, and he grabbed for it without checking the call display. "Noah Haldane," he said.

"Ah, Noah, it's—" The rest of the words died in the static of poor cell reception, but Noah recognized his boss's voice.

"Jean?" Noah said. "Is that you?"

"Yes, I am—" His voice cut out again. "Where are . . . *mon ami?*"

"We're on the road," Noah said. "About ten kilometers outside of Limoges."

"I am . . . your hotel . . . now," the crackling voice said. "Perhaps . . . can meet me?"

"Give us twenty minutes." Noah did not try to press Jean for any more information through the intermittent connection. "Twenty minutes, Jean," he repeated for good measure.

Duncan tapped Noah's headrest. "What does the boss want?"

"Poor cell reception. Must be the storm." Noah mustered a smile. "With any luck, he plans to fire us."

"Right!" Duncan moaned. "Where in God's name would he find another pair of world-class idiots to do this wretched job?"

Concentrating on the road ahead, Elise said nothing. Noah and Duncan lapsed into silence, too. Noah noticed that during the rest of the drive back to the hotel Duncan and Elise checked the mirrors as frequently as he did. They didn't spot another set of xenon headlights, but it took them more than thirty minutes to reach Limoges, and another ten inside the city limits before they pulled up in front of their hotel.

They parked on the street and stomped through the snow blanketing the sidewalk. Inside the lobby, Jean Nantal waited in his overcoat. He greeted them warmly—especially Duncan, whose hand he clutched in both of his for a silent moment—and then shepherded them to the empty bar. They sat at the now familiar corner table and ordered hot drinks: tea for Duncan and Elise, coffee for the others. Noah briefed Jean on the latest developments, including the news of the "elegant" woman seen at the Pereau farm, and how they had been followed.

Ignoring his coffee, Jean leaned forward and looked from Elise to Duncan to Noah. "We have found Georges Manet's camp."

"His camp?" Duncan said. "Not Georges?"

Jean shook his head. "We tracked his satellite phone's signal. There was a break in the weather and the Canadian Coast Guard was able to reach the research station on Axel Heiberg Island where Dr. Manet had been living."

Noah sipped his coffee, mainly to wet his dry lips. "What did they find?" he asked.

"Georges was gone." Jean raised his palms up. "But the camp . . ."

"What of it?" Duncan asked.

"A disaster, apparently." Jean exhaled a puff of air. Worry and frustration stole his usual youthfulness; he suddenly looked much older. "There were papers and documents scattered all over the station. Moreover, the hygiene was far from ideal. There were open food containers and . . . human waste . . . spread throughout the interior of the facility."

Duncan frowned. "The bugger must have gone completely mad."

"So it seems," Jean said.

"They found no trace of Georges?" Elise asked.

"It's the dark of winter in the Arctic," Jean said. "There is no light. Of course, they have searched the area carefully, but without his phone there is no way of tracking where he went. So far . . . *rien*."

Duncan slurped his tea. "First, those unhinged e-mails to his sister. Now this. Sounds to me like the poor sod's brain was loaded with your prion."

"How long has he been gone?" Elise asked Jean.

"Inside the station, the lights were still on and the generator was still running. The Coast Guard believes he left days earlier. A week, at the most."

"Left?" Elise said. "You mean died, don't you?"

Jean nodded solemnly. "I don't see how he could possibly survive, no matter what supplies he took with him."

Noah reached for his cup again. "Those papers scattered around. Did they tell you what was written on them?"

"They faxed them to Geneva," Jean said. "For the most part, they were illegible. The notes that could be read made little or no sense, but of course, I will have copies sent to you."

Noah nodded. "And his laptop? Did they find any recent notes or e-mails on it?"

Jean shook his head. "They did not find it."

Noah stiffened and slowly put down his cup. "Manet walked out into the freezing darkness with his computer but not his phone?"

"The man was losing his mind," Duncan pointed out.

"Or, at least, we're supposed to think he was," Noah said, and all eyes turned to him. "Georges seems to have spread this prion, inadvertently or otherwise, to friends and family through his ice and water. Someone, maybe Manet himself, has gone to a hell of a lot of effort to bury that bit of history. Now, our source disappears without a trace. A supposed victim of the disease he spread. But there is no body to autopsy, and probably never will be. Doesn't that strike you as incredibly convenient?"

Duncan shook his head in amazement. "You think old Georges faked a case of variant CJD and then staged his own death?"

Noah merely shrugged.

"Well," Duncan said, "it certainly wouldn't be the strangest happening in this fucking bizarre outbreak."

Elise turned to Jean. "What about Georges's glacier samples at the university in Jeremy Milton's freezer? Have you tested them for the prion yet?"

Jean held up his palms again. "They only received them late last night in Paris. It will be a day or two yet before we know."

Noah reached for his notebook in his jacket pocket. "The sample Sylvie Manet gave us that tested positive for the prion," he said, reading his scrawl. "Have they run any geological tests on the ice?"

Jean sighed. "I was told that it was typical of mature glacial ice from the Axel Heiberg region, but it is impossible to know precisely where it came from."

"It would help if we could pinpoint where Georges was drilling," Duncan grumbled.

"We are searching the area, my friend." Jean checked his watch and rose to his feet. "Please excuse me, but I can't miss my train. I need to get back to Paris before the weather halts all travel." He smiled at the others. "You have done terrific work here. All of you. I will be in touch as soon as I know more." He moved to go but stopped after a step and faced the others again. His smile faded. "What is happening in Limousin is neither normal nor natural. I will be speaking to the director of Interpol later today, but please do not take needless risks." His tone sharpened. "Am I clear?"

Duncan exhaled heavily. "Jean, if you were really

concerned for our welfare, you would ban us from any further involvement with the WHO or you."

"Always the same, Duncan." Jean chuckled, patting the Scotsman on his shoulder. *"Au revoir."* He turned and headed for the exit.

Duncan looked from Elise to Noah. "Now what?"

Noah flipped through the pages of his notebook. "Jeremy Milton told us about an engineer who worked closely with Georges." He consulted his notes. "Pierre . . . Pierre Anou. Perhaps he knows where Georges was drilling for his ice."

"Let's go see the fellow," Duncan said impatiently.

Noah nodded. "After we speak to Detective Avars."

Elise placed her teacup quietly on its saucer. "I thought you didn't trust the detective."

"I don't," Noah said, and the word "elegant" drifted involuntarily to mind again.

At the Gendarmerie Limoges a young uniformed officer, who spoke no English, ushered them into Avril Avars's roomy office. From behind her desk, she smiled apologetically and clicked her computer's mouse two or three times, as if in a hurry to close an open file, before rising to her feet. When she shook his hand, her grip was firm and dry and her eye contact steady.

Noah introduced Avril to Duncan, and then the visitors sat down across from her. She picked up a file on her desk, flipped it open, and reached for the pen that stood upright in a stainless-steel penholder. "Why don't we . . . compare notes? Is that the right expression?"

"Perfect," Noah said, still trying to decide what information was safe to share with her.

"I have interviewed several people, but so far . . ." Avril held out her hand, almost apologetically. "I did not find the old pickup truck or its owner. I have come across no reports of a suspect Audi or Mercedes sedan." She turned to Noah. "And, Dr. Haldane, I have not found any evidence to substantiate the break-in to your hotel room."

Elise leaned forward in her seat. "Detective Avars, our lab in Paris has found the prion responsible for the human infections inside Georges Manet's ice sample."

Avril nodded impassively.

"You don't seem surprised," Noah said. "Last time you implied the theory was far-fetched."

"That was the first I had heard of it," she said coolly. "I have since had a chance to interview Sylvie Manet concerning the ice and her brother Georges."

Elise pointed at Avril. "Georges. The same man who once dated Geneviève Allaire, the president of Ferme d'Allaire."

Avril pursed her lips. "That, I did not know."

"So many connections," Duncan grumbled.

"This is a small province, Dr. McLeod," Avril said.

"You know, my father hailed from Kippen. Everyone in that bloody town knew each other, and I expect a good many of them slept together, to boot." Duncan paused. "Of course, there are four hundred people in the village of Kippen, and two hundred thousand here in Limousin."

"I never suggested this is all a matter of chance," Avril said.

Noah eyed her steadily. "What do you suggest, then?"

Avril met his stare. "You paint a conspiracy that involves most of Limousin, but we still have not found a . . . smoking gun."

"How hard are you looking?" Noah asked.

"I take this very seriously, Dr. Haldane." She broke off the eye contact and looked down at her notes. "I agree that something is not as it appears. I require more time to do my job. And it does not help me to have you running the same investigation as I am."

"Yvette Pereau," Noah said.

Avril shrugged. "What about her?" she asked as she wrote the name on the page in front of her.

Noah fought back his rising ire. "Did you know that her husband owned the farm that reported one of the first cases of mad cow disease?"

"I did," she said quietly.

Duncan snapped his fingers. "You just didn't think it was worth mentioning that she disappeared right after she saw someone molesting her cows."

Avril looked up at Duncan. "Dr. McLeod, as a physician, are you permitted to discuss patients by name with other people?"

"I don't see what—"

"I am obliged to respect Mme. Pereau's privacy," she said. "Yes. I investigated her disappearance. But I also found her. And the case is now closed."

"What of Yvette's claim that she saw a stranger in her barn?" Elise asked.

Avril sighed. "Mme. Pereau told me that she was far more afraid of her husband than anyone," she said. "Apparently, his drinking made him unpredictable and violent. And paranoid. After the animals became sick, he accused her of involvement. Before she escaped with her *friend,* Yvette said, she had to invent stories to deflect the blame, including that one."

Noah silently conceded that the explanation had a ring of truth to it. "And how can we reach Mme. Pereau?" he asked.

Avril shrugged. "I doubt she's still in Amsterdam. She left me with the distinct impression that she did not want to be reached."

Duncan slapped the desk in front of him. "How bloody convenient for you!"

"Does her accusation not seem odd?" Avril asked evenly.

"Odd how?" Noah asked.

"That some woman walked onto their farm in broad daylight and started injecting cows in their barn," she said.

Duncan rolled his eyes. "When the hell is a *normal* time to waltz onto a farm and inject cows' brains full of prions?"

"That is my point, Dr. McLeod," Avril shot back. "I agree that there is more to this than we first thought. But I think it is important to separate the facts from . . . conjecture."

"And Pauline Lamaire?" Noah asked.

Avril's eyes widened momentarily. "What does Mlle. Lamaire have to do with any of this?" she asked quietly.

"You know her, then?" Elise spoke up.

"Yes," Avril said softly. "I grew up in the same town as Pauline. I used to babysit her."

Duncan looked over to Noah but did not comment.

"Do you know that she is missing?" Elise asked.

Avril nodded. "How is that related to your investigation?"

"She was once engaged to Georges Manet," Elise said.

Avril was quiet a moment and then nodded her understanding.

"This whole province is closer knit than bloody Kippen," Duncan grumbled.

"I doubt that, Dr. McLeod." Avril smiled patiently. "I agree this may not all be coincidence. I will need to investigate further, especially at Ferme d'Allaire." She looked at Noah. "With a few more days, Dr. Haldane, I will have many more answers, I promise you."

Noah found no reassurance in the promise. "I don't think we have days to wait. Besides, our director plans to take this to Interpol. Today."

"Interpol?" Avril dropped her pen on the desk. The color drained from her cheeks. "That is not necessary at this point!"

Duncan stared at her, looking as puzzled as Noah felt by her profound reaction.

"This is my investigation," she snapped. "It will not help bringing in outsiders who do not know or understand the people and culture of this region." She turned to Noah. "Believe me, Dr. Haldane. It will only make it harder for us to sort out. Give me forty-eight hours. I will have your answers. Please."

46

Limoges, France. January 21

After she shut the office door, Avril stumbled back to her desk overcome by light-headedness and nausea. She dropped into her chair and vibrated with worry. Gagging, she tasted the bile at the back of her mouth. As she clutched her head in her hands and fought back the vomit, she wondered how much longer this nightmare could last. "Antoine, what have I done?" she whispered.

Frédéric was somewhere in Limoges. *So close.* But if his abductors learned that Interpol was about to be dragged into the situation, they would surely kill him as quickly as they had Marcel Robichard. *I have to act!*

They would be phoning again soon—Avril knew it—and everything hinged on that next call. She wiped her moist hands on her trousers, reached into her jacket pocket, and pulled out her cell phone. She chose the fourth speed-dial number on her list and SIMON popped up on her cell phone's screen.

He answered on the fourth ring. "Valmont," he said before clearing his throat noisily.

"Simon, it's Avril," she said. "Where are you?"

"Lac Noir," Valmont grunted. "The suicide."

"Will you be much longer?"

"Shouldn't be. I have seen more than my fill."

"Anything unexpected?" she asked, sounding as casual as she could.

"The usual. Bullet through the roof of his mouth." Valmont's sigh turned into another throat clearing. "I hate these self-inflicted gunshots, though. I still get queasy at the sight of brain spattered everywhere."

A fresh wave of nausea swept over her as she pictured the man she had interviewed only hours earlier—the person she had hoped would lead her to her son—with a gaping hole in the top of his head. "Simon, the snow is not expected to ease up, so I am going to go to the cemetery earlier than I thought."

"When?"

"Soon as I finish up here. Maybe half an hour. I hope you can still join me. It's an important . . . occasion." She swallowed. "And I'd sooner not be alone."

He was quiet a moment. "Can you give me an hour?"

"Thanks, Simon," she said, and the tears welled up out of nowhere again.

Forty minutes later, Avril reached the cemetery on the outskirts of Limoges. As she had hoped, no one else had ventured out into the blizzard that was sweeping the region. Despite the heavy snowfall and unpredictable gusts of wind, Avril did not feel cold standing beside Antoine's headstone. As always, she was vaguely aware of his presence. Today she found it more comforting than ever.

She had already told her husband everything she had wanted to, so she stood silently by the grave, remembering those halcyon days when Antoine and Frédéric were both at home.

Her attention was drawn to a pair of headlights that cut through the gray darkness enveloping the cemetery's parking lot. She watched the shadow of the car pull into a parking stall, but the headlights switched off and she saw little else in the poor visibility. A few minutes passed before Avril spotted the outline of Valmont lumbering across the snow toward her. She saw the glow of a cigarette between his lips, but he stomped it out before he reached her.

Looking stiff and awkward, Valmont held out his gloved hand to her. "I am sorry," he said. "Antoine was a very decent man."

She shook his hand. "Thanks for coming, Simon."

He nodded and looked down at the headstone.

Avril checked over either shoulder but saw no movement aside from the constantly falling sheet of snow. "Simon, this has nothing to do with Antoine," she said very quietly.

He looked up slowly. "No?"

She shook her head. "It's Frédéric."

"And the trouble at school—"

She held up her palm to interrupt. *"They have him,"* she croaked.

Valmont frowned. "Who has him, Avril?"

"I don't know, exactly," she said. "They are the same people involved with the human cases of the mad cow disease in Limousin. The ones who abducted and killed Pauline Lamaire and Yvette Pereau."

Valmont brought his hand to his mouth. "Avril, what the hell?" he asked softly.

"Frédéric was kidnapped," she said, her voice unsteady as she spoke the words for the first time to another living person. As she summarized the events of her last two hellish days, the words flooded out.

Valmont did not interrupt to ask a question. Aside from reaching for a fresh cigarette he hardly moved while Avril spoke. "I would have told you sooner, but I didn't know how," she said. "The kidnappers are watching me at all times. And they must have a source inside the Gendarmerie. There is no other way they could have known about my investigation into the two missing women." She paused. "I think it might be Esmond."

"Esmond?"

"Whoever it is, I didn't feel safe discussing it anywhere but here."

"Of course," he said.

"It's my fault," she went on hoarsely. "I should have listened to you, Simon. This happened to Frédéric because I got too close to the truth about Yvette Pereau and Pauline Lamaire. The monsters killed those women to cover their tracks. And now they are using me to mislead the WHO doctor and the woman from the E.U."

Valmont absentmindedly tossed away the cigarette butt and reached for a new one. He stooped forward to light it. In the glow of the flame, his face suddenly looked drawn and haggard. "Did the outsiders believe what you told them today?" he asked.

"I don't know." She shook her head. "Dr. Haldane does not trust me. I don't blame him, either. There is so much to explain away, and he already knows a lot."

"What does he know?"

She shrugged in frustration. "What does it matter, Simon?"

"If I am to help you, I need to know everything they told you."

"They think Georges Manet, or maybe others, spread the human cases through polar ice or water. And they're convinced someone staged the outbreak in the animals to cover it all up. They're right, too. My theory is that there is something valuable about this ice. And these people are trying to hide its lethal side effect."

"Makes sense," Valmont grunted.

"Anyway, it doesn't matter if Haldane believed me or not," she said dejectedly.

"Why not, Avril?"

"I saw your supposed 'suicide' right before his death."

"Robichard?" Valmont asked, showing little surprise.

Avril stared at her partner. "He was lying to me. It was obvious. I knew he had to be involved in the cover-up at the farm. I think he panicked after my visit and either shot himself or more likely called his collaborators, who killed him to shut him up." She sighed heavily. "I should have confronted him then and there. Now the killers know I interrogated him."

"You were investigating, just as you told them you would," Valmont soothed.

"It gets worse, Simon." She heaved a sigh. "Dr. Haldane informed me that the WHO plans to involve Interpol."

Valmont straightened. "Have or will?" he snapped.

"Will, I think. But as soon as they do, Frédéric is as good as dead."

The creases around Valmont's eyes deepened to fissures and the bags seemed to puff under his eyes. Something looked different in her friend, but Avril was too preoccupied to give it more thought. "Listen, Simon. I need your help."

Valmont nodded distantly.

"They have not called today," Avril said. "They will, I know it. And if it's anything like the previous calls, they will send me scurrying to some public phone booth in Limoges."

"And what if they do?" Valmont asked, and then cleared his throat so long and hard it sounded as though something were caught in it.

"This might be the very last chance I have to reach Frédéric."

Valmont inhaled deeply from his cigarette but said nothing.

Avril noticed a tremor in her partner's hand. "Simon, I

need you to have the phone company track every pay phone in Limoges. I will keep the kidnappers on the line as long as possible, but we have to trace that phone call."

"That's a lot of phones to monitor," Valmont muttered. "I don't know if they will—"

"The other calls have come from Limoges," Avril pleaded. "Frédéric is in the city, somewhere close. Simon, if we can pinpoint the call, we can react right away. Surprise them. We won't give them time to do anything to him . . ."

Valmont took another long drag from his cigarette. Avril saw that his hand shook more prominently now. Then she recognized the look in his droopy eyes.

The realization hit her like a gunshot. The cold consumed her, as though she were suddenly naked in the snowstorm. She remembered Haldane's description of the anonymous farmer who tipped them off about Ferme d'Allaire. *The old beat-up truck!* Besides horse races and soccer, Simon's passion was restoring old cars, vans, and trucks. He always had at least three or four of his "projects" on his property.

No, it can't be. Her heart walloped against her breastbone. *We have been colleagues—friends—for almost twenty years!* She swallowed back another mouthful of bile and her knees shook. She thought of the gun she carried in her handbag. "Simon, can you put a trace on those phones?" she asked, stalling. "It is so very important."

He looked away and nodded.

Numb with the shock of his betrayal, Avril focused on getting to her gun. "Oh, and Simon, I came across two important e-mails that will help tie this all together."

"Really?" Valmont grunted, still avoiding eye contact.

"Yes, I have printouts in my bag." She pulled her handbag off her shoulder and reached for its zipper. "Look, you can see them now."

"Put the purse down, Avril," he said quietly.

"No, they're right here—"

"Drop the damn purse!" he snapped.

Avril's fingers froze on the zipper.

Valmont waved his cigarette over his shoulder. "Somewhere out there a man has you targeted in the crosshairs of his rifle. With any sudden move, he will shoot."

She let the handbag slip out of her hand. It landed silently on the snow. "Simon . . . how?"

His chin dropped lower. "It wasn't supposed to be like this."

She held out her hand. "Freddie considers you his uncle."

"He shouldn't be involved."

The anger surged inside her. "But he is!" she cried.

"I've had a bad year at the track. And they offered very good money," Valmont mumbled. "I was only supposed to be their eyes and ears at the Gendarmerie. Then that woman, Yvette Pereau, came to me with all her claims about the tampering at her barn." He made another hacking noise. "And every mess I cleaned up led to a bigger one—"

"They are going to kill Frédéric!" Avril spat, half accusation and half plea. "You must stop them, Simon. *You must!*"

"You should have never gone to Amsterdam." Valmont slowly looked up at Avril and met her stare. His eyes went glassy and his expression frosted over with determination. "We have to go now, Avril."

47

Martine DeGroot stared through the flat afternoon light at the monotonous countryside, made even more so by the blanket of snow covering it. In the backseat beside De-Groot, Yulia Radvogin tapped the mobile phone impatiently against her ear as she growled and snapped in Russian. She barely broke off long enough to breathe during the tirade. In the driver's seat of the Mercedes E-series sedan, her bodyguard Viktor appeared scrunched in a seat that would have been roomy for most others. Radvogin's other bodyguard, Myron, wasn't present.

Radvogin clicked shut her cell phone. "Fucking lawyers!" she snarled in English. "You pay them a fortune only to hear them tell you nothing but no."

DeGroot nodded, uninterested. "Where are we going, Yulia?"

"Not far," Radvogin said.

Radvogin's phone rang again and she answered it savagely. DeGroot turned back to the window, ignoring the impatient one-sided Russian conversation going on beside her.

They had driven another fifteen minutes without exchanging a word when Viktor suddenly pulled off onto a small side road. Only a few partially snow-covered tire tracks identified it as a road at all. At first, they drove past isolated farms, but after three or four minutes evergreens rose up on either side of the road, and soon the car was following a narrow path under a snowy canopy of firs and pines.

They came to a stop in a small clearing. Viktor climbed out and opened the door for his boss. DeGroot got out as well. She met Radvogin and Viktor on the other side of the car. "Where are we?" DeGroot asked calmly.

"I am told people come here to hike in the summer," Radvogin said.

"Are we going for a hike?" DeGroot asked with a trace of amusement.

Radvogin stared hard at her. "What have you done, Martine?"

DeGroot did not try to play dumb. "We have tried to protect your investment."

"By setting Claude Fontaine on fire?" Radvogin asked, though her tone and face showed little concern for the man's fate.

"He was going to die anyway, Yulia."

"From the prion?"

DeGroot nodded.

"That he picked up by drinking the water from Vish-nov?"

"Yes," DeGroot said. Even in the weak light, she could see that the older woman's eyes had begun to smolder.

"Interesting," Radvogin said softly. "I could swear that when we stood at the South Pole you promised me the water was safe."

"It is, once it is *sterilized* with heat and ultraviolet radiation," DeGroot stressed. "It's the same for any water supply. You wouldn't provide drinking water from a well or reservoir without carefully monitoring and treating the water. It could contain all kinds of potentially dangerous organisms."

"Not prehistoric prions," Radvogin snapped. "Besides, you told me the treatment was a precaution, not a necessity."

"I know," DeGroot said without backing down. "I thought it was best for your sake that you didn't know all the . . . less wholesome . . . details."

"I see," Radvogin said, struggling to maintain control of her tone. "What else did you think it was best for me not to know?"

DeGroot shrugged. "There has been other fallout. Unavoidable, I am afraid."

Radvogin began to pace, her boots cutting silently through a sheet of fresh snow. "*Who* else?" Her raised voice seemed to echo among the trees.

"To summarize?" DeGroot counted with her fingers. "A farmer's wife. A nosy doctor from Limoges. A spinster from a nearby town. And a panicking farm manager." She gazed off at the branches surrounding them. "Oh, and we are now about to take care of a police detective and her son."

Radvogin snorted. "I give you carte blanche, and this is how you spend my money?"

"Money well spent, Yulia." DeGroot nodded. "There are only a few others left to deal with, and then the path will be clear."

Radvogin flicked her wrist in annoyance. *"More?"*

"The main problem is a doctor from the WHO. Noah Haldane."

Radvogin grimaced and her pace increased. "Haldane? The hero of that . . . ARCS epidemic? *Him?*"

"We have tried everything to dissuade him." DeGroot sighed as if helpless to intervene. "But he will not let go of this."

"And you don't think anyone will notice?"

"Depends on how he dies, of course."

"You have a plan, I take it?"

"Weather permitting."

Radvogin blew out her lips in disgust. "I took you for many things, Martine, but never for a fool!" she scoffed.

"I know you're upset, Yulia," DeGroot said. "And I can't blame you. We never expected to come across anything like this prion. And we had no idea—until it was far too late—that Georges was passing out raw lake water like it was wine. We have had to respond to each new incident immediately. At times, mercilessly. Think of it as damage control. Or even self-preservation." She folded her arms across her chest. "Nonetheless, Vishnov is still a bottomless gold mine. In the end, this changes nothing."

Radvogin stopped pacing and spun on her heel. "It changes everything!" she hissed. "I am already facing enormous political and legal pressure. The Antarctic Treaty Consultative Parties plan to take us to court in several countries. And the ATCP has the support of every environmental lobby group you can imagine." She pointed a shaky finger at DeGroot. "Just wait until they find out that Radvogin Industries is marketing deadly water!"

"Yulia, listen to me," DeGroot said urgently. "Not only is the finished product free of the prion, it has healing properties."

"Ach. How do you know it is free of the prion?"

DeGroot rested a hand on her own chest. "Unlike Claude—who drank the water before it was treated—no one who has tasted the *sterilized* water has become ill."

"Nonsense." Radvogin shook her head vehemently. "Even if the water is safer now, someone will find out about what has happened. Believe me, Martine, you can hide only so much."

"The bottled water *is* safe," DeGroot said. "And once we take care of Haldane, and finish up our damage control, this will all be an unpleasant—but secret—footnote in the history of Radvogin Industries and the Lake."

Radvogin smiled, but there was no reassurance or warmth in her expression. "I would like to believe you, Martine. I would. But you've spun a web so thick and wide that no broom can sweep it away." Her tone hardened. "I will not let you bring down Radvogin Industries in scandal and destroy thirty years of my work." A fleck of spittle flew from her lips. "I will not!"

"Think carefully, Yulia. Bottles of the Lake are arriving as we speak. If you stop it now, you will lose hundreds of millions of dollars." DeGroot held up a hand. "Worse than that, you might actually *draw* suspicion to Vishnov by suddenly terminating production."

Radvogin stared at DeGroot for a long moment as if swayed by the argument, and then she broke into a soft chuckle. "Martine, you are so very good. And you do remind me of myself. Though you are more cold-blooded than I ever was."

"Thank you." DeGroot lowered her hand and cracked a smile of her own. "You have reconsidered, then?"

Radvogin stopped laughing. "I warned you several times about the cost of failure."

"Yulia . . ."

Radvogin shook her head slowly. "As fond as I am of you, I cannot possibly shut down Vishnov and leave you alive." She looked up at the sky. "God only knows how you might exact your revenge on me."

"Don't do this, Yulia."

Radvogin turned to her tank of a bodyguard, who had stood off to the side, motionless, throughout the conversation. "Viktor, it's time."

He casually reached into his jacket and withdrew a long pistol with attached silencer. He aimed the weapon at De-Groot.

"Good-bye, Martine," Radvogin said. "I did enjoy knowing you."

DeGroot flashed a carefree smile at the older woman. "The feeling is mutual."

Radvogin's eyes widened in sudden realization, just as Viktor redirected the gun at her.

DeGroot glanced at Viktor, and she bit her lip in an intimate smile. "Viktor works for us now. Don't you?"

Radvogin's eyes darted to her bodyguard. "Viktor? You didn't!" The color in her face drained. "And Myron? What have you done with him, Viktor?"

The giant's face remained impassive. His aim held firm.

"Myron wouldn't cooperate," DeGroot said casually. "So we had to get rid of him."

Radvogin looked to DeGroot, her eyes huge but her tone still authoritative. "How could you possibly explain my death, Martine? Who would continue to finance Vishnov?"

"I don't need to worry about either if no one knows you're gone."

"Everyone will know!"

"Over the past few weeks, we have developed an expertise in making people disappear." DeGroot ran her foot through the snow in front of her, erasing a footprint. "Besides, we have a little inside help at Radvogin Industries."

"Inside help?" Radvogin snapped, panic seeping into her tone. "Who?"

"Your man Anatoly Beria," DeGroot said matter-of-factly.

"He assures me that your absence will not be realized until we wish it so."

"Anatoly? You seduced him, too?" Her words quivered with indignation. "*Anatoly!* Fucking lawyers!"

DeGroot looked over to Viktor with a solemn nod.

"Viktor, listen to me," Radvogin pleaded. "The bitch is

using you. Do not let her mislead you with her flesh. She sleeps with everyone . . . *anyone*. You cannot trust—"

"Viktor," DeGroot cut her off.

Radvogin backpedaled in the snow, slipping and almost losing her balance, as she brought her hands up to her face. "Viktor, you must believe—" Her words were cut short by a muted thud from his gun.

The bullet ripped through Radvogin's forehead and snapped her neck back. Mouth still agape, she crumpled to her knees and toppled over. Though the impact was entirely silent, the snow around her head turned red on contact, as if the ground itself were bleeding.

48

Champsac, France. January 21

Outside the car window, the snow fell almost as hard as hail, but Noah barely noticed. He studied the cell phone in his hand, hoping for a call from home. His homesickness had mushroomed since his conversation with Gwen, which stoked not only his eagerness to return but also his impatience. He had yet to hear back from Anna and Chloe. Though he desperately missed his daughter and Gwen, he wouldn't have left France now even if Jean had offered him an out; not when he sensed they were finally closing in on the truth.

Noah looked over to Elise, who gripped the steering wheel tighter than ever. Even Duncan appeared unusually attentive to their surroundings. The threat hung heavier than ever. None of them bothered to hide how frequently they checked the mirrors or windows for a sign of a tail.

The thirty-kilometer ride from Limoges to Pierre Anou's hometown of Champsac was supposed to last thirty minutes, but they had been driving through the blizzard for more than an hour and they still had ten kilometers to go. The all-wheel drive on Elise's BMW gripped the road well. The real hazards were the other stranded

cars that impeded or blocked their way. Perhaps the greatest threat, Noah thought glumly, was the German luxury
sedans that could not be seen at all.

The cell phone vibrated in his hand. Glancing at the
screen, Noah recognized the Limoges area code. The phone
showed only one bar of reception; he knew the connection
was going to be tenuous. "Noah Haldane," he said.

"Dr. Haldane, I am Clarice Charron," she said in heavily accented English that was difficult to understand
through the earpiece's choppy static.

"Oh, Mme. Charron, thanks for returning my call,"
Noah said. "I was very sorry to hear about your husband."

"D'accord," she said.

"I work with the World Health Organization—"

"I know who you are," she said. "Jean Nantal is an old
friend of ours—of mine."

"He speaks highly of you, madame."

"Your message said you had some questions."

Noah pressed his palm against his other ear to hear better. "Is there a good time to come see you?"

"Now is the best—" Her voice cut out.

"I don't think we will be back in Limoges for several
hours."

"Why not speak over the phone?" Clarice asked.

"All right." Though reluctant to conduct the interview
over a cell phone—especially with such poor reception—he
realized that the weather might prevent a face-to-face
meeting any time soon. "I am working on the same mad
cow outbreak that Dr. Charron originally diagnosed."

There was no reply. Assuming she did not hear, Noah
began to repeat the statement, but Clarice cut him off in
midsentence. "Louis told me something was very wrong."

"It is an awful illness—"

"That is not my meaning," Clarice snapped. "My husband believed that the spread of the illness was not . . .
how do you say?"

"Random?"

"Exactly so. He found a connection between the victims. Then he went to that farm—" Her voice cut out briefly. "He met someone—" She disappeared again for another moment. "A woman, he spoke—"

"You're cutting in and out, Mme. Charron!" Noah squeezed the phone so hard against his ear that it hurt. "What farm? What woman?"

"The one from the news, Ferme d'Allaire." Her voice was choppy. "I do not know who the woman was, but she sounded important."

"Did he tell you what he found on that farm?" Noah asked.

"What?" she asked.

Noah repeated the question.

"He was going to tell me when he came home that night." She was quiet for a moment, but Noah knew it wasn't a problem with the reception. "We were supposed to have our anniversary dinner. Louis never reached home."

"He was on his way home for your anniversary dinner?" Noah repeated.

Duncan leaned between the seats. "The man was blind drunk *before* his anniversary dinner?" he whispered.

Noah shushed Duncan with a finger to his mouth.

"I don't . . ." Clarice's voice dissolved again. "Not a heavy drinker. He never . . . driving . . ."

"Mme. Charron, I am losing you." Noah articulated each syllable carefully. "What about the other times the police pulled your husband over for drinking and driving?"

"What other times?" she cried.

"We were told your husband was charged at least three times before for driving drunk."

"No! He never . . ." A pause. "Who told—" More static. "A lie—"

Noah waited but Clarice's voice never broke through the low hum again. "Mme. Charron?" he prompted.

Nothing. Noah looked down at the phone's screen and saw that the last of his reception bars was gone. The hair on his neck stood on end. He turned to the others urgently. "Do either of your cell phones get reception out here?"

Elise took a hand off the steering wheel to pick her phone out of the cup holder. She glanced at it and then shook her head. "Mine's nothing but a high-tech paperweight now," Duncan grunted.

That would add another concern for Duncan, who—judging by the number of times Noah had spotted his friend on the phone—was keeping very close tabs on his wife's condition. Noah summarized his conversation with Charron's widow for the others. "All I caught was snippets," he said. "But I know she was trying to tell me that her husband never drove while drunk."

Elise's eyes darted in his direction without turning her head. "So Detective Avars lied about his criminal record," she said in a hush.

Noah nodded. "I bet Charron's 'accident' was no accident at all."

Duncan leaned forward between the seats again. "It also means that Detective Avars—and Christ knows who else at the old Gendarmerie—is up to her neck in this."

"Explains why she didn't want Interpol involved," Noah said, fighting off a sudden chill.

"Also doesn't leave us much in the way of backup," Duncan grumbled. "If we end up in a wee pickle like Dr. Charron did, the French Foreign Legion isn't likely to ride in on their camels to rescue our sorry hides."

Consisting of three or four streets, the village of Champsac was even smaller than other towns they had visited in Limousin. Elise found Pierre Anou's quaint stone house set on a property whose landscaping consisted of a few neglected shrubs poking through the snow.

Dr. Anou answered the door in a sweater and fleece pants. Tall and skeletal, with a prominent jaw and protuberant forehead, the middle-aged engineer reminded Noah of an old black-and-white Frankenstein-like TV character. In a manner as wooden as his gait, Anou welcomed his guests into a living room piled with books and journals. Noah could barely see the computer on his desk through the stacks of paper and journals surrounding it. Anou cleared some papers off the threadbare cloth-covered chairs to make seats for everyone, but his hospitality ended there.

Elise began to explain in French that her colleagues' grasp of the language was limited, but Anou waved a big palm to interrupt. "One does not survive long in glaciology without understanding English." He viewed them circumspectly. "And you would not have driven through this blizzard unless this was very important."

"We heard you are a friend of Georges Manet," Elise said.

"A friend?" Anou considered the characterization. "Glaciology is a small field. Georges and I have worked together on numerous drill sites. I respect his work, as I imagine he respects mine. But he is a bit too wild for my taste."

"Wild?" Noah repeated.

"He is brilliant," Anou said. "But at every site I have worked with him, he has always pushed the limits too far. Always joking and fooling when it is time to be serious." He shook his head. "Perhaps that is why so often he ends up working alone."

Duncan nodded, encouraging Anou. "And the maniac was always trying to drink the glaciers he drilled on, wasn't he?"

Anou shook his head and sighed. "He thinks the nectar of the gods is frozen in that ice."

A skinny woman with wide eyes and stringy hair appeared at the doorway. She gaped at the visitors for a moment and then turned away. Noah assumed the woman was Anou's wife or partner, but the glaciologist did not respond to her fleeting appearance.

"When was the last time you spoke to Georges?" Elise asked.

Anou thought about it. "Six months ago. Perhaps longer. Late last spring, I think."

"How about e-mail?" Elise pressed.

"No different." Anou's expression darkened with suspicion again. "Why does it matter?"

"Georges is missing."

Anou frowned. "Oh? What happened?"

"They found his camp on Axel Heiberg Island, yesterday, but Georges was gone," Noah said. "They think he might have become disoriented and wandered out." Noah decided not to share his suspicion that Georges might have staged the discovery.

The engineer's prominent jaw fell and he slumped back in his chair. "*Mon Dieu!* Disoriented? Wandering outside in the dead of the Arctic winter?"

"Did you ever work there?" Noah asked.

Anou's color was wan now. "I was there two years ago with Georges and a few others from the Institut de Physique du Globe de Paris," he said.

"Georges brought back several ice samples from the region," Noah said. "We need to know exactly where the ice came from."

Anou nodded distractedly. "Georges documents his samples thoroughly."

"So thoroughly that nobody has a fucking clue where they're from," Duncan groaned.

"I do," the engineer said.

"You understand his referencing system?" Elise asked.

"Not his. Mine." Anou touched a bony finger to his chest. "He 'borrowed' it from me."

Duncan turned to Noah. "You didn't happen to record

the number in that notebook you drag around everywhere with you?"

Noah nodded, as he pulled the notebook from his pocket. He found the page and read the passage: *"Arctic, échantillon 0411B2307."*

Anou trudged over to his desk and shuffled through mounds of paper. He chose a page and brought it back to the others. It was a detailed map of the region, which he laid across his lap. Anou's slender finger came to rest on a spot slightly inland from the body of water. "That sample must come from here. Roughly five hundred meters from where we set up camp two years ago."

"Can you mark the spot for us?" Noah asked.

Anou fished a pen from his pocket and carefully marked an X on the map. "Earlier," he said, "I was not being entirely honest."

Duncan sighed. "You would have been the first one in this bloody province, if you were."

"Georges and I used to be good friends," Anou said.

Elise cocked her head. "What happened?" she asked.

Anou looked down at the map on his lap. "I blamed Georges for Vishnov."

"Vishnov . . . You mean that Antarctic lake that Claude Fontaine discovered?"

"Fontaine didn't discover Vishnov," Anou said with indignation. "He merely exploited it. Georges and I contributed as much as Fontaine did. I helped design the well that first sampled the lake. It was quite an engineering feat."

"What was Georges's role?" Noah asked.

"Originally, he was responsible for mapping the best route through the ice to the lake," Anou said. "He stayed on to study the core samples we drilled. After all, the Igloo was a glaciologist's dream."

"The igloo?" Elise gasped. "I thought we were discussing the Antarctic."

Anou laughed humorlessly. "Someone, perhaps even Georges, nicknamed the research station that, because from the outside it did look like a massive igloo," he explained. "The whole operation was privately funded. We had the best equipment imaginable. Our resources were unlimited. And the research potential there was endless."

"So how did Georges bugger up your frozen nirvana?" Duncan asked.

"He wouldn't leave Claude Fontaine alone," Anou said. "Fontaine raised the money. From the beginning, he made it very clear that it was his project. The man is arrogant and extremely vain. And Georges took every opportunity to needle him. I warned Georges, but he kept pushing the limits. He even heckled the man on film the day we broke through the ice. Fontaine was livid."

Duncan rubbed his beard. "I assume Fontaine booted Georges off the project?"

"All of us researchers, I'm afraid." Anou absentmindedly folded the corners of the map. "I was halfway through two major studies. Maybe Georges's childish behavior was not the only reason, but I have no doubt it instigated all our firings."

Noah felt the twinges at his temples as a realization began to take shape. "Did Georges ever drink the water from Vishnov?"

"Of course. He even tried to convince me to." Anou waved his big palm again. "I wanted no part of that stupidity."

Duncan's gaze shot over to Noah. "Shite, Haldane, you don't think . . ."

Noah's temples slammed steadily now. "Dr. Anou, do you know if Georges brought any water back home with him from Vishnov?"

"Barrels of it," Anou said. "He was very excited about that water. He claimed it had amazing healing properties."

"Oh, shite!" Duncan muttered.

Elise gaped at Noah. He turned back to Anou. "Do you have any idea where Georges would have stored this water?"

"No." Anou studied them curiously. "But if you're looking for a sample of Vishnov's water, you certainly don't need to find Georges."

"What does that mean?" Noah snapped.

Anou rose to his feet, passed Noah the map, and then hurried over to the kitchen. He leafed through some drawers until he dug out a magazine. He loped back to them and handed it to Noah. "My wife likes to waste money on this garbage," he said.

Though the French name meant nothing to him, Noah recognized it as a fashion magazine from the beautiful couple posing on the front cover. Bewildered as to the relevance, he studied the cover until Anou reached down and flipped it over in his hand.

Heart hammering in his ears, Noah gawked at the back cover in disbelief. The glossy, full-page, color advertisement showed a sleek stylized bottle half buried in ice with melted water dripping down its side.

The name on the bottle told him all he needed to know: the Lake.

49

Limoges, France. January 21

Arms bound behind her back, Avril lay across the back-seat of the Audi. She could see only light and dark through the scratchy hood smothering her face, and breathing was difficult. She had little concern for her own fate—if any-thing, death would come as a welcome escape from the past days of living hell—but worry for Frédéric consumed her. So did the crushing guilt. She had an unwanted flash-back to the last time she laid eyes on her son, loading his old Citro'n that frost-bitten December morning when he headed back to architectural school. Their good-byes were heartfelt, but the lingering tension over Frédéric's marital intentions overshadowed his departure. *Oh God, will that petty squabble be our last memory of one another?*

As outraged as Avril was by Valmont's treachery, she was more upset with herself for not having seen through it in time. Looking back, the clues—his secretiveness, his unexplained interest in the missing-woman cases, and the way he disappeared whenever Haldane was around—were as clear as street signs. She had let twenty years of friend-ship and her own tornado of emotion cloud her judgment. Now she was going to pay. So was Frédéric.

I have failed him as a mother and as a detective, she thought again. She mumbled a quiet prayer that she would at least have the chance to tell Frédéric how sorry she was.

Blinded by the hood, Avril listened to the hum of the car's engine and felt the vehicle drift on the snow. She had no idea who else was in the car with her, because no one had spoken a word after the massive no-neck thug slipped the hood over her head and tied her hands tightly behind her back. Through it all, Valmont had hovered silently off to the side, but he never once met Avril's accusing eyes.

After what felt like forty-five minutes, the car crunched to a stop. Avril heard the front door open and felt the cool air rush in. Voices spoke in hushed tones around her in English, but she had difficulty making out the words through her hood. At least five more minutes passed before the door at her feet opened. "Get up, Detective Avars," a woman said in French spoken with a foreign accent, possibly Dutch.

Without the use of her bound hands, Avril struggled to rise from the car seat. Someone grabbed her roughly by the upper arm and pulled her up the rest of the way. She was yanked forward and her boots broke through a soft layer of snow. Prodded from behind, she trudged about twenty feet through snow until the path cleared and she felt solid ground below her feet.

The light brightened as she stepped through a doorway and onto a floor that felt like tile. A few feet further, the same woman said, "We are going downstairs now."

Despite the warning, Avril stumbled on the first blind step. She caught her balance just before toppling down the staircase. Counting twelve stairs, she took each one carefully until the ground leveled under her feet again. She walked a few steps more before a hand tightened around her arm, halting her progress.

A door creaked open. She was shoved forward.

Suddenly, the hood flew off her head. Before she could turn around, the door slammed shut behind her in the dingy chilly room. Her eyes took a moment to adjust to the weak light, and she almost banged her head on the shelving. Seeing the low ceiling, she realized she stood in a near-empty cellar.

A voice spoke up from somewhere. "Maman?"

Avril's heart melted. "Frédéric, *darling!*" She scanned the ground frantically until she spotted her son huddled in the corner of the room, his face puffy and his shirt still covered in blood. A few feet to his left, a disheveled woman looked up at Avril with abject helplessness. Avril was so disoriented that it took her a moment to recognize the woman as Sylvie Manet.

As Frédéric struggled to his feet, Avril rushed over to her son, overcome by the intensely conflicting sense of relief and doom. She dropped to her knees, oblivious to the pain of them slamming onto the concrete floor. She leaned over to him and kissed his cheek and his swollen-shut eye.

Frédéric viewed her with a pained smile. "Maman, I am sorry." His words were slightly distorted by his swollen lip.

"You're sorry?" Tears toppled down her cheeks. "Oh, darling, this was all my fault. They used you to get to me."

He shook his head, trying to assume responsibility. "I walked right into their trap."

"God, you are so much like your father." Avril sobbed a laugh.

"Papa would never have gotten himself into this," Frédéric said. "I don't even know why I went to meet that Dutch woman. I didn't trust her from the beginning."

"Oh, Freddie, if I hadn't interfered in your love life . . ."

"You were right, Maman. And I knew it all along, too. I

was just too proud to admit it. Stéphane and I never had a chance at a real future together." He swallowed at the unintended irony of the comment. "Still, I should have never gone out with that woman! I knew she was trouble."

Avril pressed her cheek against his. "Stop it, Freddie. Don't you see? If not her, they would have gotten to you some other way. This conspiracy runs so deep." She paused. "There is nothing they wouldn't do."

"Who are *they*?" Sylvie spoke up in a faltering voice.

Avril had forgotten that she and her son were not alone. Pulling her cheek from Frédéric's, she turned sympathetically to the frightened-looking woman. "I have only scratched the surface," she said. "But apart from the Dutch woman and her henchman, they include at least a few locals."

"Which ones?" Sylvie asked.

Frédéric looked up at his mother with a pained expression. "Maman, I don't know how to tell you this, but . . . Uncle Simon is with them. I saw him once through the door."

Avril nodded. "I know, darling." She turned back to Sylvie. "Aside from Detective Valmont"—she spoke his name through gritted teeth—"a manager from Ferme d'Allaire was involved, but he's dead now."

Sylvie swallowed. "Did they kill him?"

Avril did not want to frighten them needlessly, so she ignored the question. "I am not sure if people even higher up at the farm were involved," she said. "They used the Allaire farm to stage the outbreak in cows. To pretend it came from the animals." She looked intensely at Sylvie. "But it was your brother's ice, or water, that caused the spread of this disease."

"You don't think Georges was involved in this?" she asked, horrified. "After all, it looks like he . . . died . . . in the Arctic. Maybe even from that prion disease."

"Maybe," Avril said evenly.

Sylvie picked up on her skepticism. "He's not involved!" she cried. "Our younger brother, Philippe, died of the illness. Georges would never . . ." Her voice trailed off.

After Valmont's betrayal, she was not willing to exclude anyone from suspicion. Especially not Georges Manet. However, it seemed pointlessly cruel to argue with Sylvie, so she simply nodded.

Frédéric stared at his mother with the same hurt and bewilderment she had seen in his eyes at Antoine's funeral. "Why are they doing this, Maman? What is so special about this ice or water?"

She lifted her shoulders and shook her head. "I think someone sees commercial value in that water. Maybe they plan to sell it as a kind of curative health drink. Some of the victims, Pauline Lamaire, Giselle Tremblay, and even your brother Philippe"—she glanced at Sylvie—"tried to use it as a remedy for chronic illness."

Frédéric snorted and fresh blood appeared at his nostril. "Wouldn't have much health value if people knew they could die from drinking it," he said wryly.

Avril smiled at her son. "Exactly."

Sylvie shuffled down the wall closer to the other two. Her face wasn't beaten like Frédéric's, but her cheeks were drawn and her eyes rich with fear. "You must have told someone—aside from this Detective Valmont—about what you know? Detective, if you told someone else then surely they will come looking for us."

Avril looked down at her knees. "I didn't," Avril said softly.

"How will they find us?" Sylvie asked in a whisper.

Avril didn't reply.

Frédéric leaned his head closer to hers. She smelled his stale breath. The huge welts around his eyes reminded her of his suffering, and guilt and heartache rocked her again.

"Maman, they can't afford to free us, can they?"

Avril scoured her brain for a reassuring answer. "There

have already been too many unexplained disappearances," she said. "They cannot afford to have the investigating detective, her son, *and* the sister of the man who discovered the infected ice simply disappear without explanation."

Frédéric regarded her, unappeased. "They are probably figuring out a credible way for that to happen right now."

You're too smart for your own good, Frédéric, Avril thought. "We don't know that," she said, and kissed him on the cheek again.

Sylvie hung her head, looking as if she might cry at any moment. Frédéric turned to her. "Sorry, Sylvie," he said gently. He turned back to his mother. "We might have a little time while they decide what to do with us. Maybe we can figure out a way out of here."

Avril nodded. "We have to try," she said.

"If not for us, then at least for all those people who still might be poisoned by these scum," he said. "We have to get the word out, Maman."

"I know," Avril said as the tears spilled down her own cheeks again. Despite their grim outlook, she was so happy to have found her son again. And she had never been more proud of him.

50

———

Champsac, France. January 21

By the time Noah, Duncan, and Elise left Pierre Anou's home, the dull cloud cover had disappeared in the rapidly fading twilight. The blizzard had let up, but with the break in the snowfall the temperature had plummeted. Noah shivered from more than just the cutting cold as he slipped into the passenger seat of Elise's car. He stared at his cell phone, which still did not offer a single bar of reception. Before leaving he had tried to call out on Anou's landline, only to discover it too had been knocked out by the storm. "Damn it!" he muttered under his breath.

"Bottled bloody water?" Duncan grumbled from the seat behind his. "That's what humans and cows are dying for?"

"It is a huge industry," Elise pointed out, as she pulled back onto the road, its smooth snow blanket cut by only one other set of partially covered tire tracks.

Noah nodded. "They must have put a fortune into piping that water out of Lake Vishnov."

"Who are *they*?" Elise asked.

"People who stand to make a killing off the Vishnov water," Noah said. "We'd better find out who owns the rights to the Lake."

"That shouldn't be too difficult," Elise said.

"Be easier if a single fucking phone worked in this country!" Duncan thumped Noah's headrest.

Elise looked over to Noah, her face tight with worry. "What about Georges's glacier sample that contained the prion? That was supposed to have come from the Arctic, not the Antarctic. Could it have been mislabeled?"

Noah shook his head. "It must have been a fake."

"*A fake?*" Duncan's voice squeaked. "Staging a mad cow outbreak to cover your tracks makes some demented sense. But what the hell is the point of blaming a cold plague on ice from the Arctic instead of water from the Antarctic?"

Noah glanced over his shoulder at Duncan. "No one is trying to sell ice from the Arctic."

Duncan's eyes lit with understanding. "Shite," he murmured. "If Georges Manet, or whoever, knew that we'd stumbled onto his trail, he would look for any plausible way to throw us off, wouldn't he?"

Noah sighed. "They probably hoped that the sample would be enough to send us scouring the Canadian Arctic, while they got rich selling water from Vishnov."

"But how do you fake a prion-infected glacier?" Elise asked.

"If it were me," Noah said, "I would drill holes in the ice, fill them with the contaminated water, and then refreeze."

"Wouldn't they see that in the lab, though?" Elise asked.

"That hunk of death was tested for organisms in a *microbiology* lab," Duncan said. "If it showed up at my lab I couldn't tell you if it came from the North Pole, the South Pole, or straight out of your bloody gin and tonic!"

"Duncan's right," Noah said. "And someone like Georges Manet could probably doctor the ice to fool even the experts."

"We have no proof Georges is still alive," Elise pointed out.

"I can think of several million—probably a hundred million—reasons why the bugger might have staged his own death," Duncan said.

"No doubt," Noah said.

"Christ, they're going to ship Vishnov's tainted water all over the world, aren't they? Haldane, next time we're in India or Thailand, remind me to take my chances with the tap water," Duncan quipped, but his tone belied his obvious tension.

Noah had a vivid mental image of the video footage he had seen of Giselle Tremblay and Philippe Manet. He bristled at the idea of facing countless other slobbering zombielike victims of this prion. "We cannot let the Lake get to the store shelves," he said, more to himself than to the others.

Duncan held up his cell phone and shook his head. "Still nothing. Shite!"

Elise viewed Noah out of the corner of her eye. "Who exactly should we tell? No one local, I trust."

"Jean, for starters," Noah said.

She nodded. "And I need to tell Javier."

"Are you sure you can trust him or the others at the E.U.?"

She paused a moment. "No," she admitted. "Do you not have doubts about the people at the WHO?"

"I have no doubt about Jean." Noah held her gaze. "Beyond that, I really don't know whom to trust anymore."

The creases in her forehead deepened, but Elise did not otherwise respond to the implied accusation in his tone.

"I keep thinking about that elegant woman Yvette Pereau saw leaving her barn," Noah went on. "My gut tells me we've already met her."

"Sylvie Manet, perhaps?" Elise said. "After all, she

gave us the misleading ice sample. And who is more likely to have known what her brother was up to?"

"One—possibly both—of her brothers died of the wee monster," Duncan said. "Hard to imagine she could be involved in that."

Noah nodded. "Geneviève Allaire would know her way around a barn better than Sylvie."

"True," Elise said.

Noah could no longer contain his gnawing suspicions. "Elise, if they engineered that ice sample to throw us off their trail, then they must have known we were getting close."

Elise's shoulders rose and dipped. "I imagine Detective Avars told them. We know she's been lying to us."

Noah gritted his teeth. "So how did we ever end up dealing with the one cop who is neck deep in all of this?"

"How do you know she's the only corrupt officer?" Elise said. "Maybe her boss is involved, too."

"Or maybe she knew we were coming," Noah said.

Elise's head spun to face Noah. Her lip curled. "And you think I am the one telling them?" she said barely above a whisper.

"I know that you can look very elegant."

Her lip trembled. "You bastard," she growled and then turned her gaze back to the road.

"I am sorry, Elise." His tone had softened, but he didn't change tacks. "It's just that they always seem to know where we are and what we're up to."

Before Elise could respond, Duncan leaned forward and tapped them on the shoulder. "Like now!" he said, and pointed urgently at the back window.

Noah and Elise turned in unison to see a pair of xenon headlights bearing down on them. "Move it!" he barked.

Elise punched the accelerator and the tires spun. The engine whined. She eased off, and the tires bit into the snow and launched the BMW along the white highway.

Gripping the armrest, Noah watched over his shoulder as the trailing car gained on them.

Elise sped into the upcoming bend in the road. The car drifted to the right, but made the corner. Noah squeezed the armrest even tighter. Though Elise was an able chauffeur, he had no idea whether she could outrace someone on a dark snowy highway. Nor was he totally convinced that she even wanted to. But he was only a passenger now, and that sudden helplessness bothered him more than the inherent danger.

As soon as the front end of the car straightened, Elise floored the gas pedal. The engine hummed louder. The power poles passed with steadily increasing frequency. They raced up a long hill toward a curve in the highway. Heart in his throat, Noah recalled their ride on their way to Anou's house through the same snaking section of canyon road. The route had rocks on one side and steep drop-offs on the other. "Elise, the canyon ahead—"

"I know," she said with surprising calm.

Elise eased off the accelerator only slightly as she entered the winding section. With disregard for the possibility of traffic coming from the other direction, she slid and zigzagged the car across the road. As if glued to their tail, the xenon lights stuck close behind, disappearing only for moments around the sharpest turns.

Elise slowed to round a curve, but the car still drifted into the inner lane. Noah felt a bump and then his door touched the rock wall with a grating metal kiss before slipping free. The car slid to the left, and for a breathless moment Noah wondered if they were going to plummet into the canyon. As they neared the edge, the tires caught and Elise managed to pull out of the slide.

"Too close!" Duncan said hoarsely.

The mistake cost Elise speed, and the bluish high beams flooded through the rear window. Elise punched the gas pedal again, and the engine whined in response.

But before they gained much speed they were rammed from behind. Noah's head was jolted forward and his upper and lower teeth bit hard against each other.

The car drifted again toward the rocks. *"Merde!"* Elise whispered as she fought the steering wheel to straighten out without overcorrecting.

Noah suddenly saw the dark side of the hill close up again. He shrank away from the window, expecting an impact, but just before his door reached it, Elise pulled free of the drift and steered the car back to the center of the road.

The high beams still flooded the interior and the vehicle slammed into them again. The impact propelled the car forward. Noah looked ahead in horror to see a tight curve approaching and realized they were heading for the drop-off. Out of reflex he braced his hand against the dashboard.

Elise turned hard on the steering wheel and the car fishtailed. Just before they reached the edge of the cliff, she steered into the turn and somehow the BMW stuck to the road.

"No more," Elise vowed aloud, gripping the steering wheel as though she were trying to rip it free of the dashboard. Though the bright lights were bearing down again, Elise managed to weave the car slightly from side to side, making it a more elusive target. But each time she dodged to the right or left, the car came precariously close to the road's edge—rock on one side, drop-off on the other. Temples drumming, Noah realized that they would die instantly if another car happened to materialize coming from the opposite direction.

Elise accelerated steadily as they left the canyon and the highway's curves began to level out. She drove with renewed recklessness, and the car flew down the snowy road. Despite the speed, she put little distance between their car and the blue lights.

Noah looked over his shoulder to see the xenon lights sliding to their left and realized the other car was going to try to run them off the road from the inside lane. Elise noticed, too. She turned the steering wheel. The car glided to the left, cutting off the path. Undeterred, the pursuing car aimed for the right side. Their BMW skated across to block that maneuver. For the next five hundred meters, the trailing car competed for an inside track as if the two vehicles were locked in some kind of nightmarish snow-bound Formula One race, but Elise managed to protect her flanks.

Blocking another advance, Elise wove to her right. Noah could see that she went too far, even before the other car slipped in alongside her. She reacted immediately. Leaning into her turn, she yanked the steering wheel and the car cut wildly to the left.

The back left fender of their car ground against the front right fender of the other for a long moment. Elise let go of the accelerator as the BMW swerved wildly. The back end fishtailed and the car slid off the edge of the road with a hard bump. Noah lifted out of his seat before the seat belt yanked him back down.

The car finally came to a stop in a farmer's field. He looked over to the others. "Everyone okay?"

"Better than that son of a bitch!" Duncan thumbed at the rear window.

Noah saw that the blue headlights of the car were much further behind them and pointed off in another direction. It took a moment to grasp that the car was lying on its side.

Elise did not say a word. She pressed down on the pedal and the car's engine groaned in response, but then began cutting through the thick snow toward the road. With another heavy bump, they climbed back on the highway and raced away from the upended car behind them.

"I'll say this, the French just aren't as welcoming as

they used to be." Duncan chuckled as he reached forward and patted Elise on the shoulder. "Not bad, Mlle. Renard. Not bad at all."

Noah looked down at the cell phone that he had been squeezing as though his life depended on it. He saw two signal bars. "Hey!" he said, elated. "My phone has reception again."

As Elise headed into the next turn, Noah pressed the speed-dial button on his phone and the list popped up on the screen. He reached for the DIAL button, but he froze in the sudden shower of light.

The high beams coming directly for them were less blue than the previous set but blindingly intense. Elise slammed on the brakes, but the car skidded violently. Noah dropped his phone at the same moment that the car slid into a full tailspin. As if caught in a tornado, Noah felt himself being hurled around inside the car. His ear slammed against the window, and he heard a pop followed by a louder smash. Then there was a shower of glass.

Finally, the car came to a stop perched with its front end dangling off the side of the road. Covered with glass and with his right ear ringing, Noah glanced over to Elise and then Duncan. Both appeared stunned. For a moment, he thought Duncan must be in shock. His friend stared right past him with jaw hanging open. Then Noah looked out the broken window and saw the woman standing beside the car.

Her gun was pointing directly at his chest.

51

Lac Noir, France. January 21

Wrestling with the padded restraint around her wrists, Avril began to feel a little movement and realized that she had worked more of her left palm through the binding. Encouraged, she wriggled harder, oblivious to the pins and needles from the diminished blood flow.

Suddenly, the cellar door scraped loudly against the stone floor. Avril stopped moving. She watched as three more hooded people were shoved roughly into the room. Behind the big Russian pushing them, she caught a glimpse of Simon Valmont where he stood in the hallway with a lit cigarette dangling from his lips. He held her gaze for a fraction of a second and then turned away.

The Russian yanked the hoods off the new prisoners and then stomped out of the room, slamming the door behind him. Before the masks even came off, Avril recognized Noah Haldane and his two colleagues. With their hands also tied behind their backs, all three squinted in the poor light trying to gain their bearings. As Noah's eyes fell on Avril, his face flushed with accusation. But his scowl smoothed as the implication of the scene began to register.

"Please accept my apology, Dr. Haldane," Avril said, as

she rose awkwardly to her feet. "I should have warned you somehow."

Frédéric's head swiveled to look up at her, bewildered.

"My son, Frédéric," she said to Noah.

Noah nodded slowly. "They were blackmailing you?"

"Yes."

"How could you have risked telling us?" Noah said sympathetically.

Avril took small comfort from his understanding tone. She looked down at her son. "Frédéric, these are Ms. Renard, Dr. McLeod, and Dr. Haldane." Then she switched to French even though her son spoke English. "They are the international investigators."

Frédéric mustered a smile of greeting and his swollen lip cracked in the center.

Duncan kneeled forward to study Frédéric's beaten face with concern. "Are you all right, son?" he asked.

"They're just bruises." Frédéric struggled to his feet, looking very wobbly once upright. Avril leaned closer, trying to support him with her shoulder.

Duncan shook his head indignantly as he straightened. "Blackmailing a mother with her own son," he muttered. "What a bunch our hosts must be."

Elise spoke up. "How long have you been here?"

"Maybe two or three hours," Avril said. "But Freddie has been here for days."

Frédéric nodded glumly. "Except for the bathroom a few times—and they always put the hood back on me before I go—I have not left this room."

Sylvie Manet spoke up. "I have been here only a few hours more than Detective Avars."

Elise looked down at Sylvie, who was the only person still seated. "How did you end up here?" she asked.

"I was so worried about Georges," Sylvie said. "I read through all of his recent e-mails again, and they did not seem right to me."

"In what sense?" Elise asked.

"It was almost as if . . . someone else had written them." Sylvie nodded to Avril. "I went to the Gendarmerie to discuss my concerns with Detective Avars."

Working the binding at her wrists again, Avril looked over to Sylvie. "When was this?"

"This morning," Sylvie said. "You weren't there, of course." Avril thought back and realized she would have been in Lac Noir, interviewing Marcel Robichard. "Detective Valmont approached me. He told me he was also working on the case. He followed me back to my house to see the e-mails in person." She sighed bitterly. "As soon as we came inside, he surprised me. I was overpowered before I knew it."

"Do you know where we are now?" Elise asked.

Sylvie shook her head. "They put a hood on me like the rest of you. All I know is that it was not a long drive from my house."

Avril turned to Noah. "Dr. Haldane, have you learned any more since we spoke?"

Noah stared at Avril with lingering reticence, making it clear that he did not fully trust her. Elise answered for him. "This was never about the glacier sample in Sylvie's freezer."

Avril was taken by surprise. "This infection was not in the water Georges passed out?"

"Oh, it's in the water, all right," Duncan said. "Just not in the ice."

"The water comes from the Antarctic." Elise went on to brief Avril about the well in Vishnov and the magazine advertisement for the Lake. Then she described their theory that the ice sample had been manufactured to deliberately point them in the wrong direction.

"In fact, the polar opposite direction," Duncan emphasized.

"Bien sûr," Avril said. "I knew somehow they were planning to profit from that water."

Duncan turned to Sylvie. "How did that ice sample wind up in your freezer?"

"Georges brought it back from the Arctic last summer," Sylvie said. "He asked Maman to store it in our freezer. She had done the same for him several times over the years."

"Precisely when did he leave it?" Avril asked.

Sylvie thought a moment. "Early June. Maybe late May."

"No one became ill until autumn," Elise pointed out.

"So someone must have doctored the ice after it was first put in the freezer," Duncan reasoned.

Noah stared hard at Sylvie. "Who would have known of its existence other than Georges, your mother, or yourself?"

Sylvie looked up at him, defeat clouding her features. "I suppose Georges's colleagues—or anyone who knew him well enough—would know he kept samples at home and elsewhere." She shook her head. "Georges is not responsible. If you only knew him, you would see that he would never do something like this."

"Money—especially the promise of it—changes people," Duncan said. "Your brother stands to make a king's ransom from this water."

"But how? Now that you know about the prion."

"Christ, why do you think we're imprisoned here?" Duncan exclaimed.

Sylvie's eyes widened with desperation. "Surely, you have told others about this bottled water?"

Duncan rolled his eyes. "Between the storm and your country's rudimentary telecommunication system—"

"Duncan!" Noah took a step closer to his colleague. "Someone is probably listening to our every word."

Duncan's mouth opened and his wandering eye twitched

momentarily. He said nothing, but Avril could see that he was upset with himself for the oversight.

Avril concentrated on the ligatures at her wrists. She tugged hard and felt a tad more give in her left hand. Her heart skipped a beat, as the padding slid up to the base of her thumb. *Only a few centimeters more,* she thought, working it fiercely.

Elise looked from Avril and Frédéric to Sylvie. "That Dutch woman and the Russian man, do any of you know who they are?"

"No," Frédéric said. Avril and Sylvie both shook their heads.

"Are there others?" Elise asked.

"As far as I have seen, only Detective Valmont," Sylvie said.

Avril noticed Noah studying Sylvie intently, but he remained silent.

Elise turned to Frédéric. "You have been here the longest. Have you seen anyone else?"

"No, but twice I thought I heard the Dutch woman talking to someone else. The voices were very low. But it was definitely another woman. She sounded French to me, too."

Elise viewed Frédéric evenly. "You did not recognize the woman?"

"No."

Elise indicated the door with a lift of her shoulder. "So there are at least four of them out there."

Frédéric nodded.

Avril wriggled her left hand harder. Holding her breath, she felt her thumb begin to slip further through the ligature up to the knuckle. *Not far now.*

Duncan rubbed his bearded chin roughly against his shoulder, appearing to struggle with his own bindings. "They must have collected us here for a bloody reason," Duncan said.

Elise looked over to him. "Isn't it obvious?" she said.

"They can't just make us disappear into thin air," Duncan said. He indicated Noah with a tilt of his head. "Deservedly or not, after ARCS, this one's a celebrity."

Noah said nothing. Elise sighed. "They'll find an accident or some other way," she said.

"Don't know about the rest of you, but I have a family to take care of," Duncan muttered grimly. "So I suggest we figure some way out."

Frédéric nodded eagerly. "Other days, the Russian man or the Dutch woman has brought food—milkshakes and soup—for me to drink with a straw." His voice dropped to a whisper and he glanced around conspiratorially. "Maybe when they come back, we could surprise them?"

"But how?" Elise whispered.

Duncan kicked the air with his right leg. "Our feet still work," he said.

"But they are armed," Elise said. "And the Russian looks like he's a bodyguard or a professional soldier of some sort."

"We have to try," Frédéric said.

"Bloody right," Duncan said.

Elise and Sylvie nodded. "I agree," Avril said, while still working her hands vigorously. Only Noah didn't respond. He simply continued to stare at Sylvie.

Sylvie looked around the room at the others. "If one of you had just told someone—anyone—about the Lake, we could maybe bargain our way out of here," she half pleaded and half accused.

The appeal was met by blank and helpless stares.

Avril squeezed more of her hand through the restraint, almost freeing her thumb and fingers.

"Your brother didn't write those e-mails to you," Noah told Sylvie.

Sylvie nodded. "I agree."

Noah's lips tightened. "Georges has been dead for a long time now."

"How do you know that?" Sylvie asked.

"I think he was already infected with the prion late last summer when he met Jeremy Milton for drinks. Milton described him as 'scatter-brained.'" Noah eyed Sylvie steadily. "In which case, he would have died within a month or so. I bet that's why his body has never been found. I think he's only 'existed' in sporadic e-mails to you and a few others."

Sylvie angled her head. "Why do you think that?"

"Because it fits." His tone was edgy and challenging.

Sylvie said nothing, but Avril stopped struggling with her bonds. She studied the woman with an inkling of realization.

"What fits?" Elise asked anxiously.

Noah snorted. "Why would someone pull their gravely ill relative out of a major hospital and bring them to an ill-equipped nursing home in a small town?"

"Philippe was dying," Sylvie said. "Besides, I told you, my mother was ill with a heart condition. She could not travel—"

Ignoring the explanation, Noah took a step closer. "Your little brother kept talking about the water. He said that Georges knew. That *you* knew. He was telling us that the water was poisoned."

Sylvie grimaced. "Poor Philippe had lost his mind."

"But he was aware enough to know that his death sentence came from the water. And I think the best way to shut him up was to have him die in a fire." Noah's eyes danced with a fire of their own. "You also told us Georges hadn't had a serious girlfriend in years. You neglected to mention he was dating one of the victims, Giselle Tremblay, until we discovered it."

Sylvie did not respond.

"You were the only one with access to that ice sample," Noah went on. "And it only materialized after you heard that we already knew that Georges was handing the water out to the other victims." His tone sharpened. "When you wanted to steer us away from Vishnov."

"Holy shite!" Duncan chimed in, stepping closer to Sylvie. "You're a bloody biologist, aren't you? You would know enough about prions and mad cow disease to come up with a scheme like this!"

Elise gaped at Sylvie. "You were the so-called elegant woman Yvette Pereau caught in her barn!"

From the floor, Sylvie looked up at her accusers for a long silent moment. Then she gave a sigh. Her expression bordered on relief. She pulled both hands out from behind her back and jumped to her feet. The padded ligatures dangled freely at her wrists, never attached in the first place. "I just wanted to ensure that you had not told anyone else," she said. "Thank you for confirming that. It has been so tiresome plugging every new leak."

Sylvie's hands shot out and she roughly shoved Noah and Duncan to either side, launching them off balance. Darting between them, she ran to the door and pounded on it. "Viktor . . . Martine . . . open up!" she yelled.

Avril struggled wildly at her restraint, and felt it slide further over her fingers.

Frédéric lowered his head and ran at Sylvie like he was a battering ram. She turned and saw him at the last moment. She lithely dodged to her right. Frédéric hit the door with his head, and Sylvie knocked him hard with clasped hands, sending him face-first to the floor.

"Freddie!" Avril cried. Without fully freeing her hands, she launched herself across the room at Sylvie.

Sylvie dug a small gun from her pocket. "Stop!" She aimed the muzzle at Avril's approaching head.

Avril stumbled to a halt. Everyone else went motionless. Then the door opened behind Sylvie and the Dutch woman stood in the doorway, also holding a gun. Sylvie looked over her shoulder at the woman, and they shared an amused and intimate smile. "Viktor is outside working on the cars," the woman said.

Avril tugged her arm and felt her left fingers slip free of the last of the ligature.

Sylvie turned back to the prisoners. "Your wait will not be much longer now," she said coolly. Then, over her shoulder, she yelled in French, "Oh, and Simon, get back in here and redo the restraints on the detective. Tighter this time! She almost got free."

52

⌒

Lac Noir, France. January 21

As he stared at Sylvie Manet's gun, Noah's head swam and his perforated eardrum whistled painfully. He felt as though he had yet to emerge from the tailspin the BMW had launched into back on that snowy highway.

Having regained his balance after Sylvie's shove, he stood near the far wall, reorienting himself. The Dutch woman leaned against the doorjamb, her gun hanging loosely in her hand. Sylvie stood a few feet from her, arm outstretched with the gun still pointing at Avril. To his left, Elise stared defiantly at both armed women. Frédéric lay on his side by the door where he had collapsed. Duncan rested on his knees where he had fallen after being pushed.

Avril stood still as a statue in front of Noah and a few feet from Sylvie. Noah saw that her left hand was already free but she clutched it in her right hand, pretending otherwise. Aware that she was planning to surprise the captors, he scoured his brain for a way to distract them. "You killed your own brothers, Sylvie," he said in his most condemning tone.

Sylvie's head snapped, and her eyes bored into him.

"Georges did! He drank the raw water out of the well, and then gave it to Philippe." She shook her head slightly. "What I did was merciful. I put them both out of their misery. Their brains had already rotted."

Noah shrugged his bound arms. "And all the others? What did they die for?"

Sylvie viewed him steadily. "The money, of course!" Her voice was deeper, harsher, and far more self-assured now that she had shed the pretense of being a grieving sister. "I have a doctorate and a position at the university in Bordeaux, but I cannot even afford to buy a decent apartment there. I was going to have to sell my father's prized furniture just to make my car payments.

"Then last winter Georges told me of this pure Antarctic water. He claimed that it has amazing healing powers—which it does—but even without that, I saw the value straightaway." Sylvie barked a disdainful laugh. "Georges was a socialist. He cared nothing about the water's commercial potential. So I turned to Claude Fontaine. At first, the arrogant pig wouldn't listen. I had to call upon my secret weapon." With a smile, she turned and blew a kiss to the Dutch woman. "I sent my colleague and very good friend, Dr. DeGroot, to reason with him. Within weeks, Martine convinced Claude and his backers to enter into a partnership with us." She held up her free hand. "And that would have been that—"

From his knees, Duncan scoffed, "Except you found out that your health product was, in fact, lethal."

Sylvie's gazed drifted over to Duncan. "Not lethal, Dr. McLeod. It just needed to be purified," she said. "Much of the food and drink we take for granted would be deadly without pasteurization or preservatives. Vishnov's water is no different."

"Purified?" Duncan said. "You must be out of your fucking mind, lass! Heat sterilization is used to kill living microorganisms. We're talking about a prion here."

"He's right," Noah said. "A prion is not alive in the first place. It's just a rogue protein. You cannot pasteurize something that is not living."

Sylvie seemed to waver a moment, but then her smile re-emerged. "You can, gentlemen. Heat denatures the protein. Inactivates it."

"Not consistently!" Noah said, nauseated by her miscalculation but desperate to string out the discussion for Avril's sake. "That has always been the problem with trying to sterilize prion-contaminated substances. In hospitals, people have been infected with prions from surgical tools that were both heat- and chemically sterilized between cases."

Sylvie continued as if he had never spoken. "We knew the water had to be processed from the start. But without consulting me, my foolish older brother gave out raw water to several people here in Limousin. And yes, some became ill."

Noah swallowed his outrage. "And so you buried it . . . and them," he said calmly, as he watched Avril unwind the ligature behind her back.

"What else could we do?" Sylvie shook her head as if she genuinely had no choice but evidence-planting and murder. "We had committed everything. We were desperate to explain away the prion illness before it drew attention to the Lake. So, last fall, when Georges fell ill, we flew him out to the Arctic as he intended." She shrugged. "I know my brother would have wanted to go that way."

"How did you stage the BSE outbreak?" Noah asked, trying to keep Sylvie preoccupied and allow Avril a glimmer of a chance.

"Fortunately, at labs in Paris and Berlin, Martine had access to nerve tissue of cows infected with BSE. We liquefied the substrate. It was quite simple after that." Sylvie smiled, and Noah realized with disgust that not only had she justified the twisted scheme to herself, she was actually

proud of it. "We needed our 'source' farm, and so we
turned to Ferme d'Allaire and its very greedy manager,
Marcel Robichard. We injected several of the animals—
much as you had postulated—with a needle to their thecal
sacs." She touched the back of her own neck. "Of course,
we could not wait for those calves to be sold to market.
So, with M. Robichard's paid assistance, we tracked down
a number of farms that had purchased cattle from the Allaire operation. Everything went smoothly, except at the
Pereau farm." She *tsked* her disapproval. "Yvette Pereau
was not supposed to be home the afternoon she surprised
me in the barn. Even so, she never saw the needle. And
had she not been so irrational and run to the police, there
would have been no need for her disappearance. Fortunately, Detective Valmont got wind of the complaint and
we were able to deal with it." She pointed at Avril with a
flick of her finger. "Though our luck turned for the worse
when her husband wandered into your office."

Avril said nothing, but her grip tightened on the ligature behind her back.

"But you didn't stop there, did you?" Noah asserted,
anxious to buy Avril more time. "You still had to kill
Louis Charron and Pauline Lamaire."

"Poor Pauline . . . She was something special before the
arthritis turned her into that obsessive wreck. Once
Georges gave her the first few sips of Vishnov, she was ad-
dicted. After Georges disappeared, she pestered me so
much I had to keep her supplied with water—sterilized
water—just to keep her quiet. Months passed, and I thought
Pauline was going to be all right." She touched her lip pen-
sively. "This prion is *so* unpredictable. Some people become sick right away. And others, like Pauline and
Georges, take months to show symptoms after exposure.
However, once Pauline did become confused we had no
choice." Sylvie shrugged. "As for Dr. Charron, he meddled

where he never should have. He had no business going to
Ferme d'Allaire and spouting such wild accusations."

"So you killed them both?" Elise said bitterly.

"We never planned on hurting anyone," Sylvie said, as
if it absolved her of responsibility. "We found out about
that wretched prion in our water when it was already too
late to turn back. So we did what we had to do to protect
our investment . . . our future."

"That includes murdering us," Elise growled.

Sylvie remained unrepentant. "We gave you every
opportunity to let this go. All of you." She looked at Avril.
"We went to the effort of shipping Yvette to Amsterdam,
just so she would not be considered 'missing.' But you
wouldn't listen to your own colleague." She turned to
Noah. "And, Dr. Haldane, you and your team . . . we built
you up to be the heroes of this crisis. We spent a fortune
staging events in the Arctic, but you would not accept
what the science showed."

Chest pounding with cold fury, Noah shook his head.
"It's too late, Sylvie. Too many people know," he said as
casually as he could.

"Know what exactly?" Sylvie smiled maliciously.
"They think my brother harvested a deadly glacier in the
Arctic. No one—except the people in this house—knows
differently."

"Our colleagues do," Elise bluffed.

"Do they?" Sylvie laughed. "We just saw footage on CNN
of people lined up outside a Beverly Hills spa waiting for the
first bottles of the Lake to go on sale today." She looked
from Duncan to Noah. "You think your precious WHO
would allow that if they knew Vishnov's secret?"

Simon Valmont appeared at the doorway behind De-
Groot. He mumbled in her ear, and then DeGroot called
out to Sylvie. "The snow has started to fall again." She
took a step into the room. "Sylvie, you have explained

more than enough," she said, as if the others were not even present. "It's time."

Sylvie nodded. She looked over her shoulder at Valmont. *"Simon, fixez les attaches d'Avril, maintenant, s'il tu plaît!"*

Head down, Valmont stepped around Sylvie and walked toward Avril. With his stooped posture and loping stride, Noah recognized him as the mysterious informant from outside his hotel. A new flood of rage filled him, but he fought it back. "And us?" Noah said, desperate to create a distraction for Avril as Valmont neared. "How did you keep such close tabs on us at all times?"

"Ah," Sylvie said with a wide smile. "We have a friend within—" But she didn't get any further.

Avril pounced so quickly that Valmont did not even have time to raise his arms. In a flash, she had the ligature around his neck and tightened like a garrote. Using his bloated body as a shield from the pointed guns, Avril dragged Valmont backward by his neck. He choked out a few words that were indecipherable to Noah.

"I will kill him," Avril said, as she reached Noah's side. "Happily."

"Kill him. I don't care." Sylvie stepped to her right and swung the gun toward Frédéric. She knelt down and languidly placed the muzzle of her weapon against his forehead. "But how do you feel about watching your son die?"

Frédéric stared up at Sylvie, defiantly.

Avril wavered a moment. Then her hands fell off Valmont's neck, and he wriggled free of her grip. He spun to face her. Noah heard him hiss something in her ear that ended with *garce,* the French word for "bitch."

"Simon, les attaches!" Sylvie repeated in the tone of an exasperated teacher.

Warily, Valmont slipped behind Avril and grabbed her by the forearms. But Avril did not struggle while the man who had betrayed her carefully reapplied the bindings to her wrists. He leaned forward and spat another few words in her ear, before shoving her away.

Avril looked down at her feet, never once looking up at Valmont as he walked around her and headed for the doorway. "I am going to make sure Viktor has the cars organized correctly," DeGroot said, following Valmont out of the room.

Sylvie nodded. "I would like to check the street before we leave, too." She turned and marched out of the room behind the other two.

The door slammed shut and a bolt clicked loudly into place. Avril hurried over to her son and dropped to her knees beside him. She spoke soothingly in French to him.

Duncan staggered to his feet and approached Noah and Elise. "What do you think they have in mind?" he asked them.

Noah shrugged, numb with resignation. He had a mental image of Chloe, frolicking in the gentle waves of a Mexican beach. Though he knew she would be all right with Anna and Julie, the thought that he would miss seeing her grow up stirred a ripple of despair.

Elise brought him back to the present. Her eyes clouded with determination. "That water cannot go on sale, you understand?"

Noah glanced at her with renewed affection.

"No matter what these psychopaths try, they won't be able to sterilize the prions out of that water," Duncan said. "Shite, can you imagine how many people could die?"

"I know." Noah exhaled heavily. "But how can we stop it?"

"They won't shoot us," Elise said. "They can't."

"She has a point," Duncan said. "They'll have a spot of bother trying to explain away the simultaneous shooting of every single investigator looking into this outbreak."

"That must be why our restraints are padded," Elise continued. "So they will not leave any marks on our bodies after—"

Duncan nodded vehemently. "All that drivel about the roads, the cars, and the snow. They're planning some kind of auto accident for us!"

"So they will have to walk us outside again," Elise pointed out.

Duncan nodded. "And if they can't shoot us, maybe we stand a chance if we run for it."

"Might be our best shot," Noah said, though he felt no confidence in the plan. He turned to Elise and looked deep into her eyes. "I owe you an apology."

Her lips cracked into a trace of a smile. "Not the time for apologies," she said.

"I am sorry, Elise."

Avril, who had been crouching over her son, suddenly materialized behind Noah. "Turn around and face the door," she said in a hushed tone.

Noah looked over his shoulder and saw that Avril's face was rigid with purpose. Without asking any questions, he pivoted on the spot. Avril slipped in behind him. Noah felt tugging at his restraints.

"Keep your hands where they are after they're loose," she whispered.

He craned his neck and saw Avril's unfettered hand sawing through the bindings at his wrists with what looked like a switchblade. The ligatures gave way and he could feel his hands move freely, but kept them clasped behind his back as instructed.

His heart filling with a surge of elation, he viewed her quizzically. "How?"

"*Simon,*" she whispered.

53

Simon! Even before Avril had wrapped the ligature around his neck, she understood from the quick wink Valmont flashed as he approached her that he was going to help. She did not regret choking him, though. It added to the act, and gave her a brief taste of retribution. After Valmont had slipped the blade into her hand and pretended to redo her bindings, the words he spat in her ear were: "Wait for my signal!"

Invigorated with an almost alien sense of hope, Avril moved with renewed purpose. She had already freed Frédéric's hands. After cutting through Noah's bindings, she whispered to him, "Do nothing until Simon tells us."

"You sure it's not a trap?" Noah asked, rolling his shoulders but not moving his hands.

"Absolutely," she whispered without hesitation.

Noah nodded. "What if one of the others double-checks our restraints?"

Avril had wondered the same, but she had no good answer. "Then we improvise," she said. "Make sure none of the cut material is showing."

Noah locked eyes with her. "Let me have the knife, Avril."

She shook her head firmly. "This is *my* responsibility."

Avril moved over to Duncan, cutting his ligatures as discreetly as possible and whispering for him to keep his hands in place. Duncan nodded, but said nothing. Then she went to Elise, the last prisoner to be untied. She had just knelt down behind the young woman when the door rattled noisily.

Breath caught in her throat, Avril flicked the knife shut and stuffed it as far up her sleeve as possible. She jumped to her feet and shot her hands behind her back. Her fingers frantically groped at the dangling material of the cut binding as the door screeched angrily against the floor.

Avril glanced over to Frédéric, who stood at her side with his hands behind his back. She showed a slight smile, trying to reassure him. His brief nod was almost undetectable, but it warmed Avril's heart.

Sylvie strode into the room followed by Valmont and the no-neck Russian, Viktor. In his huge hand, he gripped a stack of black material that Avril took a moment to recognize as the wool hoods.

Sylvie's gaze swept over the room, examining her prisoners. Satisfied, she turned to Viktor. "Put the hoods on," she snapped in English.

Valmont stepped in front of Viktor, and Avril tensed. She ran a finger up her sleeve, feeling for the switchblade. However, Valmont grabbed the hoods from the other man's hand. "I'll do it," he said in French.

Indifferently, Viktor looked over to Sylvie, awaiting further orders.

Valmont headed toward the prisoners. "I have to double-check the restraints, anyway," he said. "We don't need a repeat of the earlier fiasco with that bitch getting loose."

Sylvie shrugged. "Hurry, then."

Valmont reached Noah. Standing behind the doctor, Valmont yanked his shoulders so far back that Noah groaned. Nodding his satisfaction, he roughly slipped the hood over Noah's head and then moved over to Elise.

As soon as Valmont reached Avril, he made a show of tugging roughly at her arms, until her shoulder sockets actually ached. She felt his warm breath against her ear. "A little tougher to get out of this time, isn't it, bitch?" he growled. Then he added one hushed word: *"Outside."*

The room darkened as the wool scratched over Avril's face.

Valmont released her arms, and she heard his footsteps moving toward Frédéric. Beside her, she could hear him repeat the same procedure, right down to the hostile comment. "Your mommy cannot help you now, Freddie," he mocked.

Valmont trod heavily across the room toward the door. "Done," he announced.

"All right, time to go." Sylvie addressed the room. "I suggest you listen to our instructions. I think our history has shown how committed we are to sticking to our plan."

Shuffling noises surrounded Avril. She felt Viktor's meaty hands on her shoulder. Praying that no strand of her cut bindings showed between her wrists, she felt enormous relief when the oblivious giant shoved her toward the door. She took each step with care, realizing how tenuous her grip was on the switchblade tucked under her sleeve.

Increased brightness seeped through the black wool, and she knew they had stepped out of the cellar and into the hallway.

"Stairs," Sylvie barked from somewhere ahead of her.

Avril took three more short strides and her foot tapped against the first step. She climbed the stairs with deliberate caution. Halfway up, her son bumped her from behind.

She managed to regain her footing, but for a horrified moment, the knife slipped out from under her sleeve.

She desperately fumbled for it. Breathlessly, she trapped
the tip of its handle between her index and middle finger
and then pulled it back into her grip.

"Move it!" Sylvie called out.

"Sorry, Maman," Frédéric mumbled.

"It will be okay, darling," she said.

Reaching the top step, they shuffled down the hallway
toward the blowing cold. They stepped through the doorway and out into the night air. Even through the hood,
Avril could tell that the area where they walked was well
lit.

"Stop!" Sylvie suddenly cried.

Avril obeyed. Her heart pounding, she clutched the
weapon tightly in her hand. She listened intently as Sylvie
spoke to her associates in a rushed low voice. "Keep the
boy and his mother in the backseat of her car. Viktor, you
drive. But stay on the road this time." She switched to
French for Valmont's benefit. "Simon, you take the E.U.
woman and the two doctors in her car. Martine and I will
follow in the Mercedes."

Avril's fingers dug into the handle of the weapon. She
readied to pounce, waiting for Simon to give the signal.

None came.

"Move it!" the deep Russian voice growled in English.
Viktor's hand clamped down heavily on her shoulder, and
he began to shove her forward.

When, Simon? Avril wavered, trying to decide if she
should catch Viktor now with a blade to his gut. Instinct
told to her to wait for Valmont's signal, so she shuffled
along slowly on the snowy ground.

Her chest hit something hard but her belly did not meet
resistance, and she realized that she was pressing against
the roof of a car with its door open. Viktor began to push
her head down toward the door. She caught the faint smell

of the pine-scented deodorizer that she kept in her Peugeot.

"Simon, what are you doing?" Sylvie snapped, annoyed.

The pressure on Avril's head gave way like a spring releasing. She heard Viktor's feet spin on the snow.

"Get away from them, Viktor!" Valmont shouted in French.

Avril heard Viktor's boots crunch on the snow.

"Have you completely lost your mind?" Sylvie spat.

In one motion, Avril put her hand to her head and whisked off her hood. She popped open the blade of her knife and held it out in front of her. In the shadowy glow of the house's exterior lights, Avril took in the scene in an instant. Everyone except Valmont stood beside the three cars lined up at the end of the driveway off to the side of the Manet house.

Several feet away from his fellow conspirators, Valmont stood with his back to the door of the house. He swayed nervously from foot to foot as he pointed his gun at Sylvie and DeGroot. With arms at their sides and guns not visible, the women stood beside a black Mercedes at the head of the column of cars lined up on the driveway. Ten feet or so behind the women, Elise hovered near a scratched-up BMW sedan beside the two doctors. Noah had already pulled off his mask and was now removing Elise's. Not understanding French, Duncan was frozen in place, still wearing his face mask. "Duncan, your hood," Noah called to his colleague, and the Scotsman pulled it off.

At the back of the column, Avril leaned against her own car, close enough to Frédéric to hear his heavy breathing. With a quick glance over her shoulder, she saw Viktor standing nearby, very still and straight, with a hand resting perilously close to the inside of his open jacket.

"Simon, how will you pay off those gambling bets now?" Sylvie calmly asked.

"I will worry about that later," Valmont grumbled.

"There will be no later for you," Sylvie said. "Even if you could get out of here."

Valmont sneered. "Your future does not look much brighter, I am afraid."

"Simon, this is a marathon, not a sprint," she said. "Do not give up with the finish line finally in sight."

"I am sick of you, Sylvie." Valmont's shoulders sagged slightly. "You promised me all I would have to do was to be your 'eyes and ears' in the region. Nothing more. And then every week, it got worse. More and more blood."

"I didn't want any of this," Sylvie said. "It just happened. Now we have to deal with it."

"I have helped you kill three innocent people. If you think for one moment that I will let you murder Avril and Frédéric . . ." His eyes darted to Avril. "Avril, I never dreamed it would go this far. I am so sorry."

Avril nodded. Sensing danger, she raised her knife and turned to the Russian statue on her other side. Somehow, he had backpedaled a few more steps away.

"Such nobility, all of a sudden, Simon," Sylvie said. "But it's too late to find your conscience. Your only hope—ours, too—is to finish what we started."

"I am a man without hope." Valmont chuckled miserably. Then his tone hardened into a growl. "Now get down on your knees with your hands on your heads."

"That is so unnecessary, Simon," DeGroot cooed as she took a step toward him. "There is an easier way for all of us."

Valmont shook his head slowly. "You are not going to fuck your way out of this one, Martine." Then his voice rose, and he shook his gun at them. "Now get down on the ground."

Sylvie and DeGroot shared a quick glance.

"Now!" Valmont fired a gunshot over their heads to punctuate his point.

The two women began to kneel almost in synchrony.

Avril suddenly noticed Viktor's hand inching toward his jacket. She took a step nearer to him and waved her knife. "Leave it!" she yelled in English.

Valmont looked over to her. "Everything okay, Avril?" he asked urgently.

"Yes," she replied, steadying the blade in her tremulous hand without taking her eyes off the Russian.

Two gunshots erupted, and Avril whipped her head over to see Valmont stagger a step, drop to his knees, and then fall silently on his side.

Avril looked to the two women. DeGroot steadied her gun, the muzzle now pointed at Avril. "Drop the knife," she screamed.

Avril hesitated a moment. Just as she began to relax her grip on the haft of the knife, another gunshot exploded from where Valmont lay on the ground. DeGroot clutched her shoulder and stumbled back a step.

"Martine!" Sylvie cried, as she reached for her own gun.

"Just a graze," DeGroot called out. She swung the gun over and fired twice more at the fallen figure of Valmont.

"Go!" Noah yelled.

In the confusion, Elise darted between the BMW and Avril's car and scurried for the darkness of the nearby trees. Duncan followed. Noah hunched low and ran toward Avril along the row of cars.

"Maman!" Frédéric shouted.

Avril's eyes shot over to where Frédéric was wrestling nearby with Viktor. Her son had both hands clamped around the Russian's bulging arm, as he struggled to shake the gun free. Avril was already in motion when Viktor swung his free elbow viciously. It smashed Frédéric in the face and sent him reeling backward.

Avril reached Viktor before the Russian could raise the gun. In midstride, she thrust the knife's blade straight into his windpipe, feeling resistance only when it hit bone. A whoosh sounded as the blood sprayed from his neck and splattered Avril's face. His hands did not even reach the neck wound before he toppled backward.

Another gunshot roared, and air whistled by Avril's ear. She ducked and looked over to see Sylvie steadying her aim. She reached down and grabbed her son's hand. Noah appeared on the other side of him. Together, they hauled Frédéric to his feet and hurried off around the back of her car and toward the woods where Elise and Duncan had disappeared.

Shots cracked behind them.

Just as they reached the trees, Avril was hurled forward as if kicked and then felt searing pain across the back of her chest.

Avril saw stars. The world swam around her. She focused every iota of energy on staying upright, but a violent tremble overcame her legs. Her knees softened. She began to pitch forward. Just as she was about to collapse, arms wrapped around her from either side.

54

Lac Noir, France. January 21

Gasping, Avril swayed like a tree moments after the final axe blow had fallen. Arms locked behind her, Frédéric and Noah dragged her through the snow away from the gunfire and into the darkness of the woods.

The guns had quieted. Aside from the low whistle of his perforated eardrum, Noah heard nothing. The silence was more nerve-wracking than the blasts.

As they pulled Avril deeper into the tree cover, Noah desperately focused on his only previous visit to the Manets, trying to recall the property's layout. He remembered that it was the last house on the lakefront road, and the neighboring property was on the far side of the house and a long way up the road. *Way too far to drag the bleeding detective.* Noah hoped that the gunfire might have precipitated a call for help, but rather than the welcome noise of sirens, the only suggestion of a police presence was Avril's moist and labored breaths.

Noah considered making a dash for the neighboring house, but the chances of reaching it across the lit parking lot and past the two armed women seemed slim-to-nonexistent. He decided on an alternate course. "We have to get to the road," Noah whispered urgently to Frédéric and Avril. "Stop a car. Double back to the neighbors. Anything."

"I don't think . . . I cannot . . ." Avril choked and gurgled.

"Maman, it's our best hope," Frédéric encouraged her, bloody spittle flying from his freshly lacerated lips.

"We'll carry you," Noah said.

Noah glanced urgently in all directions, hoping to spot a sign of where Duncan and Elise had run, but saw nothing. Deeper in the woods, the last glow of the house lights faded and they now moved through the trees in near darkness. Branches scratched at their faces. The snow-covered ground was scattered with unexpected dips, and taller bushes poked through the snow. Noah stumbled as often as Frédéric did, but the counterbalance of propping up Avril kept them on their feet.

Noah was adjusting to the darkness. He grew more sure-footed with each step, though his sense of orientation was rapidly fading in the abyss of the lightless forest. He hesitated a moment, and then turned to his left. "This way," he whispered.

"You sure?" Frédéric asked.

"Yes." But Noah was moving purely on instinct now.

They took four or five steps and then stumbled into a thicket of hip-high shrubs. Shuffling carefully, they had barely cleared the bushes when a flashlight's beam cut across the trees a few feet in front of them.

They stopped dead. "Down!" Noah growled.

As soon as they released their grip, Avril collapsed to the ground. Frédéric and Noah dove down beside her. The beam swung directly over their heads again, focusing on the area around them. "The bushes!" Noah whispered.

His bare hands breaking through the crisp snow, Noah crawled on his stomach back toward the shrubs. He stopped every couple of feet to help Frédéric pull his mother along. She was wheezing audibly when they reached the thicket. "In here," Noah said.

With shallow and rattling respirations, Avril became a deadweight as Noah and Frédéric dragged her deeper into the bushes. Behind the tallest of the shrubs, Noah flopped back down with his chest to the ground just as the flashlight's beam swept above them.

Cheek to the ground, he did not breathe until the shaft of light moved on. He knew that between their snowy footprints and Avril's noisy breathing, the bushes would provide only temporary cover at best. "One of us has to get to the road," he whispered to Frédéric.

"I'll stay with Maman," he said.

"She will die without medical help," Noah said bluntly. "You're faster. My French is terrible. It has to be you."

"Go . . . Freddie," Avril gasped.

Frédéric wavered a moment and then said, "How?"

"I will draw them away, toward the lake." Noah pointed to the ground ahead of them, hoping his orientation was right. "You run for the road."

"All right."

Noah felt Frédéric's hand groping for his. Then Noah touched the cold handle of the switchblade that Frédéric had passed him. He wrapped his hand tightly around it.

Noah looked up. The light was moving closer, though the beam was directed up and toward the road. "Wait until she comes after me," he said to Frédéric. "Then run."

Noah took a deep breath. He rose to a crouch, counted to three, and took off with hands out in front of him, feeling for obstacles and deliberately snapping tree branches to draw attention. The beam cut across him twice before finding him. Noah could suddenly see his way lit in front of him, but that brought no comfort. He was lethally exposed now.

Two gunshots rang in his ears. He dodged to his left and right, slipping on the snow, as he ran for the nearest cluster of trees. Three more shots erupted. Louder this time. Noah felt a sting at his neck. An anxious moment passed before he realized the scratch came from a tree branch, not a bullet.

Noah tripped over a hole and fell to the ground, landing painfully on his right wrist. He scrambled on hands and knees toward the big pine tree in front of him. He found the trunk of the tree with his hand and scurried around behind it. He hopped to his feet. The pine tree was only wide enough for him to tuck completely behind in profile, so he turned to his right and leaned sideways into its base.

His hollow eardrum continued to whistle like a kettle. He pressed up so hard against the tree that the bark dug into his skin.

The light grew brighter as it swung back and forth across the tree, alternately illuminating the bushes and trees on either side of him. The pursuer was moving more slowly now. The beam dropped closer to the ground, and Noah assumed that the person was following his snowy footprints.

The shuffling feet grew louder and the noise was joined by the faint sounds of someone else's respiration. Noah held his own breath and clutched the knife tightly to his chest. The snow crunched louder. Noah had no idea on which side of the tree she would appear, but he dared not move a muscle.

The light stopped swinging. From the sound of her steady breathing, Noah guessed she was no more than five feet from him.

A moment passed, then a footstep through the snow. Noah tightened. He waited but saw nothing.

Too long!

Sensing a presence behind him, he pivoted a half turn and saw a shadowy arm rising. Noah lunged without hesitation, catching her arm just before it leveled. He knocked the gun free of her hand. Before he could move again, he felt a crushing pain in his scalp as the flashlight smashed down on his head like a club. Stunned, he fell to the ground and lost his grip on the knife. It disappeared into the snow by the base of the tree.

Blows from the heavy flashlight rained down on him. He raised his arms to protect his head and face. The flashlight cracked across his left forearm. Searing pain jolted through his entire limb. Groaning, he dropped to his hands and rolled away from the beating.

Something hard pressed into his left shoulder. *My knife!* He frantically dug it out from underneath him.

Beside him, the flashlight dropped nose down into the snow. In its faint illumination, Noah recognized the Dutch woman's contorted face and saw her hand pull the gun out of the snow.

She swept the weapon toward him.

Numb to the pain, he launched himself up and toward her with his left hand while he drove his right arm forward as hard as he could. The knife struck DeGroot in the lower abdomen. The blade tore through her belly, buried up to the handle.

DeGroot shrieked in surprise. Shocked, Noah released the knife. DeGroot stumbled back and, for a moment, stood motionless like one of the neighboring trees. Then she crumpled to the ground beside him.

Before Noah could digest any of it, a beam of light from the opposite direction locked onto him.

"Martine, no!"

Three shots followed Sylvie's shrill cry. Snow flew from nearby branches and sprayed around Noah's head. He tried to scramble for the protection of another tree but, thrown off balance, his feet slithered and he fell backward awkwardly, landing on his seat.

Helpless and exposed, a sudden calm sense of finality overwhelmed him. He remembered holding the newborn

Chloe in his arms. He had a vision of a sandy white beach in Mexico. Gwen's laughter rang in his ears. He braced himself for death.

At that moment, the second flashlight's beam fell away and he heard a dull thud.

Everything went dark and still. All Noah heard was the whistling in his ear. He wondered if he had lost consciousness. Then a voice called to him. "Noah? Are you all right?"

Elise?

Noah groped with his good hand for the upturned flashlight. As soon as his fingers found it, he swung its beam in the direction of her voice.

A few feet away, Elise was gaping at him. To her right, Duncan brandished a thick tree branch in his hand as if holding a bat. He stared down at the ground where Sylvie Manet lay at his feet. She clutched her head and rolled from side to side.

55

Of all the crime scenes Avril had attended, she had never before heard so many sirens or seen so many flashing lights. Lying on the stretcher, she noticed that all the lights were encircled with a bluish or red halo. Despite her blankets, she shook involuntarily, and her back was drenched with the stickiness of her own blood. Someone had told her that the posterior chest wound had stopped bleeding. With the oxygen mask on, she breathed slightly easier. The medication that ran through the two intravenous lines into her arm was helping, too. She was uncertain whether it was her critical injury, the painkillers, or her immense relief at knowing that Frédéric was safe, but for the first time in what felt like years, she craved sleep.

Her eyes drifted shut, but someone shook her left arm urgently. She opened the lids a crack to see her son hovering beside her.

"Maman, are you all right?" he asked.

She mustered a smile. "Just tired . . . so tired." She looked at his swirling face. Fresh blood still dripped from his nose and oozed from his lips. "Your face . . ." She tried to extend a hand to him but was too weak to overcome the tug of the intravenous line.

"It's nothing." He grinned, and she could have been looking at Antoine. "It will get me plenty of sympathy from the girls at school."

"Go easy on them," Avril murmured.

On her right, the female paramedic inflated the blood pressure cuff. "Mme. Avars, how is your breathing?" she asked.

"Fine," Avril said, though she was still hungry for air.

Two paramedics continued to swarm around the stretcher in a flurry of activity, checking lines, listening to her chest, and tightening and clicking straps and belts into place. Over Frédéric's shoulder, Avril spotted Duncan, Noah, and Elise as they viewed the proceedings with concern. She saw the bandages on Noah's arm. "Are you hurt?" she asked.

"I'm fine," Noah said with a grin. "Beaten with a flashlight. Doesn't exactly compare to being shot in the chest."

"I win," Avril mumbled groggily.

"If this is your idea of winning, then we best check *you* for mad cow disease," Duncan said.

"I did win, Dr. McLeod." Avril squeezed her son's arm. She turned back to Noah. "What of the Lake?"

Noah smiled. "We have sounded the alarm."

"We're not going to let a single bottle make it to market," Elise emphasized.

"Good." Avril eyed Noah. "And Simon?"

The doctor shook his head.

Avril felt a pang of sorrow, though in her heart she knew it was for the best: Valmont would never have tolerated the public shame of the aftermath and trial. In Avril's eyes, he died reclaiming his honor. She would mourn her friend. "And the two women?" Avril asked.

"Martine DeGroot is dead," Elise said.

"And as soon as they sew up the gash in her head, Sylvie

Manet will be heading off with your colleagues," Noah said.

"They were blinded by greed," Frédéric said, almost sympathetically.

Avril smiled again at the boy. "Your father would have been so proud of you," she said in French.

The paramedics finished strapping Avril in. "It's time, Mme. Avars," the female attendant said, as she hurried to the head of the gurney. Her partner arrived at Avril's feet.

Frédéric walked alongside the stretcher as the attendants began to wheel it toward the open door of the back of the rig. "Take care of yourself," Noah called after Avril. Duncan and Elise added words of encouragement, too, but they melted into the white noise and commotion enveloping her.

"Au revoir," she called out to them and waved weakly with a hand that never left the stretcher. Her eyes were exceptionally heavy now. She stole one more look at Frédéric before they shut again.

Avril knew that she required surgery. She expected to face a long and challenging recovery. She was not even sure if she was out of the woods. But none of that mattered. Avril felt at peace. Frédéric was safe now.

I did all right, Antoine, she thought as she drifted out of consciousness.

56

The two policemen dropped Noah, Duncan, and Elise outside the Grand Hotel Doré at 3:35 A.M. They could have come back sooner, but none of them wanted to miss hearing from the detectives who interrogated Sylvie Manet inside her heavily guarded hospital room. Elise translated the report for Duncan and Noah. According to the officers, Sylvie had spoken freely, welcoming the opportunity to unload her secrets.

As soon as Noah reached his hotel room, he picked up the phone and called Washington, where it was already after nine P.M. Anna answered on the second ring. Her tone bordered on frantic. "Noah, are you all right?" she asked.

Noah's eardrum still whistled and his arm throbbed where he'd been hit with the flashlight, but he had flatly refused to seek medical attention. "I'm good, thanks," he said as he rubbed his arm.

"It's all over the news!" she cried. "The contaminated lake water. The conspiracy. The kidnapping and murders. *A hostage!* You must have been terrified. How did you cope?"

"It's over, Anna." Though grateful for her concern,

Noah was too tired and emotionally drained to relive the experience in its retelling.

"You want to talk to Chloe, I bet," Anna said understandingly.

"I'd love to," Noah said. "I don't suppose she's still awake?"

"I just put her to bed, but I happen to know from the singing upstairs that she's still awake."

Fifteen seconds passed before he heard the excited voice of his daughter. "Daddy!" she shrieked.

His heart soared. Earlier, in the Manet cellar, he had convinced himself that he would never hear her beautiful voice again. "Sweetie! Guess what? I'm coming home tomorrow."

"Tomorrow? *Tomorrow!* That's awesome, Daddy-o!" Then she added coyly, "With a present?"

"Of course!" Noah laughed. "Now tell me about the rest of your trip."

Chloe spoke expansively of the last few days spent at her grandparents' retreat in South Carolina, most of her description focusing on the tricks learned and games played in the swimming pool. Noah took it all in, reveling in his daughter's enthusiasm and happy to have his thoughts pulled thousands of miles away from the Manets and the carnage in rural France.

"Chloe, I can't wait for tomorrow," he said.

"Me either, Daddy. Even if you don't bring a present." She paused and then added, as if only out of idle curiosity, "Can you buy Barbies in France, Daddy?"

Noah was still chuckling when he hung up. Checking his cell phone's screen, he saw that Gwen had left two messages. He retrieved both voicemails. In a calm voice that brimmed with concern, she ended her second message by saying, "Noah, I know how swamped you must be, but please let me know that you are okay as soon you possibly can."

Noah picked up the phone and dialed Gwen's cell number, but he hung up before he reached the final digit. He was desperate to vent the frustrations, confusion, and angst of the past weeks. She would understand better than anyone. But selfishly, he decided he would rather do it in person when he would have the chance to see those intelligent sexy eyes light up with empathy. He reached for his open laptop and typed out an e-mail: "Everything okay now. Hell of a story to tell you. Save some time for dinner the day after tomorrow, okay? I love you." He sent it without rereading it.

He shut his laptop and practically dove into bed, expecting sleep to come quickly. But he tossed and turned for the next few hours. He knew he should have felt proud and relieved at having helped prevent the Lake from reaching the market, but he was distressed at how easily the world had slipped to the brink of catastrophe. And he could still practically feel the pop from the knife as it plunged into Martine DeGroot's gut. The memory haunted him. Regardless of his justification, he was trained to save lives, not take them.

At 7:13 A.M., deciding to use the flight home to catch up on sleep, he rose wearily from the bed. He showered, changed, and then hurried down to the lobby. He didn't want to miss Duncan, who planned to catch the earliest flight home to Glasgow.

His bag slung over his shoulder, Duncan walked across the lobby toward Noah. "Let me guess," he bellowed. "You just heard from Nantal that we're needed in Belarus. Some daft farmer is shipping his milk inside abandoned warheads of old Soviet smallpox missiles!"

Noah smiled. "I'm not taking Jean's calls anymore."

"Finally, a few sensible words out of you." Duncan roughly scratched his beard. "Still, no regrets about coming back. It was right that we finished this."

"Agreed." They shook hands warmly. "Any word on Maggie today?"

"She seems okay . . . this morning, anyway." Duncan shrugged. "Hasn't lost her sense of humor. She told me she is desperately proud of her husband for sneaking up behind a woman and clubbing her with a branch."

Noah grinned. "I can't think of anyone who deserved a clubbing more than Sylvie Manet. I meant to ask, how did you and Elise manage to surprise Sylvie like that?"

"You."

"*Me?*"

"She chased us through the woods," Duncan said. "But when the other flashlight went down, Sylvie rushed over to help her lovable Dutch friend. We knew you were involved, so we followed. With you finally useful—as a decoy, mind you—I was able to surprise her with a pine tree to the noggin."

"You saved my hide."

Duncan waved Noah's gratitude away. "It's the least I could do for you after all the biblical predicaments you've dragged me into."

"What's next for you, Duncan?"

The playfulness deserted the Scot's face. "Now that her arm is on the mend, I am going to take Maggie home," he said.

"And then?"

"They're giving her a break before more chemo." His shoulders sagged. "We honeymooned in the Canary Islands. In spite of that, she's always loved the place. I think I might take her back there for some sunshine and knock-off British food."

Noah nodded. "Live for the moment."

"Doubt we have anything else but."

Noah swallowed away a pang of sorrow. "You're going to be okay, huh?"

"Ah, shite, things are looking a lot rosier than they did in that dank basement in Lac Noir. Enough with the navel gazing." He shifted his suitcase to leave, but before he took a step he said, "Listen, Noah, I don't know what the hell is going on between you and Elise—"

"Nothing."

"If you say so." Duncan nodded. "I have to tell you, though, I always thought you and Gwen had a decent shot of making a go of it."

Noah nodded. "I'm going home to find out if you're right."

"Good. Don't let this job fuck that up. Remember, Haldane, you're not irreplaceable." The familiar wry smile creased his features. "The world can always find another crazed woodsman."

Noah walked Duncan out the front door. The dawn skies were clear, but it was no warmer than the day before. They shook hands again, and Duncan headed off to the waiting taxi.

Noah headed back inside. He went to the restaurant and claimed his usual table in the far corner. Remembering his cholesterol, he ordered the fruit and cereal, forgoing one final crêpe with a tinge of regret. Without asking, the waiter handed him a copy of the *International Herald Tribune*. Noah opened it to discover that the story had somehow made it to press with a headline that read BOTTLED DEATH. The article was vague on details, but it was linked to a more comprehensive story that described the death of Vishnov "pioneer" Dr. Claude Fontaine, whose remains were found in a burned-out château in Switzerland. Drugs and alcohol had been implicated, but from Sylvie's confession to the police Noah knew that his death was anything but accidental.

Elise arrived at the table. Though she was dressed elegantly in a black skirt, matching jacket, and stylish pumps, her eyes were puffy and downcast.

Noah lowered the paper. "Did you sleep at all?" he asked.

"You know." She shrugged as she sat down beside him.

"Elise, I'm very sorry."

She stared past him. "So you said last night."

"I mean, about how things have worked out, you know, with . . ."

"It was my stupidity." Elise picked up the menu in front of her. "How is your family?" she asked without looking up from it.

He told her about his conversation with Anna and Chloe.

Elise smiled distantly. "Little girls always miss their fathers."

They shared forced small talk, Noah carrying the brunt of the conversation. He was thankful when her breakfast arrived and relieved him of the burden. Elise picked at her food with little interest while he downed his fourth cup of coffee. The server had just cleared the dishes when Jean Nantal and Javier Montalva appeared at the restaurant's entrance. Noah caught Elise's eye and she nodded once. The melancholy in her expression vanished, replaced with sudden purpose.

The E.U. minister wore another expensive-looking suit, but his walk lacked its usual swagger. Jean was his bubbly self again. He kissed Elise on both cheeks and hugged Noah warmly. Montalva shook Noah's hand perfunctorily, and then kissed Elise on the cheeks.

"Wonderful work," Jean gushed. "We owe you both a huge debt of gratitude for your efforts. The whole world does. Who knows how much senseless suffering you have saved us?"

"Yes," Montalva echoed. "I am going to recommend the highest recognition the E.U. has to offer. For both of you."

"And Detective Avars and her son?" Elise asked.

"Of course," Montalva said with a sweep of his hand.

"I am told Mme. Avars's surgery went well," Jean said. "She is in stable condition now."

"Good." Noah nodded with genuine relief.

Jean and Montalva sat down in the two empty seats at the table. Both refused the menus and coffees the waiter came by to offer.

"Did you get to the bottles of the Lake in time?" Noah asked.

"We think so," Jean said, though his voice showed a trace of uncertainty. "We still have to catalog the shipments, but there have been no reports of any reaching market. Even if a few did, we like to hope that the media coverage would alert potential buyers."

"Besides," Montalva added, "I understand the people involved were convinced that the purified water would be safe for consumption."

"*They* might have been convinced," Noah snorted. "I sure as hell am not. Perhaps they lowered the risk slightly, but there is no known way to reliably sterilize prions." He shook his head. "That's what bothers me the most. Sylvie is a biologist. She must have known she was rolling the dice just to hit her jackpot."

"Nothing blinds faster than greed," Jean said.

"Too true," Noah said, avoiding eye contact with anyone else at the table.

Elise looked over to Jean. "What about Lake Vishnov itself?" she asked.

"Production has been halted at the site," Jean said. "An international team made up of Antarctic Treaty signatory members is flying in today to assume control of the operation. In all likelihood, the well into the lake will be destroyed and the site dismantled."

"Good riddance," Noah grunted.

"Incidentally," Jean said, "we have learned that the operation was funded by a Moscow-based oil company by the name of Radvogin Industries."

"The CEO, Yulia Radvogin, is missing," Montalva said.

Noah shook his head. "She is not missing at all."

Montalva frowned. "Why do you say that?"

"Because she is dead," Elise said.

Montalva's shoulders squared, and he glanced from Noah to Elise. "How do you know?"

"Sylvie Manet told the detectives who interrogated her," Elise said.

"Oh, we had not heard," Jean said.

Noah looked over his shoulder and nodded once, though no one was in sight. He turned back to the table. "There are a couple of other things you haven't heard yet, Jean."

Jean glanced quizzically at Montalva and then back to Noah.

Montalva's eyes narrowed. "As the ranking E.U. official, I do not appreciate being left in the dark," he said with a tense smile.

Noah continued without acknowledging the comment. "The whole time, I had this uncanny sense that the conspirators knew what we were up to. What our next steps would be." He turned to Elise and touched the back of her hand. "I even suspected that Elise might have leaked the information."

Elise looked at the others. "It turns out that I *was* the leak," she said bluntly.

Montalva leaned forward until his elbows rested on the table. His expression was somewhere between bewilderment and wariness. "*Elise?* Is this true?"

She viewed the minister intently. "Do you not remember, Javier? You asked me to keep a very close watch on the situation. To report twice daily."

"Of course I did." Montalva pulled his elbows free of the table and sat up straighter. "This epidemic was an immense threat to the European economy. I had to know exactly what was going on."

Noah leaned back and said nothing. Jean also watched in circumspect silence.

"Of course you needed to know, Javier," Elise said. "But why did you need me to sabotage Noah's investigation? For that matter, our own investigation?"

"Sabotage?" Montalva threw his hands up, his cheeks reddening. "When did I ask you to sabotage anything?"

"'Listen, darling'"—she feigned a Spanish accent and flailed her hands in an exaggerated manner—"'Dr. Haldane will stop at nothing to make a name for himself here. Do not let him make it off the backs of the European farmers. Keep the investigation focused on the Allaire farm, from where we know this has all come!'"

Montalva's cheeks blazed a deeper red. The veins at his temples began to pulsate. "There is no need to twist my words, Elise," he said through clenched teeth.

"Twist them?" Elise said. "I know them by heart because you repeated them so often. Somehow, you convinced me I was right to undermine Noah's investigation."

Montalva shuffled in his seat. "Now, Elise." He held out his hand to her in his familiar offer-of-escape-from-a-sinking-ship gesture. "I understand how hurt you must feel about what transpired between us, but there is no need—"

"Two and a half million euros," Noah said quietly.

The comment froze Montalva in midsentence. His eyes darted over to Noah. "What are you talking about?" he growled.

"The consulting fee Sylvie Manet and her associates paid you."

"What nonsense!" Montalva spat.

"It isn't such a bad price for insurance, really. Two and a half million euros for you to ensure that the E.U. investigation would conclude that Philippe Manet, Benoît Gagnon, and Giselle Tremblay all died from BSE acquired during the outbreak at the Allaire farm."

Jean's jaw dropped. He turned to the Spaniard. "Javier, is this so?" he asked gravely.

Montalva jumped to his feet. "I don't have to listen to such absurd unsubstantiated accusations!" he barked with unconcealed hatred.

Noah smiled. "In fact, Sylvie Manet substantiated these facts for us. No doubt the forensic auditors have already found the money trail."

Montalva spun, poised to flee, but Inspector Esmond Cabot and two uniformed gendarmes trooped toward the table from the restaurant's entrance. Two other policemen suddenly emerged from the kitchen door.

Eyes bulging and face crimson, Montalva turned back to Elise. "Clearly, this is a gigantic misunderstanding," he croaked.

Elise rose slowly to her feet. She glared at him for a long moment and then, suddenly, she slapped him across the cheek with a sharp crack. Montalva recoiled from the contact. His face contorted in pain and surprise. Without another word, Elise spun on her heel and strode past the policemen and out of the restaurant.

Noah hurried after her. When he caught up to her in the lobby, she was dabbing at her eyes with a tissue. "Elise," he said.

She cleared her throat and looked down in embarrassment. "I feel like a fool, Noah."

"Montalva fooled everyone," Noah said.

She shook her head. "Not you."

"I didn't know him like you did," he said. "I had no reason to trust him . . . or to want to believe him."

Elise looked up at Noah. "I should have never have let my personal feelings intrude on my work."

"Sometimes, you can't avoid it." Noah broke into a grin

and winked. "That was a hell of a slap you laid on him. I was impressed. A tad jealous, even."

She laughed. "It did feel good."

"You going to be okay?"

"In a few days." Her eyes were dry, and her smile genuine. "Time for both of us to go home, I think."

Noah reached out and wrapped her in his arms. He held her close for a moment, then kissed her cheek lightly and let her go. He turned for the elevator without another word.

Inside the room, Noah threw his clothes into a bag. As he put on his coat, he felt the back of the notebook press into his hip, and he pulled it out of his jacket pocket. For a moment, he considered tossing it into the garbage but, more out of superstition than nostalgia, he tucked it into the outside compartment of his suitcase.

Noah powered up his laptop and saw that new e-mails had arrived. He scanned the list but opened only the reply from Gwen, which was as short as his original message: "I love a good yarn. Consider the evening yours. Welcome home. I love you, too."

Noah turned off the laptop and slipped it into his case. A fulfilling sense of closure warmed him.

It was over. And he was heading home to the people he loved.

He could not have asked for anything more.

TOR

Award-winning authors
Compelling stories

Please join us at the website
below for more information
about this author and other great
Tor selections, and to sign up for
our monthly newsletter!

www.tor-forge.com